"I'd always heard it was almost impossible for a man to deny himself release."

Adam ignored her question. "By being chaste I retain the body's energy. It builds up over time until it's transformed into the power I use to heal. I will need it, too, to survive the ordeal that awaits me in the Dragon's Cave. Would you have me squander it, just to soothe your vanity?"

She shrugged her shoulders. "It seems like an error to think you'd become more powerful by turning away from love."

"It isn't love I turn away from, but lust."

But it wasn't just lust she inspired in him. He remembered how he'd felt as she'd caressed him. She'd taught him what else a touch could carry besides lust, and made him, for the first time he could remember, long to end his solitude. She was right. His chastity wasn't just about denying the needs of the body. He'd denied other, more subtle needs, and, damn her, she'd made him feel them, too.

"You needn't fear, Lord Ramsay. I won't threaten your precious virginity again."

He sputtered. "I'm hardly a virgin. I'd become a man before I put myself under the Dark Lord's tutelage."

"Whatever the case, it's of no importance to me. Your sanctity is safe."

She turned away, though before her face was out of view, Adam could have sworn he saw a wicked smile flit across her features.

Romances by Jenny Brown

PERILOUS PLEASURES
STAR CROSSED SEDUCTION
LORD LIGHTNING

JENNY BROWN

Perilous Pleasures

AVON

An Imprint of HarperCollinsPublishers

This is a work of fiction. Names, characters, places, and incidents are products of the author's imagination or are used fictitiously and are not to be construed as real. Any resemblance to actual events, locales, organizations, or persons, living or dead, is entirely coincidental.

AVON BOOKS
An Imprint of HarperCollins*Publishers*
10 East 53rd Street
New York, New York 10022-5299

Copyright © 2012 by Janet Ruhl
ISBN 978-0-06-197607-0
www.avonromance.com

First Avon Books mass market printing: April 2012

Avon Trademark Reg. U.S. Pat. Off. and in Other Countries, Marca Registrada, Hecho en U.S.A.
HarperCollins® is a registered trademark of HarperCollins Publishers.

Printed in the U.S.A.

10 9 8 7 6 5 4 3 2 1

To everyone who has ever believed in magic

Excerpt from *Observations and Reflexions upon Afflicted Nativities*. Unpublished manuscript found in the collection of Robert Montgomery, Laird of Iskeny, tentatively dated 1792.

. . . among those who fall into the latter category [the most severely afflicted] is the man whose horoscope is ruled by planets in Pisces. Prone to brooding and melancholy, he is unworldly and gullible. Should his Pisces Sun be poorly aspected or found in the close company of other planets in this unfortunate sign, he will be prone to lose himself in drunkenness, or in dreams and delusions from which he awakens only after great suffering.

Should his Piscean planets be more favorably aspected, they may confer upon him mystical gifts, insight, and compassion. No man loves more steadily than the Pisces native, though the object upon which he confers his affections is too often poorly chosen.

Such a man is most likely to end his life as a victim or a savior. Should the wise astrologer encounter such an individual, he would do well to give him a wide berth.

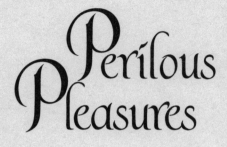

Chapter 1

London, February 21, 1803

"It is just as I thought, *ma petite*, the rent *will* be paid and I won't have to sell my rubies!"

Zoe's mother admired her still-beautiful face in the gilt and ormolu-framed mirror that filled one wall of her lavish withdrawing room before turning back to her daughter. "There was no need for your tiresome cheeseparing talk. I am still La Belle Isabelle, and there still are men of fortune who have wit enough to appreciate me."

Zoe bit her tongue. It was hardly their wits to which her mother's florid beauty appealed. But if her mother had found yet another wealthy protector, it would explain the vase of hothouse roses whose blood red hue clashed with the orange damask on the wall and filled the room with their cloying perfume, roses that cost more than she herself earned in a month of teaching at Mrs. Endicott's Select Female Academy.

She repressed a sigh. If her mother had truly found another protector, she wouldn't listen to reason now, and her extravagance would ruin them both. It had been months since the wealthy Mr. Bradburn had given her mother her *congé*, and though her mother had been assiduously exhibiting herself in all the usual haunts of the demimonde, until now no one had stepped in to take his place. Their landlady had begun to hint, not so subtly, that unless she received her payment they would find themselves and their possessions on the street. But when Zoe had begged her mother to curb her expenditures, she'd merely laughed and said that something would come up—and then demanded that Zoe dip into her hard-earned savings to tide her over until her next savior appeared.

As now, it appeared, he had.

It was wrong to feel so irritated that her mother had found yet another protector, but how would La Belle Isabelle ever learn to manage on their tiny income if she persisted in the fantasy that she would always be beautiful and indulged? She was nearing forty, and even *her* legendary career must end sometime. What would she live on when her charms finally faded and no more men could be found to take care of her—her daughter's meager earnings as a governess?

Zoe sighed. Life was so unlike morally improving fiction. Virtue triumphed only in the copybooks she read aloud to the younger pupils at Mrs. Endicott's. Everywhere else vice was far better rewarded—or at least it was while it still retained its looks.

But, as always, her mother was oblivious. She languidly lifted one graceful arm, allowing her dimpled elbow to peep from the Valenciennes lace that trimmed her sleeve, and brandished the letter from her new admirer.

"Look at his handwriting, *ma petite*! Is it not most aristocratic? Lord Ramsay! No mere 'Mister' this time. He writes he has something important to discuss with me, a private matter much to my advantage. See how wrong you were with your oh-so-serious sermons? If I had listened to you I wouldn't have bought this delicious coquelicot Swiss muslin and without an exquisite new gown, how would I captivate this Lord Ramsay?"

Zoe winced. "How could you have spent a hundred pounds on a single gown when you've owed the landlady far more than that since June?"

Her mother fixed her with an exasperated look. "Why should I throw away my money on the rent for a month that is already past? But a new gown—that is an investment! In return for the hundred pounds I paid for it, I will get two thousand pounds in jewels from this Lord Ramsay."

"And gamble them away before the month is out. You'll be begging me for another loan by Easter."

"What an unpleasant tone to take with your poor mother who has sacrificed so much for your welfare. I can't imagine where you got such a sour disposition."

"From my father, the duke."

Her mother heaved a dramatic sigh. "It's such a pity you inherited only *that* from him—and *his* looks instead of mine. If only you hadn't ended up with his enormous beak and those heavy features. It's so unjust, though the heavens know I do not complain. But even if your father *was* an ugly man, there is no excuse for the way you go on. Even an ugly woman can develop charm, and you make no effort at all."

"Perhaps I don't want to be charming," Zoe replied, but her words were cut off by a knock on the door downstairs.

"That will be Lord Ramsay, *ma petite*. Go hide yourself somewhere. I want to meet with him alone."

Isabelle sent her maid to admit the visitor and arranged herself most fetchingly on the chaise longue, stretching out her legs so that their outline could be seen through the fine muslin of her gown. It was a pose that never failed to remind her admirers of why they admired her.

Zoe headed for the door that led out of her mother's parlor.

"*Imbécile!*" her mother shouted. "Not the bedroom! Find some other place to hide yourself. *Sacre bleu*, how can you teach in a school when you can't understand the simplest thing? It is bad enough to have no charm, but to have no sense—" she shook her head in exasperation. "Well, he's here now, so there's no help for it. I shall have to introduce you to him, but once that's done, you must go."

In this, if nothing else, they were in perfect agreement. It would be a relief to return to the school, even if it meant abandoning her darling, spoiled mother to her thoughtless life of pleasure. She only hoped her mother would remember to repay her the many pounds she'd borrowed once she'd completed her negotiations with this new admirer. But it wasn't likely. Her mother would always need new gowns and new bonnets, hothouse flowers and expensive scents. That her daughter might need something never entered her mind.

Just then the door opened and her mother's visitor entered. At first all Zoe noticed was that he was unusually tall and that, despite the hint of warmth in the air that suggested an early spring, he wore a many-caped greatcoat of the sort that a gentleman would don this time of year only when preparing for dusty travel. In one hand he held a long, gold-handled cane with an odd device on the ferule that appeared to be some sort of serpent.

As soon as he entered, her mother rose to greet him, favoring him with a dazzling smile that displayed the shining white teeth of which she was, so rightly, proud. Her visitor didn't return her smile, but simply removed his tall beaver hat with a polite flourish and bowed toward both of them.

Zoe had assumed that this latest man her mother had dredged up would be well into middle age, for as her mother had grown older, her protectors had grown older, too. But the man in front of her looked unlikely to be much over thirty. Nor was he unattractive. True, his chestnut hair was cut unfashionably long, and there was the faintest haze of golden stubble on his cheek, which gave him an odd look—not at all that of a man of the *ton*. But his features were regular and fine in a way that marked him as the product of generations of good breeding. Even though there was something outlandish about the cut of his coat, she would never have mistaken him for anything but a gentleman.

But her examination of her mother's visitor came to an abrupt halt as she became aware that he was staring back at her, examining her with a curiosity equal to her own and making no attempt to hide that curiosity under a veneer of politeness. She tore her eyes away from his gaze, but not before realizing there was also something odd about his gold-flecked eyes.

La Belle Isabelle formed her lips into an inviting pout. "Your Lordship, how good of you to come. My young friend here was just on her way out."

Zoe turned toward the door. Of course, her mother wouldn't reveal their true relationship. Why trumpet the fact that La Belle Isabelle was old enough to have a daughter who was almost twenty-one?

Lord Ramsay made a perfunctory bow in Zoe's direction. "Charmed," he said, before turning back to Isabelle. "But let us get to the point. I am told you have a daughter."

"What interest can you have in a child?" Her expression betrayed her surprise. "My daughter is a mere schoolgirl."

"A schoolgirl? I must have been misinformed. I expected her to be the exact age of your young friend here."

La Belle Isabelle struggled to maintain her composure. "No. You haven't been misinformed. Not at all."

"Your daughter is a teacher, is she not, at Mrs. Endicott's Select Female Academy?" He pronounced the name in a tone heavy with sarcasm.

But how could he have known such a thing?

Clearly, her mother wondered, too. The vapid expression with which she disarmed her male admirers had been replaced for the moment with one more calculating. "How do you come to know so much about my daughter?"

"I've made it my business to know everything about you." His smile betrayed no underlying good humor. "For example, I know that your daughter is not only of the same age as this young woman here, but shares her coloring—brown hair and eyes—and is of a similar stature. Indeed, a reasonable man might conclude this young woman *was* your daughter."

Her bluff called, her mother threw down her cards. "You are very well informed, Your Lordship. Indeed. I won't attempt to mislead you. This young woman is my daughter."

Zoe felt her cheeks burn as their visitor turned the full force of his gaze on her. She braced herself for what always followed, the surprise mixed with pity that so beautiful a mother should have so ugly a child. Her mother's suitor made no reply, but the tightening of his lips revealed what he was thinking.

Her mother hurried on. "I must beg you to forgive me for not introducing her to you, your Lordship, but really, what would you have had me say, in view of the delicacy of the situation?" She shrugged one exquisite, half-naked shoulder and then blushed prettily. "Zoe, darling," she said in an unmistakably maternal tone, "make your *adieux* to Lord Ramsay."

But before she could comply, he broke in. "There is no need for your daughter to make her *adieux*, madam," he said. "I should like her to remain with us while I discuss my intentions with you."

Her mother's perfectly plucked eyebrows rose. "That seems hardly the thing, milord. She is still a young and innocent girl. This discussion is a matter between the two of us, *non?*"

"*No*," Lord Ramsay replied in an exaggeratedly English accent. "I am not French enough to dispose of a young girl's future without allowing her to be part of the conversation."

"But surely, Your Lordship, it was *our* future you've come here to discuss. It is hardly appropriate for a young child to be present at such a time."

"It is your daughter's future that concerns me."

Zoe stopped dead, her heart fluttering. *Her future?*

"Whatever could you want with my daughter?" Her mother's voice rose. "Surely you don't know her—or do you?" She stared at Zoe. "What mischief have you been hiding from your mother, *ma petite*? Lecturing me so severely and then getting up to who knows what tricks on your own."

Lord Ramsay interrupted. "The girl is blameless. This is the first time we've met. But it is she who is the subject of my interest. I must apologize if my intent was not made clear to you in my letter."

Zoe saw her mother's face fall, if only for a moment, as the import of his words struck home. What a humiliating mistake to have made! Though how understandable—until now no man had shown the slightest interest in paying court to her daughter—so ugly to start with and made all the more hideous after the smallpox had left her scarred—not that Zoe cared. She'd never had any wish to become some roué's plaything to be toyed with and later tossed aside.

But her mother was not easily flustered. Composing herself, she protested, "Your Lordship, this is so sudden. My daughter is still so young, such an innocent— I cannot bear to think of losing her."

"Your daughter is twenty and lives for the most part at a school." Lord Ramsay was no longer smiling. "Any arrangement we can come to can only relieve the anxiety you must have about her future."

"That is so true, *milord*, but still, it is no little thing to dispose of the future of a child. I want the best for her."

"I cannot doubt it." Again that undisguised sarcasm in his voice.

He reached into his pocket and withdrew a small but ornate box, which he held out toward Zoe. Compelled by his rigid gaze, she took it from him. It was surprisingly heavy. As she slowly pried it open, the glint of gold and a shimmering green stone met her eye. It was a bracelet in the form of a dragon. A large emerald formed its eye. Magnificent, but barbaric, too.

Almost as barbaric as the transaction it implied.

But before she could react, her mother swooped down and grabbed the box, lifting the bracelet off the thick gray padding it rested on and examining it greedily with the eye of one well versed in the appraisal of jewelry. Only after turning and twisting the gem to catch the light and weighing it with one hand did she restore it to Zoe and give her judgment. "Quite a nice piece. But of course there must be matching ear bobs, too. It's impossible to wear such a bauble without them, and my daughter has led such a sheltered life that, naturally, she has no other jewelry."

Lord Ramsay directed a look of annoyance at Isabelle. "The bracelet is but a token of what is in store for her, were I to find her suitable. There could be more."

Suitable for what? Zoe could barely believe what she was hearing. But her mother was taking it in stride. "She would have to have her own carriage," she demanded. "And bank shares. A girl is only a virgin once."

An unpleasant smile flashed across Lord Ramsay's gaunt features. "But that is the question, isn't it? *Is* she still a virgin?"

"Of course she is! Do you not think I would guard the virtue of my lone child like a hawk?"

"No, I do not, not in view of the eagerness with which you appear to be willing to bargain it away." He turned to Zoe. "Is your mother telling the truth, girl? Are you still a virgin?"

The avidity with which he awaited her answer was even more shocking than the crudeness of his question. "That's none of your business!" she snarled.

"To the contrary. It is essential that I know."

She refused to dignify him with an answer, returning his stare with one she hoped was even ruder. He dropped his eyes, letting his insolent gaze drift from her marred face to her thin chest and downward along her narrow flanks to her spindly legs. After a pause that stretched out so long she felt she must cry out in agony, he said, "You needn't answer. You are clearly a virgin."

She gasped, but couldn't bring herself to contradict him.

"Milord," her mother joined in. "Since you are satisfied on that point, we must discuss further these arrangements. She will need a carriage—"

"A carriage. What else?"

"The bank shares. They could be arranged?"

Lord Ramsay shrugged. "I would have to determine if the girl was worth it."

Her mother continued to bargain, as if she were negotiating with a grocer for a particularly fine joint of mutton. But she must be mad. Ugly as Zoe was, there was no good reason why a man like this would be interested in *her*—a man who was a stranger to both of them and who knew all too much about her, even the name of the school where she earned her modest living.

And his manner was so cold and sarcastic. Why did her mother persist in bargaining with him, ignoring these obvious signs of danger as she demanded that he provide her daughter with a house in town and pin money, acting, for all the world, like a mother of the *ton* negotiating a marriage settlement for her daughter.

Except, of course, that it wasn't a marriage settlement she was negotiating.

What could explain his interest in her? It couldn't be lust, whatever he might be pretending. She knew too well what lust looked like, having grown up surrounded by the men whose passions her mother so expertly manipulated. But she saw no lust in his deep-set eyes. Why would there be, with the way she looked?

So it must be something else. Perhaps she was the butt of some ill-conceived wager. Perhaps some idle pink of the *ton* had bet this haughty lord that he couldn't deflower an ugly woman. Or perhaps he needed to purchase three virgins as part of some perverted scavenger hunt. The men her mother consorted with were capable of concocting such a prank, and under other circumstances she might have even seen the humor in it—but not now. Not when she was the butt of it. Not when her mother was desperate for the rent, and Lord Ramsay was her only way of paying it.

But whatever his game was, she'd had enough of it. She was ugly, yes, and unprotected, but she deserved more than this, even from a stranger. She wondered what he'd lose were he to lose his wager, and hoped it would be a lot.

"You may go to hell with your offer." She tossed the bracelet back at him, flinging the satin box after it.

He fielded both surprisingly deftly, considering his size, then drew back. "It wasn't enough for you?"

"No offer would be enough. My virtue is not for sale."

"Ah, but that is where you are wrong," he said with an unpleasant look. "It has been sold these last nine years. There's no need for me to offer you carriages and bank shares, Zoe Gervais. Didn't your mother tell you about her bargain?"

A look of horror had swept over her mother's face, but she protested, "What are you talking about? What bargain?"

Lord Ramsay fixed her with a hard look. "You know full well what bargain. The one you made in France. The masquerade is over. I indulged myself in it because I was curious to see how low you would sink, but now that I know, there's no more reason for playacting. I've come to claim her."

"Who are you?" her mother whispered, clutching her throat protectively with her hand.

"Think back. Ignore my hair. Back then it was in a queue, and I was far younger—and much more innocent—as innocent as your daughter claims to be. Look at me more closely. Do you remember me, now?"

Her mother peered at him. Then her hand went to her mouth and she gasped out, "*Mon Dieu*, Adam Selkirk. I thought you were dead."

"You may wish I were before this day is done, but I lived—no thanks to you."

"So all this"— she gestured toward his letter—"and calling yourself Lord Ramsay—was it just a ruse to get me to admit you?"

He shrugged, sending a quiver through the many capes of his greatcoat. "Selkirk is my family name, Ramsay my title, but I didn't choose to use it in France in '93. It wouldn't have fit the temper of the times."

"No," her mother agreed. "Not with the tumbrels rolling to the guillotine, so full of men with titles."

"And with women, too—as you of all people must know." His voice was cold, but his eyes were burning.

"But it was so long ago," her mother protested. "It's like a dream to me now, a very bad dream, but still, I've forgotten so much."

"And *I* have forgotten nothing. How could I? I may still be alive, but Charlotte is not."

Her mother shrank back. "Poor child! So they killed her too. Those terrible men. May I give you my condolences?"

She stopped and turned her beautiful face toward him, filled now with the wistful expression that had always been one of her most effective.

This time it failed.

"You may give me nothing," Lord Ramsay snapped. "Except the satisfaction of knowing that at last Charlotte will be avenged. I have come to retrieve your pledge to *him*." He held up the discarded bracelet. Its serpent's eye glimmered dully.

"The Dark Lord?"

"Who else? He's on his deathbed, but before he dies he wishes to see the girl you sold him."

"Dying? Him? It seems impossible."

"He is a mortal man, despite his great powers. And you must give him your daughter."

Zoe had never seen her mother so perturbed. Her arm shook beneath its froth of lace. When she finally got command enough of herself to speak, Isabelle said, "All these years he made no claims on me. He left me in peace. He let me raise my daughter. I thought he'd forgotten all about her."

"The Dark Lord forgets nothing. And now she must come with me."

"Why you?"

He made no reply, but merely reached into the pocket of his many-caped greatcoat and pulled out a single glossy black feather that appeared to have some notches cut into it. He tossed it contemptuously on the table before them.

Her mother stared at it, openmouthed, then gasped. "Only those he drew into the darkest of his mysteries knew of the feather code. But you were hardly more than a child back then. How could you have learned it?"

"My childhood ended abruptly. And since then I've learned many things. Enough that he has decided to make me his heir."

"The Dark Lord's heir? You?" A look of horror swept over her features.

"Yes. If the Ancient Ones will accept me."

Her mother swiftly crossed herself. She was trembling visibly now.

Lord Ramsay pushed on. "I am his heir, and he has sent me to claim the pledge you made to him—"

Zoe could no longer hold her tongue. "What nonsense is this, Mama? What's all this talk of pledges, as if I were some trinket you'd pawned?"

Her mother reached for her handkerchief and dabbed at her eyes. She had always claimed nothing was so aging for a woman's skin as tears, and it appeared to be true, for she looked as if she'd just aged a decade. She held up one hand weakly and said, "He speaks the truth, *ma petite*. You must go with him."

"But that's ridiculous! I've no intention of going

anywhere with him. Surely you won't hand me over to some stranger who storms in here and behaves so abominably—"

"But she must entrust you," Lord Ramsay said softly, "to the custody of the appointed representative of your guardian. And that is who I am."

"My guardian? I have no guardian." She turned to her mother for confirmation, but she had buried her face in her hands.

Lord Ramsay went on relentlessly. "You have a guardian, as your mother well knows." He reached into the pocket of his coat and brought forth a packet of papers. "Here, see for yourself. It's all in these documents, with every *whereas* and *heretofore* the lawyers could come up with. Your mother transferred all legal right to you to one Robert Montgomery, the Laird of Iskeny, when you were twelve. And here is the letter in which he gave me the authority to come claim you."

Zoe snatched the papers from his hand. His fingers were much longer than her own, and surprisingly strong. She flung herself on the divan and forced herself to read the musty documents with their unfamiliar legal terminology. Surely this couldn't be true.

But the papers appeared to be genuine and to confirm his claim. They stated quite plainly that her mother, though given custody of her while she completed her education, had transferred the guardianship of her daughter to one Robert Montgomery, Laird of the Isle of Iskeny.

Zoe's stomach quivered and she found it almost impossible to breathe. She could not have felt worse had the floor given way, letting her plummet into the dark, malodorous shaft that had opened beneath her feet.

When she finally was able to face him again, she found that the man who now controlled her life had turned his attention to replacing the rejected bracelet in its ornate box. As he arranged it on its cushion, he gently stroked the dragon's head, then closed the lid and dropped the box back into the pocket of his greatcoat, oblivious to her dismay.

"I hope you are satisfied that all is in order. It's well past the time when I must remove you from your mother's custody. We must leave now. There's no time to lose if we are to reach Iskeny while my teacher still lives."

"Have I no choice but to go with you?"

"None." He gestured impatiently for her to return the legal papers. When she did, he carefully folded them before restoring them, too, to his greatcoat pocket. "It will be better for both of us if you don't give yourself up to strong hysterics. Where are your things? At the school?"

Zoe nodded dumbly.

"Good. I'll send a man there to fetch them."

"Won't you at least allow me to return there to say my farewells?"

"No. Your schooling is over."

"But I must bid good-bye to Mrs. Endicott. I owe her so much. I can't just leave her without a word."

"You love your schoolmistress that much?" He lowered his eyes so that she couldn't see their expression.

She took a deep breath. "The school has been the

only steady home I have had since I was ten. I love Mrs. Endicott." She forced back the rush of pain that accompanied this confession, terrified she had revealed too much. But to her surprise, something softer replaced the cold glint in Lord Ramsay's eyes.

"Then we will pay a brief call on Mrs. Endicott." He grasped his serpent-headed cane. "A very brief one. I won't deprive you of the chance to say good-bye to someone who means that much to you, even though your mother deprived me of mine." The coldness was back. "But it *will* be good-bye, Zoe. You are mine now."

His.

His hooded steel gray eyes were hidden now in the shadow of the tall collar of his greatcoat. She shivered.

Then he turned to face her mother again. "You did very well with your bargain, Isabelle Gervais, whatever it might have entailed. The old laird is leaving you a legacy, a hundred pounds. I doubt another bidder, whoever he might be, would have ever given you half so much in return for your daughter—even if she had turned out to be twice as talented a harlot as yourself."

Chapter 2

He'd failed.

Adam's hand tightened on the head of his serpent-headed cane as the hired post chaise conveyed him and the harlot's daughter to her school. He'd waited so long for his revenge, ever since that terrible day at Morlaix, nine years before, when The Dark Lord had led Adam away from the cold room where Charlotte's headless body lay and confined him in the chamber where he kept the madmen brought to him for healing.

But when time for revenge had finally come, Adam had failed to take it.

If only the Dark Lord hadn't kept him bound in restraints at Morlaix until it was too late for pursuit. Adam wouldn't have flinched from killing his sister's murderer then. But the old man had stepped in, knowing that if he'd let him track Isabelle down right after the crime, once he had killed her, he'd have turned his knife on himself.

It was only later, when Adam, exhausted from hours of raging, could finally listen to what the Dark Lord had to say, that the healer had convinced him that it wasn't too late to atone for the curse that stained Adam's soul. That was when his teacher had promised that if Adam did as he prescribed, when the time was right the Dark Lord would grant him a revenge far more satisfying than anything Adam could imagine now, for by then Adam would have cleansed himself of the fatal flaw that had made revenge necessary.

So Adam had taken the vow the healer had demanded, and when that was done, the old man had given him the serpent-headed cane, as a talisman to protect him, as he'd embarked on the grueling pilgrimage that would purify him.

For the next nine years, Adam had traveled to the great centers of learning on the Continent where he found the physicians who taught him the things the Dark Lord had instructed him to study. He'd been able to find solace in his studies, knowing they would make him more worthy to take his revenge when the time finally came. And as he mastered the skills that transformed him into a healer, the agony he felt at remembering how he'd failed his sister dwindled into an ache he'd learned to live with, like the stab of a rotten tooth.

There had even been times over the past years when he'd become so wrapped up in mastering the fine points of surgery with the scintillating Von Faschling in Vienna that he'd almost forgotten that the time for his revenge would come. Except, of course, on those nights when Charlotte's ghost came back to him in dreams, silent and reproving. Then he'd assure her, *I will avenge you*. And he'd meant it.

But when that moment had come at last, there in the harlot's rose-scented lair, he hadn't been able to do it.

"You live too much in dreams," the Dark Lord had told him when he first read Adam's horoscope, back at the very beginning, when Adam, newly arrived at Morlaix, had applied to him for teaching. The Dark Lord had been dismissive. "With four planets in Pisces, you might become a flute player, perhaps, or a drunkard. But a healer?" The Dark Lord had shaken his head. "A healer must be a man of action, not a dreamer."

And the old man had been right. For it was only in his dreams that Adam had avenged his sister. When he'd found himself, at last, face-to-face with the harlot, he'd come up short. Even though he'd followed the Dark Lord's instructions to the letter and made his appointment with Isabelle for the exact moment when the Moon eclipsed the Sun in Pisces, when he'd finally stood in her presence and had her and her cursed whelp at his mercy, he hadn't been able to do it.

The painted harlot still lived, swathed in her tawdry lace. He would never forgive himself.

He was brought back to the present as the post chaise slowed. They must have reached the school. He forced himself to get a grip. He'd have another chance to finish off the matter of the harlot once he'd come into all the Dark Lord's powers. But though he'd failed his sister today, he mustn't fail the teacher who had lodged such trust in him by choosing him as his heir. Adam still marveled that he'd done so, after all these years of separation. But in the letter that had summoned Adam to Iskeny, his teacher had explained that Adam alone of all his disciples had kept the vow the Dark Lord had enjoined on him—that vow so necessary if the heir was to survive his initiation.

The carriage stopped. When the postilion opened the door, Adam clambered out, taking care to block the entry as he took the harlot's daughter by the hand firmly enough to signal that escape would be futile. "I'll accompany you while you bid your *adieux*."

She shot him a furious look, her dark eyes blazing above her pockmarked cheeks. Her passion gave her face life, which contrasted strongly with the ugliness of her features.

Well, the girl should be thanking whatever stars ruled over *her* birth for that ugliness, for it had saved her mother's life. He'd been so shocked by his first sight of her crude features that he'd lost his momentum. Even now, he couldn't help staring at her. How could this be Isabelle's daughter? Even without smallpox's disfigurement she would have been ill-favored. Her nose was large and aquiline, her chin too strong, and her posture was ungainly. She was everything her mother was not.

For nine long years he'd pictured the harlot's daughter—that girl whose life had been saved at the cost of his beloved Charlotte's—and all that time he'd imagined her as dimpled and seductive, stupid and heartless, a pallid copy of her mother, the woman who'd ruined his life.

But the girl who had confronted him in Isabelle's boudoir was not the girl he'd imagined. The contrast had stopped him in his tracks even as he'd played through the cruel joke he'd set up to humiliate his victims—and determine if the girl had retained her virginity. She'd shown such courage. He'd expected cunning and greed from Isabelle's daughter, not bravery. But it was bravery she'd shown him, and that had made him hesitate—so much so that at that long-awaited moment when he might finally have taken his revenge, his knife had remained in its sheath.

Even now, he couldn't understand it.

He knew nothing about the girl, really. Whatever she looked like, she was still the harlot's daughter, inheriting all her cunning and her guile. She probably didn't deserve his pity. But even so, he hadn't been able to kill her mother before her eyes.

The harlot would live on—though whether her daughter would, when they got to the Dark Lord's island—he gripped the handle of his cane more tightly—well, that would be up to his teacher to decide.

When they alighted at the school, the arthritic old porter opened the heavy front door at Lord Ramsay's first knock. His wrinkled face had never seemed so dear to Zoe before, but she had no time to linger with him, as Lord Ramsay immediately ushered her into the building and stood glowering behind her, tall and spare. The porter gave him an uncertain look.

"Please inform Mrs. Endicott that Miss Gervais's guardian would have a word with her," Lord Ramsay said coolly.

The porter nodded and went off to look for his mistress. Soon the swish of her heavy old-fashioned skirts against the polished wooden floor announced Mrs. Endicott's arrival. Barely acknowledging Zoe's presence, she made her way across the room to Lord Ramsay and curtseyed deeply, as she would have done to the father of one of her wealthier students.

He inclined his head very slightly in acknowledgment, narrowly avoiding being rude. But Mrs. Endicott didn't allow herself the luxury of taking offense. Addressing him in her low, well-modulated tones, she said, "Lord Ramsay, I'm so sorry to hear that the Laird of Iskeny's illness is such that he isn't expected to live. His man of business has informed me that he sent you to bring Miss Gervais to him in Scotland."

Lord Ramsay nodded. "Yes. We leave immediately."

Zoe was appalled. Until this moment she'd been sure her schoolmistress would step in and keep her from being taken way, as she'd done in the past when her mother had tried to remove her from school to set her up in some more profitable employment. But she detected no hint of opposition in the dulcet tones with which Mrs. Endicott addressed Lord Ramsay.

Zoe shot her a look of appeal, but the schoolmistress ignored it and continued on serenely, "We will feel the loss of Miss Gervais. She has been an asset to the school. I'd hoped she might become one of our permanent teachers, in time, for she has a talent for instruction, especially with the younger girls. But of course, she will have so many more advantages under her guardian's care. It would be selfish of me to ask you to leave her with us."

Zoe could hold still no longer. "But what of my desires? I want to stay at the school with you. Surely you won't allow my mother to hand me over to some rake."

"Temper your language, Zoe," Mrs. Endicott commanded. She turned back to Lord Ramsay. "May I have a word in private with Miss Gervais?"

He nodded curtly.

Mrs. Endicott ushered Zoe into her small office, but after she'd closed the heavy door behind them, she didn't take her usual place behind the large desk. Instead she put her arms around Zoe and gently stroked her shoulder.

"Why all this wild talk, my dear? I should never have expected such vehemence from you, the most mature of all my student teachers. The Laird of Iskeny is your guardian. After having paid your school fees all these years, it's understandable he should wish to see you, especially now when he is so ill."

This laird had paid her school fees all along? This was the first she had heard of it.

"I thought my mother paid my fees."

Mrs. Endicott's eyebrows shot up. "My dear, we must speak frankly. As bright an ornament as you've proven to be to my establishment, I should never have admitted you into it had it not been for the laird's influence— not with such a mother. But the Laird of Iskeny was quite emphatic that no other situation would do for his ward, and given his rank and wealth, I was persuaded to make allowances. All the more reason you should be grateful to him, instead of treating his emissary with such rudeness."

"But if that was the case, why didn't you tell me? Neither you nor my mother ever mentioned a word about my having a guardian."

"The laird preferred it that way, and I respected his desire that I not burden you with the need to express your gratitude."

"Am I to be grateful, too, that he's put me into the power of a man like this Lord Ramsay?"

"Of course. I admit it *is* a bit irregular that he sent a man to fetch you to him, rather than entrusting you to the chaperonage of a lady. But the journey to Scotland is a difficult one and the laird's illness requires it be made in haste. If I had a maid to spare, I should send her along to preserve the proprieties, but at such short notice it isn't possible. But, even so, you should have nothing to fear from Lord Ramsay. As your acting guardian, he stands in the same relationship to you as an uncle or older brother. You need fear no stain on your reputation should you find yourself alone with him. But you must know that, Zoe. You're well aware of the rules of propriety, so well aware that I'm at a loss to understand how you could have had the temerity to call him a rake to his face. What made you speak so rudely?"

"*His* rudeness. When he presented himself to my mother, he acted as if he'd come to make me his mistress. He pretended to give me jewels and then let my mother dicker with him over terms before he revealed he'd been sent by my guardian."

"That does sound odd." Mrs. Endicott brought one finger to rest against her long chin. "Still, I've heard no ill of Lord Ramsay. The laird writes that he is to be his heir, and that he has been away on the Continent for many years studying medicine. Beyond that, Lord Ramsay's family is known to me. Their barony has an illustrious history in Scotland and stretches back to the days of the Wallace and the Bruce. You should consider yourself fortunate that he has offered to take you under his wing. It's a rare opportunity for someone whose own ancestry is so uncertain."

This reminder of her illegitimacy stung. Only long habit kept her from protesting that even if she had been born on the wrong side of the blanket, she wasn't just Isabelle's daughter, but the daughter of a duke, a man more noble even than Lord Ramsay, and that her father's illustrious blood ran in her veins, too. But she kept silent. She didn't want to see Mrs. Endicott's eyes fill with the look of pity that was all too likely to follow such an assertion.

"It *is* true," Mrs. Endicott admitted, "that the Selkirks are known to be somewhat eccentric, but then so is the laird. I'm told he has become quite mystical in his old age. But these mental oddities are often found in the finest old Scottish families. You must make some allowance for them."

"So you will entrust me to a madman because your respect for his nobility outweighs any care you might have for what happens to a whore's daughter?"

Mrs. Endicott shrank at the crude word Zoe had flung at her, but even though surprise had temporarily got the better of her, she still kept her back ramrod-straight. "There's no need for such intemperate language, Zoe," she chided, "especially from you, whom I've often held up as a model to our younger girls. Of course your future matters greatly to me."

"My language isn't any worse than what he used to my mother. He made it clear that he hates her. He means to do me harm. Why won't you help me?"

"Because I can't. Lord Ramsay comes at the behest of your legal guardian."

"Even so, he displayed a most ungentlemanly curiosity about whether I was still a virgin. He asked me, point-blank. What if he intends to ruin me?"

"Then you must pray to our Savior to protect you," Mrs. Endicott said with resignation, "and carry a knife."

She walked over to a small desk and rummaged in the drawer until she found a penknife with a pearl handle. With a single press of some invisible mechanism it flew open, revealing a surprisingly long blade. Zoe took it from her and flourished it as if she were stabbing an imaginary assailant. Its hard, smooth handle felt good in her hand.

Reluctantly, she closed it, after closely examining its mechanism to be sure she understood how it worked. When she was done, she handed it back to Mrs. Endicott, who put a long silver chain through its bail. Then she draped it around Zoe's neck as if it were a pendant, adjusting the chain so that the small knife was hidden snugly between her breasts.

"Should you find yourself in danger, the knife should be enough to protect you. But for now, we must give your guardian the benefit of the doubt. Truly, I find it hard to credit that he intends to dishonor you. You aren't at all the sort of girl who attracts men with depraved lusts. And even if your guardian's tastes did run to the debauching of young girls, well, I can't imagine that the laird would have paid your school fees all these years only to dispose of you in such a way. Our fees are quite high, and young girls may be had so cheaply—"

"So I must trust I'll be safe because I'm too ugly to tempt a rake?"

"That *is* putting it strongly, but you were always a practical girl, so I will speak plainly. One doesn't often hear of men buying young girls whose strongest appeal lies in their good sense."

The corner of Mrs. Endicott's lips turned up in a troubled smile. "Though I must hope you've misinterpreted the conversation between your mother and this man. One hears of such things, of course, but with a girl like you, it seems so unlikely."

Zoe turned away, not wishing to let her teacher see the emotions that must be clearly displayed on her scarred face with its eagle's beak and the heavy brows that were all that her father, the duke, had bequeathed her.

No one would step in to help her. She would have to go to Scotland with Lord Ramsay and hope that this man they called the Dark Lord had not, in fact, bought her to use for some unsavory purpose.

If he had, she could depend on no one to save her but

herself. But it had always been that way. Her hand flew
to the knife nestled now between her small bosoms. As
alone as she might be, Lord Ramsay wouldn't get the
best of her.

It took little time to pack up the belongings that
had made Zoe's little cubicle a home: a few books, her
summer gown, an old bonnet, some maps she had received as a prize for excellence in the study of geog-
raphy, and a rather bedraggled collection of ribbons.
She packed them carefully into her trunk, pausing
only when she came to the old doll, much the worse
for wear, that had been given to her years before by
old MacMinn, her mother's coachman. She thought of
leaving it behind, for it would take up valuable space in
her box, but decided against it. It was one of the very
few presents she'd ever received.

After she'd filled the last bit of empty space in her
trunk with her favorite books, there was no further
excuse for delay. Reluctantly, she made her way back
downstairs to the parlor, where she found Lord Ramsay
glowering, his eyes burning holes in the carpet. On
seeing her, he leapt up at once and gave the porter instructions to deposit her trunk in the hired post chaise.
Then, with no further conversation, he stood up and led
her out toward the equipage.

Though the afternoon was warm, she felt a chill as
Ramsay opened the carriage door and reached out one
gloved hand to assist her up the step. She thought of
making a break for freedom, but his grip on her hand
was surprisingly strong, giving her no choice but to seat

herself on the cracked leather upholstery of the hired post chaise, noting as she did so how his surprisingly broad shoulders blocked the doorway she'd just clambered through.

Only after she had smoothed out her brown serge skirts and settled back against the worn squabs did he take his place beside her. As he did, the energy that radiated out from him seemed to fill the compartment, like the subtle scent of some unfamiliar spice.

She half expected him to say something gloating, now that he had her completely in his power, but he showed no interest in conversation. Instead, he reached into the pocket of his many-caped greatcoat and extracted a small volume, which he began to read with the appearance of intense concentration.

Absorbed in his book, he looked strikingly different from the elegant aristocrat who had stolen her from her home. Indeed, had she not witnessed that unforgettable scene in her mother's withdrawing room, in which he had made his character so frighteningly plain, she would have guessed that the man beside her was an unworldly scholar on his way back to university.

His chestnut hair fell past his chin. It wasn't pulled back into the queue as she would have expected but hung almost to his shoulders, falling in gentle waves that reminded her of the look of a long dead medieval saint chiseled into the stone pillar of some ancient village church. He had unfastened his greatcoat upon entering the chaise. Beneath it, instead of the cravat and waistcoat she would have expected to see, he wore only a loose shirt of rough linen, open at the throat, where it revealed a tuft of reddish gold hair that glistened rather startlingly in the diffused light of the chaise compartment.

She pulled her eyes away from him and forced herself to peer through the window at the carts and wagons that were heading out of the city as their owners returned from the day's markets. But her thoughts kept returning to her companion. He was a startlingly handsome man. His face might have been called beautiful had he been a woman, but there was nothing unmanly about his beauty, just something sensuous and haunting, as if he had a dash of elfin blood mixed with the ichor of his aristocratic ancestors.

When he raised his hand to turn a page, the sleeve of the homespun shirt fell back and for a moment she thought what she saw was a trick of the compartment's dim light. She blinked her eyes to clear away the disturbing vision, but when she opened them again, it was still there. On the flesh of his forearm, the head of a serpent was picked out in delicate lines of blue. Its body entwined with that of another of its kind, rising along his arm, to where both vanished beneath the edge of his rough linen sleeve.

It was startling. Disturbing. She pulled her eyes away, wishing she hadn't seen it.

What could he possibly want with her?

The fear she'd confessed to Mrs. Endicott—that he'd kidnapped her for some carnal purpose—seemed far-fetched. The man across from her was far too attractive—and far too magnetic—to need to stoop to such a stratagem to get a woman.

But before she could pursue the thought further, Lord Ramsay interrupted her reverie. "I assume you haven't eaten." His voice was curiously melodic. "There's a hamper beneath the seat. Take what you like." He returned to his book, giving her not a second glance.

It had been a long time since she'd eaten, so despite her anxiety, she helped herself to a chicken sandwich, but her companion ignored the food as if he had no need to satisfy any earthly hunger. When she was done, she replaced the hamper beneath the seat. When she brushed against Lord Ramsay's leg by accident, he flinched and shrank away from her.

She turned her attention back to the scene passing outside the window. While she had been eating, they'd left London behind. Now they appeared to be heading north on the Great North road, the fabled route leading to Gretna Green, which was the chosen route of the scoundrels bent on abduction who were so often the villains of the novels beloved by the girls at school.

How very fitting! After all, she *had* been abducted. Unbidden, the image swam up in her mind of Lord Ramsay, transformed into just such a villain, throwing himself at her feet while making the kind of fervid declaration of love such villains were prone to. The vision was so ludicrous that, to her horror, she felt a giggle rising within her, and though she clamped her lips shut, she was powerless to suppress it.

Her captor looked up. "I see nothing humorous in our situation." His tone was quelling. "What made you laugh?"

She thought of telling him a falsehood, but given how

little respect he had already shown her, she doubted she could sink any lower in his estimation by telling him the truth.

"It was the road we are taking. The Great North Road features so heavily in the romances my school friends and I used to read to each other, late at night, when Mrs. Endicott thought us safely asleep. It amused me to find myself abducted by a nobleman, locked in a closed carriage, and headed for Gretna Green, just like the heroine of a novel from the Minerva Press. But of course, in such novels, the heroines are always great heiresses. One doesn't expect to find oneself abducted when one is the ugly, portionless daughter of a courtesan."

"Is that how you see yourself?" The faintest shadow of amusement quirked his full lower lip into a half smile.

"I know what I am," she replied. "I've always been recommended for my sense. And since you've given me no choice about going with you, why should you begrudge me what pleasure I might take from imagining the envy my situation would arouse in Miss Ecclesford, who is to have ten thousand pounds and is betrothed to a wall-eyed banker. *She'd* ask nothing more out of life than to be kidnapped by a handsome young nobleman like yourself."

Lord Ramsay peered intently at her, as if seeing her for the first time. "You haven't been kidnapped. I'm merely taking you to your guardian. I'd thought Mrs. Endicott had explained the situation to you."

"Mrs. Endicott assured me that you are descended

from a noble but eccentric race, and that, given my lack of looks and the hefty amount my guardian had lavished on my education, you were unlikely to have snatched me from my mother to make me your whore."

His eyebrows lifted, and again that half smile played at the corners of his lips. "One always wonders what women say to each other when they're out of the hearing of men, but, still, I find it difficult to believe your schoolmistress expressed herself like that. Did she really?"

"Not exactly," Zoe admitted. "Mrs. Endicott would never speak so crudely."

"But you would?"

"Why not? Being what I am, I can't expect to be treated like a lady no matter how I comport myself. So I take what pleasure I may in the liberties allowed to a courtesan's daughter."

For a moment she thought he would laugh at her wry joke, but then, as if he had forbidden himself humor, his lips tightened and he shrank away from her on the seat.

"I must thank you for reminding me of who you are," he said grimly. He sat silent for a moment, his eyes brooding. Then he set aside his book and leaned closer to her with a look of determination on his face. "What if your Mrs. Endicott was wrong? What if I *did* take you from your harlot of a mother to use in that way?"

He was trying to frighten her. It was obvious. But if so, his threat was poorly chosen. She was a practical woman and knew herself to be too ugly to raise any such desire in a man like him. Had there been the slightest question of it, the way he shrank from her touch as they rode along in the carriage would have removed it.

"She *did* sell you," he went on relentlessly. "When it was a matter of your mother's comfort and someone else's life, you know her well enough to know what choice she'd make."

Zoe shivered. She did know. And the anger in his voice made her think, too late, that perhaps her lack of looks might not matter. Perhaps he might take pleasure in hurting her, simply out of hatred. If so, she mustn't let him see her fear. There was a chance he'd only threatened her with his lust because he'd thought it would terrify her. If she behaved as if lust were a matter of no concern, perhaps he'd see no point in punishing her with it.

With as much control over her voice as she could muster, she said lightly, "So then it's true—you *do* intend to take my maidenhead." That flirting tone her mother used so well was hard to get right.

"I do *not*," he said icily.

"Then why were you so curious about my virginity?"

"I have no curiosity about it at all, Miss Gervais. I seek only to fulfill the Dark Lord's wishes. His instructions were that I should bring you with me when I came to claim my inheritance—once I'd satisfied myself that you were still a virgin. Which I did."

"So it's this Dark Lord of yours who cares about my virginity, not you?" She did her best to sound as if she held conversations about her maidenhead every day.

Ramsay's luminous gray eyes met hers again, and in them she saw again the surprise he had betrayed in response to her earlier frankness. But when he replied, his voice was grim. "My only concern is to see my dear Charlotte avenged. Your virginity or lack of it matters only to the Dark Lord. He has some use for it."

Summoning up all her courage, she asked, "Who was Charlotte?"

"My sister."

"And what did my mother do to her?"

"She sent her to her death."

The look in his eye shut down any further inquiry. Changing the subject abruptly, Zoe asked, "And this man you call the Dark Lord" —the man whose name alone had been enough to terrify her usually fearless mother—"who is he?"

The way Lord Ramsay's hand unclenched told her he was as glad as she was that she'd changed the subject. "He's the laird of the Isle of Iskeny off the Galloway coast."

"I've never heard of it before. Is it a large one?"

"No. It's quite small, and largely deserted. But it isn't the land from which the Dark Lord derives his power."

"His wealth is from some other source? Surely not from trade?"

"Hardly. His title is so ancient there are no written records of when it was first created. All that's known is that there's always been a laird on Iskeny, even before the Romans came to Britain, and that the laird has always had the power."

"What power?"

Ramsay focused his penetrating gray gaze on her. "The power of life and death."

"Over his subjects?"

"Over anyone in whom the life force flows. The Dark Lord can read a man's fate in the stars and, if he chooses, he can alter that fate.

"I find that hard to believe." Such things happened only in fairy tales.

"Believe what you will. I saw with my own eyes how he restored life to the body of a dead man. That is why I chose him for my teacher."

This was the man who'd bought her from her mother? Zoe forced her tone to give no hint of her uneasiness. "Since you are his heir, are you, too, of his ancient lineage?"

He shook his head no. "The Dark Lord's title doesn't pass down through one family. Had it done so, it couldn't have survived the millennia. Bloodlines run out or weaken, so, in their wisdom, the ancients established a better way to transmit the power of the Dark Lord through the centuries, unchanged."

"How?"

Ramsay's eyes flashed brightly, if only for a moment. "At the end of his life, each Dark Lord chooses one man from amidst his disciples. To that man is it given to descend into the Dragon's Cave and receive the Final Teaching."

"And you are that man?"

"Yes."

"Do you have powers, too?"

He shrugged. "A few—a bit of healing, a knowledge

of how to read the stars, and a slight ability to hear the thoughts of others when I exert myself—nothing like the power that he wields. But if I can reach the island while my teacher still lives, I'll endure the Final Teaching, and then"—his eyes glowed—"I'll become the next Dark Lord, with *all* the Dark Lord's powers."

This was no fairy tale to him. He believed it.

Perhaps she should leave it at that. But she could not. There was a question she must have answered before she could terminate this uncomfortable conversation. Best to get it over with. She cleared her throat. "Be that as it may, I'm still baffled as to why your master, having such great powers, would concern himself with my virginity."

Ramsay tented his long fingers together in his lap and stared intently at them. His eyes had taken on a haunted look. When he looked up again and his gaze met hers, a shock ran through her.

"I don't know," he replied. "Perhaps he thought I'd enjoy taking you from your mother, the way she took Charlotte from me. He knows how much I long for my revenge. Or perhaps he expected you to be as beautiful as she is and thought debauching you might please me."

It was getting harder to keep him from seeing her fear. But if he noticed it he gave her no sign. He shrugged. "Or it may be nothing of that kind. He is your guardian, after all. Perhaps he has some match in mind for you and wanted to assure himself that you were worthy of it. I've no way of knowing. When we reach Iskeny you'll learn more. Until then, there is no point in idle speculation."

Easy for him to say. She was no squeamish miss to go into hysterics at the thought of the loss of her maidenhead, but the brutal way he played with her fears was intolerable. Should she push open the carriage door and make a leap to safety?

No. The carriage was moving so swiftly such an attempt might end in her death. She was not such a fool as to prefer death to dishonor.

"Don't try it," he said. "Death *is* much worse than dishonor."

Had he read her thoughts? Her stomach tensed. But even if he could, she wouldn't let him get the best of her. "I don't know what you're talking about."

"You do," he replied. "And you know it. But rest assured, whatever the Dark Lord's intentions might be, *I* have no intention of debauching you."

"How very encouraging. Is that all you'll tell me?"

"Yes. The truth is, I don't know what's in store for you, only that the Dark Lord seems to have bought you from your harlot of a mother some years ago, and asked me to bring you with me to Iskeny—once I was certain you were still a virgin."

He turned back to his book, and this time she knew he would answer no more questions. She'd have to take whatever comfort she could from what he'd told her, though it was cold comfort, indeed. How ironic to learn she'd have been better rewarded had she taken less care of her virtue.

Chapter 3

Late that night they stopped at an inn. After Lord Ramsay drew forth his purse and handed a golden guinea to the innkeeper to quiet any doubts their unconventional appearance might have raised, the man led them to a private parlor attached to a suite of rooms where he supplied them with an indifferent dinner: boiled mutton and a loaf of hard bread clearly left over from last week's baking.

Her new guardian ate sparely, leaving untouched the steel implements the inn had provided and cutting his meat, instead, with a bronze knife of curious design that he had brought with him. When she remarked that it appeared to be quite old, he replied tersely that it had once belonged to an ancient Briton. But after this brief exchange he lapsed back into icy politeness, studiously avoiding any further conversation.

As soon as the inn maid had cleared their plates, Lord Ramsay guided Zoe to the chambers the innkeeper had assigned them and deposited her in the small cubicle set behind a door at the far end of his own bedchamber where she would sleep. He left her there with a single candle. She waited to find out if he would lock her door and was relieved when he didn't. But any hope that his omission might allow her to escape vanished when she realized there was no need for him to lock her in. The only way she could leave her tiny closet was by going through his bedchamber, where she could hear him moving about. She couldn't escape without confronting him. She was trapped.

But she must escape. Lord Ramsay's hatred for her mother was bad enough, but the barbaric serpents that twined up his arm, his allegiance to the ancient religion, and even her mother's terror at hearing him mention his master's name all pointed toward another reason she mustn't let him take her to the Dark Lord. She knew her history. The ancient Britons had used their knives for more than just cutting their meat. Their gods were bloodthirsty. Nothing good could await her on the remote isle where the Dark Lord held sway— this Dark Lord who worshipped the Ancient Ones and had sent his minion to bring him a virgin.

It was infuriating that it was her cursed virginity that made her so valuable to his master. If only she hadn't guarded it so closely. She'd fought off more than one of her mother's drunken guests, so that when she finally found her father, the duke, she would be a daughter he would be proud to acknowledge. How ironic it was that by defying her mother and turning away from her decadent way of life, she'd put her own life in peril.

But no sooner had that thought passed through her mind than she stopped stock-still. The idea that had just occurred to her was pure madness. She dismissed it, appalled that she'd come up with something so uncalled for. But it wouldn't go away. Its logic was irrefutable.

The Dark Lord wanted her only if she was a virgin. So the path to her freedom couldn't be clearer. She need only stop being a virgin.

Ramsay must not have considered a woman capable of thinking in a rational manner or he wouldn't have given her this vital piece of information. But, of course, he must have assumed she was a milk-and-water miss who would die before she'd contemplate earning her freedom at such a price. If so, he'd made a fatal mistake. For she was no foolish schoolgirl but a courtesan's daughter and she valued her freedom above all else.

If earning her freedom meant giving up that little flap of skin men valued so highly, so be it. She'd be the same person without it, but free. It would cost her little. Ugly as she was, and bastard-born, she had no hope of ever making the kind of advantageous marriage that motivated gently raised young women to defend their chastity.

So the path to liberty was clear, though the whole thing would have to be managed very carefully. And it would have to be done tonight, too, while an unlocked door was all that separated her from her captor's bed. If she waited too long, she might not be handed another such opportunity.

But how to achieve her end? She remembered how
Ramsay had shrunk away from her touch in the chaise.
She couldn't just offer herself to him. Nor could she
seduce him. Even if she'd been beautiful—and had
paid more attention to her mother's lessons on the
subject—she would still have to contend with the iron
self-control she sensed at Ramsay's core. Nothing so
blatant would work with him.

But there must be some other way—and within moments she saw how it could be done. One of her mother's favorite scandalous tales told of how an ugly girl
from a poor but noble family had won herself a wealthy
husband by slipping into his bed when he was sleeping
and taking things to such a point that when he finally
awakened, the man had no choice but to marry her. It
had taken place in France, of course, where men were
far easier to seduce. But still, a man was a man. Her
mother had left her in no doubt about that. And she knew
enough about men to know that if she could insinuate
herself into Lord Ramsay's bed when his consciousness
was disarmed, she might arouse him sufficiently that
even if he were to waken, nature would take its course.

Though perhaps she was underestimating the difficulty. He was a Scot, after all, not a Frenchman. And
he'd already displayed the most famous characteristic
of his nation, a quick temper. What if her plan went
awry and he became violent?

Such fears were unworthy of her. Hadn't her father,
the duke, succeeded in an even more impossible situation? Her mother had often recounted how he'd escaped the siege of Louisbourg disguised as a peddler

and come back with the reinforcements that saved the garrison. And hadn't he scaled a wall at Fort Brevard and challenged its commander to the duel that avoided a costly battle? *He* hadn't scrupled over whether his daring plans might fail.

She gave herself a moment to enjoy the feeling of her father's noble blood surging through her veins as she drew upon his courage. She would be as daring as he'd been. She had no choice. She wanted no part of the Ancient Ones and their dragon magic.

And if she roused Lord Ramsay's temper? She reached inside her bodice for the folding knife that Mrs. Endicott had given her, lifting its chain over her head. Though small, the knife was sharp, and its size, when folded, made it easy to conceal. If things went wrong, she wouldn't be entirely without protection.

But that thought led to another thought. She'd need more protection than a knife could afford her. She continued rummaging through her bag of sundries until she found the small package her mother had given her not long ago. Gratefully, she confirmed that the sponge and vinegar were still there. She didn't want Lord Ramsay's child. Once again she was glad to be a courtesan's daughter, not some innocent young miss. But of course, an innocent young miss was unlikely to have a mother who would sell her to a wizard.

That done, she stood up carefully, as the ceiling of the room in the old coaching inn was so low that her head almost touched the blackened beam sloping down the plastered wall. She wriggled out of her drab teacher's gown designed to give her the dignity needed to convince a roomful of giggling girls only a few years younger than herself that she was someone whose edicts must be obeyed. Then she unfastened her stays and slipped off her shift.

When she was finally naked, she took inventory of the tools she had to work with. Her body, illuminated by the light of the one tallow taper Lord Ramsay had left her with, was tall, yes—far too tall according to her mother and her friends. But Ramsay was taller still, so that wasn't a problem.

Her face was a ruin, of course, but it would be dark, and her mother had told her that, in bed, it wasn't women's faces men cared about. True, Zoe had no luscious curves, but though rangy, she was well-proportioned. She stroked one hand over her long thigh. The skin there was soft and unblemished, the muscles taut.

Then she went to her valise and pulled out the cast-off dressing gown her mother had given her for her last birthday. It was of ivory satin, luxurious and flamboyant like her mother herself, but more importantly, it had a little pocket inside the lining where she could stash her knife. She struggled into the gown, pulling it against her long, spare body, and tied the sash, letting its luxuriant folds fall loosely around her.

In the past, its lush sensuality had disgusted her, for the gift was just another reminder of what a disappointment she'd been to her mother. But now she hoped the sensuous gown might make up for what she lacked in dimpled curves. She slipped her knife into the pocket, checking that she could get at it easily should the need arise.

Her preparations complete, she tiptoed to the partition that separated her room from Ramsay's and placed her ear against it. It was thinner than the rest of the old inn's plaster walls, and through it she could hear sounds as he moved about his chamber. At first, it sounded as if he was pacing, as restless as she was. Then he settled into a chair—she heard him dragging it along the creaking floorboards. Sometime later, he removed his boots, which clattered against the floor as they fell. After that, she heard only the faintest rustlings as he settled, at last, into bed. He coughed once, and there was silence.

She waited another quarter hour. Then, saying a silent prayer that she might find the courage that had saved her father, she opened the inner door that led to the adjoining chamber.

Though moonlight poured in from a window, Ramsay's face was hidden by the shadows cast by the curtain hanging over his bed. As Zoe approached him, the weight of her foot caused the floorboards to groan. She halted, terrified he would awaken, but his breathing remained steady and rhythmic. Cautiously, she took another step toward the bed. The rustle of her robe and the slight scrape of her foot against the floor seemed louder than the harsh cry of the owl that pierced the darkness outside.

Still Ramsay slept. Her plan was going as she had intended.

That should have reassured her, but it didn't. In fact, it terrified her. If nothing was going to stop her from doing what she planned to do, nothing was going to *save* her from what she planned to do—and it was so very risky. She tried to ignore the quiver of uneasiness that shot through her stomach as she crossed the last few paces toward his bedside and drew aside the hangings that protected him from the nighttime damp.

Moonlight glanced off his pale skin. He lay naked under the covers, curled into the position in which she had often seen younger children sleep. Bathed in the faint light, his face looked surprisingly gentle, as if with sleep the hauteur that usually filled it had melted away. But there was nothing childlike about the sleek muscles, tight as whipcord, that ran across his flank and broad chest.

She bent over him, fascinated by what she beheld, until he stirred fitfully in his sleep. She mustn't waste time gawking at him. There was no time to delay. She crept into the bed and stretched out her thin, spare body beside his much larger one. Then, taking courage, she nestled close to him. A jolt passed through her as her skin encountered his.

It was too late now to draw back. Come what may, this was her only path to freedom.

The woman in Adam's dream was irresistible, and beautiful, the way women always were in dreams. She had no face or features to distract him, but was just a cloud of warmth and invitation that engulfed him here where he floated in the otherworld, filling him with yearning and desire. He gave himself up to the sensation. Though he must remain chaste in the world of men, here in the dream realm passion was no sin.

The dream woman's fingers, light as faerie wings, traced the veins that carried his pounding blood toward his speeding heart. Her satin gown rustled as she moved, making the tiny hairs on his arms stand up, and waking every nerve. He took a deep breath, only to find himself enveloped in her clean scent. Life surged through him, and with it came strength and hunger.

Here in the safety of a dream he could meld with this faceless beauty. He could embrace her without reproach and find, enfolded in her phantom arms, respite from the solitary life his cursed nature had doomed him to. He gave himself up to the glory of it.

The dream woman's hand drifted to his chest. Her touch felt so real he marveled at the power of his imagination. She stroked his taut nipples until they sent jolts of pleasure through his abdomen. Then her spectral fingers drifted downward, dancing their way toward his stirring prick, which throbbed now with the craving she had evoked in him.

Never before had a dream been so lucid. He'd heard tales of adepts who could walk in dreams as they did on earth and work their magic there. But never until now had he found himself in the state they had described— asleep and yet aware. His nerves and sinews tingled with the joy of it.

There was magic aplenty working here, but it wasn't his, as the dream woman's hand brushed along his hip, sending sparkles of light flickering through the darkness. He lay with his eyelids shut, savoring as the way she gingerly explored the delicate hairs from which his shaft now jutted.

He was dreaming, yet the feel of her hand was too real to be a dream. A hint of uneasiness niggled at the edges of his consciousness. He should make himself wake up. It might be dangerous to give himself up so totally to the pleasures his succubus promised.

But the glorious waves of life that pulsed through him at her touch were too intoxicating. He couldn't banish her, nor leave this realm of dreams where she enchanted him. It felt so right to lie with her, enveloped in the comfort that surrounded her. She was all he'd ever wanted, all he'd ever need. His spirit burst with life as she roused his dreaming body. He couldn't resist her, but he didn't have to. A man wasn't responsible for what visited him in dreams. He squeezed his eyes shut and allowed the irresistible dreaming to continue.

Zoe marveled that Ramsay hadn't awakened despite what she'd already done to his naked body, but still he slept. She drew her hand away from the tuft of fur from which his rod projected, teetering on the brink of a decision.

Should she grasp his organ now, and make it do its duty? Surely it was stiff enough to get the job done. She need only guide it to her *con* and in a matter of moments she would have achieved her goal. But she couldn't do it. Not yet. Perhaps in just a moment, when she calmed herself, and got control of her breathing, she could return to it. But for now, she could barely think straight. Her pulse was pounding, and the strangest thoughts were going through her mind.

She withdrew her hand and turned to something safer, stroking his muscled chest, marveling as she did how taut and unyielding his flesh was there, and how different from her own. Her breathing calmed, but not enough. He wanted her now, and she must take what he offered while she could. She ran her hand down his flank, forcing her fingers down to where they must go.

He groaned in his sleep, and as he clenched his jaw, his arms came up as if to push her away. In another moment he would waken. Would he be furious? With her free hand she reached into the pocket where she'd slipped her knife to make sure it was still within reach should she need it.

But Ramsay didn't waken, nor did he push her away. Instead, he pulled her closer. Her small breasts flattened against the hard muscles that rippled across his chest as he engulfed her. His breathing grew more ragged than her own. She could no longer delay. Steeling herself, she reached down and circled his organ with her hand, shocked by how large it had become.

She hadn't expected it to be this easy. She'd heard so much from her mother's friends about how hard it was to get their lovers' unreliable members to stand up. But this one needed no coaxing. It was hard and thick, and it swelled against her hand where she grasped it, so strongly she could barely encompass it. She squeezed it with her widespread fingers, in rhythm with the blood that pounded in her ears, sliding her hand up and down its length, amazed at how thin and flexible the skin was that covered it. Her mind began to fill with a strange madness, as pulsing waves of energy rose from his organ and made her fingers tremble.

He moaned and embraced her more tightly, nuzzling her ear with his lips and whispering something incomprehensible. His pelvis thrust against her abdomen, his organ a battering ram now, hard and demanding, and shockingly slick.

"Yes," he murmured. "Oh yes!"

She was seized with terror. This wasn't what she'd imagined. He was too strong. She'd expected to be able to control him. After a lifetime of listening to the courtesans trade tales, she'd assumed the culminating act would be just another of the subtle negotiations she'd seen her mother engage in with the men who filled her life.

But there was nothing subtle here. She couldn't control it. She was enveloped in the smell of Ramsay's arousal and helpless before the power of what she'd unleashed in him. He pulled her closer, overwhelming her, and kissed her neck and her shoulders, even as his throbbing pole pushed insistently against her body, seeking to thrust home.

There was no room for negotiation here. He was mad for her. He ground his hips so her sex rubbed against his swelling tool until, to her shock, she felt herself swelling, too, and a burst of wetness gushed out of her most private part.

How could this be? She was as wild as he was and as hungry, possessed by animal passions she hadn't ever known she could feel. In another moment she'd no longer be a virgin. She'd have done what she'd set out to do, and found her freedom. But she wasn't free now, no, not with what he'd called out in her body. She wanted him. Desire flooded through her. She forced back the cry that rose to her lips, unbidden.

Then something changed. His grip on her relaxed and his hand began to gentle her. It moved over her rigid shoulder with a touch so light, she didn't know if it was his flesh that touched her or his shadow.

He murmured what sounded like endearments, though she didn't know the language in which he spoke them. His subtle hand caressed her arm, circled her wrist, and paused as if marveling at their slimness. Yet his eyes were still pressed shut, as if he were asleep. She found herself breathing in time with his longer breaths, until her pulse matched his. Though even as she calmed, she sensed him still wanting her and needing her, and caring that she find pleasure in his touch.

Only now did he reach for her cleft and push one finger inside her, gently, stroking the tip of her cunny with his thumb. It was so shockingly intimate an invasion that she had to fight against the urge to shrink away. She'd come to his bed for this and she must do it. And yet, as his finger continued to tease her, it stirred the most extraordinary sensations, as if he knew almost before she did what kind of touch would please her. His other fingers slid over the point where all her longing burned, filling the world with bright ribbons of sensation, until, unimaginably, she found herself wanting all of what he'd soon give her.

Not because it would free her, no, but because he'd made her want it.

This was more shocking, still. She'd never known that the *woman* could want it. Surely her mother had never mentioned that in all her many lectures on the subject.

But she had no time to wonder. The hunger his hands were arousing was growing every second. The yearning that welled up now in her secret place flowed like warm honey through her entire body. His sliding fingers danced on the slickness that flowed from her desire, teasing her into madness. Then he raised himself above her and prepared for the thrust that would annihilate that need.

She braced herself for it. Huge as he was, how could she bear his entry? As she tensed, her arm jerked involuntarily, and her elbow gouged into Lord Ramsay's flank.

With a cry he awakened.

His arms, which had been holding her so gently, tensed into steel-hard bands. He twisted, nearly pushing her off the bed. Then, as if still trapped in a state between sleep and wakefulness, he shook his head, as if to clear it, and whispered in a tone of barely suppressed horror, "Who are you?"

"Zoe."

She froze, then groped around her dressing gown's pocket for her knife; though when she found it, it felt so tiny in the face of his strength—and his fury.

"What the bloody hell were you doing in my bed?"

He must never find out. She must feign a childlike

foolishness, as her mother did when *her* schemes failed. So with trembling lips—which there was no need to counterfeit—she whispered, "I couldn't stand the suspense. It was only a matter of time until you made me your mistress. I wanted to get it over with."

"I thought I'd made it damnably clear I did *not* wish to make you my mistress. The thought disgusts me. How could you ever have imagined such a thing?"

She fought back the pain his words evoked. She'd always been told no man would ever want her, but, even so, his revulsion taught her, too late, of the hope she'd been harboring that it might not be true. When he'd held her in his arms just now, he'd made her feel beautiful and desired. She'd allowed herself to dream. Now his words brought her back to earth, choking her with humiliation. But there was no time for self-pity. His anger was growing by the minute.

She forced herself to speak. "You said you might take my maidenhead, for revenge—if that was the Dark Lord's intent in fetching me."

"But if you feared that, why seduce me? That makes no sense—and I thought you prided yourself on your sense."

"I did." The words came out as a squeak.

She hung her head, as if unable to face him. She must keep him thinking she was as flighty as her mother so he wouldn't guess the truth. "I was afraid," she whispered. "I couldn't bear to wait until we reached Scotland to find out how bad it would be were you to take me—I had to find out now what kind of man you were, before there was no hope of escape."

"And what kind of man did you find me to be?" He didn't try to hide his disgust. "One who would rape his ward in his sleep?"

"No! I came to your bed of my own free will."

"And what did you find there. Tell me!"

"A gentle man. A man who whispered of love."

"Love," he said bitterly. "Only in my dreams would you hear me talk of love. I *was* dreaming, you know."

"I know," she said, contrite.

"I can't fathom it. What did you hope to gain by giving yourself to me like that?" He tilted his face so that the moonlight painted his stubbled cheeks with silver, heightening the sense that he was not of this world. His glittering eyes stabbed into hers, seeking an answer. She forced herself not to flinch as she returned his stare.

With a sigh, he let his eyes drop away first. "It wouldn't have been money. Not you. You were ready to send me away with my tail between my legs when I offered you that bracelet. But what, then, were you after? Are you so much your mother's daughter that you did it just to satisfy your lust?"

"No!" She shook her head, too ashamed to say more. He'd come too close to the truth. Whatever her original motivation had been, her idiotic scheme had taught her how strong her lust could be. She pulled her robe more tightly around her midsection, as if that could stop her shivering. "When I asked you about my fate, you wouldn't answer me."

"When you asked me about your fate, I told you the truth. I don't know what the Dark Lord's intentions were when he bought you from your mother, but I know my own. There are enough young harlots in the world, without my adding to their number. You behaved very foolishly, whatever you thought you were doing."

She shrank back, frozen by his tone. Then his eyes widened, and a look of sudden realization swept over his face. "Or am *I* the fool? Of course, that's it! I must still be more than half asleep not to have thought of it."

Beneath his blazing eyes, his pale skin had darkened with anger. Had he figured out her plan? She tightened her hold on the knife.

"You lied about being a virgin, didn't you? And when you realized you'd be caught out in that lie, you came up with a clever stratagem, so that *I'd* get blamed for deflowering you." He lunged toward her and seized her by her shoulder, forcing her to look him in the eye. She clutched the hidden knife more tightly.

"That's why you came to me, wasn't it? You *are* a harlot just like your mother, and your innocence was nothing but an act. You hoped to trick me into thinking I'd taken your maidenhead in my sleep to cover up your lie." His voice was like broken glass. "Did your mother sell you to some other man when you were young? She was eager enough to sell you to me. You can tell me the truth. I won't hold it against you. I know how little she cares about harming others. Just answer me. Did she violate the Dark Lord's bargain for a few golden sovereigns?"

She could say yes now and he'd let her go. She'd have attained her object, without the sacrifice she'd been so close to making when she'd pressed herself against his demanding body. She wanted to say it, to grasp that freedom that was so near at last. But under the pressure of his steady gaze, she could not. Pinned by those gold-flecked eyes that gleamed in the darkness like meteors falling to earth, she was incapable of anything but the truth.

Perhaps the powers he claimed were more than a delusion. She gave up the struggle. In a whisper she said, "I came to you a virgin."

"But are you one now, or did I ravish you in that accursed dream? Did I defile you?"

"I'm still a virgin."

"Thanks be unto the gods. The work can still go on."

He fell back against his pillow, the anger and energy fading from his voice. "Had I taken you, the fruit of years of labor would have been destroyed in an instant. As it is, the gods only know what purification I'll have to undergo to rid myself of this pollution."

Her gorge rose. Disgust. Pollution. That was all he'd felt in those moments when she'd felt such ecstasy. An involuntary shudder wracked her, and her knife fell from her hand. It lay on the ground, glinting in the moonlight, its blade clearly outlined against the darkness of the floor.

"What's that?" His voice cracked like a whip.

"A knife." She gulped. "Mrs. Endicott gave it to me. To defend myself."

She hadn't thought his face could show more shock than it had when he'd awakened, but she'd been wrong.

"So *that* was your plan." There was horror in his eyes. He drew his knees to his chest and pulled the bedclothes tight. "You looked like such a sweet young girl," he whispered. "But you *are* Isabelle's daughter. I should've known what you were capable of."

"I only meant to give myself to you. Not to kill you."

"Oh, not to kill me, eh? Merely to emasculate me? To rouse me in my sleep and rob me of my manhood?"

It took her a moment to grasp his meaning. Then she shrank back, though his iron grip on her shoulder made it impossible to flee. If he'd been angry at her before, what must be his emotion now?

"That never occurred to me," she protested. "And even if it had, I could never have done such a thing. I meant only to defend myself, if you turned out to be violent—in the sexual act." She added weakly, "I'd heard of that happening—from my mother's friends. And you *are* a hot-tempered Scot. So I wished to be prepared. I didn't mean to harm you."

Ramsay hauled himself up on one elbow and stared at her, unmoving, his eyes sweeping across her face as if he could read in her features the very secrets of her soul. He was prying into her most hidden thoughts and she felt terror knowing what he would learn when her soul was completely bared to him: not just the reason why she'd come to his bed, or how she'd lied to him about it, but of the shameful delight she'd felt, locked within his arms—before he'd discovered who it was he'd been making love to and sprang away from her in horror.

She sat frozen, waiting, as the seconds ticked by, each one more agonizing than the one before it.

And then he laughed.

The sound of it echoed through the room. His shoulders shook, and what looked like tears sprang at the corner of his eyes. "What a strange girl you are," he sputtered. "You've made me believe you, crazy as it sounds. If you'd meant to harm me, you'd be bragging about it now, not lying to me. You're too honest to do anything else."

Her rigid muscles relaxed. He wasn't going to strike her.

But then his voice lost its edge of humor and once again took on its customary tone of command. "Still, I'll keep your knife. Though you've been so kind as to leave me with my manhood intact, your blade can still harm me. The Dark Lord's heir must not touch iron. Not in the weeks before the Final Teaching. It destroys the ability to draw upon the powers of the earth." He gestured toward where her knife lay on the floor. "I'll dispose of it later."

He sank back onto the bed, exhausted. "Now leave me. And don't try any more of your tricks. From now on, I'll be on my guard. You may be sure of that. Whatever your scheme might have been, it failed. The power of the Dark Lord isn't mocked."

Chapter 4

The next morning, when he led Zoe down to the inn's common room, where they were served an indifferent breakfast, Adam found perverse pleasure in the discovery that his companion looked no better than he felt. Her eyes were suspiciously puffy and her usually bright features bore the heavy look that told of a sleepless night. He greeted her with a slight nod, hoping to avoid further confrontation, but the dull look of despair with which she met his eye showed she feared him even more than she had the previous day—as she should, after failing at whatever it was she'd been up to the past night.

Even so, she made a brave show of eating the leathery bacon they had been given for their breakfast. She cut it into ladylike portions and lifted each forkful slowly to her mouth, though her hand shook as she did so. He should have taken pleasure from observing her misery, but strangely, he could not. Instead, he found himself fighting the urge to reassure her. He couldn't imagine why. Her behavior had been preposterous. By behaving like a harlot, she'd proven herself to be her mother's daughter, despite the demure face she'd hitherto shown him.

And what *had* she intended with her knife? His insides contracted just thinking of it. Had he stayed asleep, she could have easily unmanned him. He had only her word for it that she'd meant him no harm. So why was he still haunted by the feeling that he'd been wrong to transfer his hatred of Isabelle to her daughter? Zoe's behavior should have strengthened his anger, not weakened it. But it hadn't.

He'd been haunted all night by the vision of her face as he had swum up into consciousness to find himself in her embrace. And he was haunted still by the memory of her touch, which had awakened such longing in his body—and in his heart. Was it to reassure *her* that he wanted to reach out and stroke her narrow shoulder? Or himself?

He *should* hate her. She was alive only because her mother had ensured his sister would die in her place. But over the years he had cultivated the ability to listen for what was unsaid, until it seemed to him sometimes that he could hear even the sound of the worms slithering in the earth beneath his feet. Now, with that trained facility sharpened by their tryst the previous night, he could hear her thoughts. He could sense what it cost her to maintain the pose of cool unconcern with which she had faced down every insult he had given her. And her courage amazed him.

She was alone, abandoned by the mother who should have protected her and helpless in the hands of her enemy—himself. But still she radiated defiance, despite the fear he felt thrumming beneath her carefully maintained façade of self-sufficiency—which he felt as strongly as if it had been his own. In the face of such courage, how wrong it would be if his revenge was to be directed at *her*.

He left his breakfast untouched and called for the chaise to be brought round. The sooner they reached Iskeny, the better. As the carriage jolted down the rutted road, he struggled to keep his leg from touching the thick fabric of Zoe's skirt, lest he remember about what lay hidden beneath it. But avoid her as he might, his flesh still tingled where her gentle hands had stroked him the night before.

If only he *had* truly been asleep. If only it had been the touch of a dream woman he'd responded to. But he hadn't been asleep, not the whole time. He'd awakened as Zoe had been going about her business, and that was what he couldn't forgive himself for. Even when he'd known she was not some phantom summoned by his loneliness, he'd allowed her to continue—nay, he'd done far worse than that—he'd *ensured* that she continue, by using his rusty lover's skills to make her want him more. The memory appalled him.

Barely a week after receiving the letter that told him he'd been chosen to be the Dark Lord's heir, he'd betrayed his master's trust and come within a hairsbreadth of violating the vow of chastity he'd maintained for nine long years, that vow whose fulfillment had made him fit, finally, to avenge his sister. No, he must be honest, he *had* violated it. That he hadn't gone on to orgasm under the girl's ministrations was unimportant. He had opened himself up to her, blended his energy with hers, and given her something that couldn't be recalled.

And the most damnable thing about it was that even now, when he knew how serious his lapse had been, the sight of her ankle peeking from behind the thin edging of her gown was causing his indomitable manhood to stir again. He still lusted for her, though he knew full well that his cursed lust was the reason he'd failed his sister. He still wanted what Zoe had offered. He, who had sanctified his manhood to earn his absolution.

Zoe stirred on the carriage seat beside him, heaving a small but poignant sigh. He wanted to be angry at her. Her behavior last night had been more than shocking. What kind of young virgin seduced her guardian in a country inn?

But his conscience had an answer for him: the frightened daughter of a woman with no morals, a woman who had sold her daughter to some stranger, a woman who had demonstrated, thanks to him, that she'd cheerfully sell that daughter once again.

He wanted to tell her not to fret. He wanted to hold her and soothe her fears—then, shocked at the direction his mind was turning, he squelched that thought. Damn him, it wasn't comfort he wanted to give her. He wanted to embrace her again, to finish off what they'd begun. His body throbbed with desire for her.

He rapped on the roof of the compartment to attract the postilion's attention and when the chaise stopped, he threw open the carriage door and lunged out into the waiting dampness. He'd ride outside. The abominable English climate would soon cool his ardor.

But even riding on one of the lead horses beside the postilion, with the rain dripping from the brim of his hat and his lust beaten back, he was haunted by the memory of the sadness he'd seen in her eyes just now, which he hadn't observed before the events of the past night. His rejection had wounded her. She couldn't know that the revulsion he'd felt had been toward himself, for the weakness that made him crave what she'd offered—and he'd take pains to ensure she never knew.

If only the journey that stretched out before them weren't so long. Once they arrived at Iskeny, it would be easier to remember what he was and what he must become: there, where the energies of the Old Ones still flowed through the standing stones, where he would become, in truth, the Dark Lord's heir, and she would become—but that thought brought him even less comfort.

He didn't want to think of what awaited her on the island. The Dark Lord knew, better than anyone, how deeply he'd yearned for revenge and he'd promised Adam would attain it soon—in the very same paragraph where he'd commanded Adam to bring him back the virgin.

No, the thought of reaching the island brought him precious little comfort at all.

* * *

Thank God Lord Ramsay had left the compartment! It had been torture to have to sit beside him in its cramped confines. Zoe doubted she could have borne it for another moment. Why did he have to look so painfully handsome in that brooding way of his, when he'd made it clear he loathed her, body and soul? And even worse, now that she knew how he felt about her, why couldn't she stop wanting him?

It must be what her mother called *maladie de la vierge*, the virgin's sickness. She'd warned Zoe about it—explaining how a first sexual encounter with an attractive man could cause a dangerous state of mental instability that made young girls long for proposals of marriage where none were possible and kept them from accepting more profitable arrangements that were.

Zoe had thought her good sense would render her immune to it. She had no romantic expectations—she'd never had them—and she'd known exactly what she was getting into when she'd entered Lord Ramsay's chamber. She hadn't dreamed the virgin's sickness would afflict her. But apparently she'd been wrong. For her body burned now with the yearnings the sleeping lord had awakened in her—though all she had awakened in *him* was disgust.

She told herself there was no point in dwelling on what she couldn't change and forced herself to stare through the raindrops that drizzled down the coach window at the monotonous moor that stretched away in all directions. But it was no use.

Why had his eyes looked so unexpectedly kind this morning? Why had he made her feel as if he could sympathize with the pain she felt—the very pain that he himself had caused?

She forced her attention back to the window just in time to see a circling raven swoop down on some invisible prey. It seemed like an omen. Could Ramsay really be a wizard? She recalled those odd words that had burst out of him when he had discovered her fallen knife: *The Dark Lord's heir must not touch iron.*

There was only one kind of creature that feared cold iron—a witch. She was too good a student of science to believe in witchcraft, but still, he *had* read her thoughts, more than once. And though he was an educated man—far better educated than she was—*he* obviously believed in wizardry. She couldn't shake the feeling that perhaps what he believed in was more than just a fantasy.

Men had been hanged for witchcraft in Scotland within living memory. There must still be some there who practiced the ancient ways, and if they did, where better to practice their grim rites than on a remote island far from the reach of the authorities? Whatever she might believe, what had taken place the past night in Lord Ramsay's darkened chamber left no room for doubt about the power *he* attributed to sexual purity—which made all the more worrisome the Dark Lord's insistence she be a virgin.

In spite of herself, she shuddered.

She couldn't allow him to take her to the island. She must flee before he brought her to his master. She would do it tonight, when they stopped at the next inn. She would have to.

At least she need not fear that when she was out on the road alone some brigand would ravish her. Lord Ramsay had made it clear that, as her mother had always told her, no man would ever want her in that way.

But that night they didn't stop at an inn. They barely stopped at all, and when they did it was only to change horses. Though Ramsay was soaked to the skin from the dreary mizzling rain that had been falling much of the day, he seemed possessed by some fury that drove him to keep on traveling.

When they did stop to change horses, he ordered hampers of food to be brought out to them, but except when she went to answer the call of nature, he didn't let her out of his sight. At their last stop before nightfall he informed her that they would ride all night. The skies had cleared and he wanted to take advantage of the full moon to make more progress on their journey.

Zoe's despair grew as the horses clattered each lengthening mile from the city. How would she ever get away?

It was close to midnight when they stopped yet again to change horses at an inn that stood in the center of a tiny village. Zoe had fallen asleep, but woke at the sound of Ramsay's voice calling out an order to the postilion. By the time she was fully roused, he was gone. Through the window of the chaise she saw him striding into the inn to make his arrangements. This was the first time all day he'd left her alone. He must have thought her still dozing.

She waited until she was sure he wouldn't immediately return. Then she made her way out of the chaise, acting as if she were merely stretching her legs in case he should be observing her. But he didn't return. She was really alone. This was the opportunity she'd been waiting for.

Their post chaise stood at one side of the moonlit inn courtyard. A lone postilion was wearily unharnessing the team. As casually as she could, she hailed him.

"It's so cold. Would you fetch my box from the chaise so I can get my shawl?"

She pointed to where it lay, atop the pile of luggage lashed to the boot of the post chaise. When the postilion handed it down to her, she reached into her purse and gave him a sixpence for his pains, which he tossed into the air, where it spun brightly in the moonlight. Then he slapped it into his pocket and headed into the taproom to exchange it for a hearty draught that would provide warmth for the long night's journey ahead.

She was alone now. There would be no cheering warmth for her for many hours to come, but if she was lucky there would be freedom. After a swift look to make sure Ramsay was still inside the inn, she rooted through her box for the things she couldn't leave behind and transferred them to the small valise she'd packed into the larger trunk. She took only a change of dress, some stockings, and a pair of sturdy shoes—she'd need those for the long walk ahead of her.

Then she picked up the old doll MacMinn had given her and gave it a furtive hug before laying it back in the box, warmed by the memory of how her mother's coachman had hugged her when she was small and sheltered her with his long, gangling body as if she, too, were a beloved doll. But this was no time for sentiment. She must make her escape.

Zoe made a bundle of the clothing she must leave behind and grabbed her old bonnet. With every sense on high alert, she reentered the chaise and heaped up the bundled garments in the corner she'd previously occupied. When that was done, she set her bonnet on top of the pile, closed the door, and stepped away.

In the gloom, the mass of cloth did look like a woman sleeping in the chaise. With Ramsay so eager to avoid any contact with her, it was unlikely he'd venture close enough to the huddled form to realize it wasn't hers. She hoisted her valise and hurried away from the center of the tiny village. Her father, the duke, would be so proud if he could see the job she'd made of her escape.

She took a path leading away from the inn, looking for some place where she could hide until the post chaise had gone. But the countryside around her was one of open fields and hedgerows offering no shelter. She didn't dare take refuge in one of the stone barns that stood behind the village houses, for if she disturbed the animals, their cries would give her away. There was no alternative but to head out into the fields.

She opened the first gate she found and began to run along the tall hedgerow that bordered it. Twigs caught in her shawl and snapped as she brushed against the bushes that formed the hedge. Soon her breath was coming in ragged gasps, but she pushed herself to keep going, feeling her heart pound. She must get far enough away from Lord Ramsay that he couldn't find her when he learned she'd fled.

Then her foot encountered an unexpected dip in the path and she tripped, falling onto the cold, damp ground. She lay there panting, clutching the leather-wrapped handle of her valise convulsively as the odor of the trampled grass assailed her nostrils. In the distance she heard a dog bark.

She resisted the impulse to leap up even as her arms broke out in gooseflesh. Was a farmer tracking her, thinking a poacher had come onto his land? She lay as still as possible, but that would mean nothing if the dog found her scent. She shivered, and not just because of the cold. The dog was getting closer. She could hear its snuffling and the scratching of its claws on the hard earth. If she were to run now, it would treat her as prey. Then, though no command had been given, it stopped, and she heard new footsteps approaching her, human footsteps. She stood up, holding the flimsy valise as if it could ward off whoever it was who'd tracked her down, knowing it was useless.

Her pursuer lumbered toward her, a short heavy man. His features were hidden by the night, but she could hear him panting with effort. She launched herself into a run but heard him gaining on her. Then, suddenly, there were more footsteps and the sound of a struggle. She heard her pursuer grunt as he hit the ground, and a wave of relief swept over her—until a voice called out, "Zoe."

Ramsay. She mustn't let *him* catch her.

She flung her valise at him, hoping to knock him down, but it fell short. With every bit of energy she had left, she scrambled away as fast as she could along the hedgerow. She heard his steps pounding behind her, louder than the sound of her own ragged breath as she raced along in the dark. Though she knew she couldn't outrun him, she couldn't stop. Her life had come down to this—that she dared not let him catch her. But he was gaining on her.

Another hedgerow loomed before her. The only way through it was a stile with a three-barred gate that glimmered in the moonlight. If she could climb over it, perhaps she might still elude him and the punishment that was sure to follow if he caught her. She threw herself at the gate with the last bit of breath she had left and set one foot onto the board that made up the lower crossbar. She was just lifting her other leg over the higher bar when the board she was standing on gave way.

Her ankle twisted and a searing pain slashed through her as her full weight fell on the gate's upper bar, cracking it and sending a long splinter of rotten wood ripping through her thigh. She fell headlong onto the ground and lay there quivering, overcome by pain, as the smell of the damp ground filled her nostrils.

Ramsay staggered toward her. He stopped, only a few feet from where she lay, looking around him like a hunting dog that had lost the scent. He sank to his haunches. Only then did he notice her lying on the cold earth where she'd fallen. As he leaned over her, the planes of his face were illuminated by the flickering moon. He was so beautiful even now. Damnably beautiful.

"Are you injured?" His voice held a note of fear.

When she made no reply, he reached for her wrist, taking it in his much larger hand with a grip that was surprisingly gentle. A thrill ran through her. Followed by confusion. How could she find such comfort in the touch of her worst enemy? And why was he, who hated her, holding her hand so tenderly? Then she remembered. He was a trained physician. He wasn't offering her comfort. He was looking for her pulse.

After finding it, his hands moved swiftly to her head where he checked the angle of her neck. Next he ran his hand along her spine. Only when his examination was complete did he gather her into his arms, pausing only to order someone following behind them to fetch her valise.

As he bore her away, she clung to him, though she hated herself for needing to. With her nose pressed against the rough wool of his shirt, she inhaled his pungent scent. She wanted to beg him to leave her here, even now, though there was no chance he would. But she couldn't make the words come out. She could barely cling to consciousness. Each jolting step he took drove more pain through her thigh.

Her last thought, as her awareness succumbed to the mist that overwhelmed her, was how strong he must be to carry her over so much ground. He looked so unworldly at times. She hadn't expected him to have such strength.

And then—it seemed like a long time must have passed—she awoke in a narrow bed. For a moment she

thought she was back in her small cubicle at Mrs. Endicott's school, but when she opened her eyes and saw
the unfamiliar cracks on the smoke-darkened ceiling,
the memories of her flight rushed back, and she knew
she must be in a bedchamber at an inn.

Someone had tended her wounds and loosened her
gown so that she could breathe after she had fainted.
Her ankle was wrapped tightly with rags, and there
was a dull throb where she had torn her thigh, but she
couldn't determine the extent of the injury, for it, too,
was bound. She struggled to sit up, only to meet Ramsay's luminous eyes.

He was seated on a spindle-backed chair by the side
of the bed. His long hair was matted with sweat, and
a deep scratch slashed through the tattooed serpents
on one arm. A wave of relief swept through her at the
sight of him, until she remembered that relief was the
last thing she should feel, now that she was once again
back in his power.

"I told you not to run away from me," he whispered.
The long planes beneath his cheekbones made him
look stern.

"You gave me no choice. Why didn't you let me go?
If you had, you wouldn't be troubled by me anymore."

"You don't trouble me."

He was lying. She did trouble him, immensely. She
could feel him resonate with her pain and with something else—something she couldn't understand.

"I pollute you," she protested. "My touch disgusts
you. Why can't you let me go? You don't want me."

"Oh, I may not want you," he said, so softly she

could barely hear him. "But I need you. You must come with me. The Dark Lord is waiting."

He looked away. A pang of longing filled her as he broke the connection, followed by despair. He felt no echo of the yearning that filled her. He loathed her and would be glad to see the last of her. He kept her beside him now only to do the Dark Lord's bidding. What was wrong with her that she couldn't keep her eyes off him, when he had made his distaste for her so clear?

She pushed herself up to a sitting position and pulled one leg out from beneath the gray sheets of the dirty bed, but the searing pain that tore through her ankle forced her to sink back onto the mattress, defeated.

"You've probably sprained your ankle." He spoke in the distant tone he must use when tending all his patients. "If so, it'll be uncomfortable for a day or two, then it'll heal. But for now, you must rest. I'll stay here with you until you fall asleep."

He stood up and fumbled in his pocket for something. A key?

She demanded, "Will you lock me in? Now that I'm your prisoner again?"

"No." He drew out his small, red, leather-bound book. Under his long, lustrous lashes, his gray eyes held something that she might have called warmth, had she not known that he hated her. "You won't be running anywhere tonight. Not with that ankle. But I'll watch over you, lest a fever develop."

She wanted to protest, to rail against him, so that he'd know he hadn't got the best of her, but she didn't have the energy. She watched as he settled himself in the spindle-backed chair, picked up his book, and began to read serenely, once again the cool aristocrat who had taken her from her mother.

She gave up the struggle. She'd had enough for one day. She'd done what she could to escape and lived up to the noble blood that ran into her veins. But, even so, she'd failed. Ramsay had caught up with her, and he'd done it so quickly, too. Perhaps he *could* read minds. Perhaps he could even control them. There was no other explanation for the relief she'd felt when she'd woken to find him watching by her bedside, even though she knew she should hate him. Perhaps his magic *was* real.

Chapter 5

She looked a lot better this morning, Adam observed with relief. Her color had improved, and she showed no sign of fever. He shook himself awake, stiff after spending the night sleeping in the uncomfortable chair by her bedside, noting with relief as he did so that his emotions were far calmer than they'd been the evening before. As they should be.

It was unlikely the previous night's misadventure had caused any lasting damage. Zoe's ankle appeared to be sprained rather than broken, and though the wound she'd taken in her thigh had caused him some concern, he'd instructed the innkeeper's wife how to clean and bandage it, and when she'd finished, she'd assured him it was nothing to worry about.

He wished he could have examined it himself, but propriety forbade that a male physician should minister to a wound in such a delicate part of any woman's anatomy. Though in the past he'd ignored such constraints, believing the patient's welfare was more important than the prejudices of small minds, after what had gone on between *this* patient and himself, he had no wish to test the bounds of propriety. The innkeeper's wife had assured him she was well versed in doctoring and had said nothing to suggest Zoe's wound was serious.

So Zoe would be fine. Indeed, in the bright light of morning, the dread that had swept over him the previous night when he'd seen her fall from the rotten stile seemed foolish. There'd been no need to stay up all night by her bedside. The exhaustion he felt now told him he'd be paying for his folly all day. A wave of annoyance swept over him. She'd had no business running from him like that. He'd been severe with her, yes, but to act with such desperation—what could she be thinking of? He was a gentleman. Surely she knew that a gentleman would not harm a young girl placed under his care.

But it struck him almost immediately that gentlemen like him hurt girls like her all the time. The gentleman's code applied only to young ladies, and though Zoe might have attended Mrs. Endicott's elegant school, she was no lady, just the daughter of a woman of the town. Hadn't he bargained with her mother for her virginity? If he'd been in earnest, he might have completed that bargain and done with her as he pleased. She had good reason to fear him.

But still, he mustn't let himself be swayed by undeserved pity. The way she'd comported herself made it all too clear what she owed to her origins. Had she not of her own free will crawled into his bed?

He beat down the surge of desire that rose unbidden at that memory. *Even after all these years he still couldn't control the lust that had already caused such havoc.* How unfit he was to accept the honor the Dark Lord had chosen to confer on him. If only he *could* send Zoe away, as she'd begged him to do. Her absence would put an end to the lustful sensations he felt in her presence. But the Dark Lord awaited them at Iskeny. They'd already lost valuable hours of travel. He could afford no more delay.

Gently, he reached out toward the narrow bed and touched the sleeping girl lightly on the shoulder to awaken her so they could prepare to resume their journey. Her eyes twitched and then shut more tightly against the morning light. Fighting against wakefulness, she arched her back, making the long, graceful arc of her body more visible under the dingy sheet, which fell back, exposing her shoulder. Adam's eye drifted to the hollow above her collarbone. It looked so vulnerable and inviting. He turned away, lest she stir again and reveal some even more tempting part of her body.

Was she merely pretending to sleep, as he'd been doing when she'd come to his bed that night? Had she shown him her naked shoulder on purpose, to inflame him? Surely she couldn't be ignorant of the effect the slightest contact with her body had upon him. She was the daughter of a woman of pleasure. Who was to say what tricks her mother had taught her?

And yet her face looked so innocent.

He jogged her shoulder to force her awake, more roughly than he'd intended. At his touch, her eyes fluttered open. As soon as she became aware of him watching her, she clutched at her bodice and pulled it closed with what looked like true modesty.

He suppressed the urge to pat her arm to reassure her all was well. He must not touch her. Not here, where she lay alone with him, half clad, in bed—in an anonymous inn chamber where so many strangers before them must have coupled.

They must continue their journey. He couldn't take much more of this.

"How do you feel this morning?" Tension made his voice sound severe, despite his desire not to frighten her.

"I don't know." She winced as she sat up in the bed, and swung her legs around so that they hung over the side. But when she attempted to put weight on her injured ankle, her face twisted in pain.

"Let me examine it," he said. "There is a small chance it could be broken."

With a look of concern, she sat back on the bed and lifted her ankle toward him, letting her skirt fall back to reveal a long sweep of naked leg.

He sucked in his breath. Her leg was smooth, pale, and muscular, rounded as only a woman's flesh could be—and disastrously arousing. He hoped she couldn't tell how strongly the sight of her naked limb affected him, but that was too much to hope. Proof of her effect on him strained against his breeches.

Struggling to regain his professional objectivity, he

motioned for her to show him her other ankle, so that he could compare it with the injured one. As she lifted it up, he caught another glimpse of naked flesh.

His groin throbbed. Disgusted, he forced himself to ignore it. What was wrong with him? He was a trained physician. Hundreds of women had revealed their bodies to him when he'd examined them.

But those women had not been this woman. They hadn't crawled into his bed and caressed him into a state of near insanity. Breathing slowly to calm himself, he took her injured ankle in his hand and gently explored it with his fingers. But as he pressed against the soft swollen flesh, he couldn't help but remember another fleshy swelling and the way Zoe had rubbed it against him two nights before, when she'd come so close to becoming one with him.

He jerked his hand away. She gave a sharp cry.

He'd hurt her. He must get a grip on himself.

"It isn't broken." He controlled his voice as best he could. "It will heal in a few days. I've rung for some food, and we'll resume our journey as soon as you finish breaking your fast." He forced himself to look stern. "Your foolishness last night cost us much time. We'll be hard-pressed to make up for it, but we must if we're to arrive at the island while the Dark Lord still lives. I'll send someone to help you down to the carriage."

Half an hour later, she joined him in the inn's courtyard, leaning heavily on the shoulder of the innkeeper's burly wife who'd dressed her wound the night before. He wished it had been possible to have the woman take another look at it, but there wasn't time. They'd already dawdled enough.

As they took their places in the post chaise, he drew away as far from her as he could on the narrow seat, taking refuge in the tiny print of the book of meditations he always carried in his pocket. But though he tried to immerse himself in reading, he kept picturing her ankle, and her leg, so pale and firm, and as he remembered the leg, he couldn't help but imagine the thigh above it, so soft and yet so muscular, and from there his mind leapt to what that thigh would feel like wrapped around him as he plunged himself into her.

Chaste he might still be by the letter of the law, but if it was the spirit of the thing that mattered, he might as well turn the carriage around and return to London. How could he face the Final Teaching when he'd failed so miserably at maintaining the chastity that was so essential to surviving it?

He forced his attention back to his book, but he had barely turned the page when Zoe stretched out her injured ankle to rest it against the far corner of the chaise. As she did so, her bare arm gently brushed his hand.

An electric spark shot through him and before he could stop himself he cried out, "Don't do that!"

"Do what? Stretch out my leg?" She pulled the offending limb back, wincing. "It was throbbing with the motion of the carriage. I'd hoped that if I could straighten it, it might hurt less."

Abashed at his own brutality, he replied, "Of course. If it pains you, you must stretch it out."

"But if it wasn't my leg you were referring to, what is it I mustn't do?"

Did she really not know? It seemed impossible she shouldn't. But if *that* was her game—to pretend that she didn't understand him so she could tempt him further—he'd put a stop to it. He took a deep breath. "You mustn't touch me, Zoe, or show me any part of your body unclothed. There's plain speaking for you. Do you understand me?"

Her face fell. "I disgust you that much?"

All the effort he'd been making to control himself imploded. What was wrong with her? Why did she persist in this pretense that he didn't want her? She was the harlot's daughter, not some innocent miss. She knew how he'd responded when she'd crawled into his bed and stroked his member with that lily white hand of hers. Hadn't she worked him up to such a pitch that it was a miracle he hadn't ravished her?

He gestured toward his crotch where the fabric strained against his hindered passion. "Does this look like disgust?" He gave her no chance to reply. "Don't play the innocent with me. You're a courtesan's daughter. You know what this means. You know that I want you. Admit it."

She shrank back against the side of the chaise, but even as she huddled at the farthest corner of the small compartment, he could still smell the faint, musky, intoxicating scent of her. "My body wants you, you little fool," he growled. "Why wouldn't it? You're an enticing minx."

"But I'm ugly, I've no seductive curves."

"You have curves enough even if you aren't rounded in the current fashion—and whether or not they're seductive—" He gestured at his crotch. "I beg to differ."

He'd shocked himself with the crudeness with which he had addressed her. There was no excuse for such behavior, not for a man who prided himself on being a gentleman. Shamefaced, he buried his nose in his book, but when he finally got up the courage to steal a glance at her, he was surprised to see that an impish look had replaced her formerly downcast expression.

"If I'm enticing as you say, why didn't you make me your mistress?"

"Because I'm the Dark Lord's heir." He didn't bother to hide his exasperation.

"So you've said. Repeatedly. As if it explained anything. But it doesn't. Why should being any man's heir make you jump away from me as if I had the pox?"

"The Dark Lord's heir must be chaste," he replied softly. "He mustn't know the touch of woman. It drains away the strength he will need to receive the Final Teaching."

"So this Teaching of yours is so great that you would unman yourself to receive it?"

"Quite the opposite. When I receive the Teaching I'll have abilities unknown to mortal men."

Her expression made it clear she didn't believe him. Struggling to find some way to convince her, he reached into his pocket, pulled out his bronze knife, and drew it from its sheath. "Perhaps *this* will help you understand it better."

He held it out toward her with the crescent-shaped blade pointing downward. It glistened with the golden shine that contrasted so sharply with the dark green patina that covered the handle.

"The Dark Lord gave me this knife when he took me on as his disciple. How old do you think it is?"

"Very old, indeed. It looks like one Mrs. Endicott found near a Roman tomb. But her knife was green with age, and its blade was almost corroded away."

He twisted his knife in the bright morning sunshine that flooded into the compartment, making the rays glance off the blade. "This knife was old when the Romans came to Britain. But it's still sharp because, unlike your teacher's knife, it was never discarded or buried in the earth. It's been passed down from each Dark Lord to his heir in an unbroken chain since the time when your Romans lived like barbarians in huts by the Tiber. Even then a Dark Lord ruled in Iskeny."

He slid it back into its sheath. "Can you imagine the wisdom that has been transmitted along with this knife?"

She said nothing, but nodded, her intelligent eyes thoughtful.

He was glad she hadn't replied with some sarcastic remark. He'd taken a risk in letting her know what he truly valued. The Dark Lord had told him once that to know what someone valued was to have him in your power, and Zoe had already gained far too much power over him.

At last she spoke. "Perhaps that *is* worth the sacrifice of your manhood." But her tone made it clear she wasn't convinced. She pressed on. "For how long have you been chaste?"

"Nine years." Nine painful years, ever since the day his cursed lust had left Charlotte unprotected from her enemies.

"That shows admirable devotion to your master."

"I didn't do it to please him."

"I'd always heard it was almost impossible for a man to deny himself release."

He shrugged, unwilling to reveal any more of his secrets than he already had. "It becomes easier with practice."

"Did your teacher tell you *why* you must be chaste?"

He had. But Adam had told her enough already. If she persisted in questioning him, he would have to ride once more outside with the postilion.

But to his relief, she said nothing more but merely folded her hands in her lap and sat quietly, awaiting whatever answer he might choose to give her.

Relenting, he rewarded her patience with an explanation. "By being chaste I retain the body's energy. It builds up over time until it's transformed into the power I use to heal. I will need it, too, to survive the ordeal that awaits me in the Dragon's Cave. Would you have me squander it, just to soothe your vanity?"

She shrugged her shoulders. "It seems like an error to think you'd become more powerful by turning away from love."

"It isn't love I turn away from, but lust."

"Of course," she said coolly, raising one fine, dark

eyebrow. "Still, I shall take some comfort in the thought that plain as I am, I can at least inspire lust. It's better than nothing."

But it wasn't just lust she inspired in him. He remembered how he'd felt as she'd caressed him. She'd taught him what else a touch could carry besides lust and made him, for the first time he could remember, long to end his solitude. She was right. His chastity wasn't just about denying the needs of the body. He'd denied other, more subtle needs, and, damn her, she'd made him feel them, too.

Pulling herself erect she raised her chin, and, proud as a duchess, said, "You needn't fear, Lord Ramsay. I won't threaten your precious virginity again."

He sputtered. "I'm hardly a virgin. I'd become a man before I put myself under the Dark Lord's tutelage."

"Whatever the case, it's of no importance to me. Your sanctity is safe."

She turned away, though before her face was out of view, Adam could have sworn he saw a wicked smile flit across her features.

They stopped at noon to change horses at a coaching inn situated in a small village that stood at a lonely crossroads on the moor. It was a poor place with a tumbledown air. Still, Zoe was grateful for the chance to get out of the cramped chaise and stretch her legs. Her ankle, though still swollen, was not as painful as it had been when she had awakened, which encouraged her to believe that Ramsay was correct that she hadn't broken the bone. But the wound in her thigh was still throbbing.

She hadn't had a chance yet to examine how it had been dressed. So after a post boy lent her his shoulder to help her hobble into the inn, she called a maid over and had her lead her to a private chamber where Zoe could attend to her needs. A few moments later the maid brought her a basin and some rough cloths, telling her to ring the bell by the door if she needed further assistance.

Drawing up her skirts and shift, Zoe examined the rough bandage that was wrapped around her upper thigh. It appeared to have been made from some old checkered material, torn and none too clean. Carefully, she unwrapped it to reveal an ugly clotted mess where the large splinter from the rotted gate had torn into her flesh. She dabbed at the ridged scab gingerly with a rag the maid had brought her, wiping away the worst of the dirt.

When she was done, the wound looked better, though it was still quite ugly. The redness that surrounded it made her uneasy. She'd tended enough wounds among the girls at the school to know it wasn't healing as fast as she might wish. Still, Lord Ramsay was a trained physician and he must have examined it when he'd tended to her after the accident. Since he'd expressed no fears that it might turn septic, she must trust that it was on the mend, though for now the nagging pain was quite unpleasant.

She certainly wasn't about to trouble Lord Ramsay with it, not after their latest discussion. She could only imagine his reaction if she were to test his chastity further by demanding he examine her naked thigh.

She'd just decided to ask the maid for a bit of whiskey with which to cleanse her wound further when she heard a sharp cry coming from outside. She dropped her skirt and turned toward the window where she saw a woman dressed in the hooded red cloak of a cottar's wife running toward the inn, wailing and stumbling in her haste.

"Ashford's bull. It's gored our Neddy. My sister's boy!" The woman's hair had fallen out of her cap and her eyes were maddened with fear. "He was a-teasing it in the pasture—heaving rocks at it—and it got loose."

As Zoe hobbled toward the inn's front door she almost collided with Ramsay, who'd sped from his chamber at the woman's cry. He muscled through the crowd that was assembling around the woman on the muddy street, calling out, "How badly is he hurt?"

At first his question elicited only a flood of tears. With a look of annoyance, he strode over to the cottar's wife and commanded, "Save your tears for later. What kind of shape is he in?"

The woman regarded him with a look of fear, but his imperious tone had had the effect he'd intended. Between sobs she gasped out that the bull had gored the child in the belly.

"Is he alive?"

The woman nodded, "Aye, they took him to his mother's cottage. But he's in such agony. His guts is all torn out." A flood of tears drowned out the rest of what she had to say.

He cut her short. "Has someone called the surgeon?"

The woman's expression grew desperate. "T'aint no

surgeon to be found here. Only old Landis, what sees to the cattle. And he's off to the market today. Oh, the poor boy!" Her voice rose in a wail.

"I've some skill at surgery," Ramsay said. "Take me to him."

The woman examined his greatcoat and well-made boots with suspicion. Clearly he bore no resemblance to any medical man of her acquaintance, "We can pay but a shilling," she whispered. "We bain't not rich folk. But if you can save my sister's boy—"

"I need no payment." He released her shoulder. Brusquely he said, "Wait here while I fetch my things." He turned back toward the inn.

Brushing past Zoe, who stood transfixed at the doorway, he said, "It sounds like a severe injury." He pinned her with his steely gaze. "I've no choice but to leave you alone while I see to the child. Remain here. Don't run from me again."

"And if I do?"

He sighed. "The boy may be dying while we stand here squabbling." His long ascetic face had gone pale, making the eyes seem brighter. Then, before she could react, he leaned over and brushed her forehead with his lips, resting them against her skin lightly and letting them linger.

The skin burned where he'd touched her. Was he truly a wizard? The touch of his lips, even so chaste a touch as this, seemed to have torn away her ability to defy him. He needn't worry that she might run away, when his kiss made her long for him to enfold her in his arms, though she knew that it was his devotion to his calling that shone in his face, not any love for her.

She fell back from him with a soft gasp. "I'll wait for you here," she murmured. "I hope you can save him."

"I hope so, too." His eyes met hers for another moment and filled her again with that mixture of joy and anguish that only he could provoke. Then he whipped around to rejoin the boy's aunt, who stood wringing her hands in the middle of the street. Her last view as he vanished around a corner was of him striding alongside the cottar's wife, his long legs taking one step for every two of hers.

It was late that afternoon when he came back. Zoe was seated by the window watching for him, when she saw him walking back toward the inn, alone. One look told her that it had not gone well. He walked slowly with his broad shoulders slumped. His hands were covered with dirt almost to the wrist, and the cuffs of his homespun shirt were streaked and stained with the same substance.

She stood to greet him, but he brushed past her without a word, stopping only to hail a waiter and command him to bring a basin of water. When it arrived, he began scrubbing his hands, over and over again, for a good ten minutes, until she began to wonder if he would ever stop. It was only when she saw the water in the basin turn a darkish red that she realized what was on his hands. Blood. The boy's blood.

"Were you able to help him?"

"No." His tone was bleak. "He's dead. I didn't have the power to heal him. He was eleven. His mother's only son."

His eyes met hers just long enough for the look in them to tear at her heart.

They were interrupted by the hostler. "Goody Mosely wishes a word with you, Your Lordship."

"Goody Mosely?"

"The boy's mother."

"Send her away. She can have no further need of me."

But before the hostler could bar her, the woman pushed past him and ran to Lord Ramsay. She looked much like her sister, save for the look of dull despair in her reddened eyes. When she neared him, she held out a shilling piece toward him as if offering food to a wild animal.

"Keep it," he snapped. "I didn't earn it." He turned to escape the woman but at the last moment he stopped and after digging into his pocket pulled out his own purse. He fumbled with it and pulled out a fistful of sovereigns. "Here," he said gruffly. "To pay for his funeral."

The woman examined the gold pieces, looking stunned, and then scrutinized his face as if searching for signs of madness. Finding none, she stuffed them into her pocket and fled.

His curtness to the grieving woman shocked Zoe. Must the Dark Lord's heir be a stranger to all human emotion? And yet, gruff though he'd been, he'd also been so generous.

When he'd dried his hands, Ramsay tore off his filthy shirt, and donned one a servant had brought him. Then, without another word, he strode out of the inn.

He'd left her alone—again. And this time he hadn't made her promise she would wait for him. Surely, it was time to make her escape. There was no reason to stay with him any longer. She'd be mad to wait meekly for his return. He was almost certain to blame her for his failure to save the boy. He'd already told her she'd weakened his magical powers by assaulting his chastity. When he came back, he would rage at her or devise some terrifying punishment.

But she couldn't abandon him now, fool that she was. She'd seen anguish in his eyes when he'd washed the boy's blood from his hands. He'd wanted to save that stranger's child so badly.

The world was very wrong to think she'd been granted good sense in the place of good looks. A sensible woman would have already left Lord Ramsay without a backward glance. But she couldn't find it in herself to do it.

She settled herself in a chair in the parlor to wait for him, but, as the minutes turned into hours, and he didn't return she began to worry. Had he changed his mind after all, and gone on alone with his journey, abandoning her here to keep himself safe from the assault of her dubious charms? But no, a quick check reassured her that their post chaise still stood in the courtyard.

So he must still be somewhere in the area, avoiding her as he dealt, alone, with his pain. But try though she might, she couldn't free herself from the feeling that she must find him, that some catastrophe threatened the two of them, which made it essential that she not abandon him. She sensed him out there, desperate and bereft—and calling to her for help.

It could only be wishful thinking. She must be the last person on earth he'd want now. And yet, like a sleepwalker, she saw herself get up and fetch her bonnet. Then, ignoring the pain in her thigh and her lame ankle, she set forth into the twilight to look for him.

It took a while to find him, but as she approached a tumbledown cottage a good half hour later, Zoe sensed Ramsay was nearby, though peer as she might through the fading light, she could see no trace of him. It was only as she came around a curve in the road by an old stone byre that she saw the flash of something golden glittering in the wan northern light. She hastened toward it. And then she saw him.

He was sitting by the byre, huddled into a ball, with his knees drawn up to his chest. He looked like a small boy, despite his height, and was holding his bronze knife before him, staring at it as if it alone could save him.

She'd never before seen him with any look on his face but anger or disdain, or, at best, a mild, distant amusement. But the man before her was not the man she'd known until now. The pain on his face was so strong that, without thinking, she walked over and gently put her arm around his shoulders, as she would have done had he been one of her pupils at school who'd just received some dreadful news from home.

He twisted out of her grasp, his face livid. "Don't touch me! Haven't you done enough damage to me already? I couldn't do anything for the boy but watch him die. His guts were spilling out and I couldn't even still his pain."

"If it was like that, then no one could have saved him."

He turned his tortured face to her. "The Dark Lord could. I saw with my own eyes how he breathed the life back into the body of a drowned child. And I might have saved this boy, too, if I hadn't betrayed what he taught me. But I squandered my strength, and when it was needed, I failed. I'm cursed, Zoe. I was a fool to think I could ever become like him."

He looked as if he might give way to tears, and again she felt the irrational need to enfold him in her arms. But she made herself resist the impulse, knowing how much he feared her touch.

She took a step back. "Don't send me away. Truly, I only meant to comfort you."

"I don't deserve comfort," he said bitterly. "I know what I must do to justify my life, but I can't do it. There's no reason why I should keep on living."

"Do you really think you're worthless because you couldn't save a dying boy?"

He nodded, his face a mask of misery.

"Then I, too, must be worthless." she said softly. "For I've never saved anyone from dying and likely never will. Indeed, I've never done more than wash off a child's cut. Does that make me worthy of contempt?"

"It's different for you. You're a woman."

"Why should that matter?"

"Because it isn't a woman's role to protect others. It's a woman's role to be protected."

"If I'd looked to anyone for protection, I shouldn't have survived my childhood. You've seen how well *I've* been protected."

That got to him. He looked up, his long russet hair framing his beautiful eyes.

"But of course," she continued, "you've made it very clear you don't think of me as a woman."

"I think of you as a woman all the time." His upper lip quirked into a bitter half-smile. "But I mustn't let myself respond." The bronze knife twisted in his hand. The golden metal seemed almost alive.

"I must be chaste." His voice was a mere whisper. "If I don't stay chaste, I'll never earn the Final Teaching. That woman's son would have *lived* if I'd known the things the Dark Lord knows. He would have lived! Would you have me give *that* up just to satisfy my appetites? To be merely a man as other men? Surely you couldn't respect a man who would be so selfish."

"Oh, I could respect such a man well enough," she said sharply, "if he offered me that protection you seem to think is a woman's due. I've never known it. But I'm only a courtesan's daughter, so I don't expect men to be as gods. It's no wonder if I should prefer a man who offered me his kindness to one who could raise the dead."

"Unless you, too, faced death—while he stood by helplessly." His eyes locked into hers. "Then you would hate him. As the boy hated me in his last moments. As Charlotte must have done."

As he whispered his sister's name, Zoe felt an unworthy burst of envy for her, dead so long, and yet so well-beloved. He'd been so loyal to her. No one would ever speak of Zoe with such yearning. No one would ever reproach himself for letting *her* down.

But this wasn't the time for self-pity. "You did your best," she reminded him. "Can't you forgive yourself for being human?"

"I can't forgive myself for being an animal." He stabbed the bronze knife savagely into the hard-packed soil. "When you touched me just now, it wasn't comfort I wanted from you, even knowing it was my lust for you that made me useless to the boy. I'm cursed. I've known it all my life. Why do you have to tempt me like this?"

"Tempt you?" Zoe shot back. "You're impossible! I didn't tempt you. I reached out to comfort you. You looked like a child who'd hurt himself, a small and helpless child who had no mother. I could never resist helping anything motherless."

"Oh, but I *have* a mother," he said quietly. "Though no female weakness ever inclined her to comfort me when I cried."

"Not even when you fell and hurt yourself?"

"Especially not then. She'd beat me if I cried, telling me it wasn't manly."

"How monstrous! Even my mother would kiss away my tears—if she was there to see them." She bit her tongue, wishing she hadn't mentioned her mother, knowing how much he hated her.

But he ignored it. He waved his hand dismissively. "Women are allowed tears, but a man must be strong.

My mother only did what was proper. My father died shortly before my birth. He left her the entire burden of turning me into a man."

"And that was how she did it? By teaching you that a man must not show pain?"

"Of course. A man must hide his pain and carry on."

No wonder he needed to be like a god! Only a god could bear to live with every human feeling bottled up inside. "Was anger the only emotion she permitted?"

He opened his mouth to reply but stopped before the words came out. He thrust his bronze knife back into its sheath, stood up and stalked away. His boots rasped against the hard-packed farmyard earth. Then he turned and faced her. "Perhaps it was. I'd never thought about it. Anger is manly."

He was thinking about it now. She took a step toward him. "Your mother was wrong. Even a man needs comfort now and then. It's for that comfort, you know, as much as for the slaking of their lusts, that men turn to women."

"It is?"

"Yes," she said. "It is. A courtesan's daughter hears much about such things. But perhaps your mother, being a lady, and innocent of the ways of the world, didn't know that."

Chapter 6

They returned together to the inn, where Ramsay paused only to order her a good dinner before barricading himself in his chamber without speaking another word. The next day, they resumed their journey, turning off the Great North Road at Newcastle and riding west on the old Roman Road that ran along Hadrian's Wall and passed through windswept moors and barren uplands. After their confrontation in the farmyard, Lord Ramsay chose to spend the long hours of their journey riding with the postilion. During the few periods when he did ride in the chaise with her, he stared moodily out of the window.

But there was no repeat of the rudeness that had marred the last day they had traveled together. If anything, he seemed to be going out of his way to be overly polite. He helped her in and out of the carriage—

touching her gingerly on the sleeve with his gloved hand. When they stopped, he made sure she had a comfortable room and tipped the inn's maidservant well to ensure she was taken care of.

Zoe could tell he was still struggling with the incomprehensible physical attraction to her he had so crudely demonstrated in the chaise and reproached her with in the farmyard. She didn't fool herself that it meant anything. He'd said himself his passions were strong, and he'd been celibate for much too long. She knew full well that to a starving man even turnips are a feast.

But it disturbed her to think he might be driven by something akin to the desire that made her want to stroke the stubble that gilded his austere cheeks, to run her hands down that muscular chest of his, and to feel once again the excitement that had filled her when she'd lain pressed against his naked body. She didn't underestimate its power. He was right to fear it, and she did not doubt that if he were to give in to it, it would end in disaster. He already hated her for being the child of the woman who had murdered his sister. He'd hate her even more if he let her steal from him the powers that meant so much to him.

She mustn't let it happen. There was no reason to give herself to him. If he gave in to his lust, it wouldn't satisfy the hunger that tormented her. Far from it. It would destroy her to satisfy her body's hunger without a deeper union of the soul. *That* was what Ramsay had made her hunger for. And that he would never give her.

So she must force herself to go back to thinking of him as the angry man who had wrested her from her mother. The rest of what she felt for him—that sense that the two of them were bound by something greater—was only a delusion of the kind that tormented foolish virgins who gave themselves to a man for the very first time. It was the virgin's sickness—whatever Zoe might have thought she glimpsed with him in those rare moments when he'd seemed to open his heart to her.

It would soon pass. Her mother had told her it always did—and that it would pass more swiftly if she took care not to give in to it. Still, when Zoe thought he wasn't looking, she'd steal glances at Lord Ramsay's handsome features. Though all too often, just when she thought him unaware of her scrutiny, their gazes would meet and lock together, and then, embarrassed, they both would turn away.

The second day after her ill-fated attempt at flight, they crossed the Scottish border and passed through Gretna Green, though they didn't alight in the town so famous for runaway marriages. Then they turned westward. The road was much rougher now that they'd left behind the smooth gravel of the coaching road. Despite the chaise's being sprung in the most modern manner, its continual jolting made Zoe's wound ache. When they finally stopped to change horses and refresh themselves, she examined it, only to find that it had opened and was weeping a bloody discharge that had soaked through the bandage. No wonder it throbbed with the dull relentless pain that seemed to beat with her anxious pulse.

She didn't look forward to riding through the night

with her wound paining her so much, but to her relief, when she came down to dinner, Ramsay told her they would have to spend the night in the tiny village where they were stopped. One of the large wheels of the chaise was not properly seated on its axle. A wheelwright would have to attend to it. She hid her relief, knowing how important it was to him to reach their destination swiftly, but it was substantial. At last she'd be able to get some rest, away from the infernal rocking of the carriage.

When the maid came to help her prepare for sleep, Zoe called for hot water and made a poultice to suck the bad humors from her wound. But the next day it was, if anything, more painful. She grimaced as she walked into the private parlor where the innkeeper had laid out an unappealing breakfast of warmed-over rabbit and bacon for her and her companion.

"Surely your ankle isn't still paining you?" Ramsay looked up from his plate.

"Not my ankle, but the wound in my leg. It's opened up again."

His brow furrowed. "How long has it been bothering you?"

"It's always ached, ever since I injured it, but since it started bleeding again, it's become much worse."

"Bleeding? When did that start?"

"From the way the bandage looks, I should think yesterday or the day before."

"Your wound's been bleeding for two whole days and you didn't tell me?" His voice rose. "Why didn't you say something? Had I known, I'd have examined it."

"After all you've said on the subject of how little you wish to be reminded that I *have* a body, I was hardly going to ask you to inspect my thigh."

"But if mortification sets in you might lose the leg." He looked horrified.

"I applied a poultice last night in the inn."

"But today the leg is worse?"

"Yes. I'm afraid it is."

Adam set down his knife and fork, fighting the feeling of doom that swept over him. He should have known better than to let some dirty inn wife dress her wound.

"Come here." He beckoned her toward him.

Zoe began to rise, then winced and plumped down again on the plain wooden chair. When he met her eyes he saw fear in them—a fear that, uncharacteristically, she was making no effort to suppress.

His heart began to pound. "I must examine your leg," he said. "There's no time to waste."

Zoe gave him a withering look. "What, and expose your purity to more of my corruption? You could hardly bear the sight of my ankle, and this injury is most certainly *not* to my ankle."

"I know very well where the injury is," he said gruffly. "But I'm not so lost to my duty as a physician that I can't overcome my own weakness when a patient's health is at stake."

"Well," she said slowly, "if you'll promise that you won't accuse me of trying to seduce you, I'll let you examine the wound. The pain is almost unbearable, and I've become rather attached to this leg. I'd be very unhappy to lose it." She smiled weakly at these last words as if to make a joke of them, but when she saw no humor reflected back from his eyes, her smile faded, and a tinge of fear colored her pale cheek.

He fought against the stabbing fear that gripped him. Fear had no place in a surgeon's heart—and he must find the surgeon within him now and set aside all else. Zoe's life might depend on it. He motioned to her to stretch out on the long, stiff-backed, old-fashioned wooden bench that stood against one wall of the private parlor where they'd broken their fast. When she had arranged herself as comfortably on it as she could, he lifted her skirt until the bandage was revealed. Then he began unwrapping it. As the cloth tore away from her wound, she gasped. An echoing pain shot through his body.

What had happened to his professional objectivity? It always hurt when a dressing was removed, and he had seen worse wounds. Yet he couldn't bear that Zoe should feel any pain. Irritated with his descent into sentimentality, he gave the bandage a quick tug. She stifled a shriek, but the rest of the bandage came off, and he could finally see what lay under it.

It was worse than he'd feared. He need no longer worry that the sight of her naked thigh would fill him with lust, not with the stench of putrefaction that wafted up from the festering wound the bandage had hidden. Though it had scabbed over, the scab had broken, and an ugly mixture of blood and pus oozed out around its edges. But it wasn't just the stench and the angry green pus that showed him just how badly his neglect had harmed her. The thin red streaks that radiated out along the flesh just above the wound were what every doctor feared: the first sign of blood poisoning.

Zoe might lose her leg. He wasn't at all sure he could save it. If she *had* weakened his healing powers with her ill-advised attempt to seduce him, she would be the one to pay the price. He might have appreciated the irony had he still been bent on revenge, but he could feel nothing now but horror at what his neglect had done to her.

"Is it bad?" She sounded worried.

He nodded, barely able to speak. "The humors have turned putrid."

A look of fear flashed across her face. "Will you have to take off my leg?"

"It hasn't come to that," he said, trying to reassure himself as much as her. In truth he probably would, and even then, she might not live. Once wound poison had reached the heart, the patient would often die. Every surgeon knew that. Still, he must give her hope. Hope was often the strongest medicine the physician could offer.

But as he had that thought, he was struck with another dreadful realization. Hope might be the *only* medicine he could offer her. He'd left London in such haste that he hadn't thought to bring with him his collection of materia medica. He had no laudanum to dull her pain, no calomel to raise the fiery humor. And out here in the wilds of Galloway, they might be many hours away from an apothecary. Yet his only hope of saving her leg and perhaps her life lay in immediate surgery. *Without laudanum.*

He gritted his teeth. The pain she'd felt when he'd removed the bandage from her wound would be nothing compared to what she'd feel at the touch of his scalpel. The alcohol the inn could supply was a poor soporific, and besides, it was so prone to depress the vital functions that it would be dangerous to give it to a woman as slender as Zoe. But what was his alternative? He must operate.

He addressed his patient in what he hoped was a calming tone. "If we're to save your leg, I'll have to open the wound and drain the evil humors."

Though he'd expected her to protest, she only bit her lower lip and nodded.

"Good, then. I'll have to go fetch my instruments. Go to your chamber and do what you must to prepare yourself. I'll meet you there in a few moments."

He turned away from her, not trusting that he could control his features any longer. He mustn't frighten her by betraying his own dismay. She'd need all her courage to fight off the poison that threatened her life. And she had courage aplenty, though it hurt to remember how many opportunities *he'd* given her to display it. She deserved better than the fate he'd condemned her to.

How wrong he'd been to even think of making her pay for her mother's crime. For he could no longer think of her as the harlot's daughter, but only as herself—brave, compassionate, intuitive Zoe, the strongest woman he'd ever known, and one he'd have been proud to claim as a friend had circumstances been different.

But they hadn't been different, and with what he had

done to her, she'd be justified in taking revenge on *him*, though the thought of her hating him sent another surge of pain shooting through his heart.

He struggled to regain the composure he would need to save her. *You must put aside all human emotions if you are to prevail over the powers of death.* Hadn't that been the first thing the Dark Lord had taught him? He must remember it.

Taking a deep breath, he strode into his own chamber and rummaged through his things looking for the instrument case he always kept with him. It held the scalpel he'd need to cut the poisoned flesh out from her wound. It was only as he was unfolding the leather case that he remembered that his scalpel was steel. Cold iron. It had been weeks now since he had touched anything of iron, ever since he'd received the Dark Lord's letter announcing that he'd chosen Adam as his heir and giving him the long list of the things he must do to prepare for the Final Teaching. To touch the iron-bearing scalpel now would drain away all the power he'd built up through his abstention. It might even make him unfit to receive the Final Teaching.

He pushed the instrument case away. He'd use the bronze knife.

But then he remembered what the instructor at the medical school in Vienna had taught him—that the touch of bronze could itself cause a festering wound. Steel cut cleanly, as bronze did not.

But, of course, the ancients had used bronze, hadn't they? And most of the patients he'd seen the Dark Lord operate on had survived—a much larger proportion of them, as he'd often recalled uneasily in Vienna, than those who yielded themselves up to Von Faschling's speedy steel blade. Surely Adam didn't need to pollute himself in order to heal Zoe? He must stay pure so he could assume the Dark Lord's powers, and once he did, he'd be able to save so many more lives and atone, at last, for what he'd done to Charlotte. How could he give all that up—to save Isabelle's child?

Pick up the bronze blade, he told himself, *and have done with it*. He'd hone the edge carefully. Surely that would be good enough to avoid contagion.

He grasped the handle of his bronze knife. The old familiar feelings flowed through him at its touch. He felt his teacher's strength, and the strength of all the unknown Dark Lords who had come before him. They beckoned him to join them. After all these years of sacrifice he was so close to becoming what he'd always dreamed of being.

But he *wouldn't* be what he dreamed of, if he let his greed for power harm Zoe.

He'd already harmed her enough by trying to husband his paltry powers. Had he not feared his own lust he would have cleaned out her wound himself and prevented it from turning septic. He couldn't make the damage worse by operating on her with a knife that could worsen the poison. If that was the price the Ancient Ones demanded for the Final Teaching, it was too high.

He shoved the bronze knife back into its hilt. He wouldn't use it.

Giving himself no time to change his mind, he

reached into his instrument case and pulled out his scalpel. Cold flowed into his fingers from the prime German steel. He tried to sense whether at its touch, some of his power had fled from him, but if it had, he couldn't feel it. The scalpel felt good in his hand, familiar. Memories of all the times he'd used it successfully flooded over him. He was an excellent surgeon. Even Von Faschling had admitted it this past fall in Vienna, and everyone knew how miserly he was with his praise.

So he said a silent prayer that this operation, too, would be added to the number of his successes, and that despite the advanced state of her wound, he would cure Zoe.

It would be a struggle. He'd have to find four strong men to hold her down while he did the operation. For surgery was a brutal art. He was one of very few gentlemen able to tolerate what the discipline required. It had taken him years to fight down the natural emotions that the surgeon must put aside so he could work serenely despite the agonized shrieks of his patients. And it would be even harder to operate on Zoe because of the sympathy that had joined the two of them since that fatal night at the inn. It would take all his fortitude—and more—to get through it, knowing as he did that, when he cut into her flesh, he would feel her agony as if it were his own.

He walked over to the washstand and carefully rinsed his hands to symbolize their purity, as the Dark Lord had taught him to do when he'd first begun to teach him the magic of healing. Von Faschling had laughed at him for following such a superstitious practice, but all surgeons had their little rituals, and the great surgeon himself wouldn't operate if a black cat crossed his path. When Adam's patients had done well after their surgeries, Von Faschling had forgiven him his idiosyncrasy.

Then Adam closed his eyes and invoked the help of the Unseen, asking that his hand be guided. He'd need all the help he could get, both seen and unseen, operating with nothing to dull her pain.

When he'd finished his prayer and opened his eyes, the first thing that caught his attention was his leather instrument case lying spread out on the table. The dog-eared corner of an old folded piece of paper peeked out of the pocket at one end. He hadn't noticed it before, so caught up had he been in his struggle to pick up the scalpel. But he knew what it was. And as he grasped the edge of the yellowed paper and pulled it out of the instrument case, his heart surged.

His prayer had been heard. For the Dark Lord had given him that paper long ago in Morlaix. It held a sacred spell he'd entrusted to Adam—one he'd claimed was more powerful than even the newfangled magnetic discoveries of Mesmer. The Dark Lord had said that this spell could send a patient into a slumber so deep that once it was invoked, you could stab the patient with a knife and he wouldn't awaken.

And it wasn't just hearsay. Adam had seen the Dark Lord use this spell to remove a gangrenous toe without eliciting even a single scream from his sleeping patient. Had Adam not seen it, he wouldn't have believed it possible. But he'd been given no chance to try it out himself, as the demonstration had taken place only a few days before the catastrophe that had destroyed Charlotte. And after that, the Dark Lord had been forced to send him away for his own safety.

It shamed him now to remember how, after leaving his master, he'd ignored that spell, even though he'd seen how effective it could be. But the Dark Lord had warned him to keep the secret teachings to himself so as not to earn the contempt of other physicians. Magic was out of fashion among the great minds of the Continent.

Now, as he read over the words his teacher had scribbled on the yellowed paper in his spindly script, and carefully fixed them in his mind, Adam remembered once more why he'd sacrificed so much to earn the Dark Lord's wisdom. For though they had taught him much that would be useful, no man of science had tools that could do what this spell could do.

As the Dark Lord had taught him, he waved the steel scalpel through a candle flame thrice, to give it strength. He would combine what they'd taught him in the operating theaters of Vienna with the Dark Lord's magic, and hope that with that potent mixture, Zoe might yet be saved.

Zoe couldn't take her eyes off Ramsay's scalpel. Its blade glittered, razor-sharp. She was lying on her bed with her hands folded primly on her abdomen as she had been doing ever since he'd sent her here to wait for him, and now he was here, with that thing in his hand, ready to cut into her flesh. She clenched her fist, struggling to remain calm, daring only to ask, "Aren't you going to give me any laudanum?"

He shook his head. "I don't have any. But even so, you won't feel the pain. I've got something much better to still it."

"Brandy?" She saw no sign that he'd brought any with the other paraphernalia he had carried into the chamber when he'd returned. Her muscles tightened. She hoped she wouldn't disgrace herself when it was time to submit to the knife.

"No, something else. Some healing magic the Dark Lord taught me many years ago in France." Her heart sank. *He* might believe in magic, but she was too practical to do so.

"It works," he assured her, "whether or not you believe in it." Once again, he'd responded to her unspoken thought, but strangely, this time instead of disturbing her, his ability to hear what she left unsaid gave her comfort.

"Is it a potion?" She saw no signs of one: no powders ground out of noxious substances, no small vial filled with healing foulness.

"No. It's a spell—a really good one. All you need do is listen to me now and do just as I tell you. Nothing else." He reached toward her. "Here, take my hand."

She did, thinking it strange that he would allow her to touch him now, when he needed his magical powers to be at their strongest. Yet as she clasped his hand a burst of warmth filled her, despite her terror. The look of concern that filled his features made her feel cared for, yet at the same time, it made him look curiously vulnerable. Indeed, something about the way the faint haze of stubble on his cheek glowed golden in the morning light made her long to stroke his cheek and comfort *him*.

It was the virgin's sickness, again. She looked away for a moment, unable to bear the sight of his sparkling eyes so full of some emotion she wouldn't give a name to. With a sharp intake of breath he grasped her hand more tightly, then dropped it almost as quickly, as if her touch had burnt him.

When she'd found the courage to look at him again, she found him facing away from her with his head bowed. Time stretched out as he gave himself up in prayer to the powers that he served. Then he withdrew his watch from its pocket. But rather than consult the time, he let it dangle from its chain with its gleaming golden back facing toward her. With a swift motion, he set it to swinging in a broad arc, back and forth, in front of her eyes.

"Observe my watch," he commanded.

She wondered why he should ask such a strange thing of her. But she did what he'd told her to do. She had no choice left now but to obey him.

Adam watched intently as her eyes tracked the arc his timepiece made as it swung like a pendulum, back and forth and back and forth again. As he did, he called upon the Ancient Ones, silently entreating them to come to his aid, despite his lapses, and his sins, and the curse he had been born with.

If he could save her, he would ask them for nothing more.

As her eyes continued to follow the rhythmic motion, her fingers uncurled and her lips parted. Her breathing became slower and beat in time with the swinging of the watch. Gaining courage, he lifted the chain and led her gaze upward, very slowly, until the subtle quivering of her lids told him the spell was beginning to work.

He felt a gust of relief. It didn't always. And if she hadn't responded he would have had no choice but to round up four strong men downstairs and get them drunk enough that they'd be willing to hold her down while he went about his brutal business. But there was no need for that yet. It was going well. Her eyes had rolled up inside their lids, leaving only a tiny margin of white exposed.

Making his voice as steady and monotonous as he could, he began to chant the magical phrases that would put her under.

"You are getting sleepy."

He said it once, and then twice, and then over and over again. And while he repeated the phrase, in his mind he said the silent, secret prayer that the Dark Lord had told him must remain unspoken.

"Your eyes are feeling heavy." His voice had taken on the droning tone he remembered his teacher using. "You're sinking deeper and deeper into a restful sleep."

He repeated these simple phrases, accompanying them with the mystical intention that would make them do their work And as he mouthed the words that deepened the enchantment, he imagined his teacher standing at his side as he had done at Morlaix so long ago, garbed in his long purple robe, with his golden wand raised high, lending him his strength.

He let his voice meander on, as he chanted word after gentle word that led Zoe into the charmed state where she'd feel little pain and where what little pain she'd feel would be forgotten once he allowed her to awaken. Soon the words seemed to be speaking themselves of their own accord, as he lost himself in the building of the spell, until, at last, subtle changes in her muscle tone told him the spell had her whole body in its power. Now he took the last step.

"Your leg feels nothing. It floats above your body, filled with peace and light. You feel warmth and comfort. Your leg is comfortable and numb." He gave himself up to the rhythm of the words, repeating this part of the charm over and over, and hoping it was true.

He laid aside the watch. The moment of truth had come.

Zoe lay supine before him, her breathing almost imperceptible. She looked as though she was deeply enchanted. He pulled back her skirt to reveal the blackened wound, picked up his scalpel, and pricked her near her thigh with its tip.

She slumbered on serenely.

The spell had worked.

Drawing a deep breath, he cut deep into the tissue around the wound, swiftly and cleanly, admiring the way the expensive German steel cut. Deftly he dissected out the infection, cutting away the swollen edges where he found the blackened nodules that had formed around the splinters that had penetrated into the wound. Von

Faschling couldn't have done it more speedily even with the screams of his patient urging him on.

Now and again, Zoe moaned, but she didn't awaken from her enchanted slumber.

As he cut out the poisoned flesh, he continued to murmur the soothing words of the Dark Lord's spell, reminding Zoe of the gentle warmth she felt coursing down her body even as the blood and pus spurted all over his hand.

When he was done cutting out the blackened tissue, he poured a vial of brandy over the wound. It was another thing he'd seen the Dark Lord do—to rouse the patient's spirit with spirits of wine—and, superstitious though it might seem, Adam had never been disappointed in its efficacy. Zoe stirred as the stinging fluid bathed the gaping wound, but she didn't awaken.

After allowing enough time for the brandy to do its work, he picked up a threaded surgical needle. Again, in tribute to his master's teachings, he waved it through the candle flame while muttering the correct invocation and sewed the wound closed.

The stitches went in smoothly. The edges of the wound were clean now, free of any traces of the blackened nodules. The spell even seemed to have controlled her bleeding.

Hope surged into his heart. He hadn't lost his powers, despite his lust, despite having touched the cold iron.

Zoe might live.

He was about to bring her out of her enchanted sleep, when he remembered something else the Dark Lord had mentioned, which might be helpful now. He'd said, in passing, that when removing the spell, it was possible to leave some lingering trace of it behind that would give the practitioner the ability to restore the patient to the entranced state almost immediately, should it become necessary, simply by uttering a Word of Power.

Zoe would undoubtedly experience considerable pain in the days ahead, for to heal her he'd had to make her wound deeper. So it would be helpful if he could easily send her back into a healing sleep if the pain became too much for her.

The instructions for extending the spell had not been on the slip of paper he had stored with his scalpel. But he was pretty sure he knew how to work it—it would require only that he add another suggestion to the ones he'd already implanted in her mind before he operated on her. And because of the hours his teacher had demanded he spend reading the ancient books, he was pretty sure he knew the correct Word of Power to use, too.

It must be *codladh*—the word for sleep in the language of the Ancient Ones.

So with his voice rising and falling in a musical manner, he gave Zoe one last command—that when she heard the Word of Power, she would return once again to this enchanted state.

When that was done, he murmured the final words that would lead her back out of her trance. As he finished, her eyes flickered open. He flung the scalpel down on the table and sank into a chair, exhausted.

* * *

Zoe rubbed one eye with her fist. She felt groggy, as if she'd been asleep for a long time, but rested, too, and strangely calm. But hadn't Lord Ramsay been about to do something terrifying? *Yes. Surgery.*

Her calm vanished. Obviously he hadn't done it yet, since the dull pain in her thigh was nothing like the agony she'd be feeling if he'd sliced it open. She braced herself for what must come next. But as the minutes ticked by, nothing happened.

Only when she heard him mutter something to himself did she force herself to open her eyes to find him sitting with his head tipped back and his eyes closed. His long, muscular torso was slumped against the backrest of a chair. He looked drained, stretched to the limit, much the way he'd looked after failing to heal the cottar's boy.

Had he failed again? A bolt of fear passed through her. Was that why she felt so little pain in her leg? It must be. He must have decided her wound was too advanced to be healed by surgery and given up the attempt. And now she'd die.

"You didn't operate, did you?" she whispered, trying to keep the fear out of her voice.

"I did."

"But there wasn't any pain."

"I told you there wouldn't be."

She blinked her eyes a few times to clear them and then, examining him more closely, saw the small droplets of blood on his hand. Her blood.

She raised her head and peered down at her wounded thigh, bracing herself for what she'd find. But the ugly sore was gone, replaced by neat stitches that drew together the edges of what now looked to be a much smaller wound. Yet she'd felt no pain.

"It is a very powerful spell," he said.

"Surely you must have given me laudanum." She wasn't sure she wanted his wizard's magic to be quite *that* real.

He shook his head. "I have no laudanum. I used only the spell. That, and my skill as a surgeon. I trained at the University of Vienna, you know." He couldn't quite keep the pride out of his voice.

"So I haven't destroyed your magic completely?"

His eyes softened. "No. Nor my skill as a surgeon. You will live, Zoe."

She felt her breath quicken. It seemed impossible that it could be true. But the calm joy she saw in his face reassured her. "I suppose I would have been well served if my attempt to seduce you had weakened your healing powers so that you couldn't save me."

His lip tightened as if her words had come perilously close to his own thoughts. "If I'd lost you. It would have been solely my fault. Not yours."

"And you would never have forgiven yourself, would you? It would have been like what you felt when you lost the cottar's boy, but worse."

"Far worse." The words seemed to burst out of him without his having any ability to censor them. "I couldn't have lived another hour if I'd caused your death."

His gray eyes were soft, as if all his armor had dropped away, revealing for the first time the emotions he'd worked so hard to suppress. But she mustn't let herself be deluded by his words into thinking he felt anything more for her than what he always had. If he was expressing emotion now, it must only be a reaction to the fear that had gripped him earlier. It would be fatal to let herself believe, for even a moment, that he was moved by anything else.

"You frighten me when you speak like that," she said in her sharpest tone. "When I recover, you'll go back to hating me. Indeed, I shan't trust that I am truly out of danger until you start snapping at me. Only that will reassure me that I'm safe."

"Then I must attempt it, if it will help you get better."

For the first time in many days, she saw him smile. Then his expression grew serious again. "But for now you must sleep. You still have a lot of healing ahead of you."

His tone was rich and resonant and made her feel engulfed in comfort, as if he'd been speaking the words of love she'd never hear from him. Then he whispered what seemed to be a foreign word, one that sounded like "collah," but she had no time to ponder its meaning, for she was overcome by a delicious sense of peace and sank back into a deep slumber where she remembered nothing more.

Chapter 7

Zoe awoke to find Ramsay again seated by her bedside, peering at her intently. "Will we resume our journey today?" she asked as she drew herself up to a sitting position.

"Hardly. It's almost dusk. You've slept the day through. But even if it weren't, surely you wouldn't expect me to make you travel so soon, after such an ordeal?" His gray eyes widened.

"Have you any choice? The moon will soon be waning and that will make it impossible to travel after dark. If we don't continue on now, how will you reach the island and begin the Final Teaching?"

"The Teaching will have to wait. Did you really think I'd force you to endure the jouncing of the carriage with your wound still tender from surgery?" His eyes were so filled with warmth, it hurt to look at them.

She must drive it away. Speaking coldly she said, "You had no compunctions about taking me from my home and tearing me away from everything I hold dear. Why should I expect you to stop your journey for me now?"

He bit his lip. "Because I'm not entirely a monster—despite the way I've treated you."

Her plan had backfired. The concern radiating from his lustrous eyes was even stronger. It tore her heart out. Then to her horror, he took her hand in his and gently stroked it.

It would be so easy to believe he cared for her—and so dangerous. If she were to let herself believe that his feelings toward her had softened, she might easily throw herself into his arms and give way to her desire for him.

She must not believe it. When the crisis was past, just as she'd said half jokingly, he *would* go back to the way he'd been before and allow himself to feel nothing for her save lust and loathing. She was still the daughter of the woman who had killed his sister. That wouldn't change. She mustn't forget it, for no matter what had made him treat her more tenderly over these past hours, he'd soon remember. Indeed, it would be better for both of them if she were to remind him of it now. Brutally.

"There's no reason you should be kind to me," she snapped. "My mother killed your sister."

He dropped her hand and drew back, as she'd intended, his lips tightening as he remembered what it was he must feel for her. Losing his regard made her feel forlorn, but she'd get over it. It was only the virgin's sickness. It would heal with time—and it would heal faster, if he'd continue treating her with his accustomed coldness.

She pressed on. "If we resume our journey now, you won't have to lose another whole day of travel."

"Why? I'd think you would take pleasure in seeing my plans come to naught, given my cruelty toward you, whatever my justification."

"I've never seen much point in vengeful behavior."

"Why not?" His tone became more abrupt. But, of course, his need for vengeance against her mother was the mainspring of *his* existence.

"Hatred only corrodes the spirit," she said primly. "And besides, I'll be safer if I give you no further reason to hate me."

"Then your behavior is motivated only by cold practicality? You'll forgive me only because to do so might make your life easier in the future?"

"What else would you expect? Sentiment can play little part in the life of one raised as I was. Would you prefer that I pretend that I act out of love for you?" She attempted a brittle laugh of the kind her mother did so well. "I think not. You've made it very clear you wouldn't wish to hear such words from me. And besides, as you say, you've given me little reason to love you."

"Can you really be only twenty?" he asked with a puzzled look.

"I'll be twenty-one at the end of August."

He shook his head. "It's hard to believe. Your cynicism makes you seem so much older."

"So you weren't cynical when you were my age?"

"I was a mooncalf fool when I was twenty," he said bitterly, "I doubt there was ever a young man so trusting and so green as I was when I ran off to France to live out my ideals."

He dropped into an uneasy silence, but once again, his hand reached for hers and she was powerless to deny it to him. When he had taken possession of it, he cradled it in his much larger one and his thumb began absently stroking the back of her palm.

Was it to comfort her this time, or himself? His voice, when he resumed speaking, was disturbed. "I earned my cynicism the hard way, as the tumbrels rolled. It must be easier to learn your cynicism at your mother's knee, as you did, absorbing it a little at a time as a matter of logic and principle, rather than to be taught it all at once as I was, by living through catastrophe. I wouldn't wish that on anyone."

"Not even the daughter of your worst enemy?" As his eyes met hers, a thrill ran through her body. She waited for the fury to sweep over his features as it always did when she reminded him of her origins, but all he did was grasp her hand more tightly, with a touch that was both delicious and disturbing. She tensed.

She must not turn to *this* man, of all people, for comfort. She must not be tempted by the intimacy she felt with him now. She must not lose herself in the unearthly beauty of his gold-flecked eyes, even now when they were softened by an emotion so different from lust or loathing.

Ruthlessly, she pulled her hand from his and shoved

it under the covers. "Yes, a courtesan's daughter is spared the pain of disillusionment, I daresay, since we start out disillusioned. But I have no regrets. It's the illusions young girls have—those foolish dreams of marriage—that ruin their lives. I'm better off without them."

"Don't you dream of being wed?"

"How could I, knowing, as I do, that men turn to women like my mother as soon as they become bored with the charms of their innocent brides. I'd much prefer a courtesan's dishonor to a wife's slavery—as you of all men have good cause to know." She shifted her tone to let him know she'd tired of this conversation. "So then, shall we continue our journey?"

"Of course not. I still cherish the hope of saving one patient this week. I beg you do nothing to make it impossible. I came in to see you just now only because I must examine your wound."

"Oh," she replied, suddenly feeling very foolish.

He motioned for her to stretch out again on the bed, then knelt down beside her and carefully uncovered her leg so that he could examine his handiwork. As she waited for his verdict she struggled to hide her anxiety from him, lest he favor her again with that caring look that made him even more handsome than before, or stroke her hand in that alarmingly comforting fashion. She had so little strength left with which to resist him if he did. But she must resist, or the virgin's sickness might prove fatal. She couldn't give in to the treacherous yearning to meld herself with him.

When he'd completed his examination, he pulled the

counterpane up over her leg. "The wound is no worse. It will be several days until I can be certain it's healing, but I'm encouraged to see no new inflammation."

He stood. "Zoe—" His voice softened as he lingered on her name.

She must make him stop before he said anything further. The emotion radiating from him was too confusing. Too tempting. Too unsafe. "If you're done," she snapped, "you may leave."

He shrank back as if she'd slapped him, but all he said was "I am done, so I'll trouble you no longer. We'll remain here another day. By then you should be well enough to travel." Then he strode quickly to the door, pausing only for a moment on the threshold, where he turned back to face her, his eyes, again, luminous.

It was too much. If he were to offer her another word of kindness, she'd have to throw something at him. But he stayed silent as he made his way to the door and closed it gently behind him. When he was gone, she lay back, exhausted, wondering why, when he had done exactly what she'd wanted him to do, she felt so suddenly bereft.

She would live, Adam told himself when he'd returned to his chamber after Zoe's abrupt dismissal. Perhaps she might even keep her leg. Perhaps, in time, only a jagged scar would remain on that soft, creamy flesh to stand witness to how close she had come to death because of his inability to control the lust she had inspired in him—and inspired in him still.

There was no way of avoiding that painful truth.

If anything, his attraction to her was even stronger, nor could he delude himself it was just lust he was feeling. Had it been, it might have been less disturbing. After all, men were lustful creatures, even those like himself who strove to become something better. But what drew him to her now was more than just the needs of his thwarted body. Her courage enticed him, as much as her long, smooth thighs.

He couldn't have enough of that cool way she dealt with the many difficulties with which her life was filled. She was so calm, so matter-of-fact. So unlike him. She wasn't tormented by an overactive imagination. And yet despite her objectivity she was so kind. She'd been willing to resume their journey because she knew what abandoning it would mean for him. She might pretend she did it cynically, but he'd felt the subtle touch of her compassion enough over these few days they'd spent together to know there was more to it than that.

He wished he had her strength. He marveled at the inner beauty that lay hidden beneath her flawed skin and crude features. Had she been anyone else's daughter—had he not been chosen as the heir—who was to say what he might have felt for her? But he couldn't change the past. She'd been right to remind him that she was Isabelle's daughter. She was the last woman alive with whom he should betray his vow and give in to his animal nature. He couldn't betray Charlotte like that.

But even so, cursed as he was—and knowing how wrong it was—his soul cried out to join itself with Zoe's.

Perhaps it was a side effect of the spell. Perhaps when he'd invaded her soul to bend her to his will he had somehow opened *his* soul to her—or given up some of his own will. Whatever it was, he hoped it would pass quickly, before he gave himself up to any more of the Piscean emotionality his teacher had so often chided him for. It might be his nature to pine for what he could never have, but he would not succumb to it.

In a few more days they would reach Iskeny, and he would find himself again in the Dark Lord's presence. But even the thought of his long-awaited reunion with his teacher brought him no comfort. For the Dark Lord had told him to bring him the virgin and had written that if he did, Charlotte, at last, would be avenged. What role would Zoe play in that Final Teaching—the virgin his teacher had summoned?

He sighed. Perhaps it was just more proof of his flawed Piscean nature, but it struck him that what he needed right now was a drink. So he made his way downstairs to the taproom and called for a pint of porter. When the bar man had pulled it and set the tall pewter tankard before him, Adam paid him and walked over to a secluded corner where a comfortable chair beckoned. It was only after he'd drunk a long, satisfying draught that he looked up and noticed that a short, burly man was making his way toward him.

The man was dressed in the characteristic costume of a lowland cottar, a shapeless hat, rough trews, and a homespun shirt with an open collar similar to the one the Dark Lord had conferred on Adam in Morlaix when he'd first taken him on as a disciple. He carried a heavy pack on his back and there were layers of dried-on mud on his boots, as if he'd recently tramped through wet fields. He must be a beggar. Adam reached into his pocket for a shilling to give him, hoping to forestall a recital of his wretched plight.

But when the man saw him bring out the coin, he waved it away. A rough smile twisted his weathered face. "Nae, keep yer siller." He spoke in a heavy Scots brogue. "I have other business with you, milord." Then, without waiting for an invitation, he dropped into a chair beside Adam and bent his face close to his. A rich odor compounded of horse and unwashed clothing filled Adam's nostrils, forcing him back against the wall.

"Who are you?" he demanded testily. "What do you want with me?"

The man smiled again, a slow, not entirely amiable smile.

"Does this answer yer question?" The man rooted around in his pocket before pulling something out and holding it up before Adam's startled gaze.

A black feather, notched in the ancient fashion, just like the one he'd shown Isabelle.

Adam took it, his fingers shaking. What message had the Dark Lord sent him now? Had the healer's powers shown him how shamefully Adam had betrayed his vow? Had he sent this message to warn Adam away from continuing on with his journey now that his impurity had rendered it pointless?

A curious mixture of emotions flowed through him at that thought: grief that the work of so many years had been wasted, relief that he might at last give up a struggle he'd begun to think he couldn't win. But though he tried to read the message encoded in the feather's notches, the rigors of the messenger's journey had caused it to become so bedraggled Adam couldn't make it out. Still, there was no doubt of its provenance. "You come from Iskeny?"

The man nodded.

"Does the Dark Lord still live?"

Reaching up to remove his hat, the man shook his head sadly. "Nae. He passed on to his reward this Tuesday last."

He'd been too late. But if the Dark Lord had died that long ago, at least it hadn't been Adam's lust and Zoe's injury that had denied him the reunion with his teacher he'd looked forward to all these years. The Dark Lord had already been dead before the two of them had even set out on their journey north.

The Dark Lord's messenger replaced his battered hat. "Since my master's passing, I've traveled hard, restin' neither day nor night to bring his last message to you."

"He left me a message? What is it?"

The man took a long, yearning look at Adam's tankard before replying. "I'll get to that, but ye must let me tell my story. The auld laird died at sunset as was the prophecy"—Adam made a gesture of reverence with his hand as he'd been taught—"but before he passed, he asked to be taken one last time to the holy stane—you know of his ways how he goes to the holy stanes and calls to Them with his magic—"

Adam did indeed. There had been a standing stone at Morlaix, set out in a field, and it was there the Dark Lord had taken him and called upon the Ancient Ones for guidance on that terrible day when he'd discovered what Isabelle had done to his sister. "I know his ways well. But get to the message that he sent me."

Then, observing the longing way the man's eyes caressed the tankard, he shoved it across the table to him, saying, "Take it, I've hardly touched it."

The man's eyes lit up. "*Slainte.*" He took a deep draught from the tankard and then wiped his upper lip with his sleeve. "It's been a long, dry journey. Now where was I? Oh yes. When we brought him back frae the holy stane, the auld laird called for me, his eyes burning like coals. 'MacMinn!' he cries—that being me name, Yer Lordship—'Find Lord Ramsay. Dinnae rest until you find him.' And he told me to follow the coaching road south until I found you."

"But why?"

"Ah, but I'm coming to that. It's the lassie, Yer Lordship. The one that he purchased frae the wicked harlot." The man fixed him suddenly with a severe eye. "You've not ravished the girl, have ye?"

"Of course not," Adam said swiftly, his blood congealing as he remembered how close he'd come to doing just that.

"Good! Then ye must wed her."

"Wed her?"

"Aye, and the marriage must take place this very night. 'When ye find him, MacMinn,' the auld laird said. 'Let not the sun rise agin afore they wed, or the

power of the Auld Ones will seep back into the earth.'
That was his charge to me, and those were his very
words."

"But he made such a point in his letter that she must
stay a virgin!"

"Well, aye," the man said slowly, pausing to take another long pull of the ale. "He wanted only the best for
you, his heir. Ye wudna wish her to be soiled, she that
would become the bride of the Dark Lord's heir?"

"So I am still his heir? Though he be dead?"

"Of course. But only if ye marry the girl."

"But the Dark Lord must be chaste."

The man fixed him with one eye. "He commanded
that ye be married, laddie. The time for chastity is over."

The Dark Lord had released him from his vow? It
was almost too much to take in. "But now that he's
dead, how can I inherit his powers? Without him, there
can be no Final Teaching. Did he mention that?"

"Och, aye. 'Twas the last thing he spake before he
could speak nae more. 'Hark ye,' says he, ''tis the harlot's daughter who holds the key to the Final Teaching
now. They must wed before the power of the Ancient
Ones seeps back into the earth. Then they must dwell
together on his ancestral lands for a year and a day, and
bide there together. He must not return to the Holy Isle
'til that time is past. For until the year goes by it wudna
be safe.' And after that he started a-babbling in some
foreign tongue and said nae more in any language we
could understand."

"So I must marry her?"

"Ye must. And ye must marry her swiftly, too, before

the power he would pass on to ye drains back into the earth. It's been seven days already since he died. Ye must not make it seven nights. It must be now."

Adam's head was spinning. He called for another pint for the messenger, who sipped at it with obvious pleasure while he tried to come to terms with the message the man had brought him. Though there could be no Final Teaching as he had understood it—no passage through the Dragon's Cave, no fearsome test—at the end of his life the Dark Lord found a way to reach out from beyond the grave. The tradition would, somehow, pass on.

He felt a pang. He'd lived for so long imagining that trip to the Dragon's Cave. The hope that he would be worthy of it had been what motivated him to keep his vow. And yet, at the same time, he felt a surge of relief. There would be no virgin on the altar.

Only now did he allow himself to admit how much he'd feared what might lie in store for Zoe on the island. But in view of the Dark Lord's last command, he saw how foolish he'd been and felt shame at how little he'd trusted in the wisdom of his teacher.

It had been his own vengeful nature that had created the ugly scenes that had flitted through his imagination. That was no work of the Old Ones. The Dark Lord had never meant Zoe to be his victim.

"Ye must marry her, laddie," MacMinn repeated after he'd refreshed himself with another swig from the foaming tankard. "And ye must do it now." He wiped his mouth. "Do not delay or the power will dribble away and the auld laird will have no heir."

"I shall do his will." Adam stood.

A broad grin spread over the messenger's features. "'Tis well that I found you in our bonny Scotland where the laws of marriage are so reasonable. I shall go now and find an anvil priest to join ye twa in the sight of the gods and men. Then off with ye to your ancestral lands, as the auld laird intended. It willna be safe to dally 'til you are home, once ye have made her yours."

The man donned his battered cap. "I imagine the girl will be relieved when she learns she's to be wed."

I imagine the girl will tear out my liver and my lights when I suggest any such thing, Adam thought, wondering how he would ever get her to consent.

Chapter 8

Adam watched with mixed feelings as MacMinn disappeared into the night to hunt up one of the blacksmiths who custom—and the lenient Scottish law—allowed to solemnize runaway marriages. But as simple as a Scottish marriage might be, the bride must still give her consent. And given the coldness with which Zoe had dismissed him not an hour ago and her bitter words about marriage, how would he obtain it?

The simplest approach—just asking—was out of the question. He couldn't delude himself that she'd accept a straightforward proposal. A gently raised girl, subjected to the humiliations he'd put her through, might welcome the wedding that would save her reputation, especially in view of the sexual encounter they'd engaged in. But Zoe didn't consider herself bound by the narrow rules that applied to a gently raised lady. She'd made her preference for freedom clear—as well as her disdain for him. With all she'd suffered at his hands, he could just imagine how she would respond were he to ask her to become his wife. He'd be lucky if she didn't fling something at his head.

But he might be wrong. He knew little about women, having taken pains to avoid their company throughout the past nine years. Perhaps she would surprise him. He was a titled lord, after all, and it was marriage he was offering. Unworldly though he might be, he knew enough to know that few women could resist the allure of a title, whatever their feelings might be for its possessor.

But he quickly dismissed that hope. He knew Zoe well enough by now to know that she was one of the small number who could. That was part of what made her so appealing—the integrity that was so evident in her character, despite her base birth.

If he ever were to marry, it would be just such a woman that he'd want, someone who saw him as more than just a way to achieve wealth and rank, an honest woman who took no pleasure in the flirtatious behaviors so common among both courtesans and debutantes. That was the kind of woman he'd want were he to marry—but that thought brought him crashing back to reality.

It wasn't a matter of "were he to marry," but of how he could persuade Zoe to marry him tonight—within the next few hours, before the power of the Dark Lord seeped back into the earth.

It seemed impossible. And yet he must achieve it.

He sighed. There was a certain justice to the old man's setting out this path for him. Perhaps the passage through the Dragon's Cave would have been too easy for him. He wasn't afraid of the things of the dark. He'd faced *them* all his life. But marriage to Zoe, whom he longed for with his body, and who, he was beginning to suspect, had touched him in his soul— to bind himself to her, for life—now *that* was truly frightening.

But none of this brought him any closer to figuring out how he would get her to go along with his plan. She had every reason to reject it. It wasn't *her* quest that made this marriage necessary. Why should she bind herself to him, after the callous way he'd treated her? Why put herself under the lifelong control of the man who had stolen her from her home with insults and threats and whose cowardice had almost cost her leg or even her life? He could barely stand to think what might have happened had he not found that paper with the spell—

But that was it. That was how it could be done.

Nothing could be simpler. He would just invoke the healing spell again. He wouldn't have to plead his case or convince her to accept him as her husband. He need only command her to assent, and she must obey. The spell would make it so. It was almost as if the Ancient Ones had planned it.

A quiet voice within whispered it was wrong. But no sooner had it made its case than he imagined the Dark Lord's scornful rebuttal. Too much was at stake for him to let himself be hobbled by Piscean sentiment. It was the time for action, not losing himself in weakening reflection. The Ancient Ones had decreed that he must marry Zoe, so marry her he would.

He'd ensure she wouldn't suffer in the aftermath. He'd give her a better life than the one she'd have had without him. As he'd told her, he wasn't a monster. Now he'd have the chance to prove it.

That decided, Adam tiptoed down the narrow inn hallway to Zoe's chamber and knocked gingerly on her door. In a whisper she bade him enter. She'd lain down as if to rest, but it was clear that rest had eluded her.

He strode across the room to where she lay. "Does your leg pain you?"

"It does, though I think it's getting better." Her face looked pale and drawn. He'd expected that by now she would be feeling her body's reaction to what he'd done to it with his surgery. But as was her wont, she was fighting hard to hide her pain.

"Perhaps I can ease it somewhat."

Her face brightened. "Can you? Were you able to find some laudanum?"

"No. But I can help you again with the healing spell. It helped you sleep after you awoke from the surgery, didn't it?"

"It did. Can you use it again?"

He nodded. But the relief that animated her features sent shame flooding through him, in view of what it was he was about to do to her. It wasn't right. Had it not been the Dark Lord's final command that Adam wed her, he'd have turned on his heel then and there and left her alone. But he had no other choice. The Dark Lord's power must not ebb back into the earth. The unbroken chain of a hundred heirs that had gone before him demanded that he assume their heritage.

He sat down on the plain wooden chair that stood at Zoe's bedside. "When you awake your pain will be gone." He looked into her warm brown eyes and smiled to allay the concern he saw in them. Then he leaned over and spoke the Word of Power.

"*Codladh.*"

Almost as soon as the breath had left his lips, her eyelids dropped over her pupils. He examined her for the signs that the Dark Lord had taught him and, finding them, was satisfied that she had, indeed, dropped back into that same state of enchantment in which he had operated on her leg.

To assuage his conscience, he began by murmuring the words that would relieve her pain. He owed her that much, as he'd told her he'd invoke the spell to soothe her. When that was done, he battled the feeling that he should stop there and not take the next, irreversible step. Conscience whispered it was wrong; prudence, that he'd pay dearly for it.

But even as he contended with his sentimental weakness, a faint smile played upon Zoe's lips, making her look so very beautiful. She glowed with an inner beauty that entranced him. He felt himself enveloped in her aura now that they were connected once again by the power of his magic. He yearned to embrace her, to enfold her in his arms, and lose himself in her.

Instinctively, he drew back, fighting the treacherous urge, only to remember that if he did what he intended

that yearning would be permitted—and not only permitted but *required*. She would be his wife. It would be
right to join himself with her and to bathe himself in
the comfort she, and only she, could give him.

"Zoe," he began, speaking with the soothing rhythm
of the ancient incantation. "When you awaken, you will
have no memory of what we speak of now. You will
feel only happiness. You will have no pain. And when
next you see me pull my watch out of my pocket"—his
voice cracked, but still he must go on—"you will be
filled with the desire to be my bride."

He paused, in case she should protest, trembling at
the enormity of what he'd done. But Zoe made no response except for the tiniest quiver at the corner of her
closed eyes. She was truly under the power of his spell.

To be certain that she had understood him, despite
the enchanted state into which she'd sunk, he asked
her gently, "What will you feel when next you see my
watch?"

Her lips parted, and in a whisper she responded,
"The desire to be your bride."

Something twisted inside him as she spoke. "And
you will feel happiness," he said urgently. "Great
happiness."

Her lips bowed in the faintest of smiles, and she
took a deep breath as if drawing in strength. He, too,
took courage from it, and went on. "A man will soon
ask if you freely consent to be my bride. Look at my
hand." Her eyes flickered open with a glazed look that
showed how deeply she remained under the enchantment. "When you see me raise it like this"—he held

it out palm up in a gesture of supplication—"you will say yes."

He stopped, overwhelmed with the wrongness of what he was doing. It would not be of her own free will that she took him, not when he employed this ancient spell to compel her assent. But he'd gone too far to stop. He must go on.

"Tell me once more. What will you do when you see me bring out my gold watch?"

"I will feel happiness." He could barely hear her whisper. "And I will yearn to be your bride."

He stretched out his hand, palm upward, in supplication. "And what will you say when you're asked for your consent?"

Her eyelids gave the minutest flutter, but she said nothing. Had he gone too far? It didn't matter, for he'd also gone too far to do anything else but continue.

"When you're asked if you would wed me, Zoe, you will say yes. Say it." His voice had become gruff with his urgency to get this over with. But she said nothing. A troubled look washed over her features.

He dropped to his knee, kneeling before the bed where she lay stretched out in the trance. Gently, he took her hand, feeling the pulse beating strongly there. He couldn't make it right—no, not with the way that he'd invaded her very spirit and bent it to his will. But he could make them more equal in what he'd done to her. He could bind himself to her the way he'd bound her to him.

"Zoe," he whispered, "in return for what I ask of you, I make you this vow: If you accept me, I will give you happiness. I will protect you with my life. I swear this to you on the blood that flows in my veins and by the power of the Ancient Ones who hear all and forget nothing."

The girl stirred faintly.

"Do you hear me? Zoe? Do you understand?"

"You vow yourself to me." Her voice was faint. "You will protect me."

"Will you accept my vow?"

There was a long pause. Her eyes flickered. He raised his hand once more, palm up in the gesture that should make her assent. But she stayed silent. Expressions flickered over her face, as if some struggle was going on deep in the netherworld where he had led her. Then finally her lips parted and she whispered, "Yes."

It had worked.

He uttered a silent prayer that he hadn't just damned them both. Then he gradually brought her out of the trance very slowly, so as not to disturb the process he had started.

When he was done Zoe shook her head. "That was so strange, I feel like I've been dreaming, and yet my leg feels so much better. What a gift you have! Much though it goes against my inclination, I vow you will make me a believer in magic." She smiled. "You give me no choice. You make it impossible for me to deny your power."

He nodded, not trusting himself to speak to her now, when he knew so much better than she did the truth of her last words.

He stood. "I'll be back shortly with some refreshment. Until then, you must rest."

She sank back against the cushions, her eyes already half closed. The comfort he'd given her with his spell made her look for a moment like a puppy. He'd never before seen her so relaxed, so unselfconscious, or so happy.

He tiptoed out the door, leaving her to the enjoyment of what might be her last minutes of contentment.

"Have you found the anvil priest?" Adam asked Mac-Minn when he found him awaiting him in the taproom.

"Aye, that be him." MacMinn gestured toward the burly man with arms as thick as fence posts who sat at a table in the corner nursing a tankard.

"Then fetch him and we'll conclude this business. Will you be the other witness?"

"Of course, and just in case, I've found a third man, too." MacMinn pointed toward a short man standing a few feet away dressed in a farmer's smock. Seizing the man by the elbow, he pushed him toward the stairs, motioning for Adam and the anvil priest to follow.

As the ill-assorted collection of wedding guests clattered their heavy way up the stairs, Adam couldn't help but wonder what madness had led him to this point. He paused at the foot of the staircase. It wasn't too late to stop matters before they went any further.

"Feeling those bridegroom nerves, are ye?" Mac-Minn asked knowingly. "It will pass. She's a lovely girl, and ye'll have no regrets for this night's work, I warrant you."

He made no reply. How could the Dark Lord's messenger know that? But even so, he followed him up the stairs.

When they all had reached the landing, Adam rapped on the door to Zoe's chamber, and after a long pause she bade him enter. He pushed it open to find her sitting up in the narrow bed, her hair loose. She'd wrapped herself in her ivory satin dressing gown—the one she'd worn that night when she'd come to his bed. At the memory, his groin tightened, and he fought his newly surging desire—only to remember, once more, that he was allowed to want her now. She was his bride.

Her eyes widened as she took in the motley collection of rustics who had entered in his wake, and when her eyes lighted on the travel-worn MacMinn, they stopped for a moment and a look of confusion swept over her face. It was understandable, the man looked like a beggar—hardly the sort of person one would introduce into a young woman's sleeping chamber. They must hasten to the matter at hand, before she had time to question why they were there.

Adam reached into his pocket and withdrew his watch, casually, as if to consult the time. A blush flowed across her cheek. The spell was working. The sight of the watch had made her feel the desire he'd implanted in her. Next, he fixed her with what he hoped was a loving look. It didn't come easily. He'd schooled himself for so long not to show any tender emotions. But as artificial as the maneuver felt, once he got past his self-consciousness it was easy. He need only relax his iron control enough to let the warmth that he felt for her flow into his features.

"It's time for us to wed," he said quietly. "These gentlemen here will witness the ceremony."

"You really wish to wed me?" Surprise made her voice rise unevenly.

"I do."

Surprise, confusion, and something that might be joy flitted across her face. Would the spell be enough to bind her?

Her eyes darted toward the witnesses who stood huddled against one wall, but when they lighted on Mac-Minn, Adam's ally just fixed her with a fierce look—one oddly like that of his master, the Dark Lord—and made a sign with his hand—probably some magical gesture his master had told him would ensure her compliance.

She nodded her head almost imperceptibly and turned back to Adam.

The blacksmith then motioned her to rise. She stood carefully, avoiding putting weight on her injured leg. As she pulled herself upright, her ivory satin gown draped itself into heavy folds around her, like the bridal gown that it was. Her rich, nut-brown hair, which had come half unbound in sleep, tumbled down her back in luxurious waves, forming a veil. When her eyes met his they were soft with desire. Even knowing it was only the desire he'd created with his spell, it still moved him. No woman had ever before looked at him with desire like this, of her body, of her heart, and of her soul.

She glanced over to him for reassurance. He clutched his watch like a talisman as the blacksmith joined their hands together and began to intone the words of the ceremony.

"Do you, Zoe Gervais, take this man, Adam Selkirk, Lord Ramsay, to be your lawful wedded husband?"

The words were so familiar. Adam had heard them repeated at many another man's wedding. But this time it was *his*. His throat suddenly felt very dry and he wondered if he'd be able to get the words out when it was his turn to reply.

But it was not his turn to reply. It was Zoe's. And she stood mute.

He must raise his palm in the prearranged signal, to make her give her assent, but before he could, the blacksmith repeated his question, more urgently now. "Do you take this man to be your wedded husband?"

Zoe's eyes darted around the room until they caught those of MacMinn, who nodded at her with a warm smile, as if urging her on. Then she turned back to Adam, her eyes filled with uncertainty. He wanted to reach out and embrace her, to reassure her that as strange as the situation was, she would be all right, but he couldn't. He felt frozen, as if he, too, were under a spell. He couldn't raise his hand. He couldn't compel her. All he could do was meet her eyes and marvel as he did so how luminous and deep they were.

If only he could tell her how truly beautiful she was. She looked to him now like a Madonna painted by a medieval Italian master, with her graceful long neck and those bright eyes, so filled with the powerful emotions she could barely withstand. But she must not withstand them. She must become his bride. The

Ancient Ones had commanded it, and his soul cried out that it was right that they had done so. He wanted her so much. If he didn't ensure her compliance now, he'd spend the rest of his life consumed with regret.

But before he could force his reluctant palm to rise, the blacksmith barked, "I haven't got all day, lassie. Do ye wish to wed or no?"

At that, as if the Ancient Ones had slashed through the bonds that held him, Adam raised his palm upward in the prearranged signal where Zoe must see it. He saw her mouth quiver but, even now, she remained silent.

Her strength was equal to that of any magic. She would elude him. He couldn't bear it.

She *must* marry him. And not just for the powers the wedding would bring him. The very strength with which her soul resisted his magic made him want her more. He leaned toward her and whispered in her ear in a tone so low so only she could hear him. "Remember what I pledged to you. I'll give you happiness. I'll keep you safe."

Her deep brown eyes met his, pure windows into her exquisite soul. Something flickered within them, though what it was, he couldn't say. Then with a tiny shudder she turned to the anvil priest.

"Yes." Her voice rang through the tiny chamber.

Satisfied, the priest nodded and turned to Adam. "Do you, Lord Ramsay, take this woman to be your wedded wife?"

"I do."

It was over.

MacMinn was regarding him now with a look of

beaming happiness. He must be relieved to know that his master's power would be transmitted to another generation. Then the anvil priest produced a piece of parchment and passed it to each of the witnesses to sign. When they were done, he handed it to Adam, saying, "This will serve as your marriage lines."

Adam handed him a golden sovereign and tossed the other witness a silver half crown. The men thanked him and quit the chamber. Only MacMinn lingered. "Ye've done all ye need do, laddie," he said in a low tone. "Ye may leave the rest of it until she's a bit stronger. It was the binding the auld laird called for, before the sun should rise, and ye are bound."

And then he, too, vanished, leaving Adam alone with his new bride.

He steeled himself for what would come next. Now that the ceremony was concluded, Adam had no idea how much power the Dark Lord's spell would maintain over his new bride. He was still holding the watch that he'd used to invoke the spell and Zoe's eyes were still fixed on it. He shoved it back into its pocket.

Released from its power, she brushed a hand over her eyes and sank down onto the edge of the bed." I must be delirious," she said at length. "Your surgery has failed and I have become feverish."

He shook his head no, not trusting himself to speak.

"Yet I don't feel hot," she said, still in the same tone of wonder. "It feels more as if I am caught up in a dream. How strange it is, to be dreaming and yet to know it *is* a dream." Her brow furrowed. "It seems so real. Who were those men, and why did it seem like one of them said the words of the marriage ceremony over us? *Am* I delirious?"

He put a gentle hand around her thin shoulders. She didn't resist it, though he could feel a quiver run through her slim frame. "You're not asleep. Nor are you out of your senses. The men were here."

Her eyes widened and her cheeks flushed with embarrassment. "But surely I must have misunderstood the words that big man said."

"You understood all correctly."

"Then I have *married* you?"

He nodded, prepared to defend himself should she lash out against him, but to his surprise, she merely sank back against her pillow. "This *is* a dream. How very odd. For a moment there I was sure I had awakened."

He didn't contradict her. She would need time to come to terms with what he'd done. For now, he must find words that would calm her and let her rest. She would need rest to complete her healing and recover the strength that would help her resign herself to what he'd done to her.

But there was little chance she would find rest this night. Just outside their doorway, people thundered up the stairs and milled about on the landing. There were a few drunken shouts, then a piper began to play an old lowland Scots wedding tune.

Word of the wedding must have spread downstairs, and the inn's denizens had decided to celebrate their union in the traditional raucous fashion. Drunken voices called out their congratulations from the hallway.

"Give it to her good, lad!"

"A son in nine months—"

"—Or in six!"

The crowd burst into a gale of raucous laughter.

"Don't be afraid," he whispered. "I'm here. I'll protect you." He stroked her cheek with his hand. "It will be all right."

"I *will* awaken, won't I?" she asked anxiously. "And your spell will wear off, like laudanum?"

"It will be all right," he repeated, avoiding her question. "I'll stay here with you all night to ensure that all is well."

He seated himself again on the chair beside her bed, as a piper wailed out the first few notes of a bawdy song about a milkmaid and her lover.

The sound reminded him of the weddings he'd attended in his youth down in the village at Strathrimmon. The same piping had accompanied the unions of the blushing girls and their hearty mates. How he had envied them their simple lives. If only *he'd* been born into a life like that, instead of into the complexities of his own—complexities into which he'd now drawn Zoe, irrevocably.

All too soon he'd have to tell her the truth. About why he'd wed her—and about the curse he bore, as all the men of his line had, for generations. Now that she was his wife, he couldn't keep it from her, much as he would have wished to. At least, now that they were wed, there was hope that when he assumed the Dark Lord's powers, he'd have, at last, the tools he needed to save them from the curse's blight.

But for now, all he could do was to send her back to sleep, using the words he'd implanted in her mind with the Dark Lord's spell. She needed sleep. She needed healing. There would be time enough to explain to her what he had done and why, later, when she was stronger.

He invoked the Word of Power to make her slumber, hoping it would be the last time he'd ever have to use it. It worked, as it always had. She was asleep in moments. But watching beside her, slumped in his uncomfortable chair, he had far less success in getting to sleep himself. If only there were someone to work a spell on *him*.

It was only long after the merrymakers were gone, in the deep silence of that hour that came before the break of dawn, that he finally remembered what else the Dark Lord had told him about the spell, so long ago in France. As powerful as it could be, his teacher had said, it couldn't be used to compel subjects to perform acts they believed would cause harm to themselves.

Adam cast his mind back to the long pause as the anvil priest had waited for Zoe's answer. He'd given her the sign that should have made her speak, but she'd stayed silent, resisting his magic, as the long minutes had ticked by. When, at last, she'd finally given in, was it because she'd been overcome by his spell—or had she made a choice?

She'd given her assent only after he'd repeated his vow. Would she have done so if she truly hated him? Had she wed him against her will, compelled by his magic? Or was the Dark Lord's teaching true? Had it been her choice?

Chapter 9

How strange it was that the dreams induced by Lord Ramsay's spell were so much sharper than those caused by laudanum. Zoe flexed her leg, pleased to find that the gash on her thigh was less painful than it had been the previous day. If only that meant the poison had receded from her blood and that her leg was saved. She lay unmoving for a long time, unable to get up the courage to examine her wound to see if the red streaks were fading.

But as she lay with her eyes closed, avoiding the start of the new day, the past night's dream flooded back into her mind. It was so lifelike, and each detail was so vivid. Nonetheless, it *had* been a dream for all of its startling clarity—a dream with the impossible logic of dreams. For only in a dream would the aloof Lord Ramsay have begged her to marry him.

She let her mind drift over the strange happenings her feverish mind had imagined: the way the chaste lord had beseeched her to accept him, and how no sooner had she given her consent than that huge man who had behaved as if he were a parson had appeared, as if by magic. And then that last detail, so clear and yet so improbable, that told her it *had* been a dream—the way MacMinn, of all people, had been standing there as one of the witnesses. MacMinn, who had been her mother's coachman back in the days when her mother could afford such a luxury and who'd always been so kind to her.

But it disturbed her to remember the joy with which her dream self had agreed to wed the Dark Lord's heir. The virgins' sickness must have penetrated even into her dreams. At least she hoped it *was* the virgin's sickness, for if it wasn't, her wound must have got much worse, and the inflammation from it reached her brain.

She wished she could ask Lord Ramsay about it, in his capacity as her physician, but how could she tell him what she'd dreamed? She could just imagine his reaction if he found out that the daughter of the woman he called the harlot was dreaming of trapping him into marriage.

But when she finally found the courage to open her eyes, the first sight that met them was that of Lord Ramsay himself, sprawled out asleep in an uncomfortable wooden chair beside her bed. His head was tipped back, his mouth open, his long legs thrust out before him.

Fear stabbed through her gut. She must have become

feverish if he'd watched by her bedside all night, and
if so, it must be delirium that explained her troubling
dream. Her earlier sense of having been reprieved vanished. Her wound must have gone bad. Perhaps the lack
of pain in her leg didn't signify that it was better. Perhaps
it had stopped hurting because the nerves were dead.

"Lord Ramsay—" She spoke quietly, hoping not to
awaken him too suddenly, but even so, at her words
he jerked awake in the chair. "Was I so ill during the
night?"

"Ill? No. Why do you ask?"

She felt herself redden, but couldn't bring herself to
mention her dream. "Why else would you have spent
the night watching by my bedside unless you still
feared for my life?"

An odd look filled his handsome features, but all he
said was "Your wound is healing well. Well enough,
that if you're up to it, we could resume our journey
after you've broken your fast."

So perhaps she really was better, for he certainly had
relapsed into his usual taciturn manner, and had ceased
lavishing on her those caring looks that had so disturbed her the previous day. Indeed, no sooner had he
informed her of his plans than he had stood and stalked
out of her chamber, leaving her alone.

She was glad she'd said nothing about her wild
dream of marrying him. Given his mood this morning
it would have been a serious mistake.

But she received another shock when she limped
down the stairway to the taproom. For the first person

she saw as she entered it was none other than Mac-Minn, who was seated at the bar, smoking a long clay pipe and looking so real that she couldn't dismiss his appearance as the figment of a dream.

Seeing her enter, MacMinn hailed her, "Guid mornin', Lady Ramsay!"

Had the events of the past evening been real? She made her way over to him, hardly knowing what to think.

"Aye, Mistress Zoe, to think ye've become a lady. I'm right proud of ye, I am, and to think that I knew ye when you were but a little thing, no taller than that." He held his hand out to demonstrate. Then, perhaps in response to the look of consternation that must be apparent on her face, he demanded, "He didna treat you roughly, did he?"

She shook her head, not sure what her old friend might be alluding to.

"No, he's not that kind." MacMinn sounded relieved, "He's a gentleman for all his mystic airs—not like the auld laird at all. He'll keep you safe."

But before she could ask him to explain, he pushed away from the bar and stood up, giving her one last look. "That's a load off my mind, I'll tell ye. But all's well that ends well, as they say. So I'll be off, now. Mind ye"—he raised one finger to his lips—"dinnae let on a word to yer fine new husband that you saw me. Mum's the word. Give him some time to get used to his sweet new wife. Do ye ken me, lassie? Not a word about meeting me here. It's important."

She nodded dumbly, her sleepy mind still trying to

puzzle out how her old friend could be standing before her bathed in the misty sunlight of a Scottish morning. But before she could ask him anything else, he tipped his battered hat and was off, leaving her alone in the empty taproom.

It got worse. She could no longer cling to the idea that she was in the clutches of a walking delirium when the maid who'd come to clean her chamber giggled and asked her if her new husband was as virile as he was comely, only to answer her own question by saying, "I daresay it will all come out in the wash." The girl curt-seyed, still giggling, and made a hasty exit.

She must have really married him. Everyone seemed to believe it.

Zoe tore the sheet off the bed, wondering what else might have happened while she'd been lost in what she had supposed to be a dream, but to her relief the sheet was as spotless as sheets in an inn could ever be. She wondered what the maid would make of that.

With growing dismay, she packed the few things she'd brought in with her and made her way out to the courtyard. Could Lord Ramsay *really* have married her?

She recalled how, when she'd confronted him the previous night and demanded to know if the bizarre events she'd sleepwalked through were real, he'd avoided her question. All she could remember him saying was "It will be all right."

Fury surged up within her. Things would *never* be all right, not if he'd tricked her into marrying him while she was under his spell. But it made no sense. Why would he go to such lengths to wed himself to the daughter of the woman who had killed his sister? And even if her mother had *not* played such a fatal role in his life, why would a man like him want to marry *her*? He was a titled lord. In his veins ran the noble blood of his august ancestors. She was only the by-blow of a woman of the town. She might pride herself that her veins, too, ran with the noble blood of her father, the duke. But no one except herself had ever been impressed by that.

So why would Lord Ramsay have bound himself to her in marriage—a sacred union that would be indissoluble once it was consummated? A crazy voice within her whispered he'd done it for love. She ignored it. That was virgin's sickness talking. And though it told her what she wanted to hear, she knew better than to believe it.

She clung to the memory of the white expanse of sheet that had covered the inn room bed. Whatever the explanation, it wasn't too late to undo what Lord Ramsay's madness had led him to do the previous night. And she'd make sure he undid it, no matter how great a magician he might prove to be.

She waited until they were jouncing down the rutted track that passed for a road in this part of Scotland before confronting him, though it had been difficult to restrain herself when she'd first encountered him in the inn's common room. The way he'd avoided her eyes when she'd hobbled into the room made his guilt plain, as did the way she caught him peering at her face intently when he thought she couldn't see him.

But when, after what felt like centuries, they were alone in the chaise, she let fly. "It wasn't a dream, then, was it?"

"No." At least he had the decency to look abashed.

"Then one of us must be insane, and I wager it isn't me. I should have believed you when you told me your family was mad."

"Not mad," he corrected her. "Accursed."

"Accursed indeed. At the inn they seemed to believe you had married me."

"I did."

"But that's infamous! Surely I didn't agree to such a thing?"

His eyelashes dropped as he looked down in expression of penitence. But all he said was "You did agree. How else could we have been wed? The law requires it."

"Then I am mad too, and we are well suited. But why should you have wed *me*, the daughter of the woman you have reason to hate more than anyone else in the world? Surely you don't wish me to believe that upon arriving at the Scottish border you were overwhelmed with the desire to unite yourself to me?"

He shook his head, his expression still penitent.

"Did you discover I was an heiress?" she said sarcastically. "Did my father, the duke, die, and leave me all his fortune? It seems unlikely as he's never before taken any notice of me, but I'm at a loss to think why else you would have taken me to Scotland and forced me into marriage."

"You aren't an heiress."

"Then why did you marry me? Why?"

"It was the Dark Lord's last wish that I do so. He's dead. He died a few days before we left London, but before he died he sent a messenger to tell me I must take you to wife."

So that was why. She was unprepared for how disappointed she felt. His marrying her had nothing to do with who she was at all. He'd only done it because it was the last wish of his beloved teacher—though if that *was* his final charge to his disciple, the man must have been raving. There was no other explanation for it.

A wave of sadness washed over her. It told her, too late, of the foolish hope she'd been cherishing in some hidden corner of her heart that Ramsay *had* been motivated by something akin to the shameful passion she couldn't stop feeling for him. But now that her hope had been exposed to the light, she saw how very foolish it had been. The power of the virgin's sickness must be even greater than she'd feared if it had made her dream, for even a moment, that Lord Ramsay could have married her for love.

She ran her fingers nervously over the cracked leather that padded the wall of the hired chaise. "*Why* did the Dark Lord wish us wed? What reason did he give you?"

He bit his upper lip uneasily. "I only know what his messenger told me—that I must wed you if I wished to inherit the Dark Lord's powers."

She forced herself to let no hint of her disappointment show. "Was that why he commanded you to bring me to the island and insisted that I be a virgin?"

"So it would seem." He spoke as if he were miles away. As if the thing he'd done to her was of no importance.

How *had* he done it? Had he drugged her? It seemed unlikely. He'd insisted he'd brought no drugs with him, and even if he'd lied, she'd swallowed no potion. How, then, could he have so bent her to his will?

It must have been the spell—the spell that had allowed him to cut into her living flesh without her knowledge. She struggled to remember what had happened in the inn bedroom after she had fallen into that enchanted sleep, but all that came to her was the sight of his handsome face with its long, sultry lashes, framed by the waves of russet hair that made him look so much like the saint he wished to be, turned up toward hers, filled with pleading.

Her hands balled into fists and she rounded on him. "You used the spell to make me accept you, didn't you?"

He nodded, looking shockingly vulnerable, as if her anger had smashed through the mask of control he fought so hard to maintain. But he made no attempt to defend himself, but just sat, shoulders slumped, allowing her to rage, looking as if he'd just sit and absorb it until at last she ran out of words.

Scolding him would be futile. She bit her lower lip to keep herself from speaking and matched his silence with her own, giving no sign of her agitation except for the way that her hand couldn't stop twisting the folds of her skirt.

When he finally spoke, his musical voice was unnaturally calm. "I had no choice. If I didn't wed you, the power of the Dark Lord would have seeped back into the earth. How could I stand by and allow all those centuries of wisdom to vanish? I had to use the spell to make you wed me. You wouldn't have done it, otherwise, would you?"

Deep within her the virgin's sickness shrieked its answer: *Yes!* But she was strong enough to ignore it. If he had asked her to wed him, she wouldn't have let herself be swayed by that raucous voice. She knew better than to bind herself to a loveless marriage, and that was all she could expect with Ramsay—no matter what his teacher had mumbled as he died. It *must* have been his spell that made her accept him. There was no other explanation.

She'd never again doubt that his powers were real—but, oh, what a price they both would pay for his use of them. She let her tone convey her bitterness. "You gave no thought, as you worked your magic, how selfish it was to wed me just to please this Dark Lord of yours. Did it mean nothing to you that I must be bound to you forever?"

"You forget," he said quietly. "I am bound to *you* forever, too."

She met his eyes for the first time, those eyes as gray as thunderheads yet soft with a gentleness so at odds with the terrible thing he'd done. But what he said was true. He, too, must live his life now without any hope of love bound to a woman he loathed. Such was the final price this Dark Lord of his had exacted of him, and he had chosen to pay it.

Despite herself, she felt a surge of compassion for him. He was a titled lord. A man of wealth. He might have wed any woman who caught his fancy had that been his pleasure. And even if he'd only been a nobody like herself, with his good looks and powerful frame, he need not have settled for a woman with her ravaged features. What woman, no matter how beautiful, would have been able to resist those gold-flecked eyes of his, had they been turned on her filled with love?

And yet he had wed himself to her, with her ruined face and her charmless disposition. What could have possibly made him willing to sacrifice so much for whatever it was his dead teacher had offered him? But she made herself stop thinking like that. Why should she feel pity for *him*? Whatever his reasons for marrying her had been, he'd had a choice, while she'd been given none.

"You did a fearful thing," she said. And it was true, for he'd made her wed him when he knew he didn't love her. But she couldn't bring herself to say those last words out loud.

"I did," he agreed, "and I won't deny it. But I wasn't entirely selfish. I gave you something in return. Don't you remember? When I used the spell to make you want to wed me, I also pledged that I'd give my life to protect you and that I'd do all that I could to give you happiness. I'm a man who keeps his vows, Zoe, as you have good reason to know."

Did she remember? Vague rustlings in her mind, like mice in the wainscoting. In her mind's eye rose the image of his face lifted to hers in supplication. Was *that* what he'd told her, that he would give his life to protect her? Was that what had made her yield?

It was. She fought back tears as the full memory of what had happened came flooding back to her. He *had* sworn he would protect her. She remembered his voice, now, low and resonant, pleading with her to have him. She remembered the joy that had filled her as he'd vowed he would give his life to keep her safe. Oh yes. That was the magic he had worked on her—to find her weakest point and offer her what she'd never had before. Protection. Care.

The thought was too painful to be borne.

She didn't need protection. She'd done just fine with no one's care. She'd taken good care of herself until now and she'd go on doing it. She needed no one—not her careless mother or her father, the duke, who had refused to visit the daughter he'd abandoned, even once.

She twisted away from Ramsay, pulling her body as far from his as was possible within the confines of the cramped post chaise. She grabbed her undamaged thigh, clinging to herself for comfort, feeling the flesh sting as she compressed it through the rough fabric of her gown.

Ramsay drew a sharp breath. Then, oh so gently, he covered her hand with his much larger one and stroked it tenderly, as if trying to enchant away its rigidity. A current began to flow between them as he touched her. Much as she wanted to tear her hand from his, she could not. He'd made her his. He'd made her *want* to be his. His magic was too strong. It was too late.

Finally, he spoke. "Give me a chance. If you truly

can't bear to stay wed to me, in a year and a day I'll send you away with whatever reward you will accept from me. I won't keep you with me against your will."

She couldn't reply. All her attention was still concentrated on the waves of longing that rose from where his fingertips had touched her. She forced herself to shake her head no. She must not give in.

The look of sadness that swept over his features at her rejection made it even harder to remember why she must not stay with him. He sighed, and his eyelids dropped. Then he said, "If you really can't bear it, our marriage can still be undone. It wasn't consummated. Whatever my sins might be, I didn't force myself on you."

She thought of the unspotted sheet. He told the truth. But she couldn't praise him for that, not when he made it so difficult for her to resist his haunted eyes.

"You cut into my body without my knowledge," she said harshly. "Why *didn't* you take me in the same way and make it impossible for me to leave you? Or did you secretly hope that I *would* leave when I learned what you had done, so that you could have the credit of fulfilling the Dark Lord's wish without the burden of a life spent married to Isabelle's daughter. Yes. That must be it. Had you really wished to marry me, you would have consummated our union while still I was under your spell."

His long, strong fingers tightened against hers. "I don't want our marriage to be undone, and not just because of the Dark Lord's wish. I felt no regret when I bound myself to you. Far from it. I wed you gladly.

Whoever bore you, you are nobody but yourself. Your honesty and courage make you the equal of any woman in the realm. But surely you know me well enough by now to know that I wouldn't take your maidenhead by force, even if it meant losing you. I pledged to make you happy and I will keep that pledge."

He turned away and stared morosely out of the dust-streaked window of the chaise for a moment, thinking. Then, after taking a deep breath, he said, "If you can't be happy as my wife, I'll set you free, no matter what it might cost me. *Is* that what you want?"

Now it was his turn to wait expectantly for her answer. And now it was she who couldn't speak. Surely there was but one course open to her now—to take the freedom he'd just offered her and ask him to annul their marriage. Then she could return to London. She need never see him again, never fear that his probing glances would uncover the shameful longings she felt for him.

But her treacherous memory repeated the words he'd just told her. *He'd felt no regret in binding himself to her. He'd wed her gladly.* How she wanted to believe these were words of love. How deluded she would be were she to do so.

It *must* be his spell that made her want to cling to him, as her body tingled with the yearnings his gentle fingers were awakening as he stroked her hand so innocently. It must be the spell that whispered that what he'd offered was enough—that she must rejoice in whatever he could give her. What else could it be? She was a practical woman, a courtesan's daughter. She knew better than to let herself believe in love.

But even so, she wanted to be his wife. Without love. Without any hope of it. Not with her mind, which fluttered weakly like a bird shot in midflight, but with her soul that he'd entangled in his spell. She couldn't break it.

She cleared her throat. He swiveled toward her, his attention utterly focused on whether she would take the freedom he'd just offered.

If only she could spend the rest of her life gazing up at his beautiful, ascetic face that made such a contrast to his muscular frame. It took everything she had not to seek the shelter of his arms or fall sobbing against his broad chest and give in to him. But if she did, she would live out the rest of her life in agony. He couldn't love her.

"How *can* I choose," she answered, "when you've made me want you so, with your enchantment?"

His face tightened. "You're right. I won't press you for a decision." He released her hand. "Just promise me that you won't try to run away from me again. If you want your freedom, tell me and I'll grant it. You must never again put yourself in peril because of me."

"And if I don't want my freedom?" she said, hearing her own voice echo within the closeness of the carriage. "If I would remain your wife? What then?" Her voice trailed off.

His eyes lit up. "Then I'll accept your sacrifice with gratitude."

"My sacrifice? In wedding you?" She stared at him. He *was* mad. "It's no sacrifice for me to remain your wife. Just think, my mother will be over the moon.

She'd have been delighted had I merely become some nobleman's toy. Can you imagine her joy on learning I have become my Lady Ramsay? She will insist that you address her as *belle-mère*."

He froze. His sharp intake of breath sounded through the confines of the post chaise. She'd done what she had to and reminded him of the price he'd pay for her capitulation. She should rejoice that it had worked and that he no longer gazed at her with the warm look of love that had so tormented her.

But somehow, she could not.

Chapter 10

When they stopped at the next inn to change horses, Ramsay asked Zoe politely if she'd dine with him. But she'd had time to recover some of her composure in the intervening hours and wasn't impressed by his civility. If he thought he could convince her to give him the rest of her life in return for a few sweet words, he'd soon learn of his mistake.

The innkeeper led them to the sparsely furnished private chamber, where they would dine. They seated themselves facing each other across the small square table that stood against one wall of the small room, and a waiter brought in a platter of meat, some crusty bread, and newly churned butter. No sooner had he left them alone than Zoe broke off a large piece of the bread and busied herself with tearing it into the smaller portions that befit a lady—until she recalled that she hadn't chosen to become Lady Ramsay and seized a large piece and stuffed it into her mouth.

Lord Ramsay's eyebrows rose. She regretted their situation was not more public so that her bad manners could further embarrass him. She attempted to tell him this, but her attempt to talk while chewing made her choke and cough. When at last she was able to speak again, she snarled, "You see, I'm not a fine lady!"

"I never imagined you were. But what has that to do with anything?"

"Because you made me your wife. Your lady wife. Surely you can see how wrong it was."

"Why? Because you chose just now to chew your bread like a cow with a particularly choice tussock of grass?" He smiled. "I've observed you enough over this past week to know you have excellent manners when you choose to use them. Mrs. Endicott did her work well."

She contemplated what was left of the chunk of bread before tossing it back onto the platter, feeling something of a fool. What had she meant to prove with that gesture?

"I see no reason why you won't make me a fine wife," he continued quietly. "You are, as you have told me more than once, supremely practical. You won't demand that I behave like a lovelorn lad. You won't look askance at my medical studies. And since you move in no social circle, I shan't have to waste my time attending frivolous social occasions, but can get on with what truly is valuable in life—"

"Which is?" She interrupted his cold-blooded recitation.

"—using my powers to help those in need."

She took a deep breath. Could he really expect her to stay married to him when he made it so clear how little he valued her? "What compelling arguments you make. I would seem, indeed, to be the perfect wife for you. Invisible, unloved, and a social outcast. I'm astonished you didn't add to the list of my virtues that I may die in childbed after giving you an heir, so that you needn't be troubled with a wife at all."

"Surely you don't think I would wish such a thing?" The shock in his eyes was real.

"No, I suppose not. It would reflect badly on your skills as a healer."

He sighed. "I would never wish you dead, Zoe. And not just for reasons of pride."

"Surely not for reasons of love. You've just assured me that it is because you need feel nothing for me that I would make you a perfect wife."

"I didn't think you'd want to hear words of love from me."

"Of course not." She shrugged. "Who knows better how unlikely it would be to find love in marriage than a harlot's child?"

"Don't refer to yourself like that!"

"Why, because it makes you remember who it is your teacher bid you wed? Your loathing of me adds luster to the fealty you've shown to him. You may take pleasure in that."

"I don't loathe you," he said quietly. "Do you loathe *me*, Zoe?"

In the silence that followed his question, he took a

bite of meat off his knife. The roughness of the gesture fit well with his homespun dress and flowing hair. How little of the elegance he'd displayed in her mother's drawing room remained now that he'd returned to Scotland. The image rose up in her mind of how he'd looked when he'd returned from tending the cottar's child with the blood dried on his sleeves. Perhaps he didn't want a lady wife after all.

"I asked you, do you loathe me?" His tone was more insistent this time.

She couldn't answer. She wished she could tell him she did, for she ought to loathe him. He'd kidnapped her from her mother to take her to some barbaric island where even he didn't know what her fate would be. He'd tricked her into marriage. But the way he was watching her now, his gray eyes soft, warm, and lustrous like the feathers on a dove's breast, made it impossible. She'd never been able to lie. It was yet another of the reasons why her mother had despaired of her future.

Frustration welled up in her. "I don't know *what* I feel for you."

Adam's heart sank. What had he been thinking when he'd made her wed him? How could he have ever expected her to think she could find happiness with him? She couldn't stand the idea of staying with him. He must let her go.

He was about to reply when a horn blared out on the road leading to the inn. It must be the mail coach announcing its arrival. Without thinking, he reached into his pocket to consult the time. As he pulled out his watch, a look of confusion washed over Zoe's features, which only the moment before had been filled with haughty rejection, and almost at once her look of disturbed dismay was replaced by one of yearning—a pained yearning, as if she was expecting to be slapped.

He looked around the parlor, wondering what could have further perturbed her, but saw nothing. Then his eye followed hers to the golden disc of his watch. *Of course.* He'd made it trigger her desire to be his bride. He jammed the watch back into its pocket. But it was too late. The damage had already been done.

Her deep brown eyes were no longer filled with yearning, but reproach. "What did you do to me?" Her voice was strained.

He could barely answer. "You have every right to hate me."

"Oh, but I *don't* hate you. As well you know. You made *that* impossible with your spell. I wish I could hate you, oh my husband. Hatred I could bear. Hatred would be easy compared to this!"

He made no reply, letting her anger rain down on him as he deserved.

"You've meddled with my soul. I have no choice but to love you." She pounded her fist on the wooden tabletop. "You must remove the spell. The feelings you've forced on me are unbearable."

"You can't bear to love me?"

"I cannot."

Her words cut him to the quick. Yet they confused him. She spoke of love, but love had played no part in the spell. He hadn't asked for it; he hadn't expected it.

Indeed, it hadn't occurred to him that she need love him at all. He'd only made her want to marry him, so she would agree to become his wife and dwell with him for the year and a day the Ancient Ones had decreed would somehow give him his Final Teaching,

But still, when she'd stated so baldly that she couldn't bear to love him, the pain that shot through him had been almost unbearable.

He reached across the narrow table and took her face between his palms, turning it gently toward his own. "Why can't you bear to love me, Zoe? Am I that difficult to love?"

She twisted her face out of his grip. "Difficult to love? You?"

He let his arms drop. "Of course you can feel nothing but contempt for me, given the circumstances under which we met. And even if I hadn't been such a brute to you, since my sister's death I've lost the art of being gracious. I've forgotten how to talk to a woman. No woman could love the man I've become since Charlotte died."

She twisted away from him. "You don't understand. It doesn't matter how you treat me. With the spell you've put me under, I would love you if you were Bluebeard himself with a string of murdered wives. You're too *easy* for me to love. It's *that* which torments me."

He studied her face as he would an ancient inscription, as if the anxious tilt of her brows was the key that would let him translate its hieroglyphics and show him his fate. But the secret that would make all clear was hidden from him. He couldn't understand her. "If I'm not repugnant to you, why is it so upsetting to feel love for me?" he asked quietly.

"Surely you must know!"

"But I don't."

"Because your magic makes me want to cling to you and gaze into your eyes like a schoolgirl in love with the hero of a great battle."

"But I've married you, so why is that so terrible?"

"Because you don't love me," she whispered. "And *I* don't have the magic to change that."

He stopped, confounded. Truly the Dragon's Cave would have been easier than this.

But this was the labyrinth he must tread, and he must tread it carefully or lose all. He could feel her deep brown eyes drilling through him, awaiting his reply. At last he said, "Would it be different if I were to love you, too?"

Their eyes met across the table. He felt the jolt he always felt when they connected. Then she turned away.

"I don't know. It doesn't matter. You *don't* love me. You never will. You enchanted me only to serve your teacher."

"That isn't true."

"Surely you won't pretend you did it for love?"

What could he say? He *had* married her at the Dark Lord's command, but it was a command he'd been all too willing to fulfill, for he had wanted her—he'd been consumed by his wanting of her—and was consumed by it still. And not just because of the way her tall, slim body felt crushed against his own—though he wanted that more than he could let himself admit. There was so much else he wanted from her, too: to bathe himself in the comfort she could give him, to follow it to its source and exult in that jolt he felt every time their eyes met, to merge himself in her and find in her cool and practical strength the balance to his own intemperate imagination.

But was that wanting love? He didn't know. The only love he'd ever known was for his sister, Charlotte. Whom he would be betraying if he spoke words of love to his new bride.

He bit his lip, unable to speak the words that filled his heart. But he must say something. Hesitantly, he forced out the words. "Forgive me, Zoe. What I did was wrong, but I was telling the truth when I vowed I would give you happiness."

"Then remove the spell!" As she slammed her fist on the table, the crockery clattered. "How can I ever be happy when I don't have command of my own heart? You must remove it!"

He breathed out slowly. There was no alternative.

As Ramsay stood and stepped away from her, relief swept over Zoe. It had been so hard not to throw her arms around him and clasp him to her breast when he sat so close, when the sweet smell of his breath intoxicated her, when she felt herself go limp inside, hearing the pleading in his melodious voice, when the softness of his lips, so tantalizingly close, beckoned like the gate to faerie land.

But she'd found the strength to resist, and make him understand, at last, the wrongness of what he'd done.

Now he'd free her from the unbearable desire that filled her and from her yearning to remain his wife.

He paced away from her, then turned and stretched out his arms in a gesture of invocation. His homespun sleeves fell back, revealing the blue serpents that twined around his forearms, their bodies forming that elaborate braid. Seeing them, Zoe felt as she had when he'd shown her the ancient knife—and knew herself to be in the presence of something ancient and not entirely benign.

She stood, as if in homage to it. His eyes met hers. Golden flecks sparkled within their grayness like rough jewels embedded in granite. Power was building up within him. The power that let him do his magic. She called out to him, "When you enchant me, give me one last wish, as magicians do in fairy tales."

"What would you have me do?"

"Make me beautiful. Can you do that with your magic?"

"You are already beautiful to me. Your soul is radiant."

"Don't lie to me. I know what I am." She gestured toward her ruined face.

"I, too, know what you are," he said softly. "And I am helpless before its power."

He reached her with three long strides. As he pulled her to him, his long hair brushed her cheek. His arms drew her close, locking her inside the circle of his serpent-wreathed embrace. His lips came down on hers, strong and demanding. His tongue thrust against the softness of her mouth, filling her with intolerable longing. She wondered if he'd claim her then and there and make their bodies one. And she knew that if he were to do so, she wouldn't stop him.

She wanted him. She wanted the life she felt pulsing in his lips and the strength that coursed through his arms. The blood pounding in her loins clamored for their joining. As he pulled her close, invisible serpents rose within her spine to meet his, ancient and implacable. It was only the spell, she knew it, but it didn't matter. Nothing mattered now but him and the union that would make them one.

But after a moment of unbearable sweetness, he let his arms drop and freed her from his embrace. "You need no magic to make you beautiful, nor to make me want you beyond bearing."

She gasped. "Are you enchanted, too?"

He nodded. "It is said that a spell misused will rebound on the one who worked it. Perhaps that is the explanation. Or perhaps you have a magic all your own."

As he stepped away from her, the air pulsed between them. With every new inch that separated them, she felt her need for him more strongly. Too strongly. She was mad to let herself love him this much, knowing he could never truly love her. If she gave in to the passion that possessed her now, she would find herself trapped in a marriage that could never satisfy her.

For he couldn't mean what he'd just said. Despite his sweet words—and what he could make her body feel—he wooed her only to keep her from leaving, because his teacher had ordered them wed. Because he wouldn't get the Dark Lord's powers unless he wed her.

She mustn't fall for it. If she let his haunting looks—or passionate embraces—seduce her, she would spend a lifetime regretting it. They were just more illusions with which he would ensorcell her. She must shatter them. Brutally. Before the desire he could arouse in her stole away the last of her will.

"I have no magic." She hurled the words at him like bombs. "I'm just a harlot's daughter, the bastard of the bitch who murdered your sister. How can you forget that?"

He flinched, and a pain knifed through her vitals. Then he took a step back, and in a voice filled with anguish he said, "You're right. We have no choice. I *must* undo the spell."

Like a sleepwalker, Zoe let him lead her over to a long wooden bench that stood against one wall. When he bade her lie back, she did so. He hovered over her for a moment, and she wondered if, like her, he was still feeling the echoes of that kiss that had bound them for a moment, despite the violence with which she'd forced him to release her.

Now, when it was too late, his words sang in her inner ear. *He found her beautiful. He wanted her past bearing.* Could he have meant them, despite everything? Had she ruined everything by striking out just now and reminding him who she was?

But if she had, it was too late for regret. The decision in his eyes told her he would end it now—whatever it was they'd begun.

In a firm tone, he bade her close her eyes. She tried

to obey, but as her lids dropped shut, she couldn't help but steal one last peek as he prepared himself, once more, to do his magic. His waves of russet hair shadowed the sharp planes of his strong cheekbones, but his gold-flecked eyes were hidden by his long lashes. She was glad she could no longer see them and imagine they held emotions it was impossible could be there. It made it easier to let him go. With a last reluctant sigh, she let her lids fall closed.

He took a deep, shuddering breath and whispered the magic word, "*Codladh.*"

She felt herself go limp as she resigned herself to letting his magic do its work. As she waited, she heard his ragged breathing. It filled the silence that stretched out after he'd invoked the spell. She heard the soft rustle of his homespun shirt and the creak of the floor as he shifted his weight from one foot to the other. In the distance, running like a silver thread through the heavy silence, she heard a coach rattle to a stop, its iron wheels clattering on the cobblestones. Harnesses jangled as new horses were brought in to replace the winded ones. It was only as she heard the passengers scattering from the coach, calling to one another as they embarked on the brief interval allotted them to eat, that it hit her. *She was wide awake.* The spell hadn't worked. It hadn't sent her back into the twilight sleep of trance.

"Lord Ramsay," she said in a small, scared voice. "I'm not sleeping."

"I know." His tone was grave. "It's just as I feared. I've lost your trust. Without it I can't put you back under the spell."

She sat up, rubbing her eyes. "Perhaps if you used a different incantation?"

"It isn't the words that do the magic, but something else—something I've forfeited through the misuse of my powers."

"But I want you to enchant me. Isn't that enough?"

He peered at her intently, raising his eyes in an odd way. Then he shook his head. "It's no use. I can't undo the spell." The note of defeat in his voice frightened her.

"Does anyone else know how to undo it?"

"Only the Dark Lord, but he's dead."

He sank down beside her on the bench as if he could no longer find the strength to stand. She could hardly bear to have him so near. Every atom of her body seemed to resonate with his, bridging the few inches that separated them as if they were connected by an electrical fluid. She was helpless before the power of the magical bond that he had trapped her in.

Her words burst out before she could control them. "If only I could put a spell on you!"

"I fear to imagine the spell you would wish on me now."

"I wish only that you might feel for me what I feel for you."

"Only that? That I should love you, too?"

"Only that. But what does it matter what I wish?" She refused to meet his eye, but stared down at the surface of the bench where long pale lines of heartwood shot through the darker grain. "Wishes accomplish nothing. When I was young I wished I might be wanted instead of always in the way. I wished that my father, the duke, might come to visit me and learn how I had struggled to make myself worthy of him. But he never did, not once. What I might wish has never mattered to anyone. Why should it matter to you?"

"Because it does," he said. "Because I vowed to give you happiness."

Why did he have to remind her of what he couldn't do?

"You've taken too many vows already," she said harshly. "I wouldn't have you feign love for me to fulfill another. Vow or no vow, you can't make yourself love me if the love isn't already there."

"How would I know if it's there or not? I've no experience of such things." He bit his lower lip. "I've been a celibate all this time, with no desire to experience love. All I know of love is what I shared with Charlotte."

"But she was your sister. That's different."

"Is it? We were twins, she and I. We shared our mother's womb."

Twins. That made his loss even more devastating, and her own plight that much more desperate. Whatever he might wish, he could never love her if her mother had killed his twin.

"I loved Charlotte and my loving her caused her death." His hands tightened into fists. "Had she not loved me so well, she might have stayed at home when I went to France and be living now. But I begged her to come join me, I missed her so. And she died there— like an animal."

He locked his hands together in his lap, where they

twisted together like thick vines. "I gave *her* that love you wish me to give you—gave it in full measure, and it killed her. Think twice before you wish my love upon yourself."

He looked the way he had after the cottar's child died. And he needed her as much as he had then. Taking a deep breath, Zoe reached over and gently untwined the fingers of his hand before taking it in her own. "I can't help but desire your love, however dangerous it might be. You've given me no choice with your spell. It's *you* who have the freedom to love or not."

"I know," he said. "And that I must make such a choice will be my punishment."

"Why punishment?"

"Because you won't be happy without my love, but if I give it to you, I'll be betraying Charlotte. You live only because she died."

So there it was. He'd admitted at last the reason he could never ever love her.

She must honor his honesty in facing it, and probe the rotting wound his words had revealed to her, as deftly as he had examined hers. The time had come to ask the question she'd never before had the courage to pose. "Tell me now," she said. "What exactly did my mother do to Charlotte?"

Her insides quivered at the risk she'd taken. But whatever she might have yearned for or he had vowed, they could not live together, married though they might be, unless they faced this ugly truth together and found some way to heal it. If they couldn't, enchanted or not, she must leave him.

His lips went white, he was pressing them together so hard. He cleared his throat, not once, but twice. Then speaking so quietly she could barely hear him, though he sat so near she could see the blood pulsing in the furred hollow at the base of his neck, he said, "Isabelle betrayed my sister to the Committee of Public Safety—the murderers who caused the Terror."

He paused, letting that sink in. Then he continued, "She did it to save her own life—and yours. She'd been accused of consorting with a marquis. A price had been put on her head. So she stole my sister's identity papers and escaped the guillotine by pretending they were hers."

Zoe's heart sank. Until this moment she'd hoped that perhaps there had been some misunderstanding. Thoughtless though her mother was, she was never intentionally cruel, and Zoe had not been able to picture her as a murderess.

But at the height of the Terror her mother might have had no choice. She'd always explained that they'd made their escape from France thanks to the influence of a mysterious gentleman, one of the many who had been enamored of her. But that was the kind of story her mother *would* tell. Especially if the truth was more unsavory. And Lord Ramsay's words made it all too likely that it was.

For Zoe remembered those papers. They *had* saved their lives, and they had come, seemingly, out of nowhere.

The memories came flooding back—how in the days before they'd left Paris, they'd been desperate, with her mother wailing that there was no way out and that they'd both soon die on the guillotine. Then everything had changed. Her mother had disappeared for several days, leaving her alone in their apartment with instructions to open the door to no one. When she'd come back, she seemed giddy with relief, but would say nothing except that she'd obtained the papers that would make it possible for them to leave France safely.

Her mother had kept the precious documents in her bosom as they fled, guarding them as ferociously as if they had been diamonds. When they'd reached the port, an official had demanded them, and Zoe remembered the long, frightening moment when he'd scowled at one document, saying it couldn't be Isabelle's. He'd let his insolent gaze sweep up and down her mother's lush form, reveling in the power he had over them. Then he'd announced that he must consult the regulations and had motioned her mother to follow him into a little cubicle behind his office. She'd done as he commanded, and after the door had snapped shut on both of them, Zoe had been left alone in the outer office, where she'd passed the time practicing the courage her eleven years had given her so many opportunities to master.

When, fifteen minutes later, the door to the little chamber had opened to disgorge her mother, the official's cravat had been crooked, and his trousers had lost their crease, but he'd let them continue on their journey to safety, unmolested.

"My mother did what it took to keep the two of us alive," she said quietly. "I can't make excuses for her.

But even so, stealing is a far cry from murder. Why do you accuse her of that?"

Ramsay took a deep breath before answering her. His hand grasped the edge of the bench they sat on and squeezed it tightly. "Your mother didn't just steal my sister's papers."

"What else did she do?"

"She knew the Committee needed a victim, so to put them off her trail, before she fled she wrote a letter to the Committee, telling them that the young woman taking refuge at the laird's estate was a noblewoman in hiding. As soon as they received it, they sent someone to arrest her. With her papers gone Charlotte had no way of disproving their accusation—and I—I who should have protected her—I wasn't there to defend her. I was in Paris. I'd told the Dark Lord I'd gone to watch the demonstration of a new surgical technique, but it was a lie.

"As I told you, once before, when I was young, my passions were very strong. I didn't want to believe what the Dark Lord had told me, that I must take a vow of chastity. So I went to Paris to find myself a woman. I told myself I must learn more about the flesh before I could renounce it. I found a beautiful, seductive woman to teach me all a well-paid Parisian whore could about my accursed nature. There was a lot to learn. It was five long days until I'd finally had my fill of her and returned to Morlaix—where I found my sister dead."

Zoe felt a wave of sadness wash over her. No wonder he so feared unleashing those passions again. But his tale just made it that much clearer that he could never love her.

She struggled to make some reply. But for a long time, none would come. At last she said, "Knowing all this, how could the Dark Lord have wanted you to wed me? How could he have asked such a thing of you?"

"I don't know and not knowing torments me. If I could ask him just one question, that would be what I'd ask. But he's gone far beyond where he can hear me. And yet"—a trace of hope lit up his features—"I *can* ask the Ancient Ones to give me counsel. He taught me how."

He strode toward the center of the room and pulled his ancient bronze knife from its sheath. Grasping it by the copper green hilt so that the golden point curved downward, he held it before him. Then he stared at it in silence as the moments crept by, fixing his gaze on the glinting blade as if he expected it to give him an answer.

At length, he let his arm drop to his side and turned back to her. "The Ancient Ones speak, but their message is confusing. Either our marriage is yet more of my penance or the Dark Lord knew some reason why I should forgive your mother which he didn't have time to tell me." He flung his knife onto the bench.

She felt a sick feeling in the pit of her stomach. How could she live with a man who believed their marriage was a punishment? But the anguish in his eyes begged her not to judge him too quickly. He was trying, and indeed, his next words reflected that.

Speaking so slowly it was as if he'd pulled each

word out of a wound in his own flesh, he asked, "If I *could* forgive your mother, would you still want your freedom?"

She turned away, unwilling to let him see the answer that must be shining from her eyes. If only she had her mother's ability to lie.

"It is as I thought," he said, and she remembered too late that he didn't need to see her face to know what was in her mind. "You *would* stay, if I could forgive your mother. But how can I forgive her, without betraying Charlotte? She comes to me in dreams, and looks at me with such reproach because I haven't avenged her. How can I love you, when you only lived to wed me because she died?"

"It is impossible," she agreed, facing him once more.

"And yet, were it not, I *could* love you, Zoe."

His words shocked her. He mustn't talk this way. His talk of love was more painful than his icy distancing, for it gave her hope that swept away all her defenses. But when she got up the courage to meet his eyes she knew he was telling the truth. His eyes glowed with it, despite the torment it cost him to admit it.

"Give me time," he said. "That's all I ask of you."

"A year and a day?" She caught her breath.

He nodded.

The love that tore through her heart now made the pain of the virgin's sickness seem like a mere scratch. She couldn't resist the hope he held out, that with time he might come to love her. As impossible as she knew it to be, hope bound her to him more firmly than chains.

It must be the power of the spell. But even now, as

she felt the last of her resistance to him melt away, she wouldn't let him know how thoroughly he had conquered her. Making her voice as light as she could, she said, "Then I'll remain your bride. What other choice do I have? The spell can't be undone, and I should be foolish to turn away from the honor you've thrust on me. A courtesan's daughter is practical. So I will take what I can get."

"And I will give you all that I am capable of," he said quietly. "Marriages have succeeded with far less."

Chapter 11

She would remain his wife. He hadn't expected it. He'd been prepared to give up everything to make up for the wrongful way he'd used the spell, even his chance to earn the Final Teaching. No power the Ancient Ones could give him would make up for ruining another woman's life.

But when he'd offered her her freedom, she hadn't taken it.

A tingle of anticipation ran up his spine at the thought. She would remain his wife. He need no longer be alone, no longer vowed to sacred isolation. What had been forbidden for so long would be permitted—more than that, it would be required. He must make their flesh one to fulfill the Dark Lord's final command. He could barely suppress the joy that filled him when he thought of taking Zoe in his arms and merging himself with her as he had longed to do, so desperately, for so long.

He was tempted to call for the landlord of the inn, to demand his most comfortable room, and order the finest food and drink to make a wedding banquet for his bride. As if she had picked up on his thoughts, Zoe asked, "Will we stay here tonight? And will you bed me?" The blood rushed to her face, giving it a glow.

"Is that what you want?" He forced his voice to sound calm.

Her blush deepened. "If I'm really to be your wife, it must be done." But then her voice trailed off. "Though perhaps it would be better to wait. We've both of us already acted too rashly—that's what got us into this predicament. Let's not compound the damage. Once our marriage is consummated, it can't be set aside."

Though he usually valued the way her calm practicality balanced his unworldliness, right now he could have done without it. He wanted her so much. But he mustn't be so selfish. She was right. Matters between them *were* too delicate to be rushed. How could he have deluded himself she'd welcome him that way so soon, when he'd just barely convinced her not to leave him. To say nothing of the fact that she was still recovering from the wound in her leg. How could he have forgotten that?

He released her hand and stood. "You're right. There's no rush. We have time."

"A year and a day," she said with a shy smile.

"And many more years after that, if the Ancient Ones will grant them."

Years. As he said the word, he imagined the joy of spending those years with this slim girl with the lustrous eyes. Warmth filled his heart at the thought of watching her go from girl to woman, and become the mother of his children. But at that thought, his veins filled with ice. He couldn't ask *that* of her. Not yet. Not until he told her about the curse. It *was* best to wait. He'd already been selfish enough.

He spoke as calmly as he could. "We won't dally here, but travel to my home at Strathrimmon, the Ramsays' ancestral seat. That, too, was what the Dark Lord wished me to do."

Her eyes lost something of their liveliness. "Of course. You must do as he asked."

He wanted to tell her there was more to it than that, but they'd already spent too much time discussing things that could not be resolved by conversation, so he said nothing.

She forced a bright smile. "How far is Strathrimmon?"

"Only another day's journey over those hills you can see in the distance from this window."

"I look forward to seeing it. I've never been to a grand estate."

"It's ancient, but far from grand. Indeed, I hope it won't disappoint you. I fear it's been sadly neglected in my absence."

"No estate that is to be mine could ever disappoint me." Her expression had become mischievous. "I never expected to ever own property—and if I did allow myself to dream of it, I contented myself with the thought of a small house in London with a tiny garden."

"Strathrimmon encompasses some five thousand acres, enough for a largish garden, I should think."

"Five thousand acres. How rich you are, Lord Ramsay!"

" 'Lord Ramsay'?" He raised his eyebrows. "Now that we are wed, you must be less formal with me. My name is Adam and I'd be honored if you would so address me."

"Oh, I shall call you Adam, if that's what you wish," she said with a twinkle, "but only if *you* will call me Lady Ramsay. You've been far too familiar with me since the outset of our connection. Now that I am to be a baroness I shall be very much on my dignity."

He grinned. "It shall be as you wish, Lady Ramsay."

As the traveling chaise made its way into the grounds of Strathrimmon, Zoe wondered how the man who was the lord of such a beautiful place could have ever left it. How could he have wandered through the world for so long with a home like this to come back to?

The Ramsay lands stretched out as far as she could see. Where the land was level, rows of stubble marked where fields of grain had been harvested the previous fall. Farther away, where the land rose in gently swelling hills, sheep fed on the greensward. Small cottages dotted the landscape, and in the distance, a tall tower rose.

"Adam, you didn't tell me you owned a castle!"

"How else would my ancestors have defended what was theirs? The Scottish borders were a lawless place. But don't get your hopes up too much. The castle is more impressive from a distance than it is when you're huddling in the drawing room in January, desperately trying to keep its stones from sucking out what little warmth remains in your body. I've often wished my ancestors had settled in a more peaceful spot where they might have built more for comfort than defense."

Zoe laughed. "It can't be any colder than some of the garrets we lived in when my mother was out of funds. You needn't fear that I'll be too nice to be your chatelaine." But that reminded her of something else she hadn't had the courage to ask him about before. "Does *your* mother still live here?"

"No. She remarried when I was twelve and went to live with her new husband farther north. Since he didn't wish to be burdened with another man's children, she left me here with Charlotte and the servants, and soon after that I was sent off to school."

How bleak that sounded. But even so, she was glad she wouldn't have to confront a new mother-in-law immediately. She couldn't imagine that any mother would welcome an unannounced daughter-in-law with much joy—especially one as basely born as herself.

Adam went on. "My father's bailiff has stayed on all these years and run things, keeping me informed by post. But the heart goes out of land when the owner isn't there to keep his eye on it. It will be good to be home again and pick up the reins."

"Then you don't plan to return to the Dark Lord's island in the near future?"

"No. It was my teacher's wish that we dwell here, and I am more than content to do so."

"It *is* beautiful country, though wild, and isolated. Will we live here throughout the year?"

"You've spent all your life in the city, haven't you?" A troubled look filled his face. "Would you hate living so far from town? I'll take you to London for the season when the year is over, should you wish it. And if that isn't enough—well, I'll find you permanent lodgings in Town."

She recoiled inwardly at his casual mention of their separating forever. But then, it was she who was bespelled into loving, not him. But when she peered more closely at his features, she saw that his lips, which had been set in a warm smile only a moment before, were tight with concern. Perhaps he'd only made this last offer in an attempt to be kind.

Acting on that hunch, she reassured him. "With a garden and dairy to keep me occupied, and some villagers to attend to, I see no reason I couldn't be very happy here."

The corners of his mouth relaxed. She had been wrong to think he was already looking for some pretext to send her away.

"Perhaps I might start a Sunday school," she added, "to teach the crofters' children their letters. Would that please you?"

"It would, but only if it pleased you. I told the truth when I said I wanted to make you happy in return for the sacrifices I've asked of you."

"It would make me happy to behave in a way that would make me worthy of the rank you've conferred on me. I want to be a wife you can be proud of—despite my origins."

"We shall get on a lot better if we look to the future, not the past," he said quietly. "I can't do anything about your origins, but you have my word, I will never reproach you for them. But that reminds me. When we spoke earlier, you said something about your father being a nobleman. Is that true?"

"Yes. A duke."

"Which one?"

She looked away, ashamed. "I don't know. My mother told me very little about him—only that he was brave and resourceful, and that he'd loved her dearly before matters of great importance had forced him to leave her behind."

"She didn't tell you his name?"

"No. I suppose she was afraid I'd seek him out. Perhaps she'd taken money from him when they parted, with the promise that he'd never be bothered by us again. I can't say for sure. She told me when I was small that he would never come to see me, but I still used to pray that he would. I worked so hard at school to learn to speak like a lady and master the manners the other girls displayed so effortlessly, because I thought it was he who'd given my mother the money for my education. I hoped that if I proved worthy of it, he would visit."

"But he never did?"

"No."

"And then, when I took you to Mrs. Endicott's, you learned it had been the Dark Lord who had paid your school fees all along. Not your father. How painful that must have been for you."

She had to look away, not just because of the shame of what she'd just confessed, but because of the sympathy she saw in his deep gray eyes. She mustn't give in to the temptation to throw herself into his arms and seek comfort there. She couldn't ask so much of him so soon. She hurried on. "My mother promised she'd tell me who he was when I turned one-and-twenty. So I still have that to look forward to."

"And when she does, what will you do?"

"Write to beg him to let me meet him. My mother said he never would, but perhaps he'll change his mind now that I'm Lady Ramsay."

"If he did, would that console you for having to be my wife?" His tone was quizzical but she was not taken in. It was a serious question about a serious matter.

She gave it a serious answer. "It has always been the deepest wish of my heart to meet him, if only once. So, yes, indeed, it would."

They turned into a broad avenue lined with tall oaks that cast their shadows across the road. Now that they were closer to the castle, Zoe saw that, as Adam had warned her, the tower was in poor repair. Windows gaped, unglazed, and many stones had fallen from the crenellations that topped it, leaving holes like the gaps in an old man's smile.

A newer building stretched beside the castle tower—Jacobean, judging from the tall, mullioned windows and the domed turrets—but it didn't look to be in good repair, either. They came to a halt in a courtyard of tamped earth, in front of an elaborate doorway crowned by a flattened arch. After asking her to await him in the chaise, Adam alighted, walked up to the oaken door, and pounded on it with the end of his serpent-headed cane.

There was a long wait until the door creaked open and an older man, whose long white hair was tied in a queue, peered out at her new husband for a moment, before rushing toward him and embracing him with the agility of a much younger man. The two conferred intently for a few moments, then Adam returned to the carriage.

"That's my bailiff, MacAlpin," he said when he rejoined her. "He's gone to assemble our retainers for a formal welcome. He's a man of the old school, and it would pain him deeply if Strathrimmon's new lady weren't to be greeted properly. I hope you don't mind the wait."

"Of course not. It isn't every day that one is welcomed as the lady of a manor. I intend to enjoy every moment of my reception. But how will they expect me to behave?"

"The servants will line up on either side of the entry. You need only smile and nod your head as we pass through. I'll introduce you to those I remember, but it's been so long since I was last here, there may not be many. Don't worry about remembering their names. There will be time to learn them later. For now all you need to do is give the people a chance to show their respect."

"But my dress! It is hardly what they will expect of a baroness." She looked down at the drab garment that was much the worse for having been worn every day of their journey.

"You're dressed like a lady. It will be enough."

And sure enough, as his servants straggled out of the castle and the tenants in from the fields, her concerns about her wardrobe vanished, in view of the rags that clothed them. Compared to the rough, ill-cut garments that enveloped the women who came to meet them, her gown was indeed luxurious. And the men! They seemed to all be wearing smocks of some rough fabric that, no matter what color it might have once been, was now the uniform tan of the soil. Both men and women wore their hair long and matted, and few of them wore shoes. Adam had not been exaggerating when he warned her that his estate might be in poor condition—not if the condition of the people who labored for him was anything to go by.

When the men and women of the estate had lined up in two ragged rows, Adam reached for her hand to lead her out of the carriage. The feeling of his long fingers against her palm made her feel suddenly breathless. As they walked together through the line of servants, Zoe smiled as graciously as possible. Adam, for his part, had again assumed the look of cool authority she was so used to seeing on his features.

Now that she'd seen the vast acres he had been born to rule, that air of authority made more sense. But she also noted how as he greeted the people of his estate, he seemed to freeze back into a kind of wooden for-

mality, which would leave a stranger thinking he was
haughty, as she had done when first they'd met. But
she knew him well enough by now to sense it was his
inner uneasiness that had deepened his reserve. This
delayed homecoming was hard for him. Very hard. It
was taking everything he had to get through it.

When, at last, all the servants and villagers had been
greeted, he took her hand and led her toward the formal
entryway, framed in oak so old it had turned nearly
black. As one of the servants sprang forward to open
the door, Zoe got a hazy impression of the dark wood
and musty hangings awaiting them inside. Then, before
she had time to realize what he intended, Adam bent
over and placed one strong arm beneath her knees, and
after wrapping the other around her shoulders, picked
her up and carried her over the threshold.

There was a scatter of applause from the servants,
and several of them raised a cheer. She was glad the
denizens of the manor couldn't see her face. It must
be the color of a well-boiled beet. Until this moment,
her wedding and all it entailed had been something private, shared only with strangers who would never see
them again, meaningful only to her and her new husband, and fragile because, despite his reassurances, she
feared he would eventually set it aside.

But with this simple, traditional gesture her husband
had made it public. He'd acknowledged her as his bride
before his people. He'd told them this was to be her
new home. Perhaps he really did want her to remain
his wife.

Still holding her in his arms, he carried her to the

center of the large, paneled reception room and set her down on her feet once again, but even then he didn't let her go. "They will expect this, too."

He leaned over and planted a kiss on her lips—a long and lingering kiss that made her go limp in his arms. Only when the last echo of the kiss had finished resonating through the most distant reaches of her body did he release her and stand back. Then he turned to face his dependents. His features betrayed only the slightest tinge of the distant, haughty look that had filled them earlier.

His eyes were warm and glowing as he said, in that rich, resonant voice of his that totally undid her, "Welcome to Strathrimmon, my dearest bride."

The rest of the evening passed in a blur. After their things were brought in, the servants saw to it that Zoe was made comfortable and given a chance to rest after the tiring journey. She napped while Adam reacquainted himself with his bailiff and his affairs. When she awakened hours later, it was to find that her dinner had been brought up to her on a tray.

She stayed awake, hoping to see her husband when he was done with his many new responsibilities, but Adam didn't come to her bed that night, though she lay awake for a long time, hoping to see him. It was only after the moon had set and all lay still in the night around her that she conceded that she was to spend her first night as the lady of the manor still a virgin.

She wondered. Despite the public way he'd claimed

her, had Adam had second thoughts, after seeing her here in his childhood home?

She told herself to stop seeing trouble where there was none. They'd made a hard journey today, traveling faster than usual, and her leg, which had felt almost normal in the morning, had started to ache. He'd noticed her limping as she'd mounted the main staircase and had commented upon it. Perhaps it was chivalry that kept him from coming to her bed, out of a fear of hurting her.

Or perhaps there was some old Scottish custom to be followed here, too—village maidens decking her out in traditional bridal robes while aged retainers muttered hoary Scots blessings. It was all so new to her. She must resist jumping to conclusions. She should be glad to have a bit of time to get some rest, alone, without the disturbing presence of her new husband to send her all aflutter.

But an untroubled rest was the last thing she wanted, for everything *was* so unsettled! Once he'd taken that last, irrevocable step that would make her fully his wife, perhaps her life would sink back into some kind of regular pattern. She would settle into her new role as mistress of Strathrimmon—as strange as it seemed now—and move on. But she couldn't relax now, not stuck as she was here, on the threshold, wife and not wife, her future still so uncertain.

But for tonight, she had no choice. Whatever his reasons, her new husband had left her alone with her thoughts, and there was nothing she could do about it.

Chapter 12

Zoe was awakened the next morning by a rap on her door. Her heart lifted. *Adam had come at last.* But a moment later she realized it couldn't be her husband. He would have come through the adjoining door that led to his bedchamber, but whoever was knocking was outside in the hallway. It must be a servant.

She called out a sleepy "Come in." At her command, the door cracked open and a small, wizened old woman entered and, without waiting for an invitation, made her way slowly toward the bed. Only when she was so close that Zoe could have touched the faded blue wool of her gown did she come to a halt and peer into Zoe's face with eyes almost as faded.

"So you are the puir wee lassie he has brought back with him." The woman shook her head. "Puir bairn."

"Who are you?" *And what gives you the right to speak so frankly with your mistress?*

"Annie MacTavish," the crone replied with an air that suggested there should be no need for her to explain something so obvious. "I was their nurse, the twa bairns, so many years ago." She leaned so close that Zoe could smell her unwashed body. "Who were *ye* before he made ye his?"

Zoe's insides constricted. Aside from the woman's rudeness, hers was not an unnatural question to ask, and they must all of them here be wondering the same thing. She must take care to answer it in a way that wouldn't lower her standing with the servants.

"I was the Laird of Iskeny's ward."

"Iskeny? Aye, that explains it then. Who else would marry one who bore such a curse as our maister?" The woman turned her head and spat over her shoulder, making a strange gesture with the fingers on one hand.

A chill ran through Zoe at the old woman's words. Adam had called himself accursed more than once, but she'd assumed he meant it figuratively. Still, the Scots *were* steeped in old traditions—superstitions, Mrs. Endicott would have called them. She must make allowances. But before she could demand an explanation, the door to her husband's chamber burst open and Adam entered. Upon seeing him, the old woman made a deep curtsy.

"Annie!" Adam cried when he recognized her. "No need to stand on ceremony with me." He came over and gently enfolded her in an embrace. "Auld Annie was my nurse," he explained before turning back to the old woman. "It's been so long since I last saw you. Too long."

"Ye had yer reasons and at least ye *did* come home, not like yer father afore ye. Anyroad, I'm still the same," the old woman shrugged. "I came to see yer bride. She's a bonny lass, though she could use some fattening up. She'll nae make it through the cold winter with so little meat on her bones."

He smiled. "I'll speak to Cook directly. I wouldn't want to lose her through such carelessness."

"Nae, I ween you wudna," the old woman agreed with no hint of a smile. "There's troubles enough awaitin' the puir lassie without that. But I'll be on my way, then, Adam, though I s'pose you being all grown I must call you my lord." Then without giving him any chance to reply she curtseyed again, very slowly, as if her joints pained her, and as she turned away Zoe thought she saw her again make that gesture with her fingers.

When Auld Annie was gone, Zoe said, "What a strange woman! Was she really your nurse?"

He nodded.

"She was quite rude. Is that the custom among servants here in Scotland?"

"No. But it's Auld Annie's custom, and she's been here too long to cure her of it."

"She seems to be full of superstition, too. Has she become that way with age?"

"No, she was always like that. She always liked to while away the long winter nights frightening young children with tales of the faerie folk and goblins who steal bad children. It kept us on our best behavior. When she tended us, I spent many a night with my eyes wide open, cowering in my bed fearing they'd soon be coming for me."

She was tempted to ask him if the curse that the old woman had mentioned was just such a fairy tale, told to keep her master's new bride out of mischief, but thought better of it. There had been something about the way the old woman had spoken of it that made her want to learn more before she confronted him about it.

He walked over to the bed. He was dressed, as usual, in a clean white homespun shirt open at the collar and in breeches of the old-fashioned sort, buttoned at the knee, which showed off the firm muscles of his long calves. The morning sun brought out the red highlights in his russet hair while deepening the hue of his gold-flecked gray eyes to a color not much different from that of the slates that covered the roof outside her window.

How handsome he was! She fought down the desire to run her fingers through his hair and explore the tempting arch of his high cheekbone. But she reined it in. It was for him to make that kind of move. She was his wife, not a woman to be taken for pleasure.

Still, she longed to put to an end the uncertainty that still hung over their marriage. He'd acknowledged her to his people. It must be time to take the final step, if only so that she need no longer torment herself wondering if he would set her aside. Their marriage must be consummated.

She felt downright brazen, so strongly did she long

for it to happen right now, despite the voice within that
counseled caution. Even if he didn't love her as some
innocent young miss might wish to be loved, what of it?
She'd never been innocent, and she couldn't remember
ever feeling young. He'd acknowledged her as his bride
in front of all his people. That was worth something.
And even if he never learned to love her, when the marriage was consummated she would have children who
would—cherished children, on whom she could lavish
her adoration, children who would have a father and a
name.

But perhaps it was the thought of those children that
explained why Adam hesitated as he approached her
bed. Despite his newfound resolution to find a way to
accept her parentage, he could have no wish to father
Isabelle's grandchild, especially not here, in the home
he'd last shared with Charlotte. Zoe could only imagine the memories he must have had to contend with on
his return here yesterday. They must have driven home,
again, how high a price he paid for doing his teacher's
will.

But even so, he'd done it, and if she was willing to
make the best of it, so must he. She couldn't bear to
spend much longer playing the role of his wife here in
front of his retainers, while knowing he could still have
their marriage annulled. If he wouldn't take the next
step, perhaps she must be the one to help him do it.

She cast her mind back to what she'd heard her
mother say on the subject of encouraging the growth of
a man's passion, but all that came to mind was her insistence that a woman must never let a man see her first

thing in the morning—not until she'd washed herself, arranged her hair, and reapplied her paint.

If that was the case, Zoe was already doomed. Adam had already seen her in her rumpled nightgown with her long tresses lying in knotted tangles around her shoulders. Suddenly self-conscious, she sat up and gathered up a few handfuls of hair to wind back into a bun, looking for her hairpins, which she remembered putting on the table beside the bed before sleep. But Adam reached out a hand to stop her.

"Leave it down" he said softly. "It's so beautiful that way. I didn't know it was so long and thick. You've always worn it up."

"I must, otherwise it becomes a rat's nest. It's far too curly."

"I think not." He reached out and stroked one long tress, beginning at her ear and then following it down past her shoulder onto her bosom. As his hand brushed by her nipple, which was covered only by the thin lawn of her nightgown, Zoe felt a wave of longing surge through her body, but she steeled herself to give no sign of it. She was to be his wife, not a woman of pleasure, and she must be careful to start as she meant to go on.

As she controlled herself, she saw uncertainty flicker in his eyes. Then he drew his hand away. Had he been disappointed with what he found? Her bosom *was* so very small, though that couldn't have come as much of a surprise, to him. He must have noticed it by now.

"Perhaps they'll grow as I get older."

"Your hair? Hair always grows." He sounded confused.

She could feel herself blushing. "I thought perhaps you found my figure disappointing. There's so little there."

He laughed. "There's more than enough. Why did you think me disappointed?"

The blush she'd felt before was nothing to the burning she felt spread across her face now. Did he really expect her to speak with him of such things? "You took your hand away."

"And you thought that meant I didn't like to touch you?"

She nodded.

He sat beside her on the bed. The mattress sagged as he put his weight onto it and she couldn't help but lean in toward him.

"I like touching you, Zoe, very much. But the situation is daunting."

"It is for me, too. I don't know how a wife is supposed to behave with her husband. Everything I've learned about such matters was taught me by my mother and her friends, and they had no wish to act like wives. The things they did were meant to captivate and enslave their men. I shouldn't think you'd want that from me."

He grinned. "I can't say. I've never been captivated or enslaved before. I might enjoy it. What does it entail?"

She pondered this. "Well, their art was mostly a matter of letting you see what you might have, while holding it back at the same time—to make you want it more."

"I'm not sure I understand. Could you could give me an example?"

She cast her mind back for some example that would not be too embarrassing. Not the tale of how Paulette had restored the admiral's ardor by dressing in a midshipman's uniform. But what? At last she said, "Well, there's that thing they would do with their bosoms— they all have such lovely ones. My mother would let her décolletage drop down like this." She pulled down the neckline of her nightgown, opening up the top buttons so that the gentle curve of her own small bosom was revealed. "Then she'd move so." She thrust out her chest and moved her shoulder in a seductive wiggle. "Then the man would reach for it and she'd laugh and slap at his hand saying, 'Foolish man' or something like that. The men always loved that, though I could never see why."

"Did your mother enjoy it?" His tone made her think he really wanted to know.

"I can't say for sure, but I think she did."

"How come?"

"Because it made the men want her more."

"But you wouldn't like it, would you?"

"No. I don't see the point of it."

"Then you must have been relieved when I removed my hand just now."

She felt herself blush again and her nipples hardened at the memory of how she'd felt when he'd touched her. "That was different."

"Why?"

She dropped her head, too embarrassed to reply. What would he think of her if he knew the truth?

He pressed on. "*Would* you have slapped my hand away, if I'd let it linger?"

Her nipples were on fire with need of him by now, but all she said was "No."

His lip turned up with mischief. "Because you'd have enjoyed it?"

Again she nodded dumbly, awash in embarrassment, wishing she had her mother's ability to lie, just this once, so he wouldn't know how unsuited she was to responding as befit a wife. "I suppose I'm very shameless."

"No." The golden sparkles in his gray eyes danced with amusement. "Just very honest. Your mother was right. You would have been a complete failure as a courtesan."

Her heart sank. "I can't help being the way I am," she said stiffly. "It was you who wanted to marry me."

"Yes. And it has long been a principle with me to only marry women who fail utterly at being courtesans."

Without another word, he reached out and pressed his long, tapered fingers where her nipple lay hidden below the thin fabric of her gown. Then he drew a languid circle around it, dragging the tip of his fingernail along the rim. When she thought she couldn't bear the sensation a moment longer, his hand dropped lower and cupped her breast. His fingers closed tightly around it for a moment, kneading the firm flesh, and then relaxed, before returning to her nipple and stroking it gently, making small circles spread out through her body like the ripples a pebble made when dropped into a pond.

She drew in a sharp breath.

"Does that please you?" he asked quietly.

"Oh yes. But why would anyone want to slap a hand away when it could give them such pleasure?"

"Because it would strengthen the man's desire if you treated him that way. You mother is right. A woman can get power over a man by denying him what he wants."

"Then I must learn to do so."

"Why?" His eyes darkened.

She wanted to stay silent, but his steady gaze forced her to speak, though her voice was barely a whisper. "So you will finally want me."

"I want you now," he said, so softly that she could barely hear him. "I'm wild with longing for you. But I mustn't give in to that longing, not yet."

"Why not?"

"We have a lifetime to spend together. There's no rush—and I don't want to frighten you."

He had let his hand drop again, leaving her taut with longing. But he wouldn't meet her eye. He was telling the truth. But not all of it. Carefully she said, "You could frighten me, still, with your anger, but not with your touch." She reached for his hand and brought it back to where it had been, on her breast.

As if her words had freed something in him, he stretched out beside her on the bed. Releasing her breast, he took her hand in his and pulled it toward him. She let him guide it toward his shirt as he pulled it up with his other hand before placing her fingers on his chest. She felt the wiry hair that guarded his nipples and let his hand guide her toward the tiny nubs that crowned them. She stroked one experimentally, wondering if it felt to him the way her nipple had when he'd touched her there.

As her fingers stroked him, he sighed with pleasure. The flesh of his nipple hardened. Hers did, too.

He reached his other arm around her and nuzzled her gently as he pressed her against his muscular chest. "It feels so good to hold you. I can barely control myself. You don't have to slap my hand away to drive me wild."

She let her hand trail downward from his nipple, over the muscular ridges of his chest. His skin there was so smooth. The corresponding parts of her own body awakened as she stroked him, as if one network of nerves connected them. Her exploring fingers drifted lower, past his chest, until she met something with no counterpart in her body—the long, silken hairs that grew in a sleek line down the center to his belly.

She teased them with her fingers, wondering at the texture of the hair, and the springy resistance it made to her touch. His stomach was so flat and hard. As her fingers encountered the curling wisps of hair, she wondered if they were the same reddish gold as the tuft that curled so bewitchingly at his throat.

It was only when she came to the barrier of his breeches and fumbled uncertainly with the edge that she felt him tense, but still he didn't stop her. He let out a long, drawn-out breath, and then reached over and quietly unbuttoned the buttons, allowing the front flap to fall open. Drawn inexorably downward, her fingers followed the soft fur farther, more hesitantly now, knowing what it would lead to.

As her fingers tangled in the thickening tuft, she made her hand veer away from the central line of his body, fearing what might happen were she to tease his rod, which already jutted against his drawers. She remembered how quickly he'd responded that night in the inn—and how quickly she'd felt overwhelmed. She wasn't ready for that, not yet, much as she wanted to be. So she contented herself with running her fingertips over the hard bones of his hip and his squared-off flank, delaying.

Then, as if reading her mind, he took her exploring hand in his and stopped its advance. "There's no need to rush," he said. "We have a lifetime together."

He brought his lips down on hers and kissed her as if he wanted to pour himself into her. At his touch, her lips melted into his. A golden light poured through her center, reaching her very heart, as she tingled with the need his lips ignited in her. Joy pulsed through her body as his lips danced with hers. His tongue, so giving and yet so firm, taught her a new kind of pleasure as she hovered on the brink of bliss.

She knew only him—the smell of his hair, like flowers, and the scent of his skin, sharp and tangy, which called her to nestle more closely against him. Their kiss dissolved into a sobbing breath as he finally released her, and she heard herself gasp.

"It's you who have enslaved *me*," she said softly. "I shall die if you don't kiss me that way again."

"Then I must kiss you." His russet lashes dropped over his steel gray eyes. "I am vowed to save life, not to end it." He brought his lips down on hers, filling her with bliss and intolerable longing. His hand stroked her ruined cheek, but even that didn't mar her joy.

She was all he'd ever wanted, more beautiful than dawn. The sweet taste of her was so perfect, he felt himself spiraling into complete abandon, wanting nothing more than to learn at last what it felt like to lose himself in the fullness of the comfort she offered.

But deep within, a voice broke through the madness that gripped him. *Would you trick her once again? And this time beyond any remedy?*

His hand froze. What had he let himself drift into, disarmed by her light tone and the unexpected flirtatiousness that had engulfed them both?

His animal nature, now fully roused, battled against the voice of conscience. His prick throbbed with wanting of her. She was his wife. It was permitted. Why shouldn't he thrust himself into her welcoming softness and be done with it? Not only was it permitted, it was required. The Dark Lord himself had commanded it.

But he'd already let the Dark Lord's command lead him to do things he'd known were wrong. He'd already violated Zoe's spirit with the spell. He mustn't take her body until she understood, as she could not now, what it would really mean.

He stroked her face, gently, one last time. Then drawing on the last of his strength that had not been consumed by desire, he pulled away from her, breathing hard.

When he opened his eyes he was amazed to realize that they were both still partly clothed. She must have had the same realization for as he released her she reached for the hem of her shift, as if preparing to pull it up over her head and discard it.

He clamped one hand on her wrist to stop her. "No. Not now."

She shrank away as if slapped. "It was my face, wasn't it? Why did you have to touch it? That ruined everything!" There was anguish in her voice.

He felt her pain as if it had been his own, and understood, too late, what caused it. "That wasn't why I stopped," he protested. "I love your face, because *you* live inside it. Didn't my kiss teach you how beautiful I find you?" He stroked her cheek again as gently as he could. "I find you *too* beautiful. It's taking all I have to rein in my longing to possess you."

She lifted his hand away. "If that's true, why must you deny it? Must the Dark Lord's heir still be chaste?"

He shook his head, no. "It isn't that."

"It's Charlotte then. Because my mother killed her."

His insides clenched at the old familiar pain, but that hadn't been the reason, so he must not hide behind it. He must tell her the truth. "It's not that, either."

Though, in a way, it *was* Charlotte who kept them apart—and would until he found the courage to tell Zoe about the curse. Yet the very comfort and content he'd felt in her arms just now made it impossible for him to do it. How could he? When she knew the truth, she would leave him. He'd be alone once more—far more alone even than he'd ever been during all the long years of exile. For in her arms, he'd tasted a hint of what it would be like to not be solitary and accursed, and that taste would make it so much more painful to go back to being that way again. He couldn't face a lifetime without her. He couldn't bring himself to ruin everything by telling her the truth.

So he only said, "MacAlpin awaits me. I promised

I'd tour the estate with him this morning, so I have to go and meet with him now, no matter how much I might wish I could stay here with you."

And with that he jumped up and left her aching and alone in her virginal bridal bed.

Chapter 13

It tormented Adam to know how much he'd hurt his bride. But it terrified him, too, that he'd almost taken her just now, carried away by passion, forgetting what it would mean to consummate their union. He couldn't trust that he would be strong enough to pull away should the same situation arise again.

If only his Pisces nature didn't make him take everything so seriously. A man born under a happier sign might have taken the easy way—and let the flirtatious mood they'd established lead them to their tryst's logical conclusion, hoping for the best. But his father had hoped for the best, and look how *that* ended. Though it had torn his heart to have had to injure Zoe by leaving her so abruptly, he was glad he'd had the strength to do what was right. But he'd only done part of it. He must finish the job.

Though that hadn't been why he'd left her, he had been telling the truth when he'd said he was supposed to meet with the bailiff, so he dressed and headed out to see MacAlpin. Of course, as he'd known it would, the route to the bailiff's offices led him past the one room he hadn't revisited since his return home. His sister's room.

Last night, he hadn't found the courage to enter it. He dreaded entering it now. But as he paused before her door, he knew he must confront what awaited him within if he were ever to fight his way out of the impasse to which he'd brought his marriage. The latch gave way easily at his touch. Only the creak of the rusty hinges gave testimony to how long it had been since anyone had entered the chamber. Once inside, he saw that nothing had changed since his sister had left it for the last time, when she'd gone to join him in Morlaix. His eyes took in her bed with its high sides, the shelf that held her books, and her crutch. He made himself look at them all, refusing to look away.

But whatever he'd expected to meet when he'd steeled himself to enter her chamber, it wasn't here. He felt a strange mixture of relief and disappointment. Though she'd left her things behind, his sister was gone. It was only his need to reach her once more that had made him think he might find her here.

He wouldn't. If he were ever to meet her again it would only be in his dreams, not here, where the poor husk that had constrained her soul had been confined. He stood quietly at the center of her room, surrounded by her things, taking deep breaths to slow his rapid pulse.

And then it struck him: he hadn't dreamed of his sister— not once— since Zoe had come to his bed that night at the inn. That was strange enough, but even stranger was the fact that he hadn't been aware of Charlotte's absence. How could he not have noticed that her ghost no longer came to him, silent and reproving, to remind him that he hadn't yet avenged her?

As he breathed in the musty scent of the room that had been Charlotte's prison, an unexpected sense of peace settled on his heart. Could he have done the right thing, after all, in making Zoe his wife?

He yearned for it to be true, but there was no way to be certain. If only he knew why the Dark Lord had chosen Zoe to be his bride. But his teacher was as dead as his sister, and neither of them would ever answer him again, plead with them though he might.

A tiny sound put him on the alert. A mouse scurried across the top of the chest that had held his sister's few treasures. He took an involuntary step toward it and stopped when he saw what lay trapped in the crack between the chest and the wall. It was his sister's knife, the folding penknife he'd given her, which she'd treasured so. It must have slipped off the top of the chest, and of course once that had happened she wouldn't have been able to get anyone to retrieve it for her. But finding it now, he felt as if she'd left it there for him.

A thrill ran through him. The knife held so many memories. It had been given to him for his birthday when he'd turned ten, a sign that he was no longer a child but a man who could be trusted to not carve his initials in the furniture. He'd thrilled with pride. But,

of course, it had been Charlotte's birthday, too, so after
he was done admiring his prize, he'd gone to show it to
her, wondering what treasure she'd received.

But she'd been given nothing. He shouldn't have
been surprised. The rest of them always did what they
could to ignore her. But their neglect ruined his pleasure in his knife, and his sister's attempt to rejoice with
him over it had only made it worse.

Late that evening, when Auld Annie had dozed off
by the fire, he'd sneaked into Charlotte's chamber and
given her his precious knife as his birthday present to
her. She'd tried to refuse it. After all, she'd never be
able to use it. But he'd insisted she keep it. He wanted
her to have the things a normal child would have, and
he'd known even then that he would be the only one
who would ever give them to her.

Now, she had given it back, a gift more precious than
his had been. He took a book from the shelf and used
its cover to pry the knife from the crack where it was
lodged. When it was out, he picked it up with a shaking
hand. The blade opened as smoothly as if it were new.
Its edge, unused, was still sharp. He slipped it into his
pocket.

His sister *had* come in answer to his summons, after
all. And as if his sister had whispered the words to him,
he knew what it was she wanted him to do with her
precious gift.

Zoe told herself that Adam *had* been telling the truth
when he'd left her so abruptly to keep his appointment
with his bailiff. She must remember that he was the

master of this vast estate with all the responsibilities it
represented. But she couldn't fully believe it, for she'd
felt the strong emotion that had swept over him, right
before he'd withdrawn from her so abruptly.

Something had spooked him. There was no reason
for him to depart so hastily. The bailiff would have
waited had the lord of Strathrimmon stayed on to dally
with his newly wedded wife in her chamber. Something else had made him wrench himself out of her
arms and flee as if pursued by furies. Though whether
it was her ugliness or her parentage, she couldn't say.
He'd denied that either was to blame, but he'd had a
hard time disguising his horror at how close they had
come to consummating their marriage. *Something* had
appalled him.

There was no point in dwelling on it. She supposed
she should be grateful that he *hadn't* taken her body
without love. That might even show some greatness of
spirit on his part. His body had certainly wanted hers.
So perhaps he was telling the truth when he'd said it
wasn't her ugliness that had driven him away.

But if that was true, it must have been her parentage. Strong as his lust had been, it hadn't been enough
to make him betray the sister to whom he'd given his
lifelong loyalty. That he was capable of such loyalty
made Zoe love him more. If only that same loyalty of
his hadn't made it impossible for him to love her. She
was tiring of paradoxes.

The sounds of the busy household outside her door
reminded her that her husband wasn't the only one who
had responsibilities to their dependents. She shouldn't

be lying here sniveling about love when she was supposed to be meeting with the housekeeper to learn more
about her new domain. As long as Adam honored her
with the role of wife, she must fill it as best she could,
and give him no reason to regret that he'd elevated her
to so high a station.

She was almost done dressing when she heard a
noise at her door. Before she could tell whoever it was
to go away, the door opened a crack, and her husband's
aged nurse hobbled into the room.

"I've brought ye something, to fend off the evil of
the curse." Auld Annie held out a branch of some shriv-
eled herb. "Though little help it may be to ye."

"I didn't ask you for help," Zoe snapped. "Nor do
I recall inviting you into my chamber." The woman
hadn't even knocked.

Auld Annie made that strange gesture with her hand
again, and her eyes hardened.

"Aye, but ye *will* have need for my help, and soon,
I ween, for he's young and healthy, our Adam, and
cannae keep his hands off o' ye. But ye're but a young
lassie and ken not what ye do. So I take no offense.
Auld Annie will aid ye when ye need her, as she did yer
husband's puir mither." Then, before Zoe could reply,
the old woman turned on her heel and made her way
out of the chamber.

Yes, clearly it was time to take on the role her husband had thrust on her. The servants had become far
too bold in their master's absence. If she tolerated such
behavior from one, soon they would all be taking such
liberties. She'd seen her pupils act in much the same

way when a new teacher had been introduced to Mrs. Endicott's school.

After dressing, she made her way down the wide staircase bordered in heavy oaken paneling that led down to the main hall, where she found Mrs. MacAlpin awaiting her at the foot of the stairs. The housekeeper stood primly, her posture suggesting she felt aggrieved at having had to wait for her slugabed mistress. Her mouth was set in a grim smile.

It *would* pose a challenge to grasp the reins of her new household. But Zoe welcomed it. It would give her something to do besides mooning over her husband like a besotted schoolgirl. But as she took in the housekeeper's tightly pressed lips and the way her fingers curled possessively around the large bunch of keys at her waist, she knew that she must go about it carefully. She needed to make her an ally, not an enemy.

"I expect you'll be wanting the keys, Yer Ladyship." The older woman made a great show of unfastening the heavy bundle of iron keys that hung from her belt.

Zoe considered taking them and dismissing the woman. She was the mistress here and wanted there to be no mistake about it. But the unvoiced resentment that radiated from every inch of Mrs. MacAlpin's wiry body reminded her of that of the girls who'd been sent to Mrs. Endicott's school against their will. She'd learned when handling them that, if she didn't make an issue of it, their resentment often abated on its own, after she'd allowed them some time to adjust to their new situation. It was understandable that Mrs. MacAlpin might fear being uprooted by the sudden appearance of the upstart who had come to take her place.

So Zoe favored her with a gracious smile. "You may keep the keys for now. I'll need your help, if I'm to do as good a job of managing the household as you've done in His Lordship's absence."

The older woman gave her a searching look. "I only did my job, Yer Ladyship." Though her voice was gruff, she looked pleased. It was comforting to learn that, as unprepared as Zoe might feel to become the mistress of so grand an establishment, her years of dealing with the many clashing female personalities to be found in a ladies' academy had taught her much that might come in useful in managing her husband's estate.

"Now I should like you to show me through my new home. There's so much I'll need to know about it that only another woman would fully understand."

Mollified, the housekeeper spent the next hour leading her through the principal rooms and sharing many valuable insights. Though Mrs. MacAlpin, like most of her countrymen, was not given to idle chatter, she'd spent most of her life at Strathrimmon and was deeply devoted not only to the family but to the manor itself. As she got over her shock at having a new mistress, she began to see the advantages of making her new mistress an ally in bringing the house back to its earlier splendor.

The housekeeper proudly showed off the Sevres porcelain urns displayed in the niches set in the walls of the main saloon, before pointing out where the Turkey carpet that covered its floor was in need of repair. She recounted who had shot the stags whose heads adorned the walls of the billiard room, and noted which chimney smoked, and what windows needed caulking. In the long gallery, she identified the various Lord Ramsays whose paintings graced the walls, and then ventured the suggestion that it was time that His Lordship's own visage should join them there.

"Is there a portrait here of his sister?" Zoe asked.

The woman's eyebrows shot up in surprise. "Nae, nae. That would hardly be proper." Then she quickly changed the subject, lamenting the depredations that woodworm had wrought on the carved ceilings that were the hall's principal ornament.

As they passed through a small withdrawing room, fitted out in a style that would have been the height of fashion thirty years before, Zoe noticed a door that led to what appeared to be a glassed-in conservatory. Her heart lifted. A conservatory would make it possible to rear some choice plants despite the short growing season.

But when they entered it, Zoe's hopes were dashed. The conservatory had been badly neglected. Panes of glass were missing, others were broken, and the stove that should have warmed it looked as if it had never been completely assembled.

"It appears the Dowager Lady Ramsay wasn't given to gardening," Zoe said.

"On the contrary, she was quite fond of it, before her marriage. His Lordship's father, Lord Ramsay that was, made this glass room for his new bride, especially to please her. And he'd ha' done far more for her after that, for he had many a plan for grand improvements. But when he learned that she was to bear him twins, that was the end of it. There was nae point in going on, once he knew the Ramsay curse had struck again."

Mrs. MacAlpin said the last words in a tone that suggested that a curse striking was something all land-owners must expect, like a bad harvest or an early frost. She added, "Next thing we knew, he'd gone off to the Continent alone, and he died there soon after, poor mannie, before the bairns were born. There was no talk of improvements after that."

"But surely when Lady Ramsay knew she was to bear twins, she must have wished to make a new nurs-ery for her children?"

The housekeeper gave her a hard look. "After the bairns were born, Lady Ramsay had nae stomach for anything to do with them. Not with them so clearly touched with the curse's mark." She pursed her lips. "Auld Annie was given the care of them, the same as had been the old Lord Ramsay's nurse. She held that what was good enough for the babes' father in his nurs-ery days must be good enough for them. And of course it was. Ye find nae fault with your husband, now do ye, my lady? Auld Annie knew her job and did it well."

Zoe had always heard the Scots were a superstitious people but until now she'd not realized how truly back-ward they were. She must straighten out this business of the curse now or she'd never hear the end of it. "Pray tell me," she demanded of the housekeeper, "what is all this about some Ramsay curse?"

"Has yer husband nae mentioned it to ye, my lady?"

"No. Though Auld Annie did, last night."

The housekeeper's face, which had relaxed slightly as she'd gone about the house displaying its treasures, froze up. Her lips were once again pressed firmly closed and her eyes shuttered. When she spoke, her voice was clipped. "If His Lordship hasna mentioned it, it's not for me to talk of such things. If ye wish to know, ye must ask him to explain it."

Though she was tempted to press Mrs. MacAlpin for more information, Zoe was unwilling to lose the small store of goodwill she'd built up over the course of the morning. So she merely nodded and let the older woman lead her back through the cavernous kitchen with its huge open hearth and large roasting spit, and then on into the dairy, where Mrs. MacAlpin pointed out how clean the basins were in which the fresh cream was set out and observed how difficult it was to find dairy maids who would do the work needed to keep them that way.

When their tour was over. Zoe gave her orders as to the dinners to be served during the week and dismissed the housekeeper. Then she returned to her chamber with much to think about.

Adam's business with MacAlpin took up the better part of the day. Much as he longed to hasten through it so he could return to his wife, his duty to his tenants made that impossible. What his bailiff had had to tell him had been sobering. Too many tenants had been driven from their holdings to open their fields to more grazing. He must put a stop to that. He had a duty to protect his people.

When he finally met up with Zoe at supper, they could only discuss commonplaces, surrounded as they were by servants. Adam rushed through his meal with almost unseemly haste, burning with impatience to get Zoe alone again. But where? What he needed to discuss with her could only be brought up in private, but the intimacy of her bedchamber would be likely to have a chilling effect on them both after what had taken place there this morning.

Fortunately the weather was fair, and there remained another hour of light. On the pretext that he wished to show Zoe some of the curiosities to be found on the estate, he invited her to join him in the gig. To his relief, she showed no hesitation about joining him, but quickly fetched her shawl.

At first, they rode in silence. It was only when they were well away from the crenellated tower of his home—and its inquisitive servants—that he steered the gig over to the side of the rough track they'd taken and brought the horse to a halt. For a moment they sat there in the silence, listening to the symphony of birdsong that rose from the hedges and enjoying the cool breeze. Then Adam said, "Sometime ago, I robbed you of something you valued. I'd like to make amends to you for taking it."

The look of surprise that swept across Zoe's face made him wish he'd phrased his words differently. Was she thinking of how he'd stolen her free will from her? He hoped not, for that he could not restore. Indeed, if he were honest, he must admit he didn't want to restore it. Not when his spell was the only thing that kept her here with him, and every new hour taught him how much he wanted her to stay.

Before she could answer, he reached into his pocket and drew forth Charlotte's knife. "I can't return the knife Mrs. Endicott gave you, for I destroyed it. But will you accept this one? It's very dear to me for it used to belong to my sister."

She took it from him, and she studied it quietly for a moment. Then her eyes met his, and in their warm brown depths he saw what he hadn't let himself hope for: approval—and something else he didn't dare to interpret.

Had she remembered how he'd taken that other knife from her when he'd brutally driven her from his bed at the inn, with words so cruel he could barely bring himself to remember them? Was he wrong in thinking she had received the silent message he'd hoped this knife would bear? Did she know his clumsy gift was an attempt to make up to her for the hurtful way he'd fled again from her embrace this morning?

For a moment—though perhaps it was only his hope that made him believe he'd observed it—he thought she did. Indeed, the glow in her eyes made him think his gift might have made her feel affection for him that didn't entirely owe its existence to his spell.

She opened the knife slowly and inspected the blade. Then she reached beneath the neckline of her gown and pulled out a long, thin silver chain. She opened the clasp and slid the chain through the bail of Charlotte's knife as if it had been a pendant. When she had fastened it again, she dropped the chain with its precious burden into the cleft between the rounded mounds of her breasts.

Then she spoke. "I'm glad you have enough faith in me now to trust me with such a fine gift, and I'll treasure it all the more because it was your sister's."

He couldn't keep himself from adding, "I found it in her room. I hope you won't think me overly superstitious when I say I think she wanted you to have it."

"No, I'm glad to hear it. Though since I find you in such a generous mood I shall presume on your good nature and take the liberty of asking you for something else."

He felt his heart contract. What more would she ask him for?

Zoe gave him a comforting smile. "Don't look so worried. It isn't something extravagant. When I spent the afternoon with Mrs. MacAlpin, touring the hall, she showed me the conservatory. It is in such sad repair that I couldn't help but wish it could be finished. It would be such a comfort to me and should cost little, as it's nearly done. Would that be too much to ask?"

Stupidly he replied, "You wish to garden?"

"I do. But there's more to it than that. Mrs. MacAlpin told me the story of how the conservatory was abandoned at your father's death, and that made me think how it must sadden you every time you pass it, for it can't help but remind you of your loss."

That was true enough, but though it was kindness that spurred his wife's request, Adam felt his chest tighten, making it difficult to breathe. What else had Mrs. MacAlpin told her about why his father had left the conservatory abandoned? Obviously, not the whole truth, or Zoe wouldn't still be calmly chatting with him.

She went on, "We must make his conservatory into a place of healing. Do you plan to keep up with your medical practice?"

The question took him by surprise. "I do."

Her face lit up. "Then I could use it to grow the herbs and simples you might use in your cures."

"Nothing would give me more pleasure."

Her offer touched his heart. He hadn't expected her to take such an interest. But even so, he wondered if finishing his father's conservatory would be tempting fate.

He snapped the reins and the gig resumed its progress down the country track. A few moments later he put his free arm around his wife. She didn't resist, but snuggled closer to him. If she wanted the conservatory rebuilt, he must do it for her. He would do anything for her that might bring that fleeting look of pleasure to her warm brown eyes.

As they drove on, he pointed to where, off in the distance, a lone sentinel stone stood, thrusting out of the barren hillside to give mute evidence that the Ancient Ones had long had his patrimony under their sway. Zoe asked him to take her closer so she could examine it. When they reached it, he reined in the horse and helped Zoe out of the gig so she could approach the stone more closely.

The sun had sunk near the horizon, bathing the close-cropped pasture around th8em with that warm golden light that lasted so briefly this time of year. He remembered loving the way that light had gilded the stone when he'd come here in his childhood—though the stone itself had filled him with uneasiness then, as it did now.

With her usual good sense, Zoe betrayed no sign of fear but marched right up to the standing stone. As she did, he noted with pleasure that she was walking normally again. Her leg was healing, and no longer seemed to pain her. When she had reached the stone she tilted her head back to examine it in the fading light and traced out the runes carved into it with her forefinger. When she was done, she walked back to him, more slowly than necessary, as if she were puzzling something out in her mind.

When she had taken her place by his side, she asked, "Is the stone the reason why your servants are so superstitious? Do they still worship in the ancient way?"

"No. They're good Christians all." The suggestion surprised him.

"Really? I thought perhaps, because you follow the ancient ways, they might, too."

"No. I learned those ways in France, when I began my studies with the Dark Lord. Such practices are no longer followed here. It would shock my tenants to know that I dabble in such things."

"I doubt that. Surely Auld Annie is no Christian."

Again his chest tightened. "What makes you say that?"

"That weird gesture she makes whenever she sees me, and her dire warnings—they're quite disquieting.

They were what made me think it was she who had first taught you about the ancient religion."

"She disturbs you, doesn't she?" The words came out before he could censor them.

"Yes. I must confess, she does. I know that respect is due to her, as your nurse. But . . ." She paused, clearly nervous about continuing.

He leapt into the silence. "But what?"

She drew in breath. "Well, I've no experience in the management of such a large household, so perhaps I'm overreacting, but I don't think she's a good influence on the other servants. Twice already she's burst into my room when I hadn't bade her enter, muttering about some family curse, and uttering dismal warnings. And she seems to have infected the housekeeper with her superstitions, too. Mrs. MacAlpin was full of disturbing hints when she took me around the manor, though she refused to explain anything when I confronted her."

"Disturbing hints of what?"

"That curse of Auld Annie's. I assure you, it's nothing I took seriously. But I do take seriously the way Auld Annie might use such superstitions to undermine my authority here. I'm afraid she's too old to learn to serve a new mistress."

"Do you want me to send her away?" He felt himself go cold.

She nodded. "If it's possible."

There was no putting it off any longer. He must tell her. But he said nothing as he led her back to the gig, he couldn't. His heart was breaking. She *would* take the curse seriously when she learned the truth, and when she did, his dream of happiness would fade like his father's. He must be grateful for the brief hours of content he'd shared with her, and take what comfort he could from knowing that, unlike his father, he hadn't let his selfishness ruin a woman's life.

He must tell her the truth, but when he did, even bespelled, he knew she'd finally leave him.

Chapter 14

What was the matter with Adam? He'd dropped the reins and sat in the gig beside her staring, as if frozen, at the barren fields. Zoe couldn't understand it. One moment he'd been so happy, when he'd given her that touching gift of his sister's knife. Then he'd withdrawn.

It must have been her ill-chosen words about Auld Annie. She should have known better than to criticize the woman who'd raised him. She wished she'd kept silent, but it was too late now. Adam had become as cold and inscrutable as the standing stone that glinted silver blue in the light of the rising moon.

She stroked his arm, hoping to defuse the tension she felt flowing through his body. But though he tolerated her touch, he didn't put his arm back around her shoulder the way he had earlier.

She took the bull by the horns. "I owe you an apology. I was wrong to ask you to send your nurse away. She has far more right to be here than I do."

He shook his head. "You have every right to wish to see her gone. I wish I *could* dismiss Auld Annie. Indeed, I'd give all that I possess to be able to do so. But the curse she referred to is real. And *it* is what makes it impossible for me to send her away. As much as I might hope I won't have to inflict her brutal ways on my own children, I might have to."

"Why? What possible hold can she have over you? Does she know some damaging secret about the family? Is it blackmail that ties you to her?"

"Nothing like that. But I may need to call on her to nurse my children—our children," he corrected himself, his face working. "Though I pray to God with all my strength, I won't."

Zoe's heart sank. So much for her dreams of having a child who would enter the world with a name and a home, a child upon whom she could lavish all the love she didn't dare show her husband lest she frighten him away.

She'd assumed that Adam would want children, too, whatever his feelings about her. A nobleman must have an heir. But her husband's last words made her realize her mistake.

"So you have no love for children?" she said quietly, hiding how much the question meant to her.

"To the contrary, I've always loved other people's children. It's only the thought of ours that fills me with foreboding."

Her heart sank further. "Because I would be their mother?"

"Never! You'd make a wonderful mother. Your children would be loved and comforted.

"But my children would be Isabelle's grandchildren. Is that why you would hate them?"

He didn't answer her directly but picked up the reins. Then he turned to face her. "Didn't you ever wonder why a man like me would have chosen to take a vow of chastity? You know me well enough by now to know the strength of my passions and the difficulty with which I repress them."

She had, but what did that have to do with curses and their children? Hesitantly she answered, "You told me that you wished to be the Dark Lord's heir, and that his heir must be chaste—or at least that's what you thought until your teacher convinced you otherwise."

"But didn't you wonder *why* I wished to be the Dark Lord's heir? Didn't you wonder why I spent so many years so far from home, living the life of an exile, when I had these beautiful green acres waiting for me where I could have lived the life of a gentleman surrounded by comfort and by others of my kind? Didn't that seem strange to you?"

"Everything about you seemed strange to me—at first." She couldn't keep the exasperation out of her voice. "But I've grown accustomed to you. You've been the Dark Lord's heir as long as I've known you, so I didn't question it. From the very first you made it clear you wished to devote your life to becoming a great healer."

"My desire to be a great healer had little to do with what I wished," Adam said softly. "If I could have had my wish, I'd have lived here all my life, tending my estate, and enjoying the simple pleasures of a gentleman with a beloved wife and my sons and daughters."

She fought against the jealousy that surged within her at the thought of that lost beloved wife whose children would have been so very wanted. "Then why then did you leave it all behind? Why *are* you the Dark Lord's heir?"

"Because of the curse," he said. "Because I couldn't bear to see it strike again. Because I hoped that something I'd learn when the Dark Lord revealed his deepest secrets could undo it."

"What curse? You're driving me mad with your refusal to explain it to me."

"The Ramsay curse." His eyes bored into hers, gleaming in the falling dusk like the flames of the beacon that warns mariners at sea of the fatal rocks that lie hidden by the shore. "In every generation of our family, twins are born, one hale and strong, like me, and one"—his voice broke—"like Charlotte."

"But you loved Charlotte. She was beautiful and good."

"I saw her that way, but I was the only one. To the rest, even to her own mother, she was only a cripple, a hopelessly damaged monster, mute and twisted."

Zoe struggled to comprehend what he was telling her. "You never told me Charlotte was crippled."

He nodded and bowed his head, letting the waves of long hair fall forward over his eyes, as if he'd hide himself from her. "She was born that way, as the smaller twin always is. Her one side was nearly useless though she could drag herself around with the help of sticks. But she couldn't speak. Or at least, not so that anyone but me could understand her."

"How sad, Adam. But why?"

"Because I'd made her so. I was the stronger twin, the bearer of the Ramsay curse. I sucked the life out of her in the womb. I've had to live with that knowledge all my life. I wouldn't wish it on my son. Better he never be born."

"But that's mad. No one sane could blame a child in the womb for the fate of his twin."

"Then you must call my mother mad, and my father, and the cottars that live on our lands, for they all believe it."

"Based on what?"

He brought his hands up to his face and rubbed at his eyes as if he could rub away the memory. "They say that ten generations ago, a Ramsay laird stole a girl from one of the neighboring clans and forced himself upon her. As he took her, she seized his dirk from his belt and plunged it into her own breast. With her dying words she laid a curse on the Ramsay laird: that his violent, lustful nature should be passed down to his sons, who would war against their siblings, even in the womb."

"But that's arrant superstition! You've been trained as a physician. How can you believe such a thing?"

His eyes met hers. "Because it's true. Every few generations a Ramsay wife has given birth to twins, one strong and hearty, the other a helpless cripple, damaged by the unseen struggle in the womb. My father was one of such a set of twins—the strong one. His twin was saved by the skill of the midwife who stayed on to nurse him, the woman you know as Auld Annie, though he lingered on for only three years before death claimed him."

He paused and took a painful gulp of air. "The pattern repeated again with Charlotte and myself, though by the time of our birth Auld Annie was more experienced, so she was able to keep my sister alive until we were one-and-twenty."

"So *that* was why you apprenticed yourself to the Dark Lord, to heal Charlotte?"

"Yes. As soon as I was old enough to be my own master, I set off to consult the finest physicians in Edinburgh, hoping to find some way to make Charlotte whole. The few who would agree to treat her subjected her to painful therapies that did nothing but increase her suffering. They bled and purged her. The most vigorous cut into her tendons. She begged me to give up my efforts, but I couldn't. I traveled to London alone to see if physicians there had anything more to offer.

"It was a doctor there, Dr. Fox, who told me that because her condition resulted from a supernatural affliction it could only be cured by a therapy of the same nature. He suggested I seek out Mesmer or the Count of Saint-Germain—some man who healed the spirit, not just the body.

"So I went to France, only to find that the Count was

dead and that Mesmer had been driven away by the jealousy of his competitors. It was one of his students who told me of a man who was a greater healer than Mesmer—the heir of an ancient tradition of wisdom, who'd improved his abilities by studying on the Continent 'til he'd also mastered all that the greatest men of science could teach."

"The Dark Lord?" Zoe asked.

"None other. Mind you, I was skeptical when I sought him out. I knew all too well how charlatans played on the hopes of desperate families. But when I arrived at his chateau in Morlaix his behavior reassured me. Unlike a charlatan, he made no grandiose claims. In fact, he applauded my skepticism about mystical powers as evidence of my intelligence, and merely bade me observe him as he went about his cures.

"When I did, what I saw made it impossible for me to doubt his power. For the first time in my life, I felt hope. But when I asked him if he could help my sister, his words were chilling: The Ramsay curse had begun with the Ramsay lust. If I was to see her cured, I must vow myself to lifelong chastity."

Adam stopped and stared silently at the horizon where the last rays of the setting sun flashed over a distant mountain. When he began speaking again his voice was almost a whisper. "I couldn't bring myself to do it. I was so young, just turned one-and-twenty, my own master at last. My passions were strong and easily gratified. I was a wealthy lord—in France— surrounded by women competing to become my mistress. I couldn't give that up. Even after what I'd seen the Dark Lord do, I couldn't make myself believe that I could heal my sister by taking a vow of chastity.

"So I begged the Dark Lord to find some other way. That was when he read me my horoscope. It showed there was no other way. My character was under the sway of four strong planets placed in Pisces. I faced a choice—to redeem myself by self-sacrifice or to suffer. If I wouldn't vow myself to chastity, my sister's case was hopeless and I must leave.

"His words left me devastated. I'd seen him cure cases that seemed far more hopeless than hers. Surely there was something he knew that could improve Charlotte's condition. I bargained with him and told him I would take the vow he demanded of me, but only if he would teach me the healer's art. I offered him a small fortune for his tuition. It took some persuading—he doubted a Pisces could find the strength it would take to become a healer. But I was persistent, and at last he took me on, but only on the condition that I would bring Charlotte to him, so he could examine her in person. To sweeten the bitter pill he'd given me, he said that if I *could* stay chaste for many years I would have made myself into one of the very few of his disciples who were fit to become his heir."

Zoe interrupted him. "So did he teach you, then, the secrets of healing those afflicted like your sister?"

His face had turned to stone. "He began to teach me the rudiments of healing, but by the time my sister had arrived in Morlaix, I sensed him holding back. I told myself it was because he was distracted by working out how he would go about healing her. But I know now it must have been because he knew I was incapable of keeping to my vow of chastity."

"But you told me that you did keep it," Zoe said. "For nine long years."

"Oh yes. I did," he said bitterly. "Starting from that day when I returned from my week of debauchery in Paris to find my sister's corpse. Only that proved to me how right he had been to demand it of me."

Zoe broke in, "And yet, on his deathbed he told you to marry me. He freed you from that vow."

Adam shook his head as if to clear it. "I know. I can only hope that at the end he saw that my atonement had been enough. It has even occurred to me that perhaps he saw that chastity had become too easy for me, and that marriage would force me to find the discipline needed to express the Ramsay passion without causing harm.

"But there is another possibility." His face darkened. "Perhaps he intended me to suffer the fate of my father before me, and father another pair of Ramsay twins, as penitence for what I'd done to Charlotte.

"In any case, after her death, there was no more time for him to teach me anything. The revolutionaries were hunting for me, too, and the Dark Lord had to send me away for my own protection. Though I studied with others, none of them knew what he knew. If we were to have a child afflicted as my sister was, I couldn't offer it any more help than I did Charlotte."

He bit his lip. "*That's* why I don't want children, and why I've struggled to contain my desire for you since we were wed. Much as I long to make you the wife of my body, I can't do it. Not knowing the cost."

Zoe's heart melted. He'd avoided her, not because he loathed her, but out of his need to protect her.

"We live in modern times," she finally replied. "And you've mastered far more of the healing art than most men. Enough to save my life. And besides, you said the curse only strikes some of the Ramsay lairds. Perhaps our children won't fall victim to it."

His lips tightened. "So my father hoped when he married my mother. He, too, was a man of enlightened principles and refused to accept that his life could be ruined by an ancient curse. He didn't tell his wife-to-be about our family history, afraid that she'd laugh at him and call him a superstitious fool. But when she quickened, and the midwife told them that she'd be bearing twins, he was forced to tell her the truth. That was when they had the quarrel that resulted in his leaving Strathrimmon before I was born. He didn't want to leave, but he had no choice."

"Why?"

"My mother drove him away. She insisted she'd never have married him had he been honest with her about the family taint. She vowed that if he stayed she'd never speak to him again and would raise his children to hate him. It was then that he fled to the Continent, hoping to find some medical man who might be able to prevent the disaster from occurring. But he died of a fever in Lausanne only a few months after he left home, and when Auld Annie delivered my sister, she was born twisted and mute, just as the cursed children of the Ramsays have always been."

He'd drawn himself as far away from her as possible on the narrow seat of the gig; his face had that wooden look again. "I should have told you before I convinced you to remain my wife. But I didn't have the courage."

"Yes, you *should* have told me," she repeated.

"I expect that you'll leave me now. But, wrong though it was"—his gray eyes grew fierce—"I've had too much happiness in my brief time with you to regret that I kept my secret. It's only for our children that I mourn."

"You misunderstand me," Zoe objected. "I didn't say that you should have told me about the curse so I could have refused to become your wife. My reasoning is quite different. You should have told me so that I could have laid your fears to rest. Or did you think my character so paltry it couldn't withstand such a challenge?"

"My parents' couldn't."

"Then I think little of their characters." She took a deep breath. "Accursed or not, your father asked no more of your mother than every man asks of the woman that he weds. Every time a man gives his seed to a woman he sets her on a path that may lead to her death in childbed. There's no magic—or doctor's skill—that can prevent it, for that is the way of the world. Eve's curse is far older than yours. So whatever you might have kept from me, I knew what I was risking in wedding you. But even though we know what it means, we women still join ourselves to men. We dare the fates.

That is the power of our love, and it is greater even than your magic."

His face held an expression hard to interpret. "But if you were to bear another cursed pair of twins, how could you not hate me for giving them to you?"

"You insult me when you suggest I couldn't love my own children."

"Even if your child were to be hideous? Lurching about, drooling, unable to speak?"

"What do you take me for? Such a child would need *more* of a mother's love, not less. And you wouldn't hate such a child. You loved Charlotte."

"I did," he said. "And I bowed in reverence before the strength of the spirit that sheltered in her broken body. But I was the only one who did, I, who was her twin. Though she couldn't speak, I could hear her thoughts with my inner ear. As we grew up together, we learned to communicate in our own fashion, in a language of hands and fingers that only we understood. So I learned who she was, beneath the deformity, and I loved her."

"As you would love a child of your own who suffered the same way. As I would, too."

A tear sparkled at the corner of his eye, and she watched with fascination as it fattened, until it grew too heavy for its perch and dropped, spattering the back of his hand.

"I thought I was falling in love with you," he said, with wonder in his voice. "But until this moment I didn't know what it truly meant to love. I'm humbled by what you've taught me."

Had Adam said he loved her?

She was filled with a mix of joy and fear. The temptation to believe it was so strong, but what if his words of love were only the product of this moment of strong emotion? She mustn't let herself be swept away. There would be time, later, to think over what he'd just said, away from his pain-wracked gaze that tore at her heart and made her want to embrace and comfort him. Only then would she dare take out his startling words and examine them, like a jeweler with newly purchased gems alone in a foreign country infested with robbers. But for now, she must just give him the comfort he needed.

"There's one thing more." His voice had taken on a different tone. "Think long and hard before you answer me." She forced herself to meet his eyes, feeling again that ache of love she always felt when they connected.

"If you could love the damaged twin," he said, "and I think you could—nay, I know you could," he added fiercely, "wouldn't you still hate the other child—the one who'd harmed his sibling in the womb and robbed it of a normal life?"

She opened her mouth to say that of course she'd love such a child, just as he would. But stopped. "Who told you that an unborn child could blight the life of its twin?" Her voice was deceptively quiet.

"Everyone. That was the nature of the curse. The lustful Ramsay heir is doomed to wound or kill his sibling in the womb. I heard it all my life, and if I had any question about its truth, the way my mother treated me would have answered it. She couldn't bear to see me any more than she could my sister. *She* knew who had caused Charlotte's misfortune."

"But that's monstrous! How could she blame a babe unborn for such a thing?"

"I sucked the life out of my sister, before she had a chance to grow," he whispered. "That was what Auld Annie told her."

"And she believed it?"

"We all believed it—except Charlotte herself, God bless her. But she was an angel."

"So you've lived all these years believing yourself to be a man who sucks the life from angels?"

He bowed his head and said nothing. The weight of his suffering filled the small carriage.

"I'll give Auld Annie her notice in the morning," Zoe snapped.

"But she's served our family all her life."

"Served them ill, I should say. How could she have said such a wicked thing to a small child? But, of course, it makes sense, if Auld Annie was the midwife, she'd far prefer to blame ancestral curses for your sister's fate than have suspicion fall upon her own clumsiness."

She paused to collect her thoughts. What she said next must be just right or she would lose him. "Adam, no babe in arms has the strength to harm another. A babe at birth is completely helpless, all the more a babe unborn. But you had no younger siblings growing up alongside you, did you?"

"No. I've had little contact with children at all. It was too painful to be around them, knowing I could never look forward to having my own."

"And you never assisted at a childbirth?"

"Physicians never do. Modesty forbids it."

"Then we shall have to remedy that, for it goes a long way to explain why you could believe something so impossible. But there's no excuse for you to continue in such a mistaken belief." She took his hand and squeezed it to give him courage. "I can't control what our children's fate might be. Perhaps you're right and there *is* some family taint that might be passed on. But if we are unlucky, and one of our children should be born suffering some misfortune, I should hope you wouldn't load such a burden of guilt on the tiny shoulders of the child who escaped unhurt. That alone I couldn't forgive. Such a child would need more of your love, not less."

He shuddered again, and she felt the air quiver around him. Then he reached over and embraced her convulsively, holding her tightly to his chest as if clinging to her for his very life. Only after a long time had passed did he finally speak.

"Our children, whatever their fate, will be blessed to have you as their mother."

"Don't make so much of it." She fought to keep her emotions under control. "Any woman with sense would have said the same thing."

But she couldn't keep herself from nestling deeper within his embrace and letting the love that radiated from him engulf her. For it was love. She couldn't doubt it. And she was hungry for it, whatever the cost might be of giving in to her hunger.

His lips met hers and brushed against them gently, in a tender kiss of the heart and of the soul. His kiss asked nothing from her but that she open her heart to him and let him in. She stroked his stubbled cheek gently, to let him know that he was safe, as they clung together in the moonlight, hearts pounding, close in a way that had moved beyond desire.

She'd feared all this time that she was only a burden to him. She'd hated loving him, thinking she wanted so much more from him than she could ever repay. But she'd been wrong. It had been her own pain that hid the truth from her. He needed her desperately and would need as much from her as she might ever take from him.

They were well matched, after all. She could love him safely, without fear.

Chapter 15

Somehow they returned to the manor, though Adam was barely aware of anything but the relief at having his lifelong burden eased off his shoulders. It wasn't gone—no, and it would never be—but the woman he loved had offered her own immense strength to help him bear it.

Fate might still deal harshly with the two of them, yes—but whatever lay in store for them, she would be there with him, soothing the terrors that sprang from his overly imaginative nature with her practical, down-to-earth insights—and the loving heart she tried so hard to keep hidden. He need only look at her ravaged face to understand why. But beneath the tough shell she'd grown to survive the rejection that had formed her personality, her heart beat strongly, and for him. Was it only the power of his spell that made her care for him, or was there something more? Would she have tried so hard to comfort him if her attachment was only the product of his enchantment? If her love wasn't real, would he have found such peace with her?

Whatever the case, he'd give her all that he was capable of and earn the love he'd stolen with his spell. And he would start now, by making her his wife at last. He would worship her with his body and unite with her in the holy rite that would join not just their bodies but their souls.

Somehow, he brought the gig back to the stables and gave instructions to the stable boy who greeted them. Then he took Zoe's warm hand and led her into the manor house, his steps springing with the joy that filled him as he ushered her to her chamber.

When they found themselves alone in its privacy, he hesitated. He was eager to consummate their marriage. But he mustn't assume that she was. With what he'd just told her, she knew now what it would mean for them to do so. She might be having second thoughts. He must not let his own relief in sharing his burden blind him to what that burden would mean for her.

Perhaps he should leave her now and give her time to think, away from his presence and the strong pull that their bodies exerted on each other. Perhaps he, too, needed to be alone, lest his passion to possess her had blinded *him* to some truth.

But the warmth in her deep brown eyes and the tender way she tightened her grasp on his hand as she led him to her bed made it impossible. It was time. It was long past time. Tonight he wouldn't leave her bed.

Not until she knew beyond a shadow of a doubt that she was beautiful and adored. And his.

Adam reclined beside her on one elbow, so close Zoe could smell the musky evidence of his arousal. As she reached toward the top button of her gown and unfastened it with shaking fingers, the fabric fell open, but only for an inch, revealing a tiny triangle of skin. He ignored it. Instead, he reached out and stroked her pitted cheek.

"Your face is beautiful," he said.

She froze. "You don't need to lie to me, to make me want to make love to you."

His fingers reached for her ruined face and stroked the craters that marred it. She went numb as she always did. Why must he do this now, when they had come so close to intimacy?

"Zoe," he said, in the voice he would have used with a tiny child. "I'm telling you the truth. I don't see things the way an ordinary man might see them. Surely you know that by now. I'm a surgeon. My knife has cut through skin of a dead woman's face. I know the name of every muscle that lies beneath this cheek. I've seen the bones."

He stroked her face again, this time with a firmer pressure that forced her to feel his hand against her skin, even through her numbness. "This body is just a shell. I've spent many a night in sleepless vigil, seeking to understand what inhabits our bodies and animates our flesh. I've learned to see with the eye of spirit and to hear with the ear of soul."

He placed his forefinger on her chest. "Can't you understand? It's *you* that I find beautiful—the you who dwells inside this gown of flesh."

She drew in a deep, shuddering breath. "If only I could believe that."

"I will make you believe it," he said gently. "I will make love to the soul that inhabits this body until you cannot doubt it."

She blinked back tears. His gaze had dropped so that his long lashes veiled his eyes. "You aren't the only one with fears," he said. "Though my body may be fair as the world judges such things—" He stopped, choked with emotion. "When my soul meets yours and is fully revealed to you, I fear that you will find *me* hideous."

"How could I? I can sense your inner beauty, too, though I don't have your training, just a woman's heart."

"We men must study long to learn what women know by instinct."

"That instinct tells me you are beautiful inside. Despite *your* scars."

He pulled her close. The wrenching feeling that came with tears rose within her, though whether it was hers or his she couldn't say. She took a convulsive breath, and a moment later, he matched it with one of his own. Then his lips brushed over her ravaged cheek and met hers in a deep and soothing kiss.

She gave herself up to it, searching for him in the touch of his lips, knowing he was there, inside the body he was wearing. His soul called out to her and begged her to join him. She must do so, despite her numbness and her fear.

She *would* be beautiful for him. She must be, if he were to find the courage to show her his deeper, hidden wounds.

When their lips broke contact, his strong hands kneaded the tight muscles of her shoulders, patiently, as if summoning her body to life. His fingers pressed on delicate spots along her neck, hard at first, until the pent-up tension released in a long, slow ache that turned to pleasure. Then they moved on with a touch so light that when he took his hand away, she could still feel his touch reaching her through the empty air.

As he massaged her, waves of energy radiated down her spine, flowing through all of her body, and awakening a new kind of hunger. It was delicate and yet compelling, peaceful and rousing at the same time. Not the gnawing ache of the virgin's sickness, or the desperation brought on by his spell, but something new that she didn't dare to name, which came from a new place, filled with trust instead of madness.

Her fingers fumbled at the next button on her gown, but they were shaking so badly she could barely unfasten it.

"May I help?" he asked.

She nodded and he undid it with fingers not much steadier than her own. As each button gave way, she felt a betraying blush spread over her body. She'd practiced shame too long to be able to entirely prevent it. But as the old familiar feeling rose, crying that he couldn't want her flawed body, an answering voice replied, *His body is just a shell.* And she knew, then, it wasn't her body that attracted him, but what dwelled within. That was what he loved, her inner self, which he saw with that wizard's eye of his.

Finally, when all the buttons were opened, she shrugged out of her gown and turned so he could untie the laces of her stays. When he'd released them, she turned back to face him, covered in only her shift. He reached toward the bed and pulled aside the heavy quilted counterpane, making a place for her. She climbed in, and safe under the shelter of the sheet, she removed her shift.

He sat up and let his legs dangle over the edge of the bed. For a moment she couldn't help but fear he'd changed his mind yet again and that he'd leave her. But the rustling as he removed his shirt and the sound of more buttons coming undone as he loosened his breeches reassured her. He'd only turned away out of respect for her modesty. She huddled more closely under the sheet, torn between a desire to see everything and the fear that she would do something to ruin the encounter.

At last, he climbed into the bed, stretched out beside her, and took her again into his embrace. She felt the hard bands of muscle on his bare arms rippling beneath the tattooed serpents as he drew her close to him. She buried her nose in the wiry hairs on his chest, no longer impeded by cloth. Yet skin-to-skin with him in naked- ness, she grew rigid. As much as she yearned to be his, she couldn't help but fear that something would drive them apart again.

But with that sensitivity that she was coming to

expect from him, he released her and said, "This time will be different. I'm yours now, if you want me."

"I do."

"Then my only wish is to give you pleasure."

"But what of your pleasure? I don't wish to make you suffer."

He laughed. "You're too late. I've been suffering ever since you climbed into my bed in the inn. At least now there's some hope that my suffering, in time, may be relieved."

She welcomed his joking tone. Somehow it made it easier to find her way to him in this perilous state where they had failed to connect before.

"I'd like to give you pleasure, too," she said, "if I knew how. But I didn't attend my mother when she offered to teach me about such matters. I didn't think I'd ever need to know of them."

He smiled. His gray eyes gleamed impishly in the candlelight. "That's probably just as well. I'd like to be the one to teach you about pleasure."

"Did you study that, too, when you learned your magic?"

He shook his head no. "Like you, I didn't think I would need to know of such matters. Until I received the Dark Lord's deathbed command, I expected to live out my life celibate." His long lashes dropped. "I hope I won't disappoint you."

"It's possible, I suppose," Zoe replied, taking up that joking tone that made it easier to be with him. "But if you would but kiss me as you did a moment ago, I imagine I should be able to make the best of my situation."

"Did you like it when I kissed you?" His voice held a note of concern.

"I may have," she replied. "But I should like to try it again to make sure."

A smile blazed up in his eyes and he brought his lips down on hers again. With delicate flutterings of his tongue he drew forth waves of longing as his hand kneaded her breast in rhythm with his kiss, his thumb stroking her nipple until she thought she must explode.

Lost in the sensations he was awakening in her, she barely noticed that his other hand had slipped beneath the sheet that covered her nether regions, until he stroked the inside of her thigh and her awareness shifted downward with a jolt. Tremors wracked her as the long, sweeping motion of his hand lit up her lower body and she found herself opening her legs to let him reach everything.

His hand made its way up her thigh, teasing the crease where her leg met her torso, dancing within her nether curls, as showers of sparks flew up from his fingers. All the while, his tongue, now one with these new and delicious sensations, stroked deeper within her mouth.

As he thrust one probing finger into the cleft in her most private place, she gasped for breath and flinched away, involuntarily. But his finger wouldn't be denied, and after drawing a lazy circle on her thigh with the tip of its nail, he invaded again that most private place of hers, brushing against her nub more gently this time. She shivered. Then he withdrew his hand, releasing her lips from his kiss, and kissed his own finger for a moment, before plunging it beneath the sheets and finding once more the warmth of her woman's cleft.

Now he glided over the delicate point hidden within her most private part, and she felt it awaken as his finger slid deliciously on the slickness it had brought with it. She felt as if she were made of silk—or water. She was breathing faster, responding to his probing touch with slickness of her own, and meeting the joy that was his hand by thrusting her hips. Her need for him grew with each rhythmic stroke of his fingers. She was wet and insistent with the craving he'd ignited. She gasped as her longing overwhelmed her. How could she bear such exquisite longing? Whatever could possibly make it right?

Again, as if reading her innermost thoughts, he pulled away the sheet and sat up. Then he knelt between her legs, with his long, well-muscled torso rearing over her, and she saw once again the braided serpents that coiled around his knotted forearms. As he stroked her in the place where he'd kindled her longing, he guided his rod toward her with his other hand, and she felt it slide against her hungry wetness. It was hard and yet giving, velvety and inexorable. He slowly pushed against her opening, gently but relentlessly, until with one last thrust she felt herself tear open and receive him.

He stopped. "Are you all right?"

She nodded, barely able to speak. The concern and kindness in his face were all she'd ever wished to see. She reached up and pulled him closer to show him without words how much she wanted him, thrusting her hips upward at the same time to drive him deeper, until he had no choice but to plow the furrow he'd made, and know that she was his.

"Zoe," he gasped, as he rocked gently back and forth within her, gently at first and then with increasing ardor. Each deep thrust increased the delicious torment of wanting him. She gave herself to the rhythm of it, until with a cry she yielded to a sudden overwhelming joy, as colors unfolded in waves within her, and she was whole, at last, complete, and his forever.

He paused, giving her time to savor perfection, then with a last few fervent thrusts he convulsed within her and fell forward, embracing her still.

When she'd floated back to earth and opened her eyes, she saw that his were closed and that his face was filled with an expression of rapture. They lay together this way for a long time. Then he gently rolled over on his side and raised himself up on one elbow. "You are my wife now. I hope you will never have reason to regret it."

"I could never regret it. You just made me feel as if I was the most beautiful woman in the world."

"You are," he said.

"It's your magic that has made me so."

"Do you wish me to remove that spell?" His eyes were soft.

"Never. I'm coming to love your magic." She'd come so close to telling him she loved him, too.

He reached over and gently stroked her cheek. His touch sent streamers of light shooting up from her skin.

He'd done what he'd promised. He'd made her know her beauty. She sighed with happiness and snuggled more closely against him.

She was his wife. She would remain with him. The long uncertainty was over.

Chapter 16

Adam dismissed Auld Annie the next morning. He did it as gently as he could, assuring her that she would receive a generous pension and a modern stone cottage located in one of the more distant villages of his holdings. She attempted to wheedle him into reversing his decision, but when he held firm, she muttered that nothing better could be expected of a curse-born bairn than that he send his aged nurse away to die alone. At that, Adam stood up and left her with a curt command that she pack up her things and be out of the manor by noon.

He couldn't believe the sense of relief he felt when he knew she was gone. He walked up and down the long corridors of the manor house, feeling as if, for the first time, the air he breathed there wasn't tainted. Silently, he blessed Zoe for her calm and earthy good sense.

She'd given him the balance that he needed. He wished he had something as valuable to give her in return.

When he'd asked her what he could give her as a morning gift, she'd replied, "You've given me the greatest gift already, by teaching me to believe in magic."

But he wanted to give her more. What would she value? Not the gowns and jewels most men gave women they loved. Those only adorned the body, but he wished to enrich her soul.

She had asked that he rebuild the conservatory. So he would, and when it was done he would fill it with the choicest flowers, to brighten the short days of winter, even as she would brighten his long nights. But that lay in the future. What could he do for her now that would show her how much he loved her?

Then it struck him. She'd mentioned more than once how she longed to meet her father. Perhaps he could grant her that. Now that she was Lady Ramsay with a generous estate of her own and a noble husband, perhaps the mysterious duke *would* be willing to acknowledge her. Adam would do all he could to make it so, but first he must find out who the man was.

But of course, to do that he would have to apply to Isabelle, as only she could give him his answer. At that thought he almost gave up his plan. But that would be unworthy of him. If his gift were to mean anything it should cost him something. So he made his way to the office and wrote a carefully worded letter to Zoe's mother in which he informed her of their wedding and asked her, now that her daughter was wed, if she would be so kind as to reveal to him the identity of her child's father.

But as he was sealing it, he had second thoughts. The truth about his wife's birth might prove unpalatable. It wasn't likely her father was really a duke, and even if he were, having not acknowledged her, he might wish to have no contact with his daughter. If that were the case, Adam would have to keep what he'd found from Zoe, so as not to cast a cloud over their newfound happiness. He had no wish to do that. Having just shared all his secrets with her, he had no desire to keep anything new from her. So he set the letter aside. He'd find something less risky to give her.

As spring turned into summer, Adam continued to bless the Dark Lord for giving him such a treasure as his wife. With Zoe's support, he was able to deal with it all—MacAlpin's grumbles, the almost constant drizzle, and even the awareness that grew with each passing day of how badly he'd neglected his patrimony.

He'd thought that he'd never again be able to enjoy life at Strathrimmon, haunted as it was by his sister's memory. But now, when he spent his days exploring his holdings with his wife by his side, he saw them through her eyes, and that gave everything a freshness that made him feel what a blessing it was to own these green, productive acres.

She'd been as good as her word about aiding him in his other work. When he'd begun to make weekly rounds to visit the ailing in the parish, she'd begged him to let her assist him. He'd been delighted to find that her innate practicality kept her from turning away from ugly wounds or growing faint at the sight of blood.

Later, after they'd returned to the hall, she would ask him probing questions. Soon they were poring together over his choicest medical books. He was surprised how much pleasure he took in using his medical skills with her by his side. It was so much easier, now that he need no longer face the hopeless cases alone.

At home, Zoe's pleasure in finding herself the mistress of his ancestral manor shone forth more clearly with each passing week, now that she was confident she would be spending the rest of her life as Lady Ramsay. Hesitantly, she'd begun to suggest ways in which the older rooms might be made warmer and more home-like, though at first she'd expressed concern about putting too heavy a strain upon his purse. But once he'd assured her that his wealth, left almost untouched during the years of his travels, was sufficient for far more than the modest changes she proposed, she began to give herself full rein.

She hired new maids and set them to washing the walls and polishing the woodwork, and called in a man to see to the smoking chimneys. She pulled down the moldering old hangings in the principal rooms and replaced them with brighter ones that let in more sun and brought out the beauty of the old wood. Though much work still remained to be done, Adam could hardly connect the cheerful home he walked through now with the somber, holland-draped chambers of his blighted childhood.

Zoe had even found a local man who was able to turn some sketches he'd done of his sister into a painting that managed, somehow, to capture the way that she'd looked. Zoe insisted he have it opulently framed, and it hung now in the long gallery, proudly claiming for his sister the rightful place that should have been hers during her lifetime

It was after that, that he sent Isabelle the letter he'd hidden away, the one inquiring about the identity of Zoe's father. His wife had given him back his family. He would do the same for her. Whoever had sired her had given birth to a treasure. Ramsay must let the man know it and bring about the reunion Zoe had longed for all her life.

As the weeks passed, his anxiety that his city-bred wife would be unhappy living in so remote a district faded. She showed no desire to leave Strathrimmon, save for the visits they made to the neighboring gentry. Though it pained him that she had only the few gowns she'd brought with her, which even he, unworldly as he was, knew did not befit her new rank, Zoe told him not to worry. There were trunks full of beautiful fabrics stored away in the attics. And sure enough, she found a bolt of sea green silk among his mother's abandoned things, and with the skill he was coming to realize she brought to everything she did, she turned it into a gown that was a masterpiece. It showed off her slim figure to perfection and brought out the beauty of her deep brown eyes. She wore it often, and he never tired of admiring her in it.

He vowed he would take her to London the next winter, where she could order a whole new wardrobe and jewels. When she tired of that, they'd visit all the best showrooms and choose new furniture with which to brighten the rooms of the old manor house. They'd bring home comfortable sofas and chairs, and the latest prints, to say nothing of new linens, and papers for the walls.

Perhaps they would buy new furnishings for the nursery, too. With the amount of time they had spent in each other's arms over these past months a child must be on the way. At that thought, he stopped, feeling a quiver of superstitious dread. His father's plans to brighten his home had been so similar—and had foundered so tragically during his mother's pregnancy. But he wasn't his father, and Zoe had proved time and again how different she was from his gently raised, oversensitive mother.

He stretched his long legs as he strode down the ancestral corridors, past the conservatory, where Zoe was busy tending the seedlings she would set out in the garden in another week, when the threat of frost was past. It was still not completely finished—workmen being what they were—but he was glad she was able to use it even in its current unfinished state. Given her love for flowers, perhaps they might make a brief excursion to Glasgow later this fall when the harvest was done. There they could find some botanical prints with which to brighten up the saloon. He relished the thought of such improvements. There was so much for the two of them to do together, here in his home, and he took such unexpected pleasure in doing it.

He'd never known that ordinary life could contain such richness. Only the other night Zoe had asked him when he planned to go to Iskeny and claim the Dark Lord's heritage. The answer that had leapt to his lips had been "Never."

He had all he'd ever wanted here. He'd learned, at last, to find happiness in his own heritage here on these Ramsay lands. The thought of receiving the Final Teaching no longer moved him, for he no longer hungered to know the secrets of the universe. He was satisfied to explore the simple things he'd ignored for so long, the human things.

But of course, some day he would have to go to Iskeny. He owed his teacher that. But he was grateful that, in his wisdom, the Dark Lord had given him this year and a day before he must take on the ancient burden, and even more grateful for the most precious gift his teacher had given him, his bride.

Adam's reverie was broken by the sound of a vehicle clattering to a standstill outside the manor. He wondered which of their neighbors was dropping by to pay a call. He made a point of being at home to everyone from the neighborhood who might seek him out, as he intended to rebuild the connections his mother had severed with the local families. As he made his way down the staircase, he heard a woman's raised voice outside. Perhaps the mistress of the neighboring estate had come to pay a call. But the vehicle he glimpsed through the window was a rough cart such as a farmer might use to go to market. Their visitor must be one of the local people needing doctoring, not a member of their local circle of polite society.

But closer inspection revealed that their visitor was not a member of *any* polite society. For the woman swathed in diaphanous rose muslin with her hair done up in the latest London fashion, who was engaged now in a loud and bitter altercation with the stolid farmer who drove the cart, was none other than Zoe's mother, Isabelle.

Adam's throat constricted. When he'd sent her the letter asking about Zoe's father less than two weeks ago, it had never occurred to him she'd respond to it by paying them a visit. But she had, so he must do his best to welcome her.

He swallowed hard and strode outside to greet her, just as Isabelle ended her exchange with the farmer by disdainfully extracting two coins from her purse and flinging them at his feet. She sprang from the box on which she'd been perched, and, as her feet touched the ground, pulled herself to her full height. After adjusting her gown, she swept majestically toward the door. Like an automaton, Adam opened it for her.

"These peasants!" she cried. "Because I am dressed *à la mode* and have the air of the Town they think they can cheat me, I who was born in the countryside and know all their ways. *Hein!* That one has learned his lesson. I paid him half a crown and nothing more. The cost of the journey was ruinous enough. Do you know what they charge to ride on the mail coach? It is a *scandale*."

She held up her reticule and with a flourish turned it upside down. "See, I have not a penny left. That robber has taken my last farthing." Then lowering her long lashes over her childish blue eyes, she continued, "But surely you don't wish to hear my sad complaints. It must be enough that I am here." She adjusted her face into a dazzling smile, as wide as it was insincere, and then, as if she'd just realized to whom she was speaking, opened her arms wide to embrace Adam, murmuring, "*Mon beau-fils!*"

My son-in-law.

"*Belle-mère,*" he responded woodenly, though with the utmost politeness.

But welcoming her didn't come easily. The lush, musky perfume she wore nauseated him. He could barely keep himself from turning away from the rounded, childlike face she turned up toward him, its look of calculation barely disguised.

"I trust I am not intruding on the nest of the birds of love?" she said archly. "But ever since I learn that my only child is wed—and to a lord!—I have been longing to see her in her new *ménage*. And such a beautiful *ménage* it is!" She craned her neck toward the high, groined ceiling of the entranceway, then turned to inspect the portraits that lined the stairwell. "Those must have cost a pretty penny! But of course," she added, in a tone of sudden uncertainty, "perhaps I'm not welcome in your so distinguished home?"

Zoe had joined them in the entry hall, and hastened to reassure her. "Of course you're welcome, Mama. But why didn't you send ahead to tell us you were coming? We would have sent the coachman to meet you at the mail stage."

"Pah, you know I can't write, and even if I could, I wished to surprise you. For perhaps you would not be so happy to see your poor mother. When Eugenie Marvelle's daughter married the earl, *her* protector, he would never allow her mother or her brothers into their home."

"Well, that isn't at all surprising, since Eugenie's boys were the most accomplished cracksmen in London. He must have feared for his plate. But surely you didn't expect me to turn you out after you'd come all this way to see me."

"I did not know," Isabelle admitted plaintively. "I wasn't sure that you would welcome me after what happened the last time we were together."

She favored Adam with a telling glare before turning back to her daughter. "You were so vexed with me, were you not? You didn't trust your mother, though I had your best interests at heart. Though, as usual, all your worries were for naught. All has worked out for the very best, though why that should be is a wonder, when you will never listen to your mother. Still, what a coup it is that you, who everyone thought must end up as nothing, so ugly, and with no charm or address, may style yourself a baroness!" Isabelle smiled as happily as if she'd arranged the match herself.

No wonder his wife had been convinced she was unlovable! Adam felt a strong urge to set Isabelle straight about her daughter's beauty and charm, but thought better of it. There was no point in wrangling with her now. So he said only, "I must apologize for my rudeness during our previous encounter. Please accept my assurance that while you are under my roof you will be treated with nothing but the respect that is due to my wife's mother."

"It is of no import." Isabelle waved one well-ruffled arm. "All has worked out exactly as I'd hoped." She took a step nearer to her daughter. "Can you imagine,

Zoe, my surprise when I received a letter from your husband? I was shocked. I was amazed. Such politeness, one might almost have thought him a Frenchman. What a gentleman he is to know what is due to the mother who raised his wife."

Zoe shot him a questioning look. "You wrote to her?"

He nodded.

Zoe's face showed the confusion he would have expected her to feel, but before she could ask him why, her mother explained, "He wished me to tell him the secret you have pestered me about all these years. About your father. But that I would tell to no one but yourself. So I am here!"

"To tell me who my father really was?" Zoe's hopeful look was almost painful to behold. Adam hoped the truth wouldn't come as too much of a disappointment.

"Of course." Isabelle waved one plump wrist airily. "Did I not just say I would? That is why I came to visit you. I knew you would wish to know it, though that MacMinn! He warned me not to come. To hear him talk you would think I was committing a crime to go visit my only child, and she a new bride. 'Lord Ramsay won't put up with the likes of you,' says he. 'His Lordship will throw you out on your backside if you impose on his hospitality.' "

Isabelle came up for air. "He is as bad as you, Zoe, for always expecting the worst. But I told him, 'My daughter knows what's due to the mother who has sacrificed everything to make her what she is today. And if she's too proud to welcome me I'll just turn around and come back home, though how I should do such a thing, when all my money has been spent on the journey, is more than I can say. But of course, you are rich now, Zoe. The cost of a mail coach can mean nothing to *you*."

Isabelle rambled on, exclaiming at the grandeur of their home, the extent of their lands, and even the handsomeness of her daughter's new husband, but to Adam, the rest of her words might as well have been spoken in the language of the barbarous Turks, for after she had so casually dropped the name MacMinn, he could hear nothing else.

Isabelle knew MacMinn. How was that possible?

Brutally he interrupted the flow of her conversation. "This MacMinn you mentioned. Is he a tall man with a kind of hangdog air about him?"

"Of course. He has never got over the pain in his heart when I refused to marry him," Isabelle replied airily. "But a woman like me can't marry her coachman. Surely he should understand such a thing."

Adam struggled to clear his mind. "MacMinn is your coachman?"

"Not now. But in the past, when I could pay." She smiled her dazzling smile. "And now that my daughter has married so well, who is to say? Perhaps he may be again. But even when I don't pay him, he still comes by to visit us, though he is always so tiresome, shaking his finger and telling me to mend my ways—when my ways are so useful and my daughter has never wanted for anything."

Adam cut her off again as the implications of what

she'd just said crashed in on him. "Did MacMinn tell you he saw your daughter wed?"

"Of course. When I received your letter, I thought it was some jest, some—how you say—practical joke. But MacMinn said it was true and swore on the Holy Book that he'd been there to see it done. How I scolded him for keeping such a thing secret from me, the mother, who should have been the first to know!"

Adam bit his lip, willing himself not to give in to the horrid suspicion that was growing in his mind. Mac-Minn *might* have come from the Dark Lord, just as he'd claimed. He *had* known the feather code. That he knew Isabelle didn't mean that he hadn't come from Iskeny. Isabelle had known the Dark Lord, too, or why else would she have given him control over her daughter? Perhaps MacMinn had made her acquaintance back at the time when that bargain had been struck. Perhaps the Dark Lord had sent MacMinn to visit Isabelle so he could keep an eye on his ward. Given Isabelle's pro-clivities, that wouldn't have been that surprising.

But as much as Adam wanted to believe that this was true, there was another, more obvious explanation for what had happened. And if it were true, Isabelle's pre-tense that she hadn't known about their wedding until now must be another of her lies.

He fixed Isabelle with his steeliest gaze. Pronounc-ing each word as if the slightest unevenness might cause it to explode, he asked, "Before MacMinn told you we were wed, when had you seen him last?"

"Oh, weeks before." Isabelle waved her hand. "The same day that you and Zoe began your journey north.

Oh, how he raged when he learned I had let my daughter go off with that terrifying Lord Ramsay!" She gave a tinkling laugh, "The names that he called me, *par foi!* But he was singing a different song when he told me you were wed. No longer does he fear you. Now you are the best husband my daughter could ever wish. It all turned out so well, that even *he* had to admit it. You are married to a lord, Zoe, and I am here, welcomed by my new son-in-law with nothing but smiles and happiness."

Adam staggered back against the wall. There was no way to deny it. MacMinn had not come from the island. He had come from London, direct from Isabelle. And the message he'd brought—the deathbed wish that had impelled Adam to wed—the Dark Lord hadn't sent it.

Zoe shot him a sympathetic look as she saw the impact that her mother's casual chatter was having on him, but he couldn't bear to meet her eyes.

It hadn't been the Dark Lord's will that they marry. Zoe had not been the old man's final gift to him—or his gateway to the Final Teaching. Nor had there been some reason known only to the Dark Lord why he should forgive his sister's murderer. Or break his vow of chastity.

He'd taken Zoe to wife at *Isabelle's* behest. He'd been tricked into it—and so easily—blinded by his raging desire for her. He had so rejoiced in the message MacMinn had brought him, thinking only of having Zoe in his arms that he had ignored the subtle clues that should have revealed the fraud.

Adam turned on his heel and lunged toward the

doorway, stumbling against it in his haste to leave the hall whose air seemed to have been replaced by a noxious gas that left him choking.

But the truth went with him. There was no escape. Isabelle's minion had tricked him into marriage, made him violate his vow of chastity—that vow his teacher had never released him from. Now he could never become the Dark Lord's heir.

But that wasn't the worst of it. With what he'd learned over the previous weeks, Adam could have found a way to live on happily just as he was. If it weren't for something else—the thing that threatened to turn all the happiness he had found with his wife into dust and ashes.

How could Zoe not have known?

He tried not to think of it, but his mind kept going back to the hour of his wedding. One thing stood out, now that he knew the truth. *She'd recognized MacMinn.* That's why her eyes had grown so wide when she had seen him enter her chamber. It was only because Adam had been so blinded by his desire that he'd told himself she'd reacted that way because the Dark Lord's messenger looked like such a beggar.

And later, when Zoe had refused to give her assent to the blacksmith's question, MacMinn had given her some sign with his hands. Adam had told himself it must be more of the Dark Lord's magic. But it was all too clear now what had really happened. It hadn't been anyone's magic that had compelled Zoe to take that fatal vow, just some secret signal from her mother's coachman.

Had she only been pretending all along that it was

his spell that made her wed him? Adam's heart broke as he got his answer. She must have been—to keep him from discovering MacMinn's ruse. He should have paid more attention when his teacher said that a spell of that kind couldn't compel its subject to do something against their will.

But if she had pretended that he'd made her wed him, and pretended, too, that painful longing to be his bride, what about her love for him—the love she never put into words, no matter how much he told her that he loved her? He'd always been so certain she must feel it. He'd excused her silence by telling himself it wasn't her nature to be demonstrative that way.

But maybe he'd been wrong. Perhaps she had feigned it all—to make the best of the marriage she'd been trapped in by her mother's ruse. Perhaps his joy in their love had been only one more self-delusion.

You will become a victim or a savior, his teacher had told him back when first he'd erected his nativity. But Adam had been so determined to become a savior he hadn't considered the other possibility. Blinded by his Pisces self-deception he'd become Isabelle's victim— two times over.

All he could do now was pray with what little faith he had left that he hadn't been Zoe's, too. Zoe, whose love he'd thought had rescued him.

Chapter 17

Her mother sank down on the sofa in Zoe's dressing room, stroked the upholstery appreciatively, and yawned like an overfed cat. "You *have* done well for yourself, *ma petite*," she said. "Whoever would have thought it?"

Zoe made no reply. It was taking all her energy not to let her irritation show. If only her mother had waited a little longer before testing Adam's patience with a visit.

How typical that it had been his kindness that had put him into this situation. He'd known what it would mean to her to find out who her father was, and to that end had put aside his disgust for her mother. But clearly, his rudeness when face-to-face with her had taught him he'd overestimated his ability to tolerate her presence and all its inescapable associations.

Had he told Zoe what he intended before he'd written to her mother, she would have gently warned him against it, just as she'd discouraged him from taking her to London in the near future. They were so happy here. Why risk it?

If only her mother would stop talking long enough to let Zoe go find her husband, wherever he had fled, and soothe the conflicted emotions Isabelle's arrival had provoked. But her mother was just getting started and showed no sign of slowing down. She was enjoying far too much her new role as the mother of a baroness.

That the man who had made her new status possible couldn't stand her didn't enter into it. Even when Adam had bolted from the reception hall, her mother had merely waved one hand and said, "Men!" in that same tone of amused exasperation one used when a puppy had disgraced itself on the carpet. Then she'd demanded that Zoe give her a tour of the manor, and after her daughter had led her through the principal rooms, she'd followed her into this, her dressing room, and after examining its furnishings as if considering their purchase, plumped down on the room's most comfortable chair.

"Now, *ma petite*, comes the difficulty," Isabelle said, raising one beautifully manicured finger in warning. "If you do not attach your husband firmly he will soon lose interest and wander to other women. There is no way to prevent it. That is the story of the wife. But now that you are no longer *une vierge*, I may teach you some helpful—how you say—tricks, so you may hold on to him a little longer. A wife must not be lazy, no! Not if she is to have any hope of keeping her man faithful. She must work twice as hard as a woman like myself. She has not the advantage that a mistress commands, for she cannot threaten to leave him if his attentions flag."

Zoe bit her tongue. There was no point in starting an argument with her mother now. "I appreciate your concern, but I need no instruction in pleasing my husband."

"So you may think, now, while still you are a bride, but in a few more weeks when the novelty of your innocence wears off? Then perhaps you will wish you had taken up my offer. I wish only the best for you, *ma petite*." Her mother reached out and took Zoe's cheek between thumb and forefinger, and pinched it in a well-remembered gesture—one she'd always hated.

"But perhaps I misunderstand," her mother added. "Perhaps you do not *wish* him to be faithful. You *are* his wife. So even when he strays, you will always be Lady Ramsay. Perhaps there is no need to keep him captivated? That must be it! There can be little pleasure to be found in tolerating the embraces of a man so ill tempered as your husband." She shook her head sagely, setting the golden curls to quivering. "Perhaps you will be glad when he looks elsewhere for his satisfaction?"

"No," Zoe said, far more forcefully than she'd intended. "I'm quite happy with my husband and he with me. We need not discuss the matter."

Her mother regarded her with a calculating look. "So, that is the problem, eh? You are above your mother now, are you, my fine Lady Ramsay? You are embarrassed that I have come to discommode your oh-so-haughty husband? If that is it, it is of no import. I shall stay this night only and walk to the village tomorrow to meet the mail coach. It was with no thought of my own pleasure that I journeyed for seven days without stop to reach you. Such is the sacrifice that a mother will make for her child. And now that I have found you well, I shall rejoice and journey seven more days to rid you of my presence."

"Mother, stop it! You know you're welcome in my home."

Her mother raised one languid hand to her brow. "It is such a thankless task to raise a child. But I must be grateful that you do not throw me out into the street, for in truth I have spent my last farthing paying that robber of a peasant, and if you aren't generous to me, the next you will hear of your poor mother is that she has been taken up for debt. I have been far too concerned about your fate these past months to waste my time finding the rent. Not when my daughter had been kidnapped by the Dark Lord!"

So *that* was really why she'd come. No surprise. "How much do you need?" Zoe asked.

"A mere trifle of two hundred pounds would see me clear."

"That is more than I have at hand. I will have to speak to my husband about it."

Her mother sighed. "I had heard this new husband of yours is very rich. Can he not spare a little for your poor mother, who has never had any thought but for your happiness? Even a hundred pounds would satisfy that vulture of a landlady for some months to come and leave me enough to buy some pretty things."

"I will do what I can, Mama. You can rely on it."

"I am glad you know your duty to the mother who raised you and made so many sacrifices for you." Her parent stood and stretched again, giving a smaller yawn to indicate that, having attained her object, she considered the interview over. Zoe led her to the room she had ordered prepared for her and then fled to her own chamber.

Zoe had scarcely had time to loosen her stays and lie back on her bed, when the door from the adjoining chamber was flung open and her husband exploded into the room.

At the sight of him, her heart lifted, as it always did when he rejoined her after an absence. She sat up and opened her arms to welcome him into her embrace. But he stood, rigid, in the doorway and made no move to join her. As she took in his expression, the warmth in her heart drained away. He was even angrier now than he'd been when he had so abruptly left her alone with her mother. The compassion she'd felt for him earlier, at the thought of what he must feel when confronting all that her mother represented, flipped over into annoyance.

"Surely you can put up with my mother for a few short days," she said, hiding her dismay behind an air of cool unconcern. "You knew whose daughter I was when you decided to wed me."

The look her husband turned on her was almost feral. "Yes, I *did* know whose daughter you were when I married you. But I had forgotten how cunning she was and the lengths to which she would go to get what she wanted."

"There's no reason to make everything into a tragedy. All she wants now is some money with which to keep her creditors at bay. That's nothing new. She's always depended on me for money when her own runs out. But there's little cunning involved."

Adam gazed at her with a look of stark incomprehension. Then he pounded one fist on the bed. "By God, Zoe, I can't bear it any longer. I must know the truth. Were you in it with her all along?"

"In it with her?" she repeated. What could he be talking about? "Not at all. I had no idea she was coming to visit. It was *you* who sent her that letter and you'd said nothing to me about it or I would have told you not to. But I *will* give her some money. You've been more than generous with me, and I can easily spare some of my pin money to give to her."

"That's not what I meant." His voice was a growl. "You recognized MacMinn at our wedding."

"But what has that to do with anything?"

"*Everything!* Has this all been a charade? Were you just pretending to be under the spell?" His eyes pried into hers and then he lunged toward her, so that his lips were only inches from her own. Surely he was not going to kiss her, as angry as he was? But just as she thought their lips must meet, he pulled away from her with one swift movement that affected her like a slap.

"You must have known MacMinn came straight from London. And yet you said nothing about his being there at our wedding, and put on such a show of pretending I had tricked *you* into marriage."

His words made no sense." Of course you tricked me into marriage, but what of it? I've long ago forgiven you."

But he had not forgiven her for whatever it was he now accused her of. His hands, balled into fists, pressed against the rough fabric of the homespun breeches that clad his long thighs, as if he were only barely restraining himself from using them.

"You had no need to become a governess," he said bitterly. "Had you gone on the stage, you might have become the greatest actress of the age."

"Adam, what *are* you talking about?"

"MacMinn." He said the word as if biting into it.

MacMinn? She tried to make sense of what he was telling her. What had her mother's coachman to do with anything?

But then she remembered: It had been only after her mother had mentioned MacMinn there in the hall that Adam had turned pale and then, a moment later, quitted them so rudely. Before that, he had treated Isabelle with politeness, strained though it might have been. But no sooner had he'd heard her mention the coachman's name than he'd undergone that transformation back into the angry man who'd first claimed her in her mother's drawing room. But why?

Adam's voice still held that furious note she'd forgotten it was capable of as he went on berating her. "MacMinn was at our wedding, I saw what passed between you."

Her heart sank. Had she been living in a dream these last few weeks when she'd come to believe her husband had found a way to love her, despite who her mother was and what she'd done?

It must be so. For a man who loved her wouldn't speak to her this way. He wouldn't snarl at her and spit his words like this. Tears sprang to her eyes, but she forced them back. She wouldn't let him see how much it hurt to learn she'd been deluded when she'd thought herself loved and safe.

Turning the energy of his attack back on him, she retorted, "I don't know what you're talking about. Of course I recognized MacMinn at our wedding. But I was under your spell and thought I was dreaming. If anyone was deceived that night, it was me!"

"But you must have known that MacMinn came from your mother. You'd just seen him a few days before. You must have known what he was up to, and yet you went along with it. You agreed to marry me after he gave you that secret sign."

She remembered it now. In that dream that had turned out to be real where Adam had begged her to wed him, she *had* held back until MacMinn had made that small gesture he used to make when she was small and her mother would lose her temper with her, the gesture that meant she shouldn't worry, that he'd take care to see that she was safe.

Woodenly she replied, "What if I did. I thought I was dreaming. And when I realized he was real, and not a figment of my imagination, the following morning, I assumed he must have followed us, after you came and wrested me from my mother. It was just the kind of thing he'd do, and I was grateful for it. Do you begrudge me that there was someone at our wedding who knew me and wished me well?"

"But once we were wed, you said nothing to me about having seen him. You kept it secret."

She had. A wave of cold swept over her as she remembered the way, the next morning, MacMinn had cautioned her not to mention their meeting to her new husband. But even so, there was no reason for Adam to be so furious about it. "Why should I have mentioned it? I didn't know how you would respond. I had little reason to trust you, then. Your moods had been so uncertain." *As they were now.* "And once you had revealed how you'd tricked me with your spell, I had other things to think about."

Adam bit his lip. "You make it all sound so reasonable." His tone was wistful. "I could almost believe you were telling the truth. But if you are, then we're both your mother's victims. For if I tricked you, it was only because her minion tricked me first. It was he who bade us wed."

"But wasn't it the Dark Lord's will that we should marry?"

"The Dark Lord's will," he said bitterly, "conveyed in his dying words, brought to me by your mother's coachman, MacMinn."

"But how could MacMinn have brought you the Dark Lord's message? He'd just been in London with us, and the Dark Lord was on his island, here in Scotland."

Adam's voice, when he answered, sounded as if it

was coming from the bottom of a deep pit. "That's just it. MacMinn didn't come from the island. He came from your mother, in London."

It finally dawned on her what he was telling her and when it did, Zoe's blood stopped moving in her veins. When she found the courage to speak, her voice was a croaking whisper. "Then it *wasn't* the Dark Lord's will that we should wed."

He shook his head slowly. "No. Never. Only Isabelle's."

"How you must hate me. But Adam. I didn't know."

"You must have guessed." His lustrous eyes were filled with agony.

"I never thought about it." How could she, overwhelmed as she'd been by the virgin's sickness which had made her love him so desperately he need not have used a spell to make her wed him? But she wouldn't make excuses to him now. Nothing she could say could make right what he'd lost.

But for her mother's ruse her husband would have become the next Dark Lord, with all the powers he had longed for. Instead he had abandoned his quest so close to its end, when they were almost on his dying master's doorstep, breaking his vow of chastity by making her his wife—devoting himself dutifully to the difficult task of making himself love a woman as flawed as she was, and doing it because it was what he'd thought his teacher had ordained.

The hopelessness she saw in his eyes was all too explainable. There was no reason for him to love her any longer. She wouldn't even ask it. He'd lost too much by marrying her. All she could do was acknowledge the injury that had been done to him. She must not ask for his pity, or make excuses for herself. He'd suffered too much at her mother's hands.

"It's over then," she said. Her voice sounded as if it were coming from a distant mountain top. "I won't hold you to your vows to me."

"Is that what you wish?" His pain resonated through her, linked as she still was to him by her love. It made her want to throw herself into his arms and comfort him, though she must not. Her own pain screamed she'd been a fool to give up her protective numbness. She must pray she could find it again. She could only go on living if she never let herself feel anything again.

She had married him in a dream, and he had loved her in a dream. Now it was time to awaken.

Chapter 18

"**Y**our husband is a very grouchy man," her mother observed. "But perhaps that is the kind of man to please a woman with your temperament."

It was the next morning. Zoe sat with her mother in the small breakfast room, watching in a state of stunned misery as Isabelle greedily devoured a full Scottish breakfast of porridge, bacon, and kippers. She envied the way her mother could ignore the stench of catastrophe that pervaded every corner of what had been, only the day before, such a happy home.

She opened her mouth to reply, but her words were cut short by the sound of footsteps in the hallway. Adam entered. He'd donned his heavy many-caped greatcoat and carried his serpent-headed cane. Once again, he was dressed for travel.

"Good morning," he said coolly to them both. "I hope you slept well."

How could she ever sleep well again without him by her side?

The words rose to her lips, but she didn't speak them. He would despise any words of love from her, now that he knew the truth about their marriage.

He paused to allow her to reply but when she didn't, he went on in a voice even more brittle and formal, "Zoe, may I beg the honor of a word with you?"

She nodded and excused herself from the breakfast table.

He led her as far as possible away from where her mother sat in the breakfast room, into the conservatory, brushing past the table full of geranium cuttings in their cheerful terra-cotta pots.

He began, "I expect you slept no better than I did."

"I slept as usual," she lied. Only the way he raised his eyebrows ever so slightly suggested that he recognized her falsehood.

She busied herself in removing a dead leaf from one of the blooms, unwilling to think about the torment she'd felt lying alone in her bed the previous night. She couldn't bear to see the coldness in his eyes and know they would never again glow with the warmth that had given her such joy in the weeks they'd just spent together.

Had it only been yesterday that she'd stood in this very spot, potting the rooted shoots, and thinking what a fine show they'd make next summer? He'd come up from behind her, unnoticed, as she'd tended to the plants, and there had been that wonderful moment when the scent of the flowers had mixed with his earthy musk, before he'd enfolded her into the most tender of embraces.

She savagely pinched off a long branch filled with blossoms though there was nothing wrong with it. Why did she have to feel this love he no longer wanted?

"*I* didn't sleep at all," he said. "I spent the night in thought." He picked up the branch she'd let fall onto the slate-topped table and examined it before adding, "Whatever the reason for our marriage, it's too late to have it set aside. It was done according to the law, before witnesses, and fully consummated."

She flinched at his choice of words, so cold and legalistic.

"Zoe, do you still care for me?"

His words took her by surprise. But she'd had hours to practice hardening herself to her emotions. She spoke in a tone as cold as his. "You no longer have any reason to love me. I can't afford the luxury of feeling anything for you."

A quiver ran through his lips, then his face hardened. "I see. But of course you no longer need to pretend to love me." His eyes squeezed shut for a moment. Their lids were heavy and reddened. "If you wish to live apart from me, I'll make you a generous allowance. I ask only that when you find some other lover you be discreet."

"If I wasn't discreet you could divorce me. Perhaps that would be the best way to end this."

"Why?" he asked savagely. "It would restore nothing

we've lost and only add more scandal to my family's name."

"So you would prefer a separation? Will you send me away?"

"My preferences have little to do with the current situation. I must play the hand I've been dealt."

"But what if I don't wish to separate?"

"Then you may remain here as my wife." Adam continued, his voice deceptively calm, "I will never again mention the circumstances we became aware of yesterday. There would be no point. What happened can't be changed. Perhaps it would be best if you did remain here, at least for the next few months. After all, you may already be carrying my heir—or a pair of Ramsay twins."

A shiver passed through her. How fitting it would be if she completed the havoc that had overtaken their lives by continuing the family curse.

"I vowed to protect you," he went on. "It's the only vow I haven't yet betrayed. So if you choose to remain, you may be confident that I'll treat you with all the respect due to a wife."

Her heart contracted within her breast. He'd remain true to their vows out of duty, despite the fact that he could feel nothing for her now but cold disdain. Was she supposed to feel gratitude for that? It maddened her, how casually he proposed to turn the home that should have been a place of safety into her prison.

Relentlessly he continued. "If you are increasing, our child—or children—will be raised with no knowledge of the trickery that led to their conception. I don't wish them to grow up, as I did, knowing their parents were estranged even before their birth."

Despair coursed through her. How could their children *not* know? Adam might have forgotten how sensitive children were to the unspoken currents around them, but Zoe knew better. Their children would grow up feeling keenly how unwanted they were. Her heart broke. She had felt such joy, when she'd thought herself quickening, thinking she'd be able to give her children the gift of being born, loved, and wanted. But it wasn't to be.

She brought one hand up to her belly, as if to protect the helpless creatures who might be growing there, and said, "If I am increasing, I should prefer a total separation."

She wouldn't let him fill her children with a wish that they had never been born. She might have to live without love for the rest of her life, but her children would be loved and valued, if only by herself.

As what she said sank in, Adam froze into an ungainly posture, as if suddenly paralyzed. She saw his tongue flick out to moisten his lips as if he were about to speak, but he remained silent. Then he turned abruptly and paced up and down the length of the conservatory, his boots crunching on stray bits of debris that littered the floor.

When he stopped, he said only, "Perhaps it would be best if you didn't give me my answer now. We're both overset. It will take us both some time to come to terms with what has happened." He turned toward the doorway. "I set forth for London today. I'll be gone for some weeks. When I return, you can give me your final answer."

So he was leaving Strathrimmon, just as his father had, and he expected her to remain here, an abandoned wife, like his mother. Would he, too, die before his return as his father had, without ever seeing her again?

The thought tore at her heart. If this was to be her last glimpse of him, she must make the most of it. She must remember every detail of his handsome face—no matter what it cost her. Pain and pleasure mixed as she allowed herself to give in one last time to the love she must learn to set aside. She drank in the way his full lower lip quirked up at the corner, the graceful curve of his eyelid with its long pale lashes, the heartbreaking golden luster of his stubbled beard.

She stored each image away against the moment when he'd be gone, hating herself for doing it, but she couldn't stop herself. She was learning now that there was an ailment far worse than virgin's sickness—the one that afflicted abandoned wives.

Only when she felt his eyes drilling into her, as if daring her to admit to what she was doing, did she let her eyes drop back to the battered plant she held in her hand and force her features to assume a mask of cool composure. She would not let him see how much she cared.

"I bid you good day, madam." He bowed stiffly. Then he pushed open the door that led into the garden and plunged through it, lost to her.

* * *

She had been so cold. So stony cold. Standing there, discussing a separation so calmly. Telling him she wished to feel nothing for him. She must never have loved him. It all must have been an act. Adam had wanted so much to believe it wasn't so, but the cool way she'd just received him made it impossible.

Even when he'd grasped the magnitude of the disaster that had swept over them both, he'd cherished the hope, foolish as it had been, that perhaps the love that had grown up between the two of them might be enough to allow them to survive it.

But the way his wife had responded to him just now in the conservatory had put paid to that. He could hardly bear to remember how much he'd hoped that she would assure him she still loved him as much as before, no matter what had led them to be married.

But she had not. Her demeanor had been what it had been ever since her mother's revelation. Cold and distant. She'd offered him none of the comfort he'd learned to expect from her. She hadn't set her cool practicality to assuaging his fears.

There was only one possible explanation. She *had* been making the best of things, seeing no alternative, caught in a trap of her mother's making as much as he'd been. But now that her mother's ruse had been exposed, there was no further reason for her to feign love for him. It must be a relief to her not to have to any longer. Indeed, she'd barely raised an eyebrow when he'd suggested they part. She'd paid more attention to the foliage in her hand than she'd given him as she'd coolly told him—as if discussing the selection of a fabric to cover the dining room chairs—that she preferred a separation to staying on with him at Strathrimmon.

A wiser man would have granted it on the spot and turned his back on her forever. But he hadn't been able to do it. Instead, he'd just mumbled something mealy-mouthed about making no decisions until his return from Town, still in the grip of that Piscean inability of his to face the truth. But he'd known, even as he spoke the words, that he was only postponing what he couldn't prevent.

Zoe had never loved him. The courtesan's daughter had feigned what she must to get by. He'd thought it a sign of her naïveté when, early on, she'd told him she'd do what it took to keep him sweet toward her. But he'd been wrong. She'd only been telling him the truth.

Zoe watched numbly as Adam made his way down the path leading away from the conservatory. A few steps more and he'd be out of sight. Then, at last, she could allow herself the luxury of tears. But before that could happen, a servant came rushing toward her husband, so fast he almost knocked Adam down.

"An urgent letter, Yer Lordship. From the post."

Mechanically, Adam took the letter from the man, but after seeing what was written on the outside of the sealed and folded billet, he froze, blinking his eyes as if he couldn't believe what he'd read. He broke the seal and unfolded the letter within. When he was done reading it, he walked, very slowly, back into the conservatory. Back to her.

"It seems I was mistaken. I'm not going to London after all."

Such was his look of alarm Zoe couldn't help but say, "I hope no one is ill—or dead?"

He responded with a harsh laugh. "No. Someone is most definitely *not* dead."

"Then what is it?"

"Here, read it yourself. I can't bring myself to read it aloud to you."

He held the letter out in such a way that his fingers avoided touching hers, but even so, as she took the paper from him, she could feel that old feeling, as if a current flowed between his hand and hers.

She scanned the letter, to distract herself. The signature was only a scrawl that meant nothing to her, but as she slowly deciphered the unfamiliar handwriting and read the lines inscribed in a spindly hand, what she held in her hand became clear.

It was a letter from the Dark Lord, sent from the Isle of Iskeny. Dated only three days before.

Its writer demanded to know if it were true that, as he had heard, Adam had chosen to dally at Strathrimmon. He lamented that his days grew short and wondered why his chosen heir had not returned to him. He wondered, too, what had happened to the virgin whose presence at the Final Teaching was so essential to them both.

Adam snatched the letter from her hand. "Is this another trick? Another forgery? Like the feather Mac-Minn showed me to gain my trust?"

"Surely you can't think that I could have written this?"

"No, I suppose not. But what of your mother? Or MacMinn?"

"My mother was never taught how to write. And why would MacMinn, who took such drastic steps to bring our wedding about, forge a letter such as this? He could have no way of knowing that you'd seen through his ruse."

Adam's eyes met hers. "If the letter isn't a forgery, the Dark Lord still lives." He shook his head. "I can hardly take it in. I've been so used to thinking him gone. But of course, I had only MacMinn's assurance that he'd died." He put the letter down. "If he lives, I must go to him."

"If he's lives, you may still receive the Final Teaching."

Adam picked up a steel pruning knife that lay on the conservatory table and ran one long finger caressingly along the side of the blade. "How could I? I've defiled myself with the touch of iron, I betrayed my vow of chastity, and married the virgin he bid me keep untouched. He can no longer wish me to be his heir."

"But without an heir, won't the ancient tradition come to an end?"

He tossed the knife back onto the table. "The tradition will continue. Someone will receive the Teaching. The ancient ways are too strong to be destroyed by the weakness of a single heir. Though I have failed, there will be someone to take my place. The Dark Lord's heritage will pass on—though not through me."

He took a deep breath. "But still, I must go to him—to let him know I failed him, so that he may appoint another to take my place before it's too late."

"And after that, will you come back?"

The look he gave her was bleak as December frost. "Would it matter?"

And then he left.

She didn't see her husband again until the midday meal, and even then, it was as if she dined only with his shadow. In her mother's presence, he spoke to her with agonizing formality, addressing her only when necessary. His coldness tore into her, all the more unbearable because she couldn't find a similar coldness within herself with which to counter it.

It must be his terrible spell that still made her love him—though love had turned out to be exactly as she had feared it would be—fickle, brief, and agonizing. She wished she had a heart as untouched as her mother's, one that would have let her merely laugh a tinkling laugh when Adam had showered her with affection and feel nothing but contempt for him later, when he changed his tune.

But she didn't. She'd let herself believe he really loved her and had dared to imagine a bright future with him. Now she hated herself for the disappointment that overwhelmed her as she realized he hadn't really loved her at all.

Her mother, determinedly ignoring the undercurrents swirling around her, chattered on merrily, though Adam made no reply to anything she said to him. As soon as the last remove had been sampled, he excused himself with the explanation that he must prepare for his journey and left them alone.

At his exit, her mother shrugged one rounded shoulder. "These marriages of the *ton* are as bad as I had heard. I thank *le bon Dieu* I need not live in such a way. Such coldness. Such lack of *joie de vivre*. But you were always a strange girl, Zoe, so perhaps such a way of life pleases you. If so, who am I to judge? But me, I am ready to return home as soon as I have the means to do so. Did you speak to your husband about the small token he might afford me, the trifle that might help me out of my current difficulties?"

"I had no opportunity to raise the matter with my husband," Zoe replied. "We had other more pressing concerns to discuss." Like the end of their regard for each other and the return of Adam's teacher from the grave.

"But your husband spoke of going on a journey. You must apply to him for funds before he leaves. Where is he going?"

"To the Dark Lord's Island. He just learned that the Dark Lord isn't dead."

"Not dead." Isabelle's face grew ashen beneath its coat of white lead and rouge. "But if the Dark Lord finds out you're married, he'll be furious."

"But wasn't it *your* doing, Mama, that I married? Wasn't it your stratagem that made Lord Ramsay think his teacher had commanded him to marry me?"

"What are you talking about? I'm not such a fool as to meddle with the Laird of Iskeny. When he sent Lord Ramsay to fetch you, I gave you to him, much as it pained me, but with the kind of man he is, what choice did I have? You can imagine my surprise when MacMinn told me he had seen you wed. He did it all on his own, and a very foolish thing it was to do, though it worked out so well."

"But if you didn't send him, why did he do it?"

Her mother shrugged. "He is very fond of you. And he has no love for the Dark Lord. Indeed, he hates him with a passion. If I had listened to MacMinn when we were still in France I wouldn't have turned to the Dark Lord for help when the Committee was after us. And then where would we be? In the grave without our heads. Pah!"

"Are you saying that the Dark Lord was the mysterious gentleman who saved our lives all those years ago?"

"Of course."

"But you said your rescuer was an admirer."

"So I did. And it was true."

"But the Dark Lord must be chaste!" Zoe exclaimed.

"Your husband doesn't know everything." Her mother shrugged. "The Dark Lord was a man as other men."

"So the Dark Lord had a *tendre* for you, and rescued us because he loved you?"

Her mother seemed to shrink into her chair. "Perhaps *tendre* is not the word for what the Dark Lord felt for me. It wasn't a matter of love. He wasn't capable of loving anyone but himself."

"Then why didn't you tell me the truth?"

Her mother shrugged uneasily. "The truth wasn't something you could easily explain to a child."

"I'm no longer a child. So you can tell me now. Why *did* the Dark Lord save you?"

Her mother sighed. "You are a married woman, so I suppose it's all right to tell you." She took another deep breath and then began to speak in a tone Zoe remembered from the rare occasions in her childhood when her mother had told her children's stories.

"When I was a young girl—a little peasant girl who tended the master's pigs—I was engaged to be married. But word of my beauty came to the lord of the estate on which we lived and he chose to exercise the *droit du seigneur* and take my maidenhead before I married. It was not the usual thing to do, by then, but he was a foreigner who cared little what the neighbors thought of him. And he was the lord of the estate, so who could stand up to him? So that was how it went, but after he had ravished me, this foreign lord, he wouldn't let me return to my fiancé. Instead, he insisted that I give up my marriage and become his mistress."

Isabelle paused in her story, her fingers suddenly clenching. "He was a cold and terrible man, *ma petite*. To be forced to be intimate with such a man—" The look of disgust in her mother's eyes was real, its authenticity all the more wrenching in contrast to the artifice with which she usually arranged her features.

"I couldn't bear it. Even though I had discovered I was carrying his child, I flung his offer in his face and told him I still wished to marry the young man I loved. At that, my master flew into a rage. He told me he had only been fooling with me and had not meant his offer. Then he spread such lies about me in the village that my intended would no longer have me.

"After that, I lived in fear. What would become of

me, shamed as I was, with a fatherless child? That was when MacMinn spirited me off to Paris one night and made sure I had a safe place to live until the child was born. He'd been my master's coachman, but he'd had enough of his highhanded ways."

"But what does all this have to do with the Dark Lord and our rescue?"

"The lord who took my maidenhead was the Laird of Iskeny. He had left Scotland and settled in France after hearing of the wealth that had been earned by other powerful magicians who had dazzled the court, like Cagliostro and the Count of Saint-Germain. He hoped to join their number. That was why he began to call himself the Dark Lord."

"But if you parted from this man with such bad feelings between you, why did you turn to him when you needed to be rescued from the Terror?"

"I had no choice. After they chopped off the head of the marquis who had been my protector, the Dark Lord was the only man I knew who had power enough to save me. Even the monsters who filled the tumbrels respected him, fearing he would use his black arts against them if they crossed him. So when I learned that the Committee had put me on their list to have my head cut off, I decided it was better to be alive, even indebted to a man who I hated, than to die on the guillotine. I returned to his village and threw myself on his mercy."

"But if he'd been so angry at you when you fled from him years before, why did he bother to help you?"

"Is it not obvious, Zoe? Use your head! He helped

me because I told him you were his daughter. That's why he saved us, though first he made me sign all those papers to make his bargain with me."

The Dark Lord was her father? He and not the courageous and resourceful duke?

Shock resonated through her, as strong as if someone she'd loved had died.

But, still. Adam revered the Dark Lord. He'd devoted his life to him. How could he have been as cruel as her mother claimed? Perhaps this story of her mother's was no truer than her earlier claim that Zoe's father was a duke, though the very ugliness of the tale argued against that. Why would her mother have made up a story that portrayed her in a role so different from that of the sophisticated La Belle Isabelle she had worked so hard to create?

Her story might be true, and if it were, it would explain why her mother had kept Zoe's origin so secret. But whatever the whole truth might be, if the Dark Lord was her father, it would explain, too, his insistence that she be kept a virgin. What father wouldn't wish to protect his daughter in that way, whatever his feelings for her mother?

And even if Iskeny's laird had been cruel to her mother in her youth, people changed. Perhaps he'd mellowed with age or come to regret his sins as he lay on his sickbed contemplating his end. Maybe that was why he had commanded Adam to bring his daughter to him on his deathbed, because he yearned to see her before he died.

She must tell Adam! She raced toward his chamber.

But when she reached it, it was empty. Nor was he in the hall. If only he hadn't already left for Iskeny. But to her great relief, she found him in the courtyard lashing a small traveling box to the gig. A groom was almost done harnessing to it his fastest horse.

She ran toward him, heedless that her long skirts were dragging in the mud. But by the time she had reached him, he'd already climbed into the gig's seat and picked up his whip.

She shouted, "Adam. Stop!"

Something flickered over his face, and for only a moment she caught a glimpse of the man who had loved her. Then just as quickly, she saw it go, replaced by the impassive mask.

"I can't." His tone was harsh.

"You must! There's something I have to tell you. Something important."

"There isn't time. And besides, we're past the point where words could change anything. Whatever it is, it must keep until I return." He flicked the whip over the horses' heads and set them cantering on their way.

She fought back tears as the gig disappeared over the brow of the hill. He'd spoken the truth, indeed. No words could change her feelings for him—even when he'd made it crystal clear he could feel nothing for her but disdain.

Why did she still keep on loving him, when he'd been able to stop loving her so easily? It must be that damnable spell. Why else would she still love this man who'd just left her without a single backward glance?

She turned back to the house and began trudging

toward it. The future stretched out, bleak. How would she survive it? She'd lost so much, and now, after her mother's revelation, she couldn't even turn for comfort to her imaginary conversations with her father, the duke. For he'd never been her father. The Dark Lord was.

But then it struck her. If the Dark Lord lived, *he* could undo the spell. It had only been because they thought him dead that they'd believed she was trapped by it forever. The Dark Lord could free her from this burdensome love. She need no longer feel helpless when pain jolted through her at the memory of how cold Adam had been as he'd driven off without a word of kindness.

The spell could be lifted. It must be lifted! And the Dark Lord—the father she'd yearned to meet her whole life long—was the very man to do it.

Chapter 19

It had been a grueling three days' ride. Adam's body cried out for rest, but he pressed on. He had tapped back into the iron self-control he'd abandoned while living in the fool's paradise of his marriage and rejoiced once again in his ability to withstand cold and hunger and go for days without sleep. Only by subduing his body in this way could he drown out that other hunger: his longing for Zoe's body and the warmth and forgiveness he'd thought he'd found in her arms.

He turned his thoughts back to the road. A few more miles would take him to the harbor village of Stanraer. There he should be able to find a fisherman to ferry him across the miles of water that separated the Dark Lord's domain from the shore. In only a few more hours he'd be reunited with his teacher, who awaited his arrival so

eagerly, unaware of how unfit Adam had made himself
to receive the powers he once craved.

He awaited the swell of bitterness he should feel
when remembering how he'd forfeited his chance to
attain those powers, but he couldn't find it. Something
within him had changed. His yearning for the superhuman powers the Dark Lord had offered him had been
replaced by something else—something shameful—an
equally strong yearning that he'd never met the man.

Upon that wish followed others even more shameful: the wish that he'd never written to Isabelle and that
the Dark Lord had truly been dead so that he could
have lived on at Strathrimmon with his wife, deluded
but content, his life filled with the simple but intoxicating joys that he'd tasted over the past months. It was
an ignoble yearning, as ignoble as the longing for his
wife's arms that washed over him any time he let his
mental guard down.

When he reached the village, he found it more difficult than he'd expected to find a fisherman willing to
take him to the island. As soon as he pronounced its
name, a wary look came over the faces of men who
had been cordial a moment before, and he saw more
than one spit to avert the evil eye. But eventually he
found a boatman whose need for the silver he offered
was stronger than his dread of the mysterious Laird of
Iskeny.

An hour later, after an unremarkable passage across
the water and a long hike up a steep hill, he found
himself at last at his long-sought destination, the Dark
Lord's keep, Torr Druidh. Dwarfed by the stark gran-

ite tower that reared up against the cloudy sky, Adam drank in the heavy silence that was broken only by a curlew's lonely call, feeling as if he were dreaming. He'd imagined this moment so often during the past nine years, but now that it had arrived, how different it had turned out to be.

Two large, muscular men, armed in the ancient fashion, admitted him to the keep. Their accents proclaimed them Frenchmen. Their deference suggested they knew the reason for his visit. Greeting him with reverence, they ushered him into a small chamber whose stone walls and high ceiling gave it the feeling of a chapel. A window barely bigger than a slit let in only enough light to reveal the altar standing in the farthest corner of the room. On it stood a goblet glowing with a dull bronze sheen. An old man knelt before it. *His teacher.*

On hearing Adam enter, the Dark Lord rose slowly to his feet. He was wearing a long robe bedizened with the dragon emblem. He was thinner than Adam remembered, and his form was bent in a way that betrayed his advancing years. When he became aware of Adam's entry he lifted up his arms in blessing. His long purple sleeves fell back, revealing the serpents that twisted around his withered arms. Seeing them, Adam felt his own serpents wake from their long slumber. A pulse of energy surged through his body, bringing with it the treacherous memory of Zoe's long, slender fingers tracing their path up his arm. Desire jolted through him.

There would be no need to explain anything now. With his great power, the Dark Lord must have just seen into his heart and learned how totally Adam had unfit himself to receive the inheritance the Dark Lord had intended for him. He must know, too, how shamefully Adam yearned for the woman with whom he had squandered the energy he should have saved up for the Final Teaching. But if the old man saw into the depths of Adam's spirit, he gave no sign of it.

As the Dark Lord hobbled toward him, a faint scent of putrefaction rose from his body and when he embraced Adam, his hold was weak. The old man could not, in truth, have much time left on earth.

The Dark Lord released him. "Thanks be to the Powers, you've come! I'd despaired of ever seeing you again. Why did you delay, my son, when I summoned you in the ancient manner? Had you forgotten the feather code?"

"I forgot nothing. I hastened to come as soon as I received your summons. But events intervened—" He didn't look forward to explaining the nature of those events, but the faster he did so, the better. At least, when he was done, the old man's wrinkled face would no longer be filled with the joy and expectation that reproached him now.

But the Dark Lord gave him no chance to explain. "Tell me your story later. You're here. That's all that matters. The time was growing short, and I feared you'd gone astray. If you had, all might have been lost. But you've come, at last, though tell me, where is the virgin? You received the instructions that I sent you about her, didn't you?"

"I did." Adam kept his voice low. "But I haven't brought her."

"You didn't bring her?" The welcoming tone had fled. "Didn't I write that you must bring her? There can be no Teaching without her."

"Then there will be no Teaching."

"What, can you say that with such calm? You have changed much since I knew you, Adam Selkirk. You used to want the Teaching more than you wanted life itself."

"As you say, much has changed."

"Well, one thing hasn't changed," the Dark Lord said harshly. "I need the virgin."

Adam felt a fist tightening around his heart but said nothing.

"Look at me!" the old man demanded. "Can't you see the ravages of the disease that has assailed me since last we met?" He pointed to his face where Adam saw now what he hadn't noticed before, the gumma that swelled from the Dark Lord's forehead and the telltale flattening of his nose.

"You're a trained physician, you know what this means."

Adam drew back in shock. It didn't take a trained physician to recognize the malady that was consuming his master. It was the pox.

"Don't give me that pitying look," the Dark Lord protested. "This is but a part of the great Mystery, the Old Ones' Ancient Plan—that I, who have mastered all the earthly arts of healing, must cure myself of this, the disease men fear the most. Only then will I become the greatest of the healer lords that ever lived."

The old man stopped, overcome by a fit of hollow

coughing. "And I *shall* heal it. I've studied the ancient writings and my way is clear. This loathsome rotting that you see is temporary. I shall be cured completely, restored to youth and health, but for that I need the virgin. Damn you, Adam, I trusted you to bring her to me. Where is she?"

"I don't know." The Dark Lord's tone had made his blood run cold.

"How can you not know? I received intelligence that you took her from the harlot's care."

"I did."

"Then where is she? I must have her. Perhaps you don't understand the urgency of my need." The Dark Lord pulled up one sleeve and pointed to the suppurating coin-sized sores that covered his flesh.

"You told me the Dark Lord must be chaste." The words burst out of Adam before he could suppress them. "That it was essential to assuming the Dark Lord's powers."

"Only the student must be chaste. I already am the Dark Lord."

The old man picked up a glass wand from a table hidden in the shadows and drew it quickly through a fold of his woolen robe. When he flicked his wrist, a shower of bright sparks flew out of it with a hissing sound. "I survived the Final Teaching, my son. I met death and conquered it. All is permitted to the man who has stood at the point where life and death meet. Indeed"—he gestured with the wand—"to such a man, all that is forbidden to ordinary men is not only permitted, it is required. It is the energy found in the forbidden that fuels the Dark Lord's power. That is the gist of Final Teaching, my heir. But before I can transmit it to you, in deeds, not words, I must restore my powers. And for that I need the virgin. Only her life force can heal the putrefaction you see within me. Tell me where she is so I can have her brought to me!"

The Dark Lord fixed him with a compelling gaze, forcing Adam's eyes to turn upward. With a start, Adam recognized what he was doing—invoking the healing spell. Except this time there was nothing healing about it. His onetime teacher was trying to get him into his power using the enchantment.

Drawing on all his strength, Adam broke eye contact. He wouldn't let himself be ensorcelled into following the Dark Lord's order, for in these past moments he'd seen something monstrous: The final stage of the disease consuming his master's body was madness. The Dark Lord was insane—and Zoe was in mortal danger.

For he knew the cure of which the old man spoke. It wasn't ancient wisdom, but a perverse folk belief, one that held that sexual congress with a virgin could heal the diseases contracted by promiscuous men. *That* was what the Dark Lord had intended for Zoe. And if not for MacMinn's meddling, that would have been the fate to which Adam, his faithful disciple, would have delivered her.

Thank God she was safe at Strathrimmon, where the Dark Lord couldn't get at her, and that he hadn't told the old man of his marriage.

But he must tread carefully. If the Dark Lord believed his survival depended on ravishing Zoe, what might be his response if he learned how he'd been cheated? Adam must give no sign that the Dark Lord's attempt to impose his will on him had failed. He must behave exactly the way the old man expected him to until he made his escape, and he must give him no hint as to where he might find Zoe.

He chose his words carefully. "It shall be as you command. She is nearby. I shall fetch her."

"Good!" The Dark Lord's response was almost a groan. "Only after you bring her to me, will you be fit to receive the Final Teaching and become as I am, like a god."

Adam forced himself to nod, wondering how he could have ever thought that the Dark Lord could see into another's heart. Was it only his malady that had dimmed the old man's powers and turned him into a madman, or had he always been that way?

Whatever the answer, as a heavy silence filled the narrow stone room, the last fragments of Adam's youthful dream shattered into a million pieces and melted away like the sparks given off by the wizard's shining wand.

But there was no time now for regret. He must act in a way that would convince the old man he was doing his will. Only that way could he escape and return home to protect Zoe from the Dark Lord and his minions.

And he *would* protect her, to his last breath. Back when he'd thought himself incapable of loving her, he'd vowed to keep her safe. Now when he loved her more than life itself, he would do so as long as life lingered in his body. It mattered not whether she loved him back.

Indeed, perhaps it was better that she didn't, now that
he knew the full nature of the catastrophe he'd almost
brought down on her.

He no longer deserved her love. All he asked for now
was her survival.

Chapter 20

Zoe could barely repress her excitement. She was finally going to meet her father. Her real father, not the phantom duke she'd longed for all these years, that stranger who had abandoned her without a backward glance, but a real man, the Dark Lord, who had paid for the education that had made her a lady and had called her to him even as he lay on his deathbed. True, it had been his intervention in her life that had left her with the painful burden of loving a man who couldn't love her back, but it was he who also had the power to free her of that burden.

She'd dressed herself in her best gown, the sea green silk that Adam once had loved, and spent every penny she owned journeying on her own to the barren Isle of Iskeny. Now, after a terrifying crossing over choppy waters in a tiny fishing boat, she stood before her fa-

ther's door, working up the courage to knock. In only
a little while, she might speak at last the words she'd
dreamed of saying all her life. "Father, it's me, your
daughter, Zoe."

The heavy door to the castle looked exactly as she
would have imagined the door to a wizard's castle
would look. Its wide timbers were bound by heavy
metal straps. In the center was a heavy brass knocker in
the shape of twined serpents. She lifted it, wondering if
a single rap would be enough to summon someone, but
before she could drop it, the door was pulled open. As
she sprang back, a man came hurtling out and almost
collided with her.

It took a moment for it to register who he was; when
it did, her heart stopped.

Adam.

In spite of everything, her first impulse was to throw
her arms around him. She'd barely quelled it when his
eyes widened with shock as he recognized her. His
mouth dropped open. Pain swept across his features.
"Not you," he cried. "Not here."

She struggled to withstand the pain that overwhelmed her at this further evidence of how much he
hated her.

"Don't let him know you're here." He sounded
horrified.

She cut him off. "I'll do what I must!" She didn't
bother to hide her anger. Though she'd felt love on
seeing her husband again, all *he'd* felt was fear that she
might spoil his reunion with his master. She tried to
push past him, but he blocked her path. She twisted

away, trying to break free, but he only tightened his grasp on her.

In desperation, she raised her knee and jabbed it where her mother had always told her it would do the most good. He yelped in pain and clutched at his groin. His agony cut her to the quick, but it was too late for regret. He'd recover in a few minutes and be even angrier with her. Seizing her chance, she raced through the open castle door and slammed it behind her to cut off his pursuit.

She'd keep silent about their marriage when she found the Dark Lord. Though Adam was lost to her, she couldn't bring herself to betray his secret and keep him from getting his heart's desire. But the agony she'd felt just now in his presence doubled her resolve. She must convince her father to undo the spell.

Despair washed through Adam as the castle door slammed shut. Not since Charlotte's death had he felt so helpless. The pain Zoe had inflicted with her well-placed blow still radiated in waves through his body, but it was nothing compared to the pain that filled his heart.

He'd delivered her into the power of a madman. He, who had vowed to protect her. But how could he protect her now? He'd come in haste, without a retinue, armed only with his wits. How could he match the power of the burly guards who surrounded his onetime teacher?

When the Dark Lord had jeered at him, so long ago in France, that the stars that ruled his birth would make Adam a victim or a savior, had his teacher known it would be *he* who would make Adam his victim? He couldn't help but wonder. But he couldn't change the stars that ruled his birth; he could only make the most of whatever gifts they'd given him. Well, Pisces's gift was delusion. He must harness it to save her now. His only hope was to keep playing the role the Dark Lord had assigned him—to behave like the eager faithful disciple he had once been and keep alert for whatever opportunity arose that would let him protect Zoe from the old man's foul plan and spirit her off to safety.

As he strode back and forth before the heavy castle door, walking off the last of the pain, he no longer knew what gods he should be praying to, but even so, he prayed for strength. When he could breathe normally again, he pushed open the door. One last time he must be the Dark Lord's heir.

As Zoe hurtled through the castle's entryway, a huge guard glided out of the darkness and barred her way with a wooden staff.

"I must see the Dark Lord," she gasped.

"No one sees him unless he bids them enter. Who are you?"

"Zoe Gervais. He will know my name."

The burly guard inspected her with heightened interest, but made no comment, merely gesturing for her to follow him down a long stone passageway. At length, he bade her halt and knocked at a closed door. A faint, querulous voice asked, "Who's there?"

"A Miss Gervais to see you, master."

"Gervais?" The voice rose at least an octave. "Zoe Gervais? Well show her in, at once!"

She took a deep breath. Here at last was the moment that she'd waited for.

The guard opened the door and through it she saw the bent form of an old man. At her entrance, he straightened, but not entirely, and hobbled toward her. "At last, you're here." He wheezed.

He was much older than she had expected, and so wizened and wrinkled, she could almost have believed he had, indeed, died—and only recently been exhumed.

He beckoned. "Come, let me look at you."

At his invitation, she took another step. He reached for a pair of spectacles and put them on before inspecting her more closely.

"You don't look a bit like your mother." His tone didn't attempt to hide his disappointment. "She was so beautiful. You're not like her at all."

She almost snapped that it wasn't her fault that she'd inherited her father's ugliness instead of her mother's beauty. But as her eyes grew more adapted to the darkness, she was glad she'd kept it to herself. What a mistake it would have been to have reproached him with his hideousness.

For hideous he was. As she gazed on him, it struck her for the first time that she'd been fortunate to have inherited only a small portion of her father's ugliness. Her pockmarks were mere blemishes compared to the buboes that ravaged his face. Still, she of all people should know better than to judge someone merely on his outward appearance. Adam venerated this man, so he must have qualities beyond those of the sort her shallow mother would have valued.

"My observation wounds you," her father observed. "How unfortunate that you got your looks from me, not her."

Had he read her thoughts, as Adam could? She hoped not, given what she'd just been thinking. But the calmness with which he continued to regard her suggested that he hadn't, but had only guessed at her emotions. Still, it would be best to think of nothing in his presence except for the reason for her visit.

"I'm surprised by your sudden appearance," the Dark Lord continued. "Ramsay told me he hadn't brought you. The boy has a curious sense of humor."

Forcing herself to smile, she said, "He told you the truth. I came on my own. He attempted to bring me, but events intervened."

"That was what he said. What caused the delay?"

His eyes bored into her. This was the power that her husband had coveted—the power her mother had robbed him of. The all-too-familiar pain flared again. If only her father's power was strong enough to free her from loving the husband who no longer loved her.

But because she still loved *him*, she must explain her predicament carefully, so as not to harm Adam's relationship with his master.

"I had an accident when we were on our journey, and took a bad wound," she answered. "It festered, and it was only through the use of his surgical skills that Lord Ramsay was able to save me."

"The boy was always good at that kind of thing. Not too proud to do surgery when a case demanded it." His tone betrayed pride in his student's abilities.

"But after he saved you, why did he dally so long? He was supposed to have brought you months ago."

Again she chose her words carefully. "There were no opiates available to him in the remote spot where he had to operate on me. So he was forced to use the healing spell you taught him."

"Spell? What spell?"

"The spell that put me to sleep and made me impervious to pain."

"Oh. *That* spell. Yes. It can be quite helpful. But what has that to do with why Lord Ramsay refused to bring you?"

"Something went wrong with the way he cast the spell. When I awoke, I found myself in love with him. He tried to enchant me again and reverse the magic, but it didn't work. So he couldn't bear to be around me—because of the love I felt for him, you see." She let her voice trail off vaguely, relieved that she'd found a way to tell her story without revealing all.

Understanding dawned in the Dark Lord's eyes. "So he fled from your charms, did he?"

"He was under a vow." She bit her lip. If the Dark Lord really could see into her mind, he'd quickly learn what had happened to that vow and how totally it had been broken.

"Well, I'm sure the boy knew better than to take your virginity—whatever temptation you might have presented to him." The old man leered. So much for his ability to read minds.

He went on, "I was most displeased with him for having failed to bring you. But after hearing your explanation, I can better understand his motive. At least you've finally arrived, whether or not he brought you. So no damage has been done."

Except to her heart.

A look of pleasure filled his ravaged features and he smiled a twisted smile. "Except, of course, to your heart."

Sheer terror. He *had* read her mind. She must be so very careful what she let herself think next. "It's painful to love where love isn't wanted," she said softly. "Can you remove his spell? Your powers are so much greater than his. If you could, I would no longer trouble Lord Ramsay with a love which he finds so distasteful."

"Nothing could be easier. Come with me to my laboratorium and it will be the work of only a few moments to undo the damage. Though it *is* odd that a *healing* spell should have so affected you. What can the boy have done to have made it go wrong that way?"

She turned away, though it was foolish to imagine that by hiding her face from the old wizard she could keep him from getting his answer. But he said nothing more as he led her down the passageway to another chamber, even gloomier than the first.

Having no windows, it received no natural light. Its only illumination was the thick candle that burned on a tall stand. Its flickering flames revealed little, just stone walls draped in heavy hangings picked out with ancient embroideries, though it was too dark to see what patterns they made.

There was an unfamiliar smell in the room, too, a

sweet smell, unlike her mother's sensual perfumes. As she breathed it in, she coughed once or twice, and then felt strangely lightheaded.

A couch was placed by the far wall of the room. It was covered with a thick velvet spread. The Dark Lord motioned her to lie down upon it. Then, from the folds of his long purple gown he pulled a shining wand that gleamed in the dull candlelight. He raised his arm in an ancient gesture of invocation. As he did so, his sleeve dropped back. Serpents twined up his wizened arm. Adam's serpents.

Unbidden, the image flooded into her mind of how the serpents had twined up her husband's muscular forearms the last time they'd made love. She'd been so lost in the bliss of it, and so sure that he, too, felt the same joy that had filled her. She could have lived on so happily with him for the rest of her life had he only continued to love her.

The memory choked the breath out of her and she coughed. The sound echoed through the smoky chamber and jolted her back to the present and why she was here.

Their marriage had been a mistake. Adam didn't want her now. Only the spell kept her loving him, and in a few more moments, that spell would be removed and she'd finally be free of the longings that overwhelmed her now. She lay back on the couch.

"You are feeling sleepy." The Dark Lord's wavering old-man's voice was reedy, but it still held a tone of command. He raised his sparkling wand, slowly and purposefully, and she felt the power emanating from him as he did so. Then his words began to weave their magic spell, and she felt herself drift off.

She'd felt just like this the first time Adam had magicked her, before the surgery. The Dark Lord's magic must be working. She'd soon be free.

His words rose and fell, bidding her to feel peace flow through her body from her feet, up to her ankles, to her thighs, and into that central place where the life force pulsed within her. She gave herself up to the enchantment, drifting inward, letting his words weave a web of magic that led her into the place of power he described for her, the holy temple of the Ancient Ones.

She could see that temple now, as his words spun the enchanted vision, with its dome and the beautiful multicolored flowers that were scattered through a meadow as fair as the fields of faerie land. Deep within that magical place, she raised her hand at his command and saw waves of light flash from her fingertips. The Dark Lord's voice was only a tiny silver ripple now, linking her back to the world from which she'd come, yet in this wondrous place where he'd sent her, she could hear it still.

"Lord Ramsay stands before you."

And he did. Adam's image shimmered before her, joined to her in this magical world where she peered one last time into the eyes she had loved so much, whose color was like highly polished pewter. But this time, when she met his gaze, he didn't flinch. His angry mask was gone. His eyes met hers and a torrent of love and warmth flowed from them into her, until she could nevermore deny it: He was her mate. Her love. Her only one.

"Lord Ramsay is nothing to you." The Dark Lord's voice was gentle and beguiling. "You feel nothing for him. He is a stranger to you."

But in the magical place where the wizard had brought her, Adam's eyes pulsed with life and with love—and the love that surged within her pulsed back toward him in response. How could he ever be a stranger to her, with all they had shared?

The Dark Lord's voice droned on. "Lord Ramsay is fading away. You are releasing him. He is a stranger to you. You do not know him."

But she *did* know him. She knew the strength of his lithe body and the kindness in his heart. She knew the struggle he'd gone through to learn how to love her. And she knew more. She knew of the pain he had lived with all his life, thinking himself his sister's destroyer, and of the healing he had found when, daring to be an ordinary man at last, he'd reached out and opened his heart to her.

She couldn't let him go. What they'd shared had bound them forever. Not even the Dark Lord had magic enough to change that.

"Do you hear me, Zoe?" The Dark Lord's voice was soothing and relentless at the same time.

She nodded. She had heard him. But the words he'd spoken were lies.

"Lord Ramsay means nothing to you. Repeat it to me, now."

As she opened her mouth to tell him that his spell was not working, in the magical world Adam reached out and touched her lips to still them, and a wave of peace coursed through her at his touch. With the tiny bit of herself that remained in the world of men, she summoned her strength to nod in response to the Dark Lord's question, giving him no sign that his magic had failed.

"Good. For *I* am your master now, Zoe. You shall do all I wish. My will shall be your will. My body, your body, and you thrill with the desire to have me fill you with my seed."

With a shattering crash, the glorious colors of the magical world where the Dark Lord had taken her vanished, as the meaning of his words forced her out of the trance.

Had she gone mad under the spell?

But as the old man's soothing voice repeated the obscene suggestions that had propelled her from her trance, she knew it was not she who was insane— and that Adam wasn't the only one who bore a cursed heritage.

All her life she'd had contempt for her mother and taken comfort in thinking she resembled the unknown father whose nature she knew she must share. But now that father had brought her here to ravish her. If she were to escape, she must hope that, along with his cursed nature, she'd inherited some small trace of her mother's cunning.

Chapter 21

A guard informed Adam the Dark Lord had taken Zoe down the hallway into his laboratorium. As he paced down the cold stone hallway to the laboratorium's heavy oaken door, Adam refused to allow himself to speculate on what might be going on behind it. He would rescue her. That was all he needed to think about.

Another guard blocked the door. Adam's fists curled. He cursed himself that he'd brought no better weapon, but as he approached, the guard bowed deferentially and stepped away from the door. There had been no need for violence. The Dark Lord's minions still believed him to be their master's anointed successor.

He turned a haughty face toward the guard and nodded slightly, the way one nodded toward a despised servant, reinforcing that belief. Then he knocked gently on the heavy door, tapping out the pattern the old man had taught him in Morlaix.

There was no answer. He rapped again, more loudly. As he stood waiting, the pounding of his heart seemed to fill the empty hallway, until he thought it strange the guard didn't seem to hear it.

The wait was intolerable. He longed to throw himself against the door and to smash himself into a bloodied pulp, anything that would get him inside—and to Zoe. But destroying himself wouldn't save her. He must lull the old man into thinking he was still his dupe. He rapped on the door again, this time so hard his knuckles started to bleed. The pain grounded him, reminding him that he must stay calm, but how could he stay calm when *she* was in there with *him*?

He sized up the guard. Could he take advantage of his inattention to wrestle him to the ground and grab his sword? Probably not. The man outweighed him by at least three stone, and the sound of their struggle would attract others. But even so, that might be his only hope. Each passing moment made it more likely that his worst fears were coming true. He was about to drop into the crouch from which to make his desperate move, when the door cracked open. The Dark Lord had opened it. Adam shouldered his way in.

Zoe lay on a couch. Her eyes were closed, her limbs relaxed. She was dressed in her beautiful sea green gown. He wasn't too late. He uttered a silent prayer of thanksgiving.

As he entered, the Dark Lord took a step back. His long velvet robe swirled around him. "Don't wake her!" he said in an annoyed whisper. "I'm not done with her."

Adam composed his features into an expression he hoped looked like worshipful obedience. "Excellent! I was hoping I wasn't too late to observe you exercise your skill." It was a miracle the words didn't choke him as he spoke.

The old man's expression brightened. Clearly, he was pleased by his student's servile tone. And clearly, too, he'd lost the ability to read minds.

"Did the girl tell you of the spell that went amiss?" Adam struggled to keep his tone casual. He must find out how much she had already told him.

"Yes indeed—and of the annoyance she caused you with her unwanted admiration." The Dark Lord chuckled. It wasn't a sound Adam ever wanted to hear again. "But you'll not be troubled by her unrequited passion any longer. I've undone the spell and relieved you of that burden.

She hadn't told him of their marriage. Only of the spell.

"She is an ugly creature, isn't she?" The Dark Lord sneered. "I don't imagine she posed much of a threat to your chastity. You've withstood far greater temptations. But it's hard to fathom how she could have turned out to be so ugly with such a delicious mother and such a distinguished sire."

"You knew her father?"

"I *am* her father," the Dark Lord said with satisfaction. "That's why she, and she alone, will cure my wretched affliction."

Zoe was the Dark Lord's daughter?

Adam choked as his throat closed up. What was it the old man had said? *The energy of the forbidden fuels the Dark Lord's powers.* So *that* was why he'd wanted Zoe so badly. It hadn't been just any virgin his perverted beliefs required, but this one, the child of his own begetting.

It was impossible that Adam's revulsion didn't show on his face. But the old man's voice went on, dry and grating. "I released her from that misguided spell you bound her with. What were you thinking of to use it on her? I don't wonder that you botched it. That kind of spell is very difficult to control. There are far simpler ways to make a woman do your bidding."

"I have not your art, master." Adam forced his tone to remain humble. "It seemed like the easiest way at the time. The girl was rebellious and repeatedly tried to escape."

"Well, then perhaps you weren't so misguided. Love will control the most obdurate of females. Though I would have preferred it if you hadn't meddled with her emotions. I wish them to be all mine." He shrugged. "Even so, it's no great matter. I undid the spell you set and replaced it with one that will make the girl love *me*. Though it's a shame she's so damnably ugly. I've carried her mother's image in my mind all this time I've been awaiting her." He sighed. It sounded like bubbling gasses rising from a marsh. "But there's no help for it. I must do what I must to heal myself."

There was a rustle from the couch where Zoe lay. Hearing it, the old man paused abruptly. "We will talk more about this later. I'm not yet done with her. I've implanted my commands in her spirit, but now I must make her forget all that I have done to her and bring her back to life."

"Will you use her as you planned when she awakens?" Adam struggled to keep his voice even and uninvolved.

"Of course not." The old man shook his head. "You always were so rash, Adam. Always wanting to rush ahead. But as I've told you, time and again, these things must be done right. There are rituals to be observed, and the energy of the universe must be in the correct alignment. Only a fool would take her now, when tomorrow the Dragon's Tail conjuncts the Sun and Moon."

"There is an eclipse?"

"Indeed there is, a solar eclipse. The second of the year and most propitious for our ends. Have you forgot all that I taught you and stopped consulting your ephemeris each morning to check the aspects? It was because of the proximity of this eclipse that I was so disturbed when you arrived without the girl. It is a very rare alignment, with Mercury combust and Jupiter on the ascendant at the very moment that it culminates. Nothing could be more conducive to my purposes. I shall take her when it reaches totality."

"And then?"

The Dark Lord smiled, perhaps already imagining himself healed. "Then it will be time for you, my boy, at last. You will have your revenge against her mother—the harlot who sent your sister to her death—and it will be all the more delightful for having been so long postponed."

How much joy those words would have given him had he heard them pronounced a few short months ago, before that last eclipse when he had gone, as instructed, to claim the Dark Lord's virgin. He felt disgust for the man he'd been then, who had let hatred so overpower him that he'd thought nothing of making a victim out of an innocent girl. But his self-loathing wouldn't save Zoe. He must find some way to get her away from the Dark Lord before he carried out his wretched scheme.

Doing his best to keep control over his voice, he said coolly, "So you will give me the girl then? To do with as I wish?"

The Dark Lord's eye, unnaturally bright, drilled into Adam's. "Not exactly as you wish, but as you must. Do you forget that I summoned you here to receive the Final Teaching? Once I have robbed her of her virginity, she will be of no further use to me. I'll give her to you then, so that by practicing on her the ancient sacrificial rite you may observe closely the process by which the life force flickers and leaves the body. It's by doing this, in the manner passed on from each Dark Lord to each of the Dark Lords' heirs, that you will cultivate the ability to rule over death. Your Teaching begins now, my heir. The Dragon's Cave awaits you. Your long apprenticeship is over."

Surely this must be a nightmare. It couldn't be real. But Zoe couldn't wake up any more than she'd been able to waken from that dream wedding at the inn. She could only lie silent, with her eyes clamped shut, pretending to still be enchanted, while her husband and father discussed in their cultivated tones the terrible fate they had planned for her.

Pinned against the soft cushions that cradled her body, she felt her hand go numb, as if she were already beginning to leave the body whose future was to be so short and hold such horrors.

The father she'd longed for all her life would rape her. Then, when that was done, the husband she'd adored would make her the sacrifice that would transfer to him his master's unholy powers. Could this be the same Adam she had loved? Whom she had married? Whose child—or children—she might be carrying even now?

The numbness had crept up her arms now. Soon it would reach her heart. If only it would move more swiftly. How could she have felt love, even bespelled love, for a man who could discuss her ravishment and death so calmly? How could she have reveled in his touch? Had he known all along that as the Dark Lord's heir, his hands were meant to take her life?

Love was as terrible as her mother had warned. Worse. For even her mother hadn't warned her of this kind of betrayal.

The old man's hesitant footsteps turned back toward her. Then he swiveled around to face Adam. "There's one more thing." He wheezed. "While she's still entranced, I must seal her to me with a Word of Power. When next she hears it, she will lose her own will and yield herself to mine. Observe me well, my heir, as I complete the magic, so that you don't bungle it when next you use the spell."

The Word of Power. The blood in Zoe's veins turned into ice. Adam had used one to make her sleep. And she *had* slept—and then he had used it to make her love him.

"Can you hear me, Zoe?" the Dark Lord asked. Despite herself, she heard her voice reply, "Yes."

"You are the Dragon's Child. When you awake and hear me call you by that name, you will open your soul to me, ready to do my bidding. My will shall be your will. You shall live only to fulfill my commands. You will feel joy as you give yourself to me. Do you understand me, Dragon's Child?"

Filled with revulsion, but paralyzed, she heard herself answer, "Yes."

He had made her his.

The last bit of her will drained out of her. The Dark Lord had stolen her soul, and Adam had let him.

He must act now, whatever it might cost. As chancy as it would be, he could save her no other way. Adam took a deep breath, and putting his hand on his master's shoulder said, "It won't work."

The Dark Lord's face hardened. "Of course it will. Why would you doubt it?"

"Because she is no virgin."

"What? Did you winkle out of her that she had taken to her mother's ways?" A look of distaste swept over his features. "What an irony it would be if she, too, were to turn out to be diseased. Where then would I turn for healing? But if she defied me thus, the little baggage, I'll teach her to disobey the Dark Lord's will!" His face had turned an unhealthy purple against which his sores stood out dark red.

Adam cut in. "She attempted to do your will. It was I who was at fault. She lost her virginity when I forcibly made her my wife."

"Your *wife*?" The Dark Lord's eyes widened. "You stole her from me? *You*? But that explains why you wouldn't bring her to me. I knew you weren't telling the truth, though I couldn't tell why. But why did you defy me like that?"

"I didn't do it to defy you," Adam said, keeping his voice dangerously quiet. "I was tricked by Isabelle. She was wilier than I credited. She sent a messenger to convince me that it was *your* will that we marry. By the time the truth came out, it was too late. The deed was done. The girl knew nothing of it. I used a spell much like the one you just set upon her to bend her to my will. That was the spell she begged you to undo. So if you must blame someone, blame me. The girl was blameless."

"That damned whore Isabelle." The Dark Lord growled. "I should never have saved her life. If I'd let the Committee kill her and taken her daughter afterward, I could have kept the child locked up somewhere and then none of this would have happened."

The Dark Lord had saved Isabelle. Did that mean what Adam thought it meant? He couldn't let himself think out the implications. He didn't dare let himself react. All that mattered now was getting Zoe away safely.

From the corner of his eye, he saw her body twitch

on the couch where she lay enchanted. Dark Lord noticed it, too. His lips tightened in irritation.

Adam continued. "What's done is done. But as the girl is worthless to you now without her virginity, I'll take her away with me and you won't be troubled with either of us again."

The Dark Lord shrugged. "The loss of her virginity is a heavy blow. But still, she *is* my daughter. To mate with her, virgin or not, may release energies sufficient perhaps to heal me. I must use her. I have no other recourse."

Adam's heart sank. He'd thrown the dice and lost. Deception would not take him any further. It was time to speak the truth. "You'll have to kill me before you touch her."

The Dark Lord's hands flew up in surprise, revealing the tattooed serpents. "Surely such an ugly chit can't mean that much to you, a man who has trained for years to assume the sacred heritage?"

"She means more to me than life itself. She is my life, my one true love. No power you could give me would make up for losing her."

"You would choose her over all that *I* could give you?"

"I *have* chosen her. Now let her go."

The Dark Lord peered at him as if seeing him for the first time.

"So that is how it is." He wrinkled his nose in disgust. "I should have known. Though you were a Pisces, with all the sentimental tendencies of that sign, I thought you'd grow out of the worst of them once I'd rid you of that pathetic sister of yours. It was so providential that you brought her over with a fresh set of traveling papers just when I needed to get Isabelle and her whelp off to safety. And once I'd disposed of that crippled millstone hanging round your neck, you settled down and dedicated yourself to the great work, just as I meant you to. You had a knack for it, despite your Pisces mawkishness. I thought sending you to learn surgery would harden you to human suffering as nothing else could and make you fit for the role I had chosen for you. But I was wrong. Without me by your side to keep you on the path, your Piscean tendencies grew stronger. Now they've destroyed you. You aren't fit to be the Dark Lord's heir."

"No. I'm not. So let her go and I'll trouble you no longer."

The Dark Lord's thin lips twisted up into a sordid equivalent of a smile. "You *won't* trouble me any longer—you can be sure of that. But I still need the girl. I need her life force."

"Take mine instead."

"You'd offer up your life to save hers?"

"I do. My life is yours, if only you'll let her go free."

The Dark Lord sneered. "You are such a Pisces, with all the Piscean hunger for self-destruction. But such gestures, like so much that is associated with your sign, are effective only in the imagination. You couldn't give me a fraction of the energy I will get from her. Even if mating with her doesn't heal me, she still holds the life force I once gave to her. I shall drain her of it and then, when I've rejuvenated myself, I'll extract your life energy from you, too, exquisitely slowly, as the Ancients decreed should be the fate of a failed heir. Your youth, too, will invigorate me and give me the strength I'll need to survive now that I have no heir."

There was only one hope left. Adam launched himself at the Dark Lord and wrestled him to the ground, choking with the stench of him. The guards would be here any moment, but perhaps Adam could kill him first.

But even as he felt his hands closing in on bones of the old man's sinewy neck, strong arms pulled Adam off and pinioned his arms behind his back. He twisted and jabbed with his knees, but it was no use. The guards were bigger and stronger.

As one of them helped the Dark Lord to his feet, the old man rasped, "Put him in the dungeon." His hand clutched at his throat. "But don't kill him yet. I want to do it myself, after I'm done with the girl."

It had all happened so fast Zoe hadn't been able to help him. She'd still been lying paralyzed, with her eyes closed, afraid to give any sign she wasn't entranced, when Adam had spoken his fierce words of love and flung himself at the Dark Lord. At his scream, she'd struggled up on one elbow, fighting her way back into her body, so she could help him, but it had been too late. The guards were already in the chamber, too many of them. Now she heard only the sound of his body being dragged down the corridor. Her Adam. Who loved her. Who'd offered his life for hers out of that love.

His words still rang in her heart. *She is my life. My*

one true love. Her vision had not been a lie. Adam loved her. Though that was little comfort when her husband lay in the Dark Lord's dungeon where a painful death awaited him. He'd not been able to kill her hell-born father, and there was no one left to stop the Dark Lord from carrying out his madman's plan.

A thudding sound told her that her father was limping back toward her. She froze. Would he attempt to take her now? Inflamed as he must be with bloodlust after Adam's ill-fated attack, would he invoke the Word of Power that would render her will useless? Would he force himself on her?

Or would he wait as he'd said he would, for tomorrow's eclipse. She tensed in preparation for his approach. If he thrust himself upon her, she would do all she could to take him with her before the guards who surrounded him now finished her off.

But Adam's attack seemed to have drained the old man's energy. He was breathing unevenly as he chanted the incantations meant to bring her out of the trance, taking deep gasps of air, and breaking in midphrase, even as he reminded her that she was his and bid her forget all that had happened in the trance. As if she ever could!

With an eerie whistle he summoned a wiry hag as muscular as his bodyguards. He muttered to her in an unknown tongue, and the woman grasped Zoe by the wrists, as the Dark Lord hobbled away, leaning heavily on the shoulder of his bodyguard. The hag pushed Zoe through the open door and led her down the musty passageway, motioning her into a small cell. After mumbling a few incomprehensible words, she left, slamming the door shut behind her. A key squealed in the heavy lock, then Zoe was alone in the silence.

Alone and doomed.

And yet, her heart swelled with the certainty that Adam loved her. He'd always loved her. He loved her enough to give his life for hers. She'd given her love where it had been wanted, after all. She would go to her death treasuring that knowledge.

But then it struck her. Not only did Adam love her, but she still loved *him*. And that meant the old man's magic hadn't worked. He hadn't been able to break the spell or replace it with his own. Nor, in that terrifying period when Adam had been playing the role of his devoted heir to try to get his teacher to let her go, had the Dark Lord seen into Adam's heart any better than she had.

The Dark Lord had no more power than she did. Perhaps less. For her soul swelled now with a new power all her own, the power of her love—made invincible by Adam's sacrifice.

Chapter 22

The dungeon was a dark pit carved out in the earth. The only way in was the trapdoor that gaped, twelve impossible feet above his head. There was no escape.

Adam lay in the muck, checking his body for broken bones. Though he was bruised and battered, everything still seemed to work. For now. It mattered little. Through his blindness and stupidity he'd delivered Zoe to a madman. Back when they'd been safe in Strathrimmon, she'd waved off his warning about the Ramsay curse. But she must believe in it now, and she'd die hating him for leading her to so terrible an end.

Had he been able to hold off the guard for only another moment he might have killed the old man and prevented some of the horror in store for her. But he'd failed. The Dark Lord lived, and tomorrow the eclipse would come. Had he more strength, he would bash his head against the damp stone walls of his prison and silence the voice that told him how utterly he'd failed to protect the woman he loved. But he couldn't even succeed at that.

How blind he'd been, to put his faith in a man who would rape and kill his own child to prolong his life—a man who served only himself, and prided himself on his inhumanity. It was only now that Adam could see the truth: The source of the Dark Lord's strength had been his inability to feel the pain of others.

He shifted his bruised body on the damp floor. He'd been prepared to sacrifice all that he had to earn the Final Teaching that he'd believed would make him superhuman like his master. Now, in this foul dungeon, he'd been given that Final Teaching: That it was better to be human than a god. That even the greatest of happiness could disappear in the flicker of an eyelid, so one must love with a full heart and revel in whatever joy one found.

But of course, he had learned it all too late.

He lay in the darkness, as the hours crawled by, measured by the dripping moisture coursing down the walls of his dungeon and by the inflow and outflow of his breath. The next thing he knew, he felt a woman's touch.

He must be dreaming. He cursed himself that his last dream should be so unworthy. For he wanted no woman's touch but Zoe's, and this was not her hand. It was too small and rounded, and it wouldn't stop tugging at his battered shoulder, sending jolts of pain up into his neck. But even as the pain dragged him back to wakefulness, the woman was still there.

"Wake yourself, Lord Ramsay," she hissed in a husky whisper. "This isn't the time for sleep!" Then her slap stung his cheek, and his eyes flew open. Though even now, he knew he must still be dreaming because the woman who hovered over him, her golden curls illuminated by the light that streamed through the open trapdoor, while her frilly gown soaked up fetid water from the muddy floor, couldn't be real. But real or not, when she raised her small white hand to deliver another slap, he sat up, protesting, "I'm awake! Don't strike me!"

"*Merci á le bon Dieu!*" exclaimed his mother-in-law. "I was so scared. You slept like one who was already in the grave. But now all will be well. Here, stand up!"

Still unable to trust the evidence of his senses, Adam drew himself up, painfully, to a standing position. Only then did he see the rope ladder that dangled from the edge of the trapdoor. Without a word, Isabelle grasped it, gathered her ruined skirts with one hand, and began to climb. Dazed, he followed her.

Isabelle had rescued him. The woman he gladly would have fed to the ravens in small pieces with his own hand.

When he reached the top of the ladder, Isabelle pulled it up and motioned him to be silent. "The guard will give me an hour before he raises the alarm. We must move swiftly."

"Did you bribe him? If so, we're still in danger. He'll get more from his master for turning us in."

"Do you think me a fool? He gets his reward only when I'm satisfied he's done what he promised."

"But I thought you had no money."

"I am La Belle Isabelle," she said with satisfaction, "and though I'm not as young as I once was, I still need no money to get a normal man to do my bidding. But there's no time for talk. You must come away with me. There's a boat hidden by the landing."

"You take it. I can't leave Zoe alone with that monster."

"Zoe will be safe. MacMinn followed me to Strathrimmon, and when he heard where you and my daughter had gone, he set out after you. He will bring help in from the mainland."

"But what if he fails? We must get Zoe out of the castle before the Dark Lord can do what he has planned for her."

"She is no longer in the castle. The guard told me they'd already taken her away. But you're as bad as my daughter with all your worrying. Everything will work out well. It always does. MacMinn will think of something."

The sun was setting when the old woman came for Zoe. She brought with her a scarlet robe of rough woven homespun and gestured to Zoe to remove her gown and dress herself in it. The woman spoke with a lilting accent that suggested English was not her native language. For one wild moment, Zoe thought of begging the woman to help her escape, but she quickly dismissed the idea. The woman served the Dark Lord. He wouldn't have entrusted his prize to anyone he believed capable of treachery.

Before undoing her bodice, Zoe turned away out of modesty. As she unfastened it, her fingers encountered Charlotte's knife hanging between her breasts on its chain. Her attendant hadn't seen it. Carefully, she draped the rough homespun robe over her shoulders to hide it. When she was done, she turned around, lowering her head as if she'd lost all hope.

"Come," the woman said. "It is time."

"They go to the place he called the Dragon's Cave—a barrow," Isabelle explained as Adam led her to a copse of trees not far from the dungeon, large enough to hide them. "That's what he told me, this guard. He pointed that way." She waved her hand vaguely in a direction away from the castle. "But where it might be, this Dragon's Cave, I do not know."

Adam's heart sank. There was no time to canvass the entire island looking for the place where the Dark Lord would perform his abomination. But before he had time to begin his search, the castle gate creaked open and an unearthly keening sound rose into the air like the cry of a dead soul. The hairs rose on his neck. A moment later a lone piper emerged from the gateway, his ancient instrument the source of the haunting skirl. A few elderly women followed in his train, robed in long black gowns like nuns' habits.

Zoe followed, dressed in a gown the red of flowing blood. She was flanked on each side by three burly guards. Adam struggled to keep himself from rushing to her. It wouldn't save her, but it took all the strength he had to stay rooted where he stood. She walked slowly, as if dazed. Had the Dark Lord given her some drug to make her passive?

He yearned to give her some sign that he was there, to let her know that if she were to die, she wouldn't die alone, and that, if nothing else, they would enter the next life together. But he held back. With how she must hate him now, he couldn't bear it if his last vision of her before the guards got to him was of her face filled with the loathing she must now feel for him. So he kept silent, drinking in every detail of the procession, waiting for that one moment when he might make his move.

It wouldn't be easy. The guards who flanked her were dressed in what must be ancient armor—thick plates of hardened leather that completely covered their broad chests. Each bore a bronze short sword made in the ancient manner, but the gleam of their weapons' edges showed they were sharp and ready for hard use.

He sighed. How he had treasured his own bronze knife. The antiquity of the Dark Lord's ways had meant so much to him. It hadn't occurred to him that evil, too, might be passed on from generation to generation.

Now he must confront it, unarmed. When he did, he would die, one more sacrifice to the Dark Lord's dark gods. It didn't trouble him. He was more than ready to die, as long as he brought the Dark Lord down to hell with him.

The Dark Lord followed Zoe in the procession. He was preceded by two elderly men carrying torches and was garbed in a richly bordered robe of the same blood red color as the one that clothed Zoe. On his head he wore a shining golden diadem made in the shape of twined serpents. He moved slowly but steadily and in his upraised arms he bore a gleaming sickle.

More guards followed him and a few more women. The gate swung closed behind the last of the procession as it crept slowly down the dirt track that led away from the castle, in time with the wild keening call of the piper.

A shadow crept across the face of the morning sun. The eclipse. Birds began to twitter, as the sky took on the color of twilight, not at the horizon, but in midsky.

Adam gestured to Isabelle to remain hidden until the last of the trailing guards were almost out of sight. Then he motioned her to follow as he moved forward, staying in the shadows, but keeping the procession in sight.

The birds fell silent as the indigo sky devoured the last of the sun and turned to night. The procession had reached an earthen mound that rose at the edge of a steep cliff overlooking the gray Irish Sea. The piper halted and, after letting forth one last wavering blast like the cry of a wounded seabird, he let the pipes fall silent. The Dark Lord raised his arms and, turning to face the sea, called out an invocation in the ancient tongue.

The hair prickled on the back of Adam's neck. But he edged closer, taking advantage of the way all attention was turned toward the old man. There must be some way to save Zoe. Hidden as he was by the shadows, he was able to come within a few yards of the procession, close enough to see that there was an opening in the mound that in the eclipse-light looked like the black mouth of a cave.

When the old man's last words had vanished into the stiffening wind, two guards took positions on either side of the mouth and raised their swords. Then the Dark Lord limped toward Zoe and muttered something. Her shoulders slumped, then, like an automaton, she extended one thin hand toward her destroyer.

It must be the Word of Power.

Cold sweat broke out on Adam's brow. He fought down nausea. He'd used one on her, too, fool that he'd been; had he not, she wouldn't be here now. Had he not given in to his selfish desires, she wouldn't have wed him and come to this cursed place to end her life in horror.

As the Dark Lord prepared to take her into the barrow, Adam eyed the flanking guards. If he were to make his move, it must be now. In another moment, it would be too late. He tensed his muscles to spring. The bruises from the guards' beating protested, but he ignored them. He wouldn't be needing this body much longer. His death was only a breath away, or two, but he would make it a good one.

But just as he was about to hurl himself toward the old man, he was grasped from behind.

"No!" Isabelle's nails dug into his shoulder. "Would you commit self-murder? Wait!"

"I'll kill him. My life doesn't matter."

"Don't be a fool. You may wish to die, but I don't! You can't get to her with all those big men around her, but if you try, they will find me and kill me, too."

He froze. She was right, but there was no help for

it. She must sacrifice her life to save her daughter. He twisted around to tell her. She stood silhouetted against the purple sky—Isabelle with her golden curls and tawdry magnificence. The woman he had hated for a decade. Who had just risked her life to save his.

He stopped. He couldn't make her die against her will. Not unless he would become as heartless as the man he wished to kill.

"Be patient," Isabelle implored. "MacMinn will come. He'll save her."

"It's too late for that."

But it was also too late for him. Isabelle's appeal had robbed him of his opportunity. During the moments he'd wasted debating with her, the Dark Lord had drawn Zoe into the barrow. Only the last bit of her scarlet robe was visible now, trailing on the ground. Her six guards, their swords crossed, stood impassively, blocking the opening.

The piper began his damned skirling again, and any cries his beloved might have made as she confronted her fate deep within the earth were drowned out by the tormented pipes.

Zoe fought for air, choking on the smell of damp. The Dark Lord was leading her down a long passageway dug into the mounded earth of the barrow. In the uncertain light of the burning brand he'd brought with him, she could just make out the ancient inscriptions incised into the walls in some barbaric script. She shivered. The air inside the cave was much colder than it had been outside.

The silence was broken by the sound of rustling wings. The old man's fingers dug into hers as a flight of bats rushed past them. As his clawlike grip tightened, she tried to hide her revulsion. He believed she was under his spell. She must let him continue to believe it. If only it didn't become true.

When he'd called her Dragon's Child outside the cave, she'd waited in a near panic, wondering if the Word of Power would wrest away her will and make her love him, as Adam's spell had done.

But it hadn't. She still hated her father, as much as she had when he'd first revealed his plan for her in his laboratorium. His magic had failed, but who was to say what other ancient secrets he might draw upon before this day was over?

She thought of making her move now, before the Dark Lord could do anything more to bend her to his will. But the passageway was too narrow, and the old man was moving surprisingly swiftly for one as hobbled as he was by age and disease.

She must wait. The moment must be perfect.

The Dark Lord led her deeper into the barrow, moving more slowly now and stopping at times to rub his hands over the incised carvings as if reading them. Finally they came to a place where the passageway opened up into a chamber whose smoke-blackened roof rose many feet above them. At the center stood a raised stone platform, its edges lined with geometric carvings. Something pale lay upon it. As she drew closer, Zoe saw bones.

Then the Dark Lord spoke. His voice was like the

rustle of dry leaves. "Await your master here, O Dragon's Child, in the high place of sacrifice."

The air squeezed out of her lungs. Dragon's Child. *His* child. The Word of Power.

But still nothing changed.

She swayed toward the old man, trying not to gag as the rank smell of his rotting breath wafted toward her. His dark magic hadn't stolen away her will. It was still hers to command. And now her own power surged through her, that power born of the love that joined her to the man who'd offered his life for hers. She lurched toward the old man and fell upon him, as if by accident, and knocked the torch from his hand.

She heard his sharp intake of breath as the light was extinguished. *Good.* Then in the sudden darkness, she reached inside the neck of her robe and found her knife—*Charlotte's knife*—hanging on its chain. With a liquid motion she lifted the chain over her head and flicked the knife open. Then she braced herself against the raised platform, feeling the icy touch of the stone against her naked leg.

"Dragon's Child, make yourself ready to receive me." The Dark Lord's voice quavered in command.

There was a faint rustle as he divested himself of his robe. She tried not to imagine his nakedness—that cursed nakedness in which her own life had begun. The reek of his corrupted flesh forced the breath out of her lungs, as he moved toward her with uneven steps.

Then he stopped. "Speak to me, daughter. So I may find you in the darkness."

He would find her in the deepest darkness, for

they would enter hell together. But if fate was kind, she would have a choice of *which* sin would send her there.

"I am here, Father." She gripped Charlotte's knife more tightly. "Come to me."

Chapter 23

Adam hoped she'd been drugged, or that the spell had blunted her to the horror of her fate. As he gazed helplessly at the empty mouth of the barrow, he prayed that something had kept her from suffering in those last dreadful moments of her life.

All that kept him from throwing himself at the guards now, and letting them put him out of his misery, was the knowledge that he had no right to betray Isabelle's presence to them. She'd risked her life to save his. He wouldn't condemn her up to a death she hadn't chosen. But for himself, death would come now only as a welcome release.

Isabelle's eager whisper broke through his stupor. "You see, over there, to the east? MacMinn comes, at last! And he's brought help—just as I said he would!"

She swung around and pointed back in the direction

from which they'd come, and sure enough, in the distance a dim glow resolved into torchlight. A company of men marched toward them, armed not with ancient weapons of bronze but with serviceable muskets.

"He's brought the militia!" Isabelle exclaimed. "See? He is always so clever!"

But it was too late. Too much time had passed since Adam had seen his wife vanish inside the barrow's entrance. All must be over now—her violation and the final sacrifice. But he said nothing to dampen Isabelle's hope. She'd learn her daughter's fate soon enough. But for himself, he couldn't bear to look at the troupe of men as they marched toward him. Had they come only minutes earlier, Zoe might have been saved.

The Dark Lord's guards saw the advancing militia, too, and no sooner did they take in their muskets and determined faces than they dropped their ancient swords and ran like the bullies they were, leaving the opening of the barrow undefended. Adam ran toward it, stopping only to pick up one of the discarded swords before racing into the gaping maw. At least he would have this satisfaction: It would be his hand that ended the Dark Lord's life.

A few moments later, he heard muffled footsteps coming from deep within the barrow. His unspeakable deeds done, the Dark Lord must be returning to his minions. Adam advanced another few paces to block the narrow passageway with his broad shoulders. Then he raised his sword.

The footsteps came closer. Swift footsteps, not the hesitant limp of an old man. Having replenished himself at the well of life, the Dark Lord moved like a young-ster. White-hot rage filled Adam. The demon laird must take what pleasure he could in his newfound youth now, for when he reached the opening of the barrow, Adam would end his life and send him straight to hell.

Then he heard a cry coming from deep within the earthen passageway. His flesh crawled, for the voice was Zoe's voice. Had the Dark Lord stolen not only her life force, but her body?

But as Zoe's tall form lurched toward him, her face lit by the flare of a militiaman's torch, it was no specter that he saw, no spirit-filled corpse, but his wife, alive, and whole. A shout tore from his throat as he lunged forward to embrace her, but she dodged away from him, her eyes wild.

"Don't touch me!" she cried.

It was only what he deserved, but the joy drained out of him at her rejection. He couldn't bear to meet her eyes.

As he backed away she gasped, "I've killed my father." Then his wife, her hands stained red with blood, collapsed before him in a dead faint.

He stood frozen, unable to move. It was Isabelle who, ignoring the horror of the bystanders, picked up her daughter and, by slapping her gently on the cheek, brought her back to consciousness.

"What nonsense is this, Zoe?" she demanded. "Your father is most certainly alive."

"No. I stabbed him with Charlotte's knife." A shud-der ran through her body.

Comprehension filled Isabelle's features, and she smiled. "Did that pig's arse tell you he was your father?"

Zoe nodded. "But so did you! You told me he rescued you from the Terror because you told him I was his child."

"And so I did," Isabelle replied with a charming smile. "But of course, I lied. His child died at birth, thanks to *le bon Dieu*. You were born a year later."

"Then am I truly the duke's daughter?" Zoe's face filled with an expression more beautiful than any Adam had ever seen.

"Well, no." Isabelle's smile dimmed.

"Then who *is* my father?"

Zoe's expression told Adam how terrified she was of what the answer might be. Before Isabelle could reply, he broke in. "Whoever he was, I pity him for missing out on the pleasure of seeing you grow into so brave a woman."

Zoe's reply was a look of such warmth that, for a moment, he began to think matters between them were not as hopeless as he'd thought. But before he could take advantage of the goodwill his words had won for him, Isabelle said, "What are you talking about, milord? Her father has had plenty of opportunity to enjoy his daughter throughout her life."

Zoe's voice rose. "For God's sake, then, tell me. Who is he?"

"I can't believe you haven't tumbled to it by now," Isabelle said dismissively. "But here. Let him tell you himself. MacMinn, come introduce yourself to your daughter and her new husband."

"*MacMinn* is my father?" Zoe's eyes widened in surprise. "But why didn't you tell me before?"

"And have you go through life burdened by the knowledge that you were the bastard daughter of a coachman? I wouldn't have done that to you, the child of my heart. So I gave you a duke for a father instead, and you see, I was right. You've grown as proud and noble as any duke's daughter!"

"But MacMinn isn't married. You could have married him."

"And become a coachman's wife?" Isabelle's distaste showed in her wrinkled brow. "Surely you haven't forgotten everything I've taught you. I am La Belle Isabelle. How could I marry a coachman? MacMinn is a very good sort of man and he saved me from that swine who called himself the Dark Lord. But he wasn't at all what I would look for in a husband."

The lanky coachman had come to join them now. He eyed his daughter and Adam with a sheepish look. "I did my best to watch over you, Zoe," he said. "But your ma was right. It would have only lowered you to think I was your da. And that starchy Mrs. Endicott, she'd nae have let you go to school alongside her young ladies if she knew your father was only a servant. Still, though Belle wouldn't marry me, I did what I could to keep an eye on the both of you."

"And you saved your daughter's life—twice—after I'd put her into the gravest danger." Adam held out his hand. "I'm honored to make your acquaintance."

MacMinn tugged his forelock and twisted it uneasily. "I didn't like to have to fool you the way I did to make ye wed, Yer Lordship, but I saw no other way. You believed in him so strong, you wouldn't have trusted me had I told you it was he that stole your sister's papers. But he did, and that's why he sent you off straightaway to foreign lands when you came back and found your sister dead—to make sure none of us could betray him to you."

Adam bowed his head. No wonder his sister's shade had haunted him. She hadn't been thirsting for revenge, but trying to warn him that he'd put his faith in the man who had murdered her. Well, she could rest easy now. His eyes, at last, were open.

He turned to Isabelle. "I owe you an apology," he said quietly. "When I finally confronted you in London, I condemned you without ever giving you a chance to defend yourself. Had I let you explain, none of this would have happened." He gestured toward the barrow. "Can you tell me now what really happened?"

Isabelle's eyes dropped and a serious look filled her usually vapid features. "He told me the papers belonged to a woman who had died before he could treat her, and that I must take them and tell everyone I was her. That's all I know."

"And that letter that was sent to the Committee and made them come for Charlotte? Who wrote it?"

"He must have. I knew of no such letter. And besides, I can't write, except to sign my name. My talents lie elsewhere," she added with a certain pride. "But I can assure you, I wouldn't have taken those papers had I known it would cause your sister's death. I am a practical woman, but I'm not a murderess."

"But *I* am," Zoe said softly. "Whoever he was, I killed the old man back there in the barrow. I had no choice."

"Never think it, Zoe," MacMinn said with a broad laugh that broke the somber mood of the gathering. "You didn't kill him, you just gave him enough of a scare that he won't be troublin' anyone again with his black magic and ugly ancient ways."

He gestured to where two militiamen were carrying the old man out of the cave on a hurdle. "He's been stricken with a fit—cannae talk or move nary a limb. He'll die in the natural way, soon enough, but it's his own fear that killed him. You only sliced a bit o' skin off his chest with that wee knife of yours. Aye, you're a game one to get yourself out of such a pickle on your own. But then you always were braver than a pit bull on a Sunday." He paused and wiped his brow. "You aren't too disappointed, lassie, to find out ye're my bairn?"

"Disappointed?" Zoe exclaimed. "There is no man alive I'd rather call father. You've been there all my life, playing with me when I was little and getting me out of scrapes when I got older."

"But I am but a coachie, and all this time you've been thinking your father was a duke."

"A rotten, nasty, child-abandoning duke." She sniffed. "Who never expressed the slightest interest in me. I'd much prefer to have you as a father. You're braver than any duke and twice as resourceful. Why, you must have saved my life a dozen times all told, not to mention all the sweetmeats that you bought me when I was young. For shame. I know *she* is a snob." She pointed to her mother. "But I hadn't expected that kind of thinking from you."

MacMinn came over and embraced her warmly. "You're a good girl, Zoe, and it does my heart good to hear you say that." He turned back to face Adam. "But it's you who will be troubled by her birth, I'm thinking, being a lord and all. Ye needna worry. I'll nae be showin' my face at your castle in the bonny north or asking the little lordlings to call me grandpa. I know my place."

Adam smiled. "Your place will be with us, whenever you choose to visit. I may be a lord, but I'm not nearly as big a snob as Isabelle. Our children will be lucky to have such a fine grandfather to look out for them."

But as he spoke those words, a shadow fell over his heart. For it wasn't likely Zoe would be staying with him in the bonny north. The Dark Lord had removed the spell that had bound her to him, and after all the suffering he had caused her, she had little reason to love him. So he must say what must be said and give her back, at last, the freedom he'd so wrongly stolen from her.

He lowered his voice so that only she could hear it. "My offer still holds. You need never see Strathrimmon again. I won't hold you to our marriage. If you choose to live on your own in London, I'll do whatever I can to make you comfortable while I look into applying to Parliament for a divorce. Our circumstances are so unusual, it's possible they might grant one."

"So you still wish to send me away?" The light had fled from Zoe's deep brown eyes, but whether it was because she was sad that the time had come to admit to the failure of their marriage or from something else, he hadn't the courage to ask.

Isabelle shot her daughter a look of surprise. "What have you done, child, to have so displeased Lord Ramsay that he sends you away after only a few weeks of marriage? Had you listened to me and done those things I told you of, he would be enchanted now, instead of taking a disgust—"

"Your daughter could never do anything to displease me," Adam shot back. "But I won't force her to live with me if she doesn't love me. If you'd allow us a word in private—" He turned to his wife and drew her from her parents, guiding her away from the opening of the barrow toward the edge of the cliff that looked out over the sea.

The eclipse was almost over now. The sky had lightened and the sun's face was regaining its glory. They watched together as the waves rolled beneath them in the waxing light of day. For a long time, neither spoke.

Then Adam cleared his throat. "I don't want to send you away. But I love you too much to ask you to stay in a marriage you didn't choose with a man who isn't worthy of you. Now that the Dark Lord has released you from my spell, you're no longer bound to me by the black arts he taught me."

He stopped, barely able to go on, but honor demanded he continue. "How could I hold you to your vows? They were made under compulsion. Nothing I could ever do will make up for what I did in forcing you to wed me, but I will do everything I can to ensure you don't spend the rest of your life trapped in marriage with a man you cannot love."

"But if I should wish to remain with a man whose love I treasure?" She looked up at him, her eyes crinkling at the corners with what could only be mischief. "If I wish to return with you to Strathrimmon and do something about the execrable upholstery in the dining chamber?"

His heart quaked. "Would you really? Do you still love me, even without the spell?"

Her voice was so quiet, he could hardly hear it. "It wasn't the spell that made me love you, Adam. I had started to love you long before you had enchanted me. But I'm as proud as my mother. So I blamed the spell for my desire for you, rather than admitting that it rose from my own heart. I couldn't bear to love you, when it seemed so impossible that you could ever return my love."

"But I did," he said. "I do. I always will."

A gull swooped toward the cliff on whose edge they stood. Adam flung his arms around Zoe to shield her. As he gathered her into his embrace, she nestled against him. He could barely speak, so great was his joy in having her back in his arms where she belonged.

He buried his lips in her hair and stroked the rough skin of her beloved features. "I don't know when it was I started to love you. Perhaps it was in my dream that first night when you came to me—I had lived so much of my life in other realms. But you brought me to earth and taught me how to face reality. By the time Mac-Minn told me we must wed, I was wild with love for you. How could I not have been, when you gave me so much comfort and understanding, despite the way I treated you."

"Never had I seen a mortal so in need of comfort. I would have had to have a heart of stone not to care for you." She bit her lip. "But I didn't expect you to love me, simply because I was kind to you. It was only at Strathrimmon that I dared hope you might return my love, after we truly became man and wife."

A delicate blush had stolen across her cheeks, making her so beautiful he longed to stop her words with a kiss, but she wasn't done. "Even then, I didn't dare trust that you really loved me. What you had chosen to give me, you could take back, so I still fought against admitting how much I needed you. I made myself believe I loved you because of the spell, not because I'd chosen to. It was only when the Dark Lord enchanted me and attempted to transfer my affections to him with the selfsame spell that I had to admit that a spell couldn't create love unless it was already there."

Her mention of the Dark Lord brought him back to earth. "But that's the hell of it, Zoe. Even if you loved me then, how can you love me now, when I led you to the Dark Lord's lair and did nothing to save you?"

She drew herself up to her full height. "How could I love you? With all my heart and soul. You offered your *life* for mine. But, you know, Adam, it was probably for the best that you didn't save me just now. You've spent too much of your life trying to be a hero and if you'd been one today, you might still think I'd only love you when you were strong and successful. Now you can be certain that I'll love you no matter what happens."

"Can you really love me even when I fail?"

"Of course. That's when you need my love the most."

He drew her closer. "What could I ever give you, in return for so great a gift?"

"You've already given it. You made me believe in magic."

She opened her lips for a kiss. He pressed her close and nuzzled her ear, and the wonderful scent of her hair filled him with joy as he bent down to take what she so freely offered.

Across the way, her mother shook her head. "She'll never learn," she observed to MacMinn. "But then, she always was a stubborn child. It's a mystery how she managed to marry a lord, when she went about it so clumsily. I ask you, can there be anything more absurd than her falling in love with her own husband? No good can come of it. I've told her that a million times, but the foolish girl, she never listens."

A Word to the Reader

For those of you who would like to consult his chart, Adam was born on March 17, 1773, at 12:51 P.M. at Selkirk, Scotland. Though he was trained in astrology, which was taught as part of the medical curriculum well into the eighteenth century, he wouldn't have known of the grand trine that forms such a striking feature of his chart, as it involves the three new planets, Uranus, Neptune, and Pluto, the last two of which had not yet been discovered.

Discovered or not, these transpersonal planets clearly played a strong role in Adam's life, as they aspected his Moon and various other personal planets. They go a long way to explaining why he was so dominated by survivor guilt, and why he sought comfort, as so many Pisces do, in renunciation and in losing himself in erroneous beliefs about supernatural powers.

Those planetary configurations also explain why Adam had such a need to purify himself and undergo a life-threatening initiatory ordeal. As you probably noticed, Adam did, in fact, receive the Final Teaching that his years of pilgrimage had prepared him for. His purity of heart allowed him to learn wisdom, even from a flawed teacher. The compassion he'd learned through his sufferings kept him from risking Isabelle's life at the barrow. Had he been willing to sacrifice her, he would have died at the hands of the guards. But because he did what was right, he survived his ordeal and lived on to spend the rest of his life with the woman who really did turn out to be his gateway to enlightenment.

The opposition between Pluto and the Moon conjunct in the Sixth House and his Twelfth House Mars also explains why Adam made such a good surgeon, a profession you might not otherwise find a Pisces pursuing.

Zoe, whose down-to-earth practicality made her such a good foil for him, was, as you have probably guessed, a Virgo. She was born August 29, 1782, at 6:51 P.M. at Nanterre, France. Her concentration of Virgo planets in the Sixth House with its emphasis on service made her the perfect mate for Adam, as it gave her the ability to ground him and make it possible for him to learn to appreciate the things of this world rather than lose himself in the hidden mysteries so intoxicating to his Pisces nature.

Zoe's challenge was to avoid becoming *too* grounded. Adam taught her to see past her limitations and dis-

cover the faith she needed if she were to express her
Pisces Ascendant through action, rather than suffering.

As they grew older, the two of them would have
become a powerful team of healers. Together they
would have used their practical skills to heal those patients whose ailments could be cured while letting their
mystical compassion ease the way of patients whose ill-
nesses could not be healed by the limited medicine of
their day.

Like all those living on the cusp of the scientific age,
Adam and Zoe would have found it difficult to distin-
guish magic from science. The hypnotism that the Dark
Lord taught Adam—which is, of course, what he was
using when he cast the "healing spell"—would have
seemed like magic to anyone of his era, and indeed,
hypnotic techniques had long been used by holy men
in India and elsewhere, and were considered forms of
magic.

The historical record reports that hypnotic trance
was indeed used as anesthesia by several surgical
practitioners throughout the late eighteenth and early
nineteenth centuries, until it was replaced by the newly
discovered anesthetic gasses. But it wasn't until the
1840s that hypnotism came to be understood as a con-
crete, repeatable physiological phenomenon, through
the work of another Scottish surgeon, James Braid.

Though Mesmer is often thought of as having used
hypnosis, and even gave his name to the practice, his
healing practice involved the use of imaginary electrical
fluids and did not employ actual hypnotic techniques.

The Dark Lord is fictional, but I based his character on those of charlatans like Cagliostro and the legendary Count of Saint-Germain, who were active near the time of the French Revolution and were believed to have mystical powers. The way the Dark Lord exploited a wealthy young man whose emotional wounds were so close to the surface is all too typical of how religious cult leaders behave, even today. They win followers by blending a powerful mixture of real truths, psychic ability, and charisma with appealing lies that offer hope to friendless people like Adam, who are struggling with difficult emotional conflicts.

Should you ever find yourself falling under the spell of any religious teacher, examine closely the direction that energy—and money—flow between that teacher and his followers. Real adepts give, they don't take. If they have psychic powers, they use them reluctantly and without calling attention to themselves. They don't ever ask for money. They give to the poor and heal those in pain without asking for anything in return. Most importantly, they don't create a cloud of awe or fear around themselves.

When people leave the presence of a truly illuminated being, their hearts are filled with peace and understanding. Such people walk the earth today as they always have. They show up when you are ready to receive their teaching, give you what you require, and then quietly disappear.

Next month, don't miss these exciting new love stories only from Avon Books

Kiss of Pride by Sandra Hill
A Viking vampire angel? Reporter Alexandra Kelly thinks Vikar Sigurdsson is either crazy or just trying to maneuver her into his bed—until he does something unexpected, and even she begins to wonder if perhaps he is everything he says he is.

Wicked Road to Hell by Juliana Stone
With the legions of the underworld gathering and chaos close at hand, sorcerer Declan O'Hara's deadly skills will be tested. But nothing will sway him from his duty...except perhaps beautiful vampire Ana DeLacrux. Together they will travel the wicked road to hell.

A Warrior's Promise by Donna Fletcher
Bryce can't afford distractions on his quest to restore Scotland's true king to the throne. When a desperate urchin steps in his path and turns out to be oh so much more, will Bryce turn away from love in order to fulfill his duty, or will he discover that promising your heart is the bravest mission of all?

The Fireman Who Loved Me by Jennifer Bernard
Melissa McGuire and Fire Captain Harry Brody have just one thing in common: they're both convinced they're perfectly wrong for each other. But when Melissa's matchmaking grandmother wins her a date with Brody at a bachelor auction the sparks fly.

Give yourself a Christmas present
any time of year with these delicious stories by
New York Times bestselling author

LORI WILDE

CHECK OUT HER E-BOOK STORIES FROM AVON IMPULSE:

The Christmas Cookie Chronicles: Carrie

The Christmas Cookie Chronicles: Raylene

The Christmas Cookie Chronicles: Christine

AND DON'T MISS HER OTHER JUBILEE, TEXAS, NOVELS:

The Sweethearts' Knitting Club

The True Love Quilting Club

The First Love Cookie Club

The Welcome Home Garden Club

Available in print and as e-books from Avon Books!

LW 0412

At Avon Books, we know your passion for romance—once you finish one of our novels, you find yourself wanting more.

May we tempt you with . . .

- **Excerpts** from our upcoming releases.

- Entertaining **extras**, including authors' personal photo albums and book lists.

- Behind-the-scenes **scoop** on your favorite characters and series.

- **Sweepstakes** for the chance to win free books, romantic getaways, and other fun prizes.

- Writing **tips** from our authors and editors.

- **Blog** with our authors and find out why they love to write romance.

- **Exclusive content** that's not contained within the pages of our novels.

Join us at
www.avonbooks.com

AVON

An Imprint of HarperCollins*Publishers*
www.avonromance.com

FTH 1111

Give in to your Impulses!

These unforgettable stories only take a second to buy and give you hours of reading pleasure!

Go to *www.AvonImpulse.com* and see what we have to offer.

Available wherever e-books are sold.

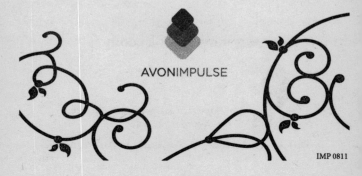

AVONIMPULSE